D0261818

David the Prince

David the Prince

Nigel Tranter

HODDER AND STOUGHTON
LONDON   SYDNEY   AUCKLAND   TORONTO

British Library Cataloguing in Publication Data

Tranter, Nigel
    David the prince.
    I. Title
823'.9'IF   PR6070.R34D/

ISBN 0 340 24622 7

Hodder and Stoughton Editorial Office: 47 Bedford Square, London WC1B 3DP.

PRINCIPAL CHARACTERS

In Order of Appearance

DAVID MAC MALCOLM: Sixth son of Malcolm the Third and Queen Margaret the Saint.

HUGO DE MORVILLE: Younger son of a Norman baron and a Saxon mother.

HERVEY DE WARENNE: Youngest son of Norman Earl of Surrey and of Gundred, an illegitimate daughter of William the Conqueror.

EDGAR, KING OF SCOTS: Fourth son of Malcolm Canmore and Margaret.

COSPATRICK, EARL OF DUNBAR: The second so-called. Great Scots noble.

RANULF FLAMBARD: Lord Chief Justice of England, a cleric.

WILLIAM THE SECOND (RUFUS): King of England. Second surviving son of William the Conqueror.

PRINCE HENRY BEAUCLERC: Third son of the Conqueror. Later Henry the First.

PRINCESS MATILDA (or MAUD): Eldest daughter of Malcolm and Margaret, and sister of David. Later Good Queen Maud.

PRINCESS MARY: Younger daughter of Malcolm and Margaret.

SIMON DE ST. LIZ, EARL OF NORTHAMPTON: Great Norman noble.

ANSELM, ARCHBISHOP OF CANTERBURY.

ROBERT, DUKE OF NORMANDY: Eldest son of the Conqueror.

SYBILLA: Illegitimate daughter of Henry the First. Later Queen to Alexander the First of Scots.

ETHELRED MAC MALCOLM, EARL OF MORAY, ABBOT OF DUNKELD: Third son of Malcolm and Margaret.

ALEXANDER MAC MALCOLM, EARL OF GOWRIE: Fifth son of Malcolm and Margaret later Alexander the First.

MADACH, EARL OF ATHOLL: Great Scots noble related to the royal house.

MATILDA, COUNTESS OF HUNTINGDON: Wife of Simon de St. Liz. Countess in her own right. Great heiress.

EARL HAKON CLAW OF ORKNEY: So-called Governor of Galloway.

FERGUS MAC SWEEN, LORD OF GALLOWAY: Great Scots noble.

RALPH, PRIOR OF PENNANT-BACHY: Tironensian cleric. Later first Abbot of Selkirk.

GRUFFYDD AP CYNAN: Prince of Gwynedd.

JOHN, BISHOP OF GLASGOW: David's former tutor.

EADMER: A Saxon monk of Canterbury, later Bishop of St. Andrews.

ROBERT DE BRUS: First Norman Lord of Annandale.

MALCOLM MACETH: Son of Ethelred. Later Earl of Moray.

RANDOLPH DE MESCHIN: Norman Governor of Cumbria.

CARDINAL JOHN OF CREMA: Papal legate.

THURSTAN, ARCHBISHOP OF YORK.

STEPHEN OF BLOIS, COUNT OF BOULOGNE: Nephew of Henry, later King of England.

ROBERT, EARL OF GLOUCESTER: Illegitimate son of Henry the First.

MAUD THE EMPRESS: Daughter of Henry the First.

ALWIN: A Saxon cleric, David's later chaplain.

HENRY MAC DAVID, PRINCE OF SRATHCLYDE: Son of David the First.

ST. MALACHY O'MOORE: Bishop of Armagh.

LORD WILLIAM OF ALLERDALE: Son of the briefly-reigning Duncan the Second.

MALCOLM MAC HENRY: Elder son of Prince Henry. Later Malcolm the Fourth (The Maiden).

WILLIAM MAC HENRY: Second son of Prince Henry. Later William the Lyon.

Part One

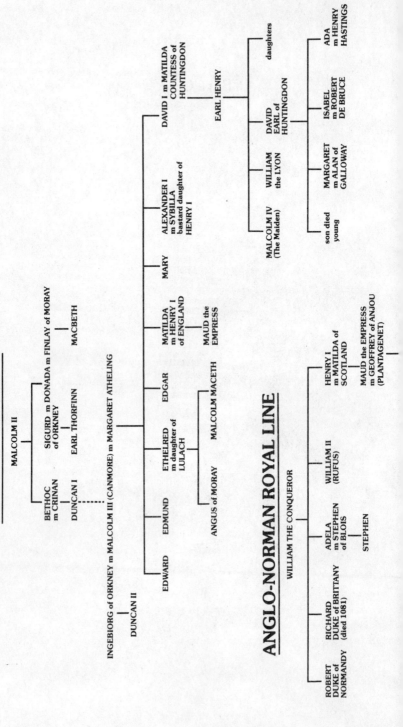

SCOTS ROYAL LINE

MALCOLM II

BETHOC m CRINAN — DUNCAN I

SIGURD m DONADA m FINLAY of MORAY of ORKNEY

EARL THORFINN

MACBETH

INGEBIORG of ORKNEY m MALCOLM III (CANMORE) m MARGARET ATHELING

DUNCAN II

EDWARD

EDMUND

ETHELRED m daughter of LULACH

ANGUS of MORAY

MALCOLM MACETH

EDGAR

MATILDA m HENRY I of ENGLAND

MAUD the EMPRESS

MARY

ALEXANDER I m SYBILLA bastard daughter of HENRY I

DAVID I m MATILDA COUNTESS of HUNTINGDON

EARL HENRY

MALCOLM IV (The Maiden)

WILLIAM the LYON

DAVID EARL of HUNTINGDON

daughters

son died young

MARGARET m ALAN of GALLOWAY

ISABEL m ROBERT DE BRUCE

ADA m HENRY HASTINGS

ANGLO-NORMAN ROYAL LINE

WILLIAM THE CONQUEROR

ROBERT DUKE of NORMANDY

RICHARD DUKE of BRITTANY (died 1081)

ADELA m STEPHEN of BLOIS

STEPHEN

WILLIAM II (RUFUS)

HENRY I m MATILDA of SCOTLAND

MAUD the EMPRESS m GEOFFREY of ANJOU (PLANTAGENET)

1

THE THREE YOUTHS splashed across the stream in a great splatter of spray and shouts of laughter – laughter from the two in front, at least, as the one slightly behind got soaked from their commotion, on the smaller, shorter-legged mount. Clambering up the willowed bank beyond, Hervey shouted back.

"A race! Race you to the ridge. We may see them from there. Race you, I say!" And without waiting for agreement from the other two, he dug in his heels and spurred his fine Barbary black up the long grassy slope.

"A plague on you!" Hugo de Morville called after him. "Wait! Start level, at least . . ." But when the other drove on without pause, he kicked his beast into a canter, beating with his clenched fist on the grey's rump, spattering clods of the damp brook-side earth in the face of the third youth. "Come on, David!" he yelled.

That individual, the youngest by a full year, at fifteen, said nothing but bent doggedly over his stocky skewbald's shaggy neck, urging it on with a convulsive gripping and stroking action of his fingers, and hissing slightly in the silky ear. It was not a very notable horse, in looks or breeding, with only a modicum of the prized Arab blood in it, but he was fond of it, and it was his all.

It was no race, of course – Hervey de Warenne saw to that, with both a major start and the best mount. But then, he liked to win, was used to it and good at it; after all, he was the son of the famous Earl William de Warenne of Surrey, one of the richest and most powerful Norman nobles in all England; and more important still, his mother had been the Lady Gundred, daughter – albeit illegitimate – of the late and mighty King William the Conqueror, which made him the nephew of the present Red King, William Rufus. So the winning was, as it were, in the blood. He covered the half-mile slope to the rolling Hampshire ridge, with a good seventy yards to spare, and reined up his steaming black on the summit, turning in the saddle to grin back at the others, not scornful but well content.

Hugo came up, his grey snorting through flaring nostrils. "You are an oaf, Hervey!" he exclaimed. "Always were. A race

9

is no race unless there is a fair start." But he spoke without rancour, an open-faced, easy-going lad of sixteen years, strongly-built, with curling fair hair unusual in a Norman – but then his mother had been daughter of a Saxon ealdorman. He scarcely glanced at his companion however, but stared out over the suddenly wide vista of the rolling Hampshire downland, eastwards by north, which flanked the shallow fertile vale of the Itchen, Tichbourne below, Cheriton Great Wood away on the right. "I do not see them," he added.

"No. They are late. Plaguey slow. Probably lost!" the other said. And added, grinning again, as the third rider came up. "After all, they are only Scots!"

"My uncle will be with them," Hugh reminded. "*He* knows this country sufficiently well."

The youngest boy, David, seemingly unconcerned at being last, as so often, was already scanning the farther scene with a steady, methodical, quartering gaze. He pointed.

"There they are," he said. "Beyond that village. On the hillside with the open woodland. Two miles – more, three." He spoke Norman-French also, but with a carefulness which indicated that it was not his native tongue, and with a slightly sing-song accent which could much amuse his friends.

The others peered through narrowed eyes, in the early afternoon September sunshine. After a few moments they both saw the distant movement which at that range, was really what was to be seen rather than the men and horses of a large cavalcade.

"You have the eyes of a tiercel!" Hugo declared.

"Say a kite!" Hervey amended. He was the oldest by months, nearly seventeen, as well as the most eminent, and was apt to be at pains to show it. But not too unkindly, to be sure, or the trio would not have remained friends. If young David was something of a butt he was still a good fellow, however limited by his circumstances, birth and curious upbringing. "A kite – eh, David?"

That one shrugged, not rising to the bait. He was a slender, slightly-built youth, dark of hair and eyes, large, fine eyes, pale of complexion, almost delicate of feature, but with a strong jawline which redeemed the sensitive mouth from any hint of weakness.

"It is not better eyes that you need, Hervey," he said mildly. "Only the wits to tell you what your eyes see. There is a difference, I think."

"Ha!" Hugo de Morville exclaimed, laughing, and punched his grey's arching neck, urging it into movement again.

10

They set off down the long eastern slope, towards the Itchen's cress-flanked windings, at an easy canter now. Even so, inevitably David fell a little behind. But he was used to that.

The two parties, large and small, drew together in wet splashy meadow-land, between the Alres ford and Cheriton village, where the Tich bourne joined Itchen, mallards rocketing up from the reeds and water-cress-beds on every hand. The company coming from the north-east was fully fifty strong, richly-dressed men in front, with an escort of armoured fighting-men, all travel-stained and dusty, under a great banner which bore the device of a hunched-backed boar. Suddenly the three youths seemed very callow and unimpressive, however fine two of their mounts.

As they approached, it was Hervey and Hugo who held back a little, and the younger lad who rode ahead.

In the forefront of the large cavalcade, a fair-haired young man rode directly under the boar-banner, flanked by somewhat older men just a head behind. He was paying no real attention to the trio before him when, abruptly, at about fifty yards, he leaned forward in his saddle, staring. Then his rather sombre features lightened and he raised a pointing hand.

"Davie!" he exclaimed, and not in Norman-French. "Davie – yourself it is! By all that's holy – you, here!"

The other smiled, waving, and spurred forward. "Edgar – my lord King! Oh, it is good to see you," he cried. "It has been so long – two whole years. Edgar – at last!"

They reined up alongside each other, leaning over to grasp each other's forearms in warm greeting, both still on the young side for anything so emotional-seeming as an embrace – although Edgar mac Malcolm was nine years older than his youngest brother. Thus close, side by side, the family resemblance was evident in the all-but-delicate lines of their faces, the shape of head and carriage of person, although one was fair and quite tall and the other dark and slight.

"Two years, lad, yes – I am sorry," the elder said. "It has not been possible. I would have sent for you – but . . . all has been difficult. In Scotland. Still is – or, God knows, I would not have come! But – how you have grown, Davie! You were but a halfling when last I saw you. Now you are almost a man!"

Kind as it was of his brother to say so, David wished that he had not done so. He would be left in no doubt that it was not true, by his two companions, later. That thought reminded him, however, of the necessary courtesies.

"These are my friends, my lord," he said. "This is Hervey de

11

Warenne, a son to the Earl of Surrey. And this is Hugo de Morville, from the Honour of Huntingdon."

The two other youths made jerky bows from their saddles.

"We greet Your Highness," Hervey said.

"Your servant to command, Sire," Hugo mumbled.

The King of Scots inclined his head. "Friends of Davie's are friends of mine," he said. "The Earl of Surrey I know – a great lord. Is he behind, somewhere? And de Morville is an honoured name in my kingdom." He turned. "Sir Eustace – is this young man some kin of yours?"

A middle-aged, heavy-made man just behind, Eustace de Morville, newly-made Great Constable of Scotland, nodded. "My brother's youngest son, Highness. If this is the Prince David – I could say that he is not in the best of company!"

Into the laughter, Edgar spoke. "My brother, friends – David of Scotland. Come to greet us. We wondered when someone would!"

As salutations were murmured amongst the men behind the King, David bowing right and left, scanned the ranks of the riders. They were a mixed lot, in appearance as in dress and age, some, like the Constable, with the cropped heads and shaven chins of Normans, some with the almost shaggy flaxen to fair hair and beards of the Saxons, some with the darkly Celtic looks and thin down-turning moustaches of the Scots. The face for which the youth looked was not there.

"Where is Alex?" he asked.

A frown flickered on his brother's brow for a moment. "Alex is ... Alex ..." he returned shortly. And then, as though recognising that this might sound unsuitable in front of all these others, he went on, "He asked to be excused the journey. And it was as well that one of us should remain in Scotland. Lest men of ill-will should think to take advantage of my absence. Alexander at least will keep his sword drawn, willingly enough!"

David could not hide his disappointment. He had a strong family-feeling and liked his next brother even though he was the most vehement and aggressive of the Margaretsons, some five years older than himself as he was.

An older man spoke, behind the King, whom David recognised as Gillibride, Earl or Mormaor of Angus, one of the *ri*, literally lesser kings of the Celtic realm, as distinct from the *Ard Righ* or High King of Scots.

"Are you sent ahead of King William, David mac Malcolm? You *boys*!" he demanded.

12

David moistened his lips. "No, my lord," he admitted. "We come . . . of ourselves."

"Kind!" the Earl gave back, with something not far from a snort. "But where then is the King? We cannot be more than five or six miles from Winchester. We had thought to see him before this."

The boy answered nothing.

"Well, Davie?" Edgar prompted. "We have looked for a welcoming embassage from William all this day. Since Farnham, where we slept. To bring us to the King himself. We are near to our journey's end. Yet here come only my own brother and two young friends. You are come from Winchester, I take it? Where is William?"

David swallowed. "My lord – King William is not here. He is . . . hunting."

"Hunting!" That came out in an explosion of breath – although it was scarcely to be heard in the sudden volley of exclamation from behind. "*Hunting*, you say?"

"Yes. I, I am sorry . . ."

"Did he not know that I was coming? Today? My messenger . . . ? He must have done – since *you* knew to come."

"He knew, yes, Edgar. But . . . went hunting."

His brother spoke through clenched teeth. "And he sent *you* to meet me?"

"No, my lord King. He sent none. We, we came of ourselves."

"You mean . . . God in His Heaven, you mean that William Rufus knew that I was approaching his city, and at his own request, and sent none to greet me, the King of Scots?"

Unhappily David nodded.

"This is . . . insufferable!" Edgar turned to look at the men behind him. None, Scot, Norman or Saxon actually met his eye, although all looked shocked, unbelieving, angry.

"Turn back, man!" Gillibride of Angus shouted, hotly. "He is an oaf! He did this once before, mind – to your father. At Gloucester. I was there. The same year Malcolm died, six years back. He summoned Malcolm – and then when he came, refused to see him. The man is a churl. Son of a bastard, the Bastard of Normandy, who knows not how to behave!"

Some of the Normans present looked distinctly uncomfortable at that, but none raised voice.

"Aye, turn back, Highness," young Cospatrick, Earl of Dunbar and March urged, second-cousin to Edgar and David. "This is an insult."

Edgar chewed at his lower lip. His was not a strong face, more rugged than David's but lacking that firmness of jawline.

"I can scarce do that," he muttered. "We are three hundred miles and more from Scotland. And, and . . ." He scarcely required to finish that. All there knew the position well enough, Angus included. Without the army William Rufus had lent him three years ago, to march on Scotland, Edgar would still have been an exile, like David, and not wearing the Scottish crown today. He would never have unseated his uncle, Donald Ban, on the throne without English help. And, with much of Celtic Scotland still eyeing him askance, Edgar might need that English aid again, at any time. To turn back now might mean that he would never get it.

"We could halt here, and wait," Sir Eustace the Constable suggested. For a Norman that was a stout gesture, indicative of how closely he at least had thrown in his lot with the Scots king, in three years. "There is a small monastery a little way to the west, beyond Kilmeston. But two miles or so. I know it well. We could wait there, Highness. Until King William thinks better of it."

Edgar shook his fair head. "I think not, Eustace. It would not serve. If William, later, does *not* think better of it, I should look the greater fool, sitting there. William has done this of a purpose, I swear! He will not change his mind. No – we must go on."

Men murmured, but they rode forward again.

The King was silent, preoccupied, for a while, and David and his companions fell back amongst the less important of the company, unsure of their position. But presently Edgar summoned his brother to his side.

"Tell me of William, Davie," he said. "Does he do this to scorn me? Why ask me to come? What ails the man?"

"I do not know. I see him but little. He is a strange man – an evil man, men say . . ."

"What is the talk at his palace? About me?"

The other hesitated. "I have been at Winchester Castle only since yesterday. Brought from Romsey especially. With Matilda and Mary. For this Crown-wearing ceremony. I do not speak with many of the King's people. But . . . folk speak scornfully of all Scots, I fear."

"Including myself?"

"Ye-e-es."

"Then why am I summoned here? He sent *requiring* me to come. And, God pity me, I dared not refuse."

"Why, Edgar? I am glad to see you, so happy that you come. But . . . I had rather have seen you in Scotland! Come to you, not you to come here. Why must it be?"

"Do you not understand, Davie? You are all but a prisoner here. But, so am I, in one way! William seated me on our father's throne, three years ago – just as he had seated our half-brother Duncan on it three years before that. He can *unseat* me, as easily. So long as Scotland is so divided as it is. I sit anything but secure, lad – and Rufus knows it all too well. And uses the threat of it against me."

"But what could he do? Against you? If he sent up another army to invade Scotland, then surely the Scots would unite to throw them back? All would rally to your aid, then. They would have to, or be conquered. And that the Scots will never allow."

"You think so? Davie – you are old enough to understand, surely? Why think you I have not brought you, and our sisters, back to Scotland? Not for lack of love. I know well that you all would be free of our Aunt Christina at Romsey. I do not, because I cannot. William insists that you remain. Hostages. As I said, all but prisoners. And why? So that, at need, he could *use* you. Against me. He chooses to consider Scotland a vassal kingdom. It is not – but he would have it so. His father sought the same. And Canute before him. All would bring Scotland beneath England's heel."

"How could he use *me*? I am not important – and would never be used against you, Edgar."

"I fear that you would have scant choice, Davie. He would declare me deposed, if I refused to do his will, calling himself Lord Paramount – as he did with our Uncle Donald. Nominate *you* in my place, and march north with you, at the head of a great army, calling on all Scots to support you and unseat me. He threatened as much when last I saw him, two years ago. That is why Alex would not come south with me. *He* does not wish to be so used. So William keeps you, to be used if need be. And he can rely on the Scots to be sufficiently divided to play his game, North against South, Highland against Lowland, Celtic Church against Roman. The house of MacBeth, in Moray and Ross, would leap at the chance to bring down our father's line and replace it with their own. They attempted it against Duncan, and when they failed in war, had him assassinated. Half Scotland, all the North, would support them. William knows it. I walk in that shadow, lad."

There was silence between the brothers for a space, David tight-lipped.

"So William will not let you leave England, Davie," the elder went on. "And he summons me south to carry his Sword of State at his Crown-wearing, knowing that I dare not refuse to come. But this, of neither coming himself to greet a fellow-monarch, or sending a deputy, is bad, bad – an open affront. I fear that there may be worse in store."

"Perhaps he is but careless, heedless, Edgar? Means no special ill. He loves hunting above all else – save perhaps young men!"

The King glanced sidelong. "You . . .? He has never looked that way? Towards you?"

"No, the saints be praised! I see but little of him. He never looks at me, never visits Romsey Abbey although it is but ten miles. Besides, he has a sufficiency of young men to pleasure him, eager and willing enough!"

"M'mm." Edgar changed the subject. "How goes it with you, then? At Romsey Abbey. Is Aunt Christina as harsh and sour as ever? *I* hated it there."

"Sour, yes. Is it not strange that our mother should have had so different a sister? So stern. Holy, yes – but unloving. It is worse for Matilda and Mary. Matilda hates her. She treats them just as she does her other nuns and serving-sisters. She can do little with me, now. When I was a child it was different. But now I am largely in our tutor, Brother John's hands. With my friends. We are scarce ever in the women's part . . ."

"I am sorry for it all," the King of Scots sighed. "What a broil it all is! We can only hope for better days, Davie – hope."

"Hope – and pray," the youth said simply. "I pray a lot."

The King did not comment on that. Not all the Margaret-sons were as pious as their sainted mother had been. But then, their father had been no saint.

Presently the cavalcade came down the long hill to reach the walls of Winchester, on its slope above the Itchen, capital city of England and favourite seat of the monarchy, presided over by the twin magnificences of the largest castle and greatest cathedral in the land, whose thrusting towers had drawn all eyes for miles back. Those of the visitors who had not been here before were duly impressed, some even over-awed by the size and grandeur of it all, the extent of the walled town, the jostling spires and turrets and gables and the riot of fluttering flags and banners which flew everywhere in honour of tomorrow's occasion. When they had to join a long queue of folk, however, noble and poor, priests and beggars and chapmen, to get in at the heavily-defended gatehouse, the admiration wore off somewhat. The leaders of the party were too preoccupied with their possible reception to be impressed.

But here, at least, they were expected, for as they neared the portcullis arch a captain of the guard and two soldiers, roughly pushing aside the people before them in the queue, came forward to demand if they were the Ecossais party? On this being admitted, he proffered no greeting or any mark of respect, but shortly told them to follow his two men, who would lead them to their quarters. He then turned on his heel to leave them – when Sir Eustace de Morville could contain his proud Norman temper no longer.

"Sirrah!" he rapped out. "What respect is this to pay to my lord King of Scots? And his lords."

The captain turned at this peremptory tone, in his own language, and perceiving the style of the speaker submitted a grudging salute – but to this recognisable authority that he was prepared to accept, not to the fair-haired figure under the boar-banner, who wore the simple, slender golden circlet around his brows.

"Respects, sir? I but obey orders from Monsieur Flambard."

In through the thronged and narrow twisting streets of the city they followed the two soldiers, in little more than single-file now, even though their guides sought to open a way for them ungently with the staffs of their halberds. The place was crowded to a degree, with folk of all sorts and conditions, notably many armed men wearing the colours and badges of lords and knights arrived for the festivities.

They had proceeded only a short distance when David, behind his brother, turned to look back unhappily at his two friends. They were heading *downhill*, away from the high ground towards the West Gate where towered the royal castle-palace. Yet the two guides obviously knew exactly where they were going, clearing the way in no uncertain fashion still. They were, in fact, heading down towards the poorest quarter of the town.

Sir Eustace voiced his own recognition of this fact. "This is not the way to the castle, fools!" he called. "Where are you taking us?"

The older soldier looked back. "The Hospice of St. John, sir. Orders."

"Whose orders, by God?"

"Monsieur Flambard's, sir."

David considered his brother's stiff back in some agitation. St. John's was a hospice for the poor, founded by St. Birinus, the Roman who had converted the Saxon King Cynegils in the seventh century, set down in Winchester's most wretched area, half-a-mile from palace and cathedral. The city was crowded, to be sure, but the castle itself was vast. Even he and his friends and sisters were installed there, however modest their quarters. And there were other hospices and friaries in the town less lowly than this poors'-house. He said nothing, however.

They came to the place – which indeed was none so ill a building, quite large and well-constructed. But the air of poverty was all about it, the smell of poverty also. And there was a notable lack of stabling for over fifty horses. The crowds thronging outside seemed to consist only of the aged, the disabled, the blind, beggars and the like. They were received by an elderly friar, who looked defeated and apologetic.

Angus burst out into profanity, and others took up the resentful complaint. But the King made no comment. Dismounting, he stalked inside behind the friar. It was quite the poorest accommodation they had experienced in all their long journey from Scotland.

David's two friends, embarrassed, decided to remove themselves back to the palace, but he elected to remain with his brother meantime.

*   *   *

At least there was a sufficiency of food, plain fare as it was, with light ale to wash it down. After they had cleansed themselves, changed from their travelling clothes, and eaten, Edgar announced that he was now going up to the palace. He certainly was not going to wait humbly down here in this kennel until such time as he was summoned to appear before Rufus, like some wretched suppliant. Some argued that this could lay him open to further embarrassment, but most agreed that it was better to grasp the nettle thus.

So, with only some half-dozen of his senior supporters, and David, he mounted, to ride uphill again, in the early evening.

In the event they had no least trouble in passing through the castle gatehouse-pend and entering the palace precincts. The place was astir with nobles and knights and clerics and men-at-arms, coming and going, few sparing more than a glance at the newcomers, these less handsomely dressed than many there. Grooms took their horses readily enough, but otherwise they were ignored. David led the way to the Great Hall.

This proved to be an enormous, pillared cavern of a place,

quite unlike the hall of any castle, rath or hallhouse in Scotland, fully two hundred feet long by half that in width, the walls hung with tapestries and arras. Down the two sides, quite near the walling, servitors were setting long tables for a banquet, leaving a wide space open in the centre. At the head of the great apartment was a raised dais with another table, crosswise, already set with gold and silver vessels. In a minstrel's gallery above the bottom end, musicians were tuning up their instruments.

Edgar pointed, wordless, to the dias, and led the way, to climb on to it – watched askance by the servitors but not interfered with.

"I shall await William here," he declared, sitting on a bench.

"I think that he cannot be back from the hunt, yet," David said. "I have seen none of his friends."

His brother nodded. He beckoned one of the servants. "Fetch us wine, fellow."

The man looked doubtful. "The Deputy Chief Butler dispenses the wine, sir. Later."

"Aroint you, fool – wine!" Sir Eustace barked. "Are you telling the King of Scots to *wait?*"

"Eh . . . no. lord! Yes, lord!" Bowing, the man hurried off.

There was some considerable delay before the wine appeared, nevertheless. And when it did, the servants were accompanied by two or three others, richly garbed, the foremost of whom was a fleshy but smooth man of early middle years, round-faced, balding, smiling, with shrewd small busy eyes.

"Flambard!" David groaned into his brother's ear. "Now the King's chiefest minister and right-hand. A man hateful."

"Ah – here is a surprise," the newcomer said, his voice high and light, but pleasingly modulated. "Do I see the Lord Edgar of Scotland? You take us unawares, my lord."

"Do I? It might almost have seemed so – only the keeper of your poors' asylum here was ready for us, at least! Under instructions from one Flambard, it seems."

"That is my humble self, my lord. I hope that you found all to your comfort at St. John's? The town is plaguey full, I fear, folk roosting in every corner. But you will have all St. John's Hospice to yourselves, I promise you. The . . . inmates have been removed."

Edgar made no comment. "Where is King William?"

"His Grace has just returned, my lord. From Somborne Forest. I heard his company ride in but a few minutes ago. Let

19

us pray that he has had a good day's sport so that he is in genial temper!" Despite the lightsome voice there was a grating behind that somewhere, a warning or threat.

"We had looked to see him before this," Edgar said flatly.

"Your patience will soon be rewarded, my lord."

"My patience is not the best of me, Monsieur . . . what was the name?"

"Flambard, sir – Ranulf Flambard. His Grace's humblest servant."

"Are you, then, this Deputy Chief Butler?"

"Ah, no. Scarce that. I am, all unworthily, the Lord Chief Justiciar of England, my lord."

"Indeed. I am . . . surprised."

For a moment those small eyes gleamed daggers. Then the man bowed. "Here is wine for your refeshment, my lords. But – may I suggest that you drink it otherwhere? This dias-table is set and reserved, you will understand, for the King's Grace." Flambard backed away.

"I am sufficiently comfortable here, sir," Edgar told him. "And it is usual to name a monarch Highness or lord King."

"Ah – but there is only one lord King in England . . . Highness!" the other asserted, smiling, and swept out.

"That low-born scullion Chief Justice!" Sir Eustace exclaimed. "A priest's bastard, from the Cotentin. Red William must have run mad!"

"He is named the most cruel man in England, as well as the Justiciar," David said. "But – that was well-spoken. I wish that I could speak like that, Edgar. You, you are not going down from this dias?"

"No."

"Good lad!" the Earl of Angus chuckled. "Er . . . Highness."

So they sat drinking, as the hall filled up, seeming at ease but wary-eyed. They were stared at, as guests came to take their seats at the lower tables, but none actually came to speak with them, although there was much whispering and head-shaking. No women were present. William Rufus did not like women. They all had quite a lengthy wait, with only the Scots party drinking. The musicians played now.

Then, at last, the music stopped and a trumpeter appeared in the gallery, to blow a loud and stirring fanfare. All men rose – all men, that is except the King of Scots.

A door was thrown open behind the dais area, and as the trumpet-notes faded, a herald cried, "Attend on the King's Grace!"

There was a pause, quite prolonged. Then laughter could be heard from beyond the doorway. The herald stood aside, and bowed low. Two men came strolling in, one of middle years with his arm around the shoulders of one much younger. Both were chuckling, one deeply, the other in more of a high giggle. After a slight interval came a casual gaily-clad group of about a dozen, Chief Justice Flambard prominent amongst them.

The leading pair were, of course, immediately confronted with the Scots group occupying the dais platform, the older man affecting not to notice at first, although his companion, a beautiful young man most elaborately dressed, contrived to look both alarmed and determinedly amused at the same time. Then, when he was within a few feet of the Scots, William fitz William halted, arm still around his friend, to stare.

Edgar rose from his bench, at last. "Greetings, Cousin," he said into the profound hush.

"On my soul – Edgar of Scotland!" the other monarch exclaimed. He stuttered somewhat. "S'so you have answered my s'summons with becoming promptness!"

William the Second was scarcely an impressive figure, a short-legged, stocky man with a prominent belly but strong shoulders. He had a notably red face, clean-shaven, the colour blotchy – hence his by-name of Rufus, for his hair, which he wore long and straight contrary to the Norman normal, was fair-to-sandy, although greying now. But seeing him for the first time, it was the King's eyes which were apt to make the most impact, strange, narrow, spotted eyes, appearing to be of differing colours – although it would be hard to decide what those colours were. But they were keen and intelligent eyes, there was never a doubt as to that. He was richly but untidily dressed.

"I accepted your kind invitation for tomorrow's ceremony, yes" Edgar nodded. Compared with the other he looked young, almost boyish. "I might have been less prompt had I known how occupied you were, Cousin, with today's . . . activities!"

"Ah, yes." Rufus grinned. "We had a good day. Excellent sport. Did we not, Ivo?" And he turned to his companion, squeezing those shoulders.

"Excellent, Sire," the beautiful youth agreed, with a nervous laugh.

"Yes." Switching off his smile, William looked behind him. "Ranulf – have the Lord Edgar and his people conveyed to their due place," he snapped, the crispness almost emphasised by the hint of stammer.

21

The King of Scots was as brisk. "No need," he asserted, as Flambard stepped forward. "I have already chosen where we shall sit." And ignoring the Justiciar and all others, he turned and stepped down from the dais, to stalk down the open central space towards the foot of the hall, almost as though he was going to leave altogether, his party following. But near the foot he halted, swung on his friends, and pointed to the lowest table of all.

"Clear me this," he ordered. "And move it there." He gestured sideways, crosswise, into that central space.

Grinning, Angus actually guffawing, his supporters did as he said, some roughly pushing away the still-standing diners there, others, including David, laying hands on the table, to heave and push it aside, at right-angles to its former position, so that it became islanded out in the middle of the hall, certain beakers and cups spilled in the process. Then its complement of benches were grabbed and dragged out. Edgar sat down centrally, beckoning David to his right hand. Angus seated himself on the King's left, Cospatrick of Dunbar on David's right, the others where they would. The dispossessed guests, looking mortified, unsure, had to go and re-seat themselves where they could.

Up on the dais, William was glaring down at this unprecedented scene, powerful shoulders hunched, his arm dropped from his favourite now. Then abruptly he laughed loudly, and sat down. Relievedly, in most cases, all others sat also.

Flambard pointed towards the minstrels' gallery, and music started again, if somewhat raggedly. The long lines of waiting servitors filed in bearing laden trays, platters and dishes.

"That was good!" David said to his brother. "Splendid! I wish my friends could have been here to see it. I would never have thought of that."

"It is but the first move," Edgar said heavily. "Rufus has all the cards." Proof of this assessment was speedily forthcoming. A resplendent character wearing a white, lace-edged linen towel over his left forearm – no doubt the Deputy Chief Butler – came hurrying down from the dais, giving orders to the servants. Swiftly it became evident what those orders were. No food or drink was brought to the Scots table.

By the time that the last, and lowliest, of the other guests were served, Edgar's face was expressionless but his knuckles gleamed white, while his friends looked grim. William, chatting and joking with his close companions, did not so much as glance in their direction.

"Walk out!" the Earl of Angus suggested, loudly, and there were murmurs of agreement from others.

The King of Scots sat still, very still – and none could move until he did.

Everywhere men watched, all but holding their breaths.

Then there was a diversion. Up at the dais-table a man three seats from William's right rose to his feet, and rounding the table-end, stepped down and walked towards the Scots. He was in his early thirties, short-legged and wide-shouldered also, but with close-cropped dark hair and sallow angular features.

"Henry. Henry Beauclerc," David said. "He is better. Has shown me favours at times."

This man came up, and bowed to Edgar, not low but civilly. "I greet you well, my lord King," he said. "We have not met, I think? I was long in Normandy. But I know this young man, the Prince David. I am Henry fitz William."

"Your renown is known to me, Prince Henry," Edgar acknowledged carefully. "We might have met under, under kinder circumstances."

"No doubt. We may not always choose our circumstances – but we may perhaps mend them a little. Or bend them!" He smiled faintly. "If you can make room at your table, Highness, I would esteem myself honoured to sit with you?"

Edgar drew a quick breath – as did others there, who heard. "That would much pleasure me, sir," he said, and there was no disguising the relief in his voice. He gestured to his side, his right, and David eagerly moved over, closer to the young Earl of Dunbar, to provide space.

Henry came and sat, every eye in the hall on him. He patted David's shoulder and murmured a word or two to Edgar, then, looking up, gestured peremptorily to the nearest servitors, pointing at the empty platters. Glancing uneasily at each other, at the Deputy Chief Butler and up towards the dais, these hastily brought meats and wines. They dared not disobey the King of England's brother.

"How is Your Highness's other brother, Alexander?" the prince asked. "Him I *have* met. And there are two others, are there not, still alive?"

"Alexander, Earl of Gowrie, is well – if unruly!" Edgar answered. "Yes, Ethelred and Edmund still live – both older than I am. But they are churchmen. Ethelred – he now names himself Hugh – always has been. Edmund's . . . reform, is more recent!"

"Ah. Brothers can present their problems!"

At the other end of the hall King William shrugged off his glaring, and resumed his converse with his associates.

The banquet proceeded more normally.

Presently William clapped his hands for entertainers, and after a moment in filed a troupe of dancers, about a dozen of them, in colourful and fairly diaphanous dresses, long-haired pretty creatures, girlish, none over seventeen by the look of them, cheeks rouged, bared shoulders powdered white. The musicians struck up a languorous rhythmic melody, and the dancers proceeded to swan gracefully in couples up and down the central space – with the Scots table inevitably somewhat in the way. At first all was most decorous and pleasing, the performers willowy, supple but virginal, schooled to perfection in step and timing – although their efforts were greeted by hoots and catcalls from the all-male gathering, led from the dais. Then the music began to speed up and to change its character as well as its tempo. The dancers responded, their chaste and artistic movements becoming jerkier, more angular, less restrained. Soon the dance had become quite wild, although still in fair time with the music, with much kicking and bending and parting of legs. This exercise revealed that the long flowing skirts were, in fact, slit front and rear, almost all the way from ankles to waists, frequently displaying much or all of the said active legs. But revealing more than that, as the high-stepping and cavorting became ever more abandoned and the dancers were apt to be bared momentarily right up to their crotches, where all were seen to be possessed of male genitalia, the bouncing breasts above proving to be skilfully artificial.

Now the performers, panting with their exertions, slowed with the music to a less violent exercise, replacing it with a disciplined but lewd and highly indecent posturing, in pairs still, thrusting and weaving, bending and twisting to each other. The watchers cheered and egged them on with both advice and insults.

The Scots party sat uncomfortably throughout. There were no prudes amongst them, and most were necessarily fairly tough in their attitudes. But this sort of behaviour was new to them, unthought of for entertainment. Edgar in especial looked unhappy, frequently glancing sidelong towards his younger brother. They had been strictly brought up by a determined saintly mother.

"You do not admire my brother's tastes and diversions, Highness?" Henry Beauclerc wondered. "Yet you, like he, remain unwed."

24

Edgar reached for his wine beaker and did not answer.

David spoke. "Is this not evil, my lord Henry? Against all God's laws? Can a realm prosper when such as this is practised openly by rulers?"

"Do not ask me, young man – since none others ever do! What is evil? Is there such a thing as evil? Or are there but offences to others, inconveniences, inexpediencies and the behaviour of others contrary to one's own?"

"There is evil!" the boy said, with certainty. "Is not disorder evil? Untruth? Worst of all, cruelty, unkindness, man's inhumanity to others. So our lady-mother taught us – and she *knew*."

"Ah, the good and clever Margaret! Perhaps not all of us had your . . . advantages, lad. And yet – did not His Highness your brother, here, act with scant kindness towards your uncle, as I heard? King Donald. I heard, even in far Normandy, that when he defeated him in battle, he put out his two eyes and sent him to his kitchens to act as the scullion. For the rest of his life. Was that evil? Or was it . . . justice?"

It was the youth's turn to remain silent. He had wept one sleepless night when he had heard of that dire deed of his brother, three years before. He could by no means defend it.

Edgar did, if abruptly. "Would you have had me slay him? Take his life? My own father's brother. It was that – or what I did. He had twice grasped the throne. Once from Duncan, our half-brother, once from myself. He would have done so again. Is he better in my kitchen? Or in the grave?"

"So it was justice and expediency – not evil." Henry waved a hand towards the dancers. "And this – this could be folly, misdemeanour, *balourdise* – but is it evil?"

"Yes," the two brothers said.

The dancers retired, to loud applause, and a single singer with a lute came in. There was no doubt about the sex of this one, at least, for dressed in the height of fashion, he nevertheless wore an enormous image of an upright male organ strapped to his groin, flesh-coloured, perhaps three times the size of even the most ambitious, and this he waggled and flapped as he minced and capered, strumming his lute the while. As he broke into a song, catchy and tuneful but quickly evident as obscene as his appearance, Edgar mac Malcolm suddenly rose to his feet.

"Enough!" he jerked.

All his party rose also, of course, even Henry, although he delayed for a moment.

25

"I thank you, my lord Henry, for your courtesy," the King of Scots said, shortly. Then drawing himself up, he looked towards William at the dais, and nodded his head in the merest suggestion of a bow. Turning, he stalked to the nearest door, his people after him.

Unknown as it was for any guest to leave the monarch's presence lacking express permission, none could confidently assert that this applied to another monarch, even William. That man, as abruptly, laughed loudly – as dutifully did most of his supporters. The singer sang on.

The Scots party returned to St. John's Hospice. David went to his own palace quarters, where were his sisters. And Henry Beauclerc walked back to his place at the dais-table and resumed his seat, ignored by his brother.

*   *   *

The next day's Crown-wearing ceremony was, in fact, something of an anti-climax, certainly nothing worth the Scots having made all their long journey to attend. But then, it was not meant to be. It was merely an excuse, to remind them and all others that William was master and that the King of Scots must come at his bidding. Any other pretext would have served equally as well. It was not directed only at the Scots, of course, but at all Rufus's feudal vassals, the Norman baronage in especial, which his father the Conqueror had set up and which by its very nature was liable to become uppish and out-of-hand. The native Saxon chiefs and ealdormen were now little trouble, fairly thoroughly cowed. But some of the new Norman earls and lords had waxed altogether too powerful for the King's liking, some owning as many as two hundred manors. William greatly blamed his father for so lavishly rewarding his old comrades-in-arms – or allowing them to reward themselves. So every now and again he held a Crown-wearing demonstration, just to remind all concerned of their true position, of *his* powers and their subordination, at which it was obligatory to attend, on summons. It was, in reality, just a sort of repeat of the coronation, much foreshortened. There had not been one for four years.

A herald came that morning to command that the King of Scots be in position in the forecourt of the cathedral by one hour before noon. Edgar treated this instruction with reserve, especially when young David arrived at the hospice with his two sisters, shortly after, and mentioned that they had been told that they must be in their place inside the church only twenty minutes before noon. So it was evident that their elder brother was going to be kept hanging about outside, like some underling, for almost an hour, with the ceremony itself not starting until mid-day. He decided to delay his appearance considerably.

The two Scots princesses, from the nunnery at Romsey Abbey, aged nineteen and sixteen years, were attractive girls, however unflatteringly dressed – as was to be expected in daughters of the beautiful Margaret Atheling – but very different in appearance as in character. The elder – actually she had been christened Eadgyth, given a Saxon name like all Margaret's children, but had always been called by her second name of Matilda – was a tall and very lovely creature, fair-haired, well-built, prominently-breasted, with a quick wit and equally quick temper. Whereas Mary was more like David, slight, dark, quiet, with fine eyes and a thoughtful expression. They greeted their elder brother warmly enough, but they did not really know him very well, for one way or another most of his life had been spent apart from them. And they held it against him somewhat that he had never managed – if he had really tried – to get them out of the clutches of their Aunt Christina, Abbess of Romsey, and a monastic life which Matilda in especial loathed. They were not nuns, in fact, but had long been treated almost as such by their sternly pious aunt. This was hardly the occasion for much discussion on that long-standing problem, and William Rufus's part in it, but the subject did not fail to come up, if briefly.

In due course, as it drew on towards mid-day, the herald arrived back in some agitation, to demand, in the King's name, why the lord Edgar of Scotland had not appeared, as commanded, before the cathedral. He must come, at once. The herald was considerably more upset before, some time later, the royal party, with the other Scots notables, set out eventually in a distinctly leisurely progress through the climbing streets, thronged even more notably, to the higher part of the city.

Edgar found Flambard the Justiciar in charge outside the great church, who greeted him coldly but with a hint of relief. The group of notables assembled there were no more forthcoming. But then, none of them looked particularly happy or pleased to be present anyway. Edgar recognised only a few, including the Earls of Surrey, Shrewsbury and Warwick, but most were unknown to him. He guessed that all were in much the same situation as himself. These three he knew certainly were not William's friends, so probably the others were not either. None, so far as he could see, had graced the dais-table last night. Like himself, they were being used, forced to take a prominent part in this ceremony, as indicative of their dependence upon and subservience to King William.

David and his sisters were hurried off by one of Flambard's minions, to take their allotted places in the cathedral. The rest of the Scots party were ignored entirely.

David was surprised to find himself being led up through the already crowded church of St. Swithin to quite a prominent position near the chancel-steps, amongst the great ones. This was a new experience, for hitherto his family had been almost entirely disregarded by the Red King and left in no doubts as to their unimportance. After last night's performance, it would be foolish to imagine that this represented any change of heart. So, when he and his sisters were placed at the front of the chattering, richly-clad throng in the south transept, facing into the crossing, he decided that they were there to be seen, for William's own purposes – and these were unlikely to be kindly. He perceived, directly opposite, Henry Beauclerc standing, a little way apart from the rest in the north transept, but with two ladies, both over-dressed and neither beautiful. The prince waved a greeting to David.

"Who is that?" Matilda asked. "Someone prepared to know us!"

"Prince Henry, the King's brother. The one we told you of, who aided us last night. I do not know the women."

"The taller one is the Princess Adela, Countess of Richmond and of Blois. She came to Romsey with another sister, the Abbess of Caen, in Normandy, last year. I do not know the shorter one. Probably another of the King's sisters."

They gazed around them at the vast congregation – although it was not really that, for almost certainly this was not to be any occasion for worship. William was wholly irreligious, hating all priests and priestcraft; and the chattering, noisy company gave no indication of being aware that they were in a sacred edifice. No doubt the cathedral was being used merely because it was the largest building in Winchester.

Henry surprised again by coming strolling over to them. "A good day to you," he nodded, casually friendly. "Not improved by wearisome waiting! For myself, I mislike all such mummery." He was speaking to David but his eyes were on Matilda. "I vow that your royal brother, too, will be glad when it is over.

Is this . . . are these beautiful creatures your princess sisters? Make me known to them, I pray you."

"This is Matilda. And here is Mary, my lord Prince."

"Ah, yes – Matilda. And Mary. I am lost in admiration." He took Mary's hand and raised it to his lips, and then Matilda's – and hung on to it. "My eyes feast. I swear that I am going to enjoy this day's tiresome nonsense after all!" He looked into the older girl's eyes, frankly admiring.

"You cozen, my lord," she said, gently withdrawing her hand. "Amongst all your Court beauties, male as well as female, we are not for your notice!"

"Ha!" he observed. "That is the way of it, is it? Wit, as well as loveliness! *My* tastes, I would assure you, Princess, are not my brother's! Nor any of my family's, for that matter." He grimaced, and turned back to David. "Do you tell me, my young friend, that you have been hiding away this, this treasure in Romsey Abbey all these years?"

"We have been there, yes, for six years, my lord. As to hiding, I know not."

"Being hidden, perhaps," Matilda amended quietly. "Not of our choice."

"So-o-o! You would be out therefrom?"

"Yes."

"I think, then . . ." he began, when the blare of trumpets interrupted him, a stirring fanfare echoing and rebounding amongst the lofty stone walling.

Henry bowed to the girls, shrugged ruefully at the same time, and walked unhurriedly back to his own place just as his brother made his entry from the chapter-house doorway.

William was dressed magnificently today in cloth-of-gold seeded with pearls, beneath a scarlet cloak trimmed with miniver and thrown back, a jewel studded belt around his ample waist. He had an ungainly walk as he strutted to his throne-like chair placed isolated just above the chancel-steps and in front of the screens which partly hid the choir and high altar. Behind him trooped his personal entourage.

Sitting, and the others arranging themselves behind him, a motley crew, mainly men younger than himself, the King raised a hand for silence.

"I greet you, I greet you all," he said, "on this the twelfth anniversary of my accession to this throne of England. In token whereof I command this Crown-wearing. Let all my friends rejoice. And let all my unfriends take heed, and tremble."

"God save the King's Grace!" Bishop Maurice of London,

the only cleric present in evidence, intoned in a mellifluous voice, so much better attuned to the cathedral acoustics than William's high-pitched stammer.

Everywhere the shout was taken up. "God save the King's Grace. God save the King's Grace!"

Another flourish of trumpets was the signal for the great west doors to be flung open, to admit the procession. First came the King's Champion, a knight in full armour, white-painted, mounted on a huge pure white destrier or war-horse, white lance held high. Behind him came the royal Standard-Bearer, similarly mounted, bearing aloft the St. George Cross banner of England. The horses' iron-shod hooves clattered and slithered and drew sparks from the stone flags of the central aisle, as folk stared and gasped at such sight and sound in a church, some hastily crossing themselves. The two horsemen were followed by a splendidly-dressed double file of soldiers, on foot, halberds shouldered, marching to the rhythmic clash of cymbals, stamping the time.

There was only a slight gap before Chief Justice Flambard appeared, bearing before him a purple velvet cushion on which rested the Crown of England, a heavy, open gold band heightened with four spikes topped with trefoil heads, all studded with pearls. Flambard walked alone. Behind him the others came two by two, William de Warenne, Earl of Surrey, Hervey's father, carrying the sceptre or baton; and beside him, Robert de Bellême, Earl of Shrewsbury with the orb topped by the cross. Next came Simon de St. Liz, Earl of Northampton with the golden spurs on another cushion; and Henry Beauchamp, Earl of Warwick with the ring. These were followed by the two Montgomery brothers, Roger and Arnulf, Earls of Lancaster and Pembroke, each holding a glove, and looking distinctly offended to be so doing. Then, walking alone, was the King of Scots bearing upright the two-handed sword of state. These represented all the coronation symbols to be paraded. But not all those Rufus wished to be seen as supporting them. A group followed, carrying nothing, led by Gruffydd ap Cynan, Prince of Gwynedd and Richard, Prince of Cornwall, with a number of others including Saxon ealds and thanes – none of especially high rank, for all such were dead or imprisoned. Finally there was another file of the soldiers, with more cymbal-clashing.

This illustrious column might well have looked highly impressive. But it was not intended to do so; and the desired end was achieved in two ways – by packing the individuals close together, so that they were all but treading on each other's heels, and by the soldiers, front and rear, forcing a very quick pace, timed by the cymbals. The result was an undignified, hurrying shuffle, which duly produced mocking smiles from some of the watching audience, frowns from others – and open laughter behind the King's chair. The horses of the Champion and Standard-Bearer misliking the cymbals, snorted and blew and sidled.

This travesty of a coronation procession was hustled, almost like a file of prisoners in a Roman triumph, up to the chancel-steps, where Flambard lined up the token-bearers in front of William, the soldiers standing at either side. When all was in order, the cymbals fell silent and Flambard stepped forward to the King's left side, bowing low, with the crown on its cushion. The Bishop of London moved round from back to front, bowed in turn, and ceremoniously taking the crown, placed it carefully on William's head. Rufus presumably did not find it comfortable for he promptly took it off again, looked at it and replaced it – to titters of amusement from behind. The Bishop stepped back, raised a hand high, and pronounced a resounding benediction. Bishop Maurice was the only prelate readily available for this service; for Anselm, Archbishop of Canterbury, was banished the realm, Archbishop Thomas of York was sick, and anyway in disgrace, and most of the other sees, including Winchester itself, either deliberately kept vacant or their occupants in prison.

Flambard then summoned forward each of the symbol-bearers in due order, almost with a snap of his plump fingers. First Warwick with the ring, which he was stooping to place on the third finger of William's left hand, as signifying his marriage to his kingdom, when Flambard barked out for the Earl to kneel as he did it. Scowling, Warwick went down on one knee, to complete his task. Then Northampton was pointed forward, with the spurs – and since there were two of these, Gruffydd of Wales was gestured up to buckle one on the King's heel whilst Northampton did the other. This involved kneeling anyway, however sour the Welsh prince looked about it. Then the Montgomery brothers, Lancaster and Pembroke, were signed to put the gloves on the King's hands, again at the kneel. They obeyed stiffly, with ill-grace, Rufus grinning at their clumsy efforts to fit the things over unhelpful fingers. Then it was Shrewsbury's turn, to place the orb in the royal right hand and Surrey to put the sceptre in the left, William again making it difficult for the kneeling earls, with his gloved fingers fumbling.

31

Finally Edgar came forward with the sword. At Flambard's order to kneel, he turned slowly and stared for a long moment at the man, features expressionless, so that even the Justiciar blinked. When he looked back at Rufus, he inclined his head and bent one knee barely perceptibly, before stepping over and thrusting the long hilt of the heavy sword towards the other. But William had the sceptre in his left hand and the orb in his right, and sat, unmoving. The two monarchs gazed into each other's eyes, with mutual loathing. Timeless moments passed thus, until at last Rufus put the orb into his lap and reached for the sword. Edgar stepped back, lips tight.

William waved the sceptre at Flambard, who raised his voice again.

"God save the King!" he cried.

Over and over again that cry was echoed by the assembly, those behind the throne, with the soldiers, leading – although it was noticeable how little lip-movement there was amongst the group in front of the monarch. At another signal from Flambard, the trumpets sounded again, and Rufus rose to his feet. He had difficulty with the orb until the Justiciar took it. Then he stepped over to the first white destrier, the Champion having dismounted. That man took sword and sceptre meantime, and two soldiers assisted the king up into the vacated saddle, and the two symbols were handed up to him. The sword he rested over his shoulder, because of its weight. The Champion took the beast's bridle and began to lead it down the central aisle, the Standard-Bearer and his banner close behind. The file of soldiers and the cymbalists followed on. Flambard hurriedly marshalled his party of humbled notables, cushions abandoned, and herded them along, in any order, the second party of soldiers immediately at their heels.

So the King of England rode out of Winchester Cathedral into the sunlight to commence his parade through the city streets, wearing his crown. He was met in the forecourt by a band of mounted musicians playing a stirring marching tune; also by lines of gaily-caparisoned horses for his personal friends. There was one for Flambard now – but the former token-bearers still had to walk between the ranked and quick-marching soldiers.

There was some cheering by groups of men-at-arms, but by and large the populace in the streets watched in silence.

David mac Malcolm hurried and weaved his way through the crowd inside the church and seeking to leave, to the west doorway, to be in time only to see the royal procession leaving the forecourt area. Biting his lip at what he saw, and hastening after, he was nevertheless some time in catching up, on account of the crowds choking the narrow streets. But when he managed to do so, some way down the hill of the principal street, he was surprised to see that Edgar was no longer amongst the glumly-marching earls and lords. Gazing about him, he could see no sign of his brother. Turning he commenced to push his way back to the cathedral.

In the forecourt, where privileged folk now strolled and chattered, he found his two friends Hugo and Hervey with his cousin Cospatrick of Dunbar and other Scots, all looking depressed and at a loss.

"Edgar – my brother. The King – he is not there!" he panted. "He is not with the others, any more. I think that he must have slipped away. Lost himself amongst the crowd. Before the soldiers could stop him. It would be quite easy. The streets are throng with folk."

"A God's name – where is he now, then?" Dunbar cried. "The King – lost in this rabble!"

"He would make for St. John's, I think, surely? The Hospice . . ."

"Then let us go. At once. We were waiting here for the execrable procession to return. Come . . ."

"Where are my sisters? I must tell them . . ."

"They are well enough," Hugo de Morville assured. "Henry Beauclerc has them in hand – a hand in each arm, indeed! He was escorting them back to the palace, the last I saw . . ."

"Was my father there?" Hervey de Warenne demanded. "With the procession?"

"I do not know. I looked only for my brother. But – yes, I think that he was . . ."

"Come!" Dunbar exclaimed. "Back to the Hospice. There is Angus. Tell him."

"And my Uncle Eustace," Hugo said.

So the group beat their way through the crowds, downhill as they had come, through the poorer quarters. Being mounted it was easier, David on Edgar's horse, Hervey pillion behind, Hugo with his uncle, the flats of their swords driving a way for them.

At St. John's they found all in a stir, men saddling horses and strapping on gear. Edgar was already there, set-faced and urgent with his commands. They were leaving, and at once. He would not stay another hour in this accursed city. Rufus would be some time making his damnable procession – their going

33

would not be noticed. There was to be another banquet after. It would be hours before they were missed. They would out-distance any pursuit – although Rufus might well not seek them. He had had his infamous Crown-wearing . . .

Dunbar and Angus were loud in agreement, the Constable also. Unfortunately, however, some of the Scots party had not yet returned.

"You will wait and send them on after us, Davie?" the King said.

"But . . . I would rather come with you. Back to Scotland."

"That is not possible. I am sorry, lad – but it cannot be," Edgar told him. "That *would* bring Rufus after me. You are here as something of a hostage. And have you forgot our sisters?"

"No. But . . ."

"It cannot be, David. Not yet. One day, I may be able to contrive it . . ."

So, only minutes later, the three youths watched the Scots group ride off to the East Gate and out of Winchester, spurring fast as soon as they were beyond the great drawbridge.

"So that is . . . all!" David said, almost bitterly for he who was seldom bitter. "The end of our hopes."

"*Your* hopes," Hervey said. "We will never get away. We are prisoners, that is all. None want us, not even our own kin, sufficiently to risk the King's wrath."

"So it will be back to Romsey," Hugo sighed. "To tutoring and Latin and nuns and watered ale. Your brother did not serve much to get us out of there. What of Henry Beauclerc? He seems friendly towards you and yours. Would *he* not aid to get us free of Romsey Abbey?"

"I do not know. Would King William heed him? They also are unfriends . . ."

2

THE GREEN-CLAD cavalcade drew rein at Bramshaw Mill, as hitherto. This was the fourth New Forest hunt the three friends had attended; and the others had halted here also, for brief refreshment after the dozen-mile ride from Winchester, before dispersal to the various favourite glades of the vast forest area where the best sport might be looked for – the King, of course, choosing the most hopeful. It was a pleasant enough place to rest, by the stream-side, where the horses and hounds could drink, with greensward along from the mill for grazing – although the mill itself was rather disfigured by the beam which projected above the hoist in the gable from which dangled four bodies in chains, creaking and swaying in the breeze, one quite new by the look and smell; these were Saxons almost certainly, since the arms were handless and the eye-sockets empty, the prescribed punishment, before hanging, for Englishmen caught trespassing anywhere in the King's forests. But then it was quite difficult to find spots where there was grass and water and shelter, suitable, around the New Forest's perimeter, these days, which were not so decorated.

The youths sat a little way apart, to eat their plain oaten cakes and dry old cold mutton from the satchels – which was all that the nuns had provided for them – not mixing with either the royal hunters' party nor with the Norman foresters and men-at-arms drafted for the day's beating, local folk not being permitted to enter the forest precincts even as beaters.

"Your friend Henry might at least offer us a mouthful of his wine!" Hervey declared, as they watched the King and his companions eating and drinking very differently from themselves.

"If the Princess Matilda was with us, it would be different!" Hugo said.

"He must not seem to show us too much favour," David pointed out. "Or the King might not allow us to come at all. It is good of him to consider us and get us out for these hunts."

"He only does it as an excuse to call at the Abbey, coming and going, and so see your sister, who appears to have smitten him!"

"Perhaps. But it is good, for us. Better beating for the hunt in the forest than sitting in Romsey Abbey under Brother John, learning Latin!"

Neither of the others could deny that. "We should be *hunting*, not beating," Hervey asserted. "We are not children any more. And better bred than most of these! I am almost eighteen years."

That was an old story and required no comment.

Presently the King rose and called for his horse. Immediately there was a stir as hunters moved and coalesced into their groups for the dispersal, the Chief Huntsman, Le Chiene, marshalled his beaters, to allot to each group, and the hounds moved in on the royal scraps. This was always a tense moment amongst the guests. For Rufus, who was an expert and practised hunter, preferred to have only the one companion with him in the forest, for the sake of better sport and less noise. Whom he would choose was an important matter for those at Court – and it was not always the monarch's reigning favourite, who might be a poor marksman or feeble horseman. Ivo de Vesci was the darling still; but he was by no means the best shot with a crossbow, and after the last hunt William had blamed him hotly for having missed a hart which he had graciously left for him.

The King enjoyed keeping people on tenterhooks and he grinned at his party as Le Chiene allotted the beaters, assigning to the monarch three seasoned foresters, who would know the best places and be more skilful at driving the deer. The other groups could make do with the men-at-arms. Prince Henry beckoned the three from Romsey over to himself and Sir William de Breteuil, the Treasurer, who was one of the few friends he had at his brother's Court.

"Walter," the King called, at length, gaily. "Walter Tirel – you will accompany me today. And see that your shooting is better than was Ivo's last week!"

The beautiful de Vesci looked daggers, even though the King turned to clap him on the shoulder consolingly before mounting. Walter Tirel, the Sieur de Poix from Ponthieu, had been the favourite whom de Vesci had dispossessed some eighteen months before, a handsome dark man some eight years his senior.

As the others were mounting there was a diversion. An officer of the royal guard came riding in from the north, where lay Winchester, with a monk uncomfortably astride a spirited horse behind.

"Sire!" he cried, saluting. "Monsieur Flambard sent me with this clerk. He has a message for Your Grace. The Chief Justice believed that you might wish to hear it."

"A message, man? When I am hunting! From a monk?" Rufus snorted. "What foolery is this?"

"No foolery, Sire," the cleric, a sturdy, sober man of middle years, declared. "I am Ulfric, Sub-Prior of St. Peter's Abbey at Gloucester. I have ridden all this way from there, near thirty leagues, these two days, at great discomfort . . ."

36

"Well man – well! I am not interested in your discomforts. What has happened at Gloucester?"

"It was a dream, Sire – a most notable dream. My lord Abbot Serlon said that for Your Grace's sake I must come and tell Your Grace . . ."

"God in His Heaven – give me patience! Dreams, now!"

"I pray you to heed me, Sire. For your own good. For it was a sore dream, a sore omen. I dreamed three nights ago that the Lord Christ sat upon His throne in Heaven . . ."

"Rot your bones, clerk – *you* dreamed! You say your name is Ulfric? Ulfric, was it? So you are an Englishman, a Saxon! And you dare to come to *me*, the King, with your wretched dreams! I have a mind to have you flogged, fellow!"

"The dream concerns your royal self, Sire. And my Abbot sent me – who is a good Norman." The monk spoke quietly, determinedly, an obstinate, stolid man. "And the Chief Justice sent me on . . ."

"Then Flambard should have had greater sense! He grows addle-pated as well as fat. Well, fool – out with it. But be quick about it. What of Christ in Heaven?"

"The Lord Christ, Highness, sat on His throne amidst the cherubim and the seraphim, all wings and eyes. And a holy angel brought three women to the golden steps, amongst the four-and-twenty elders. Poor women – Englishwomen, Lord King. And these tore their hair and beat their breasts. And they cried, they cried . . ." Even the stalwart cleric's voice faltered for a moment. "They cried 'Saviour of the human race, look down! Look down in pity on Thy people. Who groan, Lord God, who groan . . . under the yoke . . . of William!'" He almost choked on that last word.

The King also all but choked. For the moment he could find no words.

"And . . . and the Lord Christ answered them, Sire," the other forced himself to continue. "He said, He said, that He had seen the sufferings of His people and was not heedless. He said that He sorrowed greatly – but sorrowed the more for William, His disobedient servant. Who, who had sworn in his coronation oath to protect His people, not to persecute them. He said that . . . this day . . . William must choose."

Despite himself, Rufus leaned forward on his horse. "Choose? Choose what, man?"

All there stared, hardly believing their ears.

"Choose good or evil, lord King. Choose to turn from the ill. To go on your royal knees, in the nearest church of God, and repent you. Or to go on in your cruel sin – and pay the price! That was the Saviour's words."

"Fiend seize you!" William raised a trembling fist – but the trembling was not from fear but from fury. Corpulent, for a moment or two it seemed as though he might take a seizure, his red features turning to purple. Then he mastered himself and produced a strange whinny of a laugh. "Oaf! Clerkly dolt! Saxon lout!" he stammered. "You think to frighten me, William, with your befuddled dreams? Do you take me for such as yourself? An Englishman who frights at shadows? Think you that I am such as abandons his course because old women dream dreams and Saxon churls start at fancies? Does the King pause when an Englishman sneezes in his sleep! Begone, fool – begone, while I yet spare you. Begone, before I have you strung up there beside these other cattle! I will not have my day spoiled by such as you. Away!"

He turned in his saddle. "Come, Walter de Poix – mount you. To horse, all. Chiene – the new arrows, I had made. Give them here. These, now, are excellent. See – they will serve us well this day, I swear." He took six arrows held out by the Chief Huntsman, weighing them in his hand, then handed two to Tirel, keeping four. "On, my friends – on. I make for Bignell Wood for the first draw. Go you all where you will – so as you do not spoil my sport, by Christ! Return here by four after noon. On, I say."

Dispersing, the hunters set off in little groups, with their beaters, heedful to give the King's personal party a wide berth. Prince Henry chose to take the line nearest to that of his brother on the west, saying that they would make for the Malwood, where he knew of a hopeful spot. The three youngsters, de Breteuil the Treasurer and a single forester rode with them, with three deerhounds.

When they were out of sight of all others, Henry reined back to let the youths come level. "That was an unedifying scene, was it not?" he said. "The man was a fool indeed, to think that William would pay him heed."

"But brave," David said.

"Bravery can also be folly, lad. But . . . I liked it not."

"Why did Flambard send him on?" de Breteuil asked.

"That I wondered also. He would know how it would be. And he is scarce a godly man, though a priest."

Eager as they were to discuss the incident, the trio could scarcely do so in front of Henry, who referred no more to it. He spoke to them of the area to which they were heading, just over a mile southwards where, in the Malwood Shaw, there was a large mire he knew of where the great harts liked on occasion to lie up in the cool mud of the August heat, spared the flies. This swamp was surrounded by scrub oak, into and through which the beasts could be driven. There were two lanes cut through the scrub where the hunters could hope for a shot.

Soon they were in the thicker woodland, and presently they passed the former charcoal-burners' village of Canterton, now only roofless walls and rioting vegetation, burned like all the other of the New Forest settlements, and the folk driven out, to improve the preserve. There were scores of such sad sights in the forest. Soon after, they came to the vicinity of Malwood Mere. Now they dismounted, to lead their horses quietly through the trees. Presently they split up. The forester took the three hounds forward, to reach the southern limit of the marsh, when he would slip them. The young men were to make for the mire's northern flanks, there to seek to prevent any deer which the hounds put up from breaking out east or west through the surrounding thick scrub, to ensure that they bolted down the north-stretching ride where Henry and de Breteuil would be waiting with their crossbows. In this dense woodland the horses would be of little use, and were to be left at this central point, one of the youngsters to stay with them and bring them swiftly to the hunters should three blasts on a horn summon them. The lads drew lots for this boring task and Hervey, drawing the shortest grass-stalk, was left behind.

Picking their way quietly through the tangled brushwood and undergrowth, to avoid disturbing any game there might be, and with the ground growing ever more soft and water-logged beneath them, David and Hugo came to open space where it was so wet that no trees would grow, although reeds stood high, an area perhaps six hundred yards by four hundred yards. David elected to go round to the far, eastern, side.

They waited opposite each other.

Alone now, and silent, David listened to the hum of the insects and the soft croodling of the woodpigeons in the warm August air. It was eleven months since the disastrous Crown-wearing, and as ever, he longed for the wider landscapes, the stronger air, the hills and white foaming rivers of Scotland.

They did not have to wait long today, at least. All the warning they received was, first a flight of mallard exploding from the reeds and as the wing-beats faded, the sound of a faint rustling and splashing – for the deerhounds did not bay as they worked. Then three deer suddenly were leaping lightly, gracefully, through the reed-beds in a shower of spray. But a glance showed that these were females, a hind and two almost-fully-grown calves. They were speeding down the centre of the mire and made no attempt to break out, left or right, before continuing out into the northern ride, to disappear down its green aisle.

Another hind came shortly after, alone, this nearer Hugo's side. Perhaps it got a whiff of his scent on the faint westerly air, for when almost abreast of him it abruptly swerved and came bounding over to David's side. He jumped up, waving his arms, but silently, and the beast slewed round again and raced for the ride directly ahead. That was satisfactory enough – but it was not hinds which the hunters sought.

There was a pause. They could hear the hounds now at their long-legged tireless quartering of the swamp. Then, at a stiff, bucking, head-down run, a large, heavy-shouldered boar crashed snorting through the reeds, hidden by their height most of the time. It was near David's side. He glanced swiftly about him for a climbable tree, for if the brute scented him, a wild tusker could be highly dangerous for an unarmed man. When he looked back, however, the boar was seen to be hurtling on in the wake of the vanished hinds. David wondered whether to blow his horn, the one blast which would warn the hunters that an especial quarry was approaching; but that thought was dismissed by the appearance of three more deer a short distance behind, the first an old grey hind, then two stags, one mud-plastered, with a shaggy mane and a handsome pair of antlers, the other younger. To wind the horn now might scare these away from the ride. The first of the hounds broke cover as the deer disappeared down the grassy lane – which would mean that there was not likely to be any more game behind.

David called in the hound, and a second which appeared, signalled to Hugo to join him, and hurried off to the ride, at a trot.

They found the marksmen about three hundred yards along, part elated, part frustrated. The boar and the big stag had appeared before their hiding-places almost side-by-side, and for precious moments each man had hesitated. The Treasurer would have allowed the Prince first shot, of course, or the best of two. But he could not tell whether Henry would choose the stag or the totally unexpected boar. The Prince, for his part, was equally doubtful. He shot at the boar, in the end, and brought it down – for he was an excellent crossbowman; but by that time the longer-legged, bounding stag was a less good target. To complicate matters, the second stag was now in view, and de

Breteuil hesitated again, whether to take the new and poorer beast or still to try for the other. He chose the latter, despite the extreme range. He scored a hit but not a kill. The wounded hart went on at a scrabbling run, the bolt projecting from its ribs. Neither man had time to string a new arrow before the second stag was gone also.

Henry had put the dying, kicking boar out of its gnashing misery, with a cut throat, when the youths ran up.

"My horse!" the Treasurer shouted. "The hounds! I have wounded my beast. I must follow it up. Quickly!" That was the law of the chase.

David blew three blasts on his horn, the signal to summon Hervey.

It was some time, of course, before these could be brought up. Meanwhile the forester and his hounds arrived and were sent off on the wounded stag's trail. Henry was pleased with his shot, and his tusks for trophy.

When the horses came, Hugo and Hervey were left with the boar, to gut it and bleed it, then to hoist the carcase on to one of their mounts and carry it back to Bramshaw Mill. The three others, with the forester's horse, mounted to go in search of the wounded beast. There was a spattered trail of blood to lead them.

They trotted for half-a-mile northwards by east before they found the forester waiting where the long ride forked into three. He declared that the hart had taken the right-hand, easternmost lane. It was going heavily now. It would not last much longer, he thought. It would probably go to ground deep in a thicket. Henry was a little anxious. This line, so much to the north and east, was bringing them into territory where others might be operating.

The forester proved to be right. Soon the hounds, and the blood-spatters, led them off into the thicker woodland, due northwards. They were dismounting, to leave David with the horses, to go after the stag on foot, when the drumming of hooves turned all their heads eastwards. Round a bend in the lane ahead came a single horseman riding fast, much faster than was wise on that uneven terrain. He slowed to nothing as he came up with them but pounded on and past, head down.

They stared after him, astonished.

"Tirel!" Henry exclaimed. "Walter Tirel de Poix! What in God's name is he at?"

"He follows no deer," de Breteuil said. "And did not wish to see us."

Nonplussed, they were discussing this strange development when, faintly through the constriction of the trees, north by east, they heard the high notes of a hunting-horn. Four times it sounded, then a pause and four more – the accepted signal for alarm, trouble.

"Some mishap," Henry said. "In that direction."

"Perhaps the Sieur de Poix was hastening for help?" David suggested.

"Why did he not seek *our* help, then?"

As the horn sounded again, urgently as it seemed, they decided that de Brcteuil and the forester should continue on after the wounded hart, their horses tied to a tree here; and Henry and David should ride eastwards, to investigate the horn-winding.

They did not have to go far, not much more than a quarter-mile along the ride, before they could hear the horn quite close on the left. A track led into the trees here – and there were new horse-droppings on it. This quickly brought them to an open glade, green and gold in the afternoon sun. Two men and a horse occupied that glade – and one of the men lay prone. The other was Le Chiene, the Chief Huntsman, horn in hand.

"My lord Prince!" the latter cried, starting towards them. "Praise God – my lord Prince! The saints have mercy upon us – the King!"

Henry jumped down and strode over to his brother's side. William Rufus lay on his back, sightless eyes staring up through the canopy of the branches, a crossbow-bolt projecting from his chest.

It did not require the huntsman's repeated desperate assertions to convince that the King was dead; the arrow obviously was embedded in the royal heart.

Henry looked down, wordless, as David came up. It was the boy who found his voice first, even though it was a tremulous voice. "What . . . what happened?"

"Dear God alone knows, lord," the man Le Chiene gabbled. "Mercy on my soul – I know not. I put up a fine hart. In Bartley Shaw there." He pointed eastwards. "Not far. The King's Grace and my lord Walter waited here. The hart bolted this way. I sent the hounds to flank it. I heard a scream, that is all. I came, hastening. I found . . . I found the lord Walter kneeling. Over the King's body. When he saw me coming, he jumped up, ran to his horse and rode off. Fast. No doubt to seek help, my lords. The King was . . . was already dead."

42

"Tirel!" Henry said, not in anger or anguish, but thought-fully. "Walter Tirel!"

"Why did he not stop? To tell us?" David wondered. He was looking resolutely away from the staring corpse.

"Fool! Would he come confessing that he had murdered my brother?"

"Murdered . . .? Oh, no. Not murder. An accident . . ."

"Accident, you say?" Henry barked. "Tirel is one of the best marksmen in all Normandy. William is shot through the heart. That was no accident." He straightened up, turning to Le Chiene. "Where are your other foresters?"

"They went further east, my lord Prince. Towards Bird's Walk Wood. To drive those coverts. They would not hear my horn . . ."

"Where is the nearest house, man? Or farmery? We need a cart. For this . . . body."

"A cart? A cart, yes. The charcoal-burners have a cart. At Shave Green. We have used it to carry deer . . ."

"Very well. Go get it. Bring it. David – go find and tell de Breteuil. But – tell none other."

"Yes. Bring him here? To you?"

"No. Tell him that I have returned to Winchester."

"*Winchester*? But . . ."

"Winchester, yes. Tell Breteuil to come there, to me. At once. No delay. Le Chiene – off with you. To Shave Green, for the cart. Bring his Grace's body to Winchester thereafter. You will not win there, with a cart, this night. Rest at Romsey Abbey. There is no . . . haste. For that!" And he strode over to his horse.

As David mounted his own beast, he looked back. The glade was already empty, deserted, save for the dead monarch, who lay as they had found him. Biting his lip, he hurried in search of the Treasurer. It occurred to him that this was, in a way, like father like son. William the Conqueror, too, when he had died twelve years before, at Rouen, had been deserted, even by his own sons, left lying on the floor of his bedchamber for the dogs to nuzzle. *He* had no cause to love William Rufus – but it was an unchancy way to die.

*   *   *

It was early evening when David, accompanying de Breteuil, arrived back at Winchester. The town was quiet, with no signs of alarm – the palace too, when they reached it. An officer met

43

them at the gatehouse, however, to say that the Prince Henry awaited them in his own bedchamber. To go, at once.

They found the Prince pacing the floor, still in his green hunting-clothes. "Well my friends," he greeted them. "Here is a notable to-do. You have been commendably swift. As well, for there is much to be done."

"It is most terrible, shameful . . ." the Treasurer began, when Henry raised hand to cut him short.

"Save the lamentations for the funeral!" he jerked. "If lamentations there should be. William was a bad king – and is gone. The realm will have a better, now. You have told none, as yet?"

Both shook their heads.

"That is well. I shall announce the death myself, presently. Meanwhile, to business. And, first of all my Lord Treasurer – the keys."

William de Breteuil stared. "Keys . . .?" he echoed. "Which keys, my lord Prince?"

"The Treasury keys, to be sure. What do you suppose?"

"But, but . . ."

"But nothing, man. Those keys – I want them."

"Henry – I swore a solemn oath. As Lord Treasurer of this kingdom. That I would keep them secure, never leave them from off my person. Save to hand them, when required, to the rightful King of England."

"*I* am the King of England now, Will. Have you not thought of that? Give me them."

The other gazed at him, whilst David gulped. They were seeing a new Henry Beauclerc.

"Henry – my lord Prince – how can that be?" de Breteuil demanded. "You are the youngest son. Robert, Duke of Normandy, is older. He should succeed. In the treaty between your brothers it was decided. That Robert should have Normandy and William the greater England. But that if William died, lacking heir, Robert should be King . . ."

"Robert is far away. On this great Crusade to the Holy Land. Moreover, Robert is a fool, and weak. England needs a strong king, with wits – and here present! Now. Think you that this realm of fierce, proud lords and warring factions can be held together by aught but the presence of a determined monarch who knows his own mind? If I do not grasp the throne *now*, there will be war within weeks and no kingdom of England within months!"

"Nevertheless, Henry, you are *not* the King. Not yet. Not

when there is a more senior heir, and named so by treaty. Not until you are accepted as such by at least a great number of the lords. And until you are I cannot give you the keys."

"You *will* not?"

"No. I am sorry. I am your friend – but this I cannot do."

"So-o-o!" Henry turned, to where his sword hung from its belt on a peg beside his bed. He whipped it from its scabbard. "Will – I will have those keys. They are on your person. We are friends, yes – but a kingdom's weal is more important than one man, even a friend. Give me them – or, as God is my witness, I shall strike you down and take them!"

For a long moment they eyed each other starkly, while David gripped the girdle of his tunic tightly.

Then de Breteuil inclined his head, and reaching up, loosened the silken scarf around his neck and drew out the three keys in a soft leather pouch which hung on a golden chain. Slipping the chain over his close-cropped head, he handed it, warm from his body, to the prince.

Henry nodded. "Now – to the Treasury. David – yonder is another sword. Draw it, and follow me. Will – you also. Come."

Leaving the bedchamber they strode through the long vaulted corridors of the castle-palace almost to its other end, Henry beckoning imperiously to any guards or others they passed to fall in behind. They had collected quite a little crowd by the time they reached the North Tower. There, isolated, a special guard of three men, throwing dice, started up in some confusion at the eruption, reaching for their weapons; but seeing that it was the prince and their own master, the Treasurer, they straightened up in salute.

Henry handed the sword he was carrying to David, who now had two. The Prince selected the largest of the three keys, to unlock the heavy door of the tower basement. As it creaked open, he signed to all but de Breteuil and David to remain outside. Voices rose in question and exclamation as the door was closed again in their faces.

The stone-vaulted cellar was only dimly lighted with three slit windows, but sufficiently to reveal the stacks, from floor to curved ceiling, of iron-bound chests, scores of them. Henry stepped over, loosed the hasp of one and threw up the lid. It was filled with silver pieces. He tried another. This was as full, but of gold coins. He picked up a handful of these, and let them trickle through his fingers.

"The sinews of a kingdom!" he said. This was the Conqueror's treasure, looted from all England and half France, added to by Rufus's penal taxation and extortions from Holy Church.

Slamming down the lids again, Henry took the middle key and opened an inner door, which led into an adjoining and smaller chamber. As well as more chests, this one was shelved, and on the shelves were piled hundreds upon hundreds of vessels and ornaments in gold and silver, cups, chalices, pattens, crucifixes, plates, candlesticks, images of saints and the like, many jewel-encrusted. Opening one of the chests here, the Prince showed that it contained unnumbered rings and brooches, necklaces and loose gem stones. Another was filled with gold chains and belts.

But it was to a special solid-silver chest, banded in gold, placed in the deep single window-embrasure of the thick walling, that Henry made his way. With the third and smallest key he unlocked this. Inside, on the padded velvet cushions, lay the symbols they had all last seen eleven months before at the Crown-wearing – the crown itself, the orb and sceptre, the ring and the spurs, gleaming dully in the thin slantwise evening sun.

Henry picked out the crown, looked at it for seconds on end, and then, transferring it to his left hand, shut the lid again and relocked it. "Enough!" he said.

Neither of the other two had spoken a word throughout.

They went out, locking the two doors behind them. Henry kept the keys. Beyond the outer door they found the crowd grown. There was a great indrawing of breaths and a swell of comment when they saw what the prince was carrying.

He raised his voice. "De Comines – go find the Justiciar Flambard. Tell him to have everyone of any quality in this palace assemble in the Great Hall. At once. The castle guard to muster and come to me. At the dais entrance. And send wine. Now. You have it?"

"Yes, my lord Prince," the Chief Butler said, agitated. "But . . . the King's Grace . . ."

"Do as I say, man. Forthwith. I speak with the King's voice. Heed it!"

Henry now led the way to the hall, speaking to none. David felt distinctly foolish with his two swords. De Breteuil walked grim-faced behind.

So they came to that same dais platform. All but the three principals were sent curtly down into the body of the hall. Henry remained aloof. But when wine and beakers were brought, he dismissed the servitors and poured for his two companions.

"That New Forest," he said, in a voice different from that he had been using. "It is accursed. I shall never hunt there again. This is the third of our line to die there. My brother Richard, gored by a stag. My half-brother broke his neck, thrown. Now William. That monk from Gloucester spoke truly . . ."

Flambard appeared from the dais-entrance, looking concerned. His glance went straight to the crown, which Henry had placed on the table.

"My lord Prince – what is this?" he exclaimed. "Where is His Grace the King?"

The other did not answer, not in words at any rate. He pointed a finger at the Chief Justice and then jabbed it down towards the lower level of the hall-floor. Flambard hesitated, then, compressing his lips, descended the dais-steps.

Henry poured himself another beaker of wine.

The hall was filling up now, and agog with talk. Reginald de Lucy, the commander of the royal guard, appeared from the dais-doorway. "The guard is assembled, my lord Prince," he announced. "Is this the King's command?"

"Yes. Have a file of them in here. Behind me. The rest round to the door of the hall. When the horn blows, none to enter or to leave. Save on my orders. See to it."

De Lucy looked doubtful but did as he was told.

At length Henry turned. "A blast on your horn, David."

When the wailing notes died away, the prince raised his voice. "My friends – and, it may be, my unfriends also! I have tidings for you, important tidings. Heed well what I say. King William, my brother, is dead. Slain by an arrow, in the New Forest . . ."

The commotion in the hall halted him, and he let the noise prevail for a little, expressionless. Then he raised hand for silence.

"My brother was slain by a bolt shot by Walter Tirel. Whom all know. Who was alone with him in the wood. Whether of intent or accident is yet to be established. But . . . Tirel has fled!"

Again the uproar drowned his words. Henry turned to David and pointed to the horn once more.

The high notes of it gained approximate quiet.

"You will remain silent!" Henry cried "The next to raise his voice unbidden will be removed by the guard. Heed you – and fail to do so at your peril! There has to be a King in England. I, Henry, have assumed the crown." He picked up the golden circlet and held it aloft. "From this moment, I am King Henry.

My brother Robert of Normandy is a thousand miles away, fighting the heathen. England cannot wait for him. Besides, he is not of the stuff of kings. And I am, my friends – I *am!*" He stared round the gathering, head thrust forward a little, crown held against his chest now.

There was not a sound in the hall. Men scarcely breathed.

"I shall make you a good king – but a strong one," he went on. "All shall be changed. This realm shall be ruled as a kingdom, not a tyranny – and not a playground for pretty boys! Nor yet, see you, for Norman adventurers! I am an *Englishman*. I was born here, at Selby in York. I shall rule England as an Englishman. Normans, Saxons, Danes, each and all are assured of my goodwill – so long as they keep my peace." He paused, and glanced round at David again. "In token whereof – and that the reign of catamites and favourites is past, I announce to you that I intend to take as wife the Princess Matilda of Scotland . . ." He held up his hand as the noise swelled. "I said silence! The Princess Matilda, sister to Prince David of Scotland, here. This is my decision. She is daughter of Margaret, who was daughter of Edward, who was son of King Edmund Ironside, of the ancient line of the Kings of England. Myself, I am son of a cousin to both Edmund and Canute, who replaced that line. So I shall unite all three royal houses. So England will be ruled by England indeed." He took a sip of wine. None other raised voice – although David mac Malcolm at least had difficulty in keeping silent.

"There will be changes, I say," Henry went on. "You all are Normans here – or most." And he smiled faintly at David. "You will suffer nothing for being so. But the persecution of the English shall cease. And their lords will again take their due place in my realm. Mark that! As will Holy Church. For long the Church has been ravaged and slighted. No longer. I shall bring back Anselm, Archbishop of Canterbury, exiled at Bec. Others likewise. And justice will now prevail in my courts – justice not persecution, infamy, corruption. This I swear on my royal oath! As I now give you sign and token." He turned. "Sieur de Lucy – arrest me the man Flambard, formerly Chief Justice, and miscreant! And confine him in your deepest pit. Until my further pleasure be announced."

Now there was tumult indeed, and this time Henry made no attempt to stop it. The guard-commander took four of his men from the back of the dais and descended upon the alarmed Ranulf Flambard, to march him out, protesting.

"Enough for this present," Henry declared, after an interval which allowed the excitement to subside somewhat. "You shall hear my further decisions in due course. William de Giffard, until now Chancellor, you will take a troop of men and bring me back Walter Tirel de Poix – if he has not already reached the sea and taken vessel to Normandy. He was fleeing southwards. A council will be called for two days hence – no, three. Most of the hunt is not yet returned. When these do, some shall join Flambard! The late King William's body will lie at Romsey Abbey this night, and be brought here tomorrow for burial in the old minster of St. Swithin. There will be no ceremony. Tomorrow, also, the bells of all churches and monasteries will ring all day. Not for my accession but because Holy Church is free again in England." Henry held the crown above his head again for a moment, and then turning to de Breteuil, he handed it to him. "My Lord Treasurer and chief minister!" he said. "Come, sir. And you, David."

As they moved over to the dais-door, someone shouted "God save the King! God save the King!" And immediately the cry was taken up on all hands, even if doubtfully in many quarters of the hall. They strode out, to its chant.

"That was . . . splendid!" David exclaimed enthusiastically. "Splendid. Was it not, Sir William? Are you truly King now?"

"Scarcely, lad. It takes a little longer! But – near enough. Tomorrow I ride to London, with this crown. For Bishop Maurice to crown me. I cannot wait for the Archbishop's return. Someone else can bury William! You shall come with me, if you wish."

"Oh, yes, yes. And, and Matilda? You meant that truly? That you would wed her? It was not just a sudden whim?"

"Think you that I would have announced it to all, as I did? That was no whim, David. It has been my desire to marry her these many months. But William would have seen it as a danger to himself. Threatening his position, for myself to be wed to one of the old line. Now, it is best, suitable." He smiled. "Think you that she will have me, lad?"

Gravely David inclined his head. "I believe so, yes. I know that she esteems you greatly."

"You much relieve me!"

"I perceive that you have thought it all out very well," de Breteuil remarked. "All this has not come into your mind since this afternoon's slaying, I think?"

"Can you not bring yourself to call me Sire, Will? No – I have had sufficiently long to consider it all. With William unmarried and lacking heir, I saw it coming. He was well hated. One day it

49

would happen. Slighted and replaced catamites are unchancy companions! I have but waited my time . . ."

They came back to Henry's bedchamber. "I must have a better room than this, now," he said looking round its modest dimensions. "Not that I would wish to occupy William's – which would stink in my nostrils! Besides, I shall soon need a bedchamber large enough for two – eh? How would this one serve *you*, David?"

"*Me*? You mean . . . ?"

"To be sure. You have long wished to be out of Romsey Abbey and the nuns' clutches, have you not? And if you are going to be the Queen's brother, you must have a certain style. The room is yours."

"I thank you, I thank you. But, Henry . . . my lord . . . Sire – my friends, Hugo de Morville and Hervey de Warenne. They hate the Abbey . . ."

"Yes, yes – bring them with you. We shall find a corner for them. There will be many empty chambers in Winchester Castle after this day!"

"And Matilda? And Mary?"

"Ah, now – that is different. Eh, Will? We shall have to go discreetly there. To consider the princesses' reputation. Much as I would wish to have Matilda here, I think that meanwhile she must remain with the good nuns. But not for long, lad – tell her, not for long. When I get back from my coronation in London, my first call shall be upon her . . ."

3

So LIFE CHANGED entirely for David mac Malcolm. From being a sort of hostage, personally unimportant, to be ignored when he was not actually slighted, he abruptly became the King's friend, and only a little less suddenly the Queen's brother – for Henry and Matilda were wed that St. Martin's Day, only three months after the hurried coronation. All about the Court now treated him with some degree of deference. It was a very

different Court, of course, with all Rufus's young men, favourites and hangers-on, sent packing, many of his principal minions imprisoned, and most of the nobles who had supported
him retired to their estates and replaced by such as the men
whom he had humiliated at his Crown-wearing – Warwick,
Surrey, Pembroke, Lancaster, Chester and the rest. If all these
great earls did not exactly genuflect before David, at least they
treated him with a decent respect – admittedly not so much as
the brother of the King of Scots as the brother-in-law of the
King of England.

Not that all this in any way went to that young man's head,
for he was of a modest and unassuming nature, and gave
himself no airs. He was, in fact, more aware of the reaction of
his two friends, Hugo and Hervey, whose attitude towards him
underwent a change quite as pronounced. From being the
junior of the trio and something of the butt, he became, as it
were overnight, if not the senior at least the most influential and
prominent. There was nothing of the obsequious offered or
expected; but David's wishes and preferences now tended to
have priority – it would have been strange otherwise, with all at
Court, from the King down, treating the other two as being
more or less in the Scots prince's train. Even their tutor, the
Benedictine Brother John, a pleasant if rather sober young
man, less than ten years older than themselves, treated David
differently, having come with them from Romsey to Winchester.

The wedding was a notably joyful occasion, much more so
than most royal matches. For although Henry was well aware
of the political advantages of marrying the senior female representative of the Saxon royal line, he was much attracted to
Matilda personally, and she to him – as near a love-match as
any prince was likely to approach. Even though he insisted on
her name being changed to Maud, the English diminutive, on
account apparently of his hatred of some female relative of that
name who had bullied him as a child. His new Queen did not
mind, her true baptismal name being the Saxon Eadgyth, or
Edith, anyway. She would have put up with much more than
that to attain this wedded bliss – for obstacles were indeed put
in her way. The marriage was not popular with the Norman
nobility, even those who were close supporters of Henry. They
conceived it to be a mistake, an unnecessary encouragement of
the Saxon element in the kingdom, which might well become
uppish, and a consequent danger to their own French supremacy. Some of them went beyond mere murmurings in the

51

matter. They raised the objection that the princess was in fact a nun, already wedded to Christ and therefore unable to marry the King. Vehemently she protested that this was not so, that she had never taken the veil, had only dwelt, and unwillingly, amongst the nuns in the care of her abbess-aunt, Christina, at Romsey. But the objectors got Christina, a distinctly soured character, to testify that once, when they were younger, she herself had thrown veils publicly over the heads of her two nieces to protect them from the advances of licentious soldiery – which could be construed as an initiation of sorts. It became the gentle but firm Anselm's first task, on his return from exile in France, as Archbishop, to declare this as invalid and the princesses no nuns. He improved on this by personally marrying the happy couple a week later, in St. Swithin's, David giving away the bride. The King of Scots' agreement was taken for granted.

After the wedding, David found himself in something of a dilemma. Hitherto he had been little better than a prisoner-at-large. Now he was the Queen of England's brother and the King's friend. Yet his heart should be back in Scotland. Presumably there was nothing now to prevent him from going home? But was it his duty? Could he better serve his country, back in Scotland or here at the court of England? He was under no illusions that Edgar was anxious for his return. Edgar showed no real interest in his youngest brother. As for Alexander, he went his own way, never communicating with him or his sisters. What place would there be for him in Scotland? Moreover, would Henry permit him to go? Henry clearly assumed that he would remain, even seemed to want his company, finding roles for him to fill. Might he not serve best by acting as voice for his brothers here, meantime at any rate? Besides the fact that Matilda and Mary would not hear of him going. And his friends were here. Scarcely admitting it to himself, David found a reluctance to leave. Later, to be sure . . .

Apart from the Norman disagreement with his marriage, Henry's taking of the throne was remarkably painless, virtually unchallenged. William had made so many enemies, and chosen his friends from amongst the baser sort, that most of the men of real power and influence – that is, the Norman nobility – found the change so much for the better that even those who agreed that the elder brother, Robert of Normandy, should have had the crown and that Henry was really a usurper, did not press the matter. Robert, all knew, was an amiable weakling. And while such, on the throne, would almost certainly have allowed the nobility a free hand, most recognised that the kingdom was infinitely more secure with a strong hand at the helm. The Saxon majority, of course, high and low, greatly welcomed the new regime. And the churchmen supported Henry to a man. So there were no uprisings and revolts, no conspiracies – none to reach the stage of action, at any rate.

Until nine months later, that is, with the Queen already four months pregnant, when, without warning a Normandy fleet appeared in Southampton Water, with a large army. Duke Robert was back from the Crusade and calling upon all loyal Englishmen to rally to his cause and dispossess his usurping brother.

It was a dire situation, as dangerous as it was totally unexpected, no word of the Crusade's end having reached England. Henry had no forces mustered and Robert was only a mere fifteen miles away. It would take days to collect an army sufficiently large to defeat the sea-borne force – by which time Winchester could have fallen. Dissident Anglo-Norman barons would almost certainly take the opportunity to rise, which would inhibit Henry's supporters locally. Moreover, Robert was proclaiming that he had brought Edgar Atheling with him – he also had been on the Crusade – and he was calling upon all Saxons to support the Duke's cause likewise with the promise of great if unspecified privileges. Edgar was David's and the Queen's uncle, their mother's brother and grandson of King Edmund, so rightful claimant to the Saxon throne – although he had many times undertaken to renounce any such claim. But ineffective and now elderly as he was, the blood-link was strong and could influence many of the Saxons.

Henry called a hasty council, at which David, now seventeen, attended. It was no large gathering, for it was harvest-time and most of the lords were at their own demesnes and manors superintending the ingathering of their lands' wealth. A worse time could hardly have been chosen – or a better, from Robert's point-of-view. Anselm, the Archbiship was, fortunately, on a visit to the palace, and present; as was Gundulf, Bishop of Rochester, famous for his building skills, who was at Winchester for the King's scrutiny of plans for a great new castle or tower at London. A third Bishop was William de Giffard, still Chancellor but now given the vacant see of Winchester itself. Simon de St. Liz, Earl of Northampton, was the only earl present, although there were a number of lesser lords, including de Breteuil, now chief minister, and

William de Pont-de-l'Arche who had succeeded him as Treasurer. Also Reginald de Lucy. It made a less than warlike council.

After Anselm had opened the proceedings with a brief prayer, Henry spoke. "My friends – you all know the situation. My brother Robert has four thousand men, I am told, landed at Itchen-mouth – normally no great host. But these are mainly veterans of his Crusade, now at a loss for employment, hard and experienced fighters. They lack horses, which is our slight advantage. But I can only muster barely one thousand two hundred! I have sent summons to all lords and knights within a day's journey, to assemble and march with all speed. But it will be a week, at least, before I have an army strong enough to challenge Robert. What do you advise, my lords?"

"Delay," Northampton said. "Somehow we must delay him. To give time. Some device."

"Easily said. But how? Robert will perceive the situation as well as do we."

"Use what forces we have, Sire, to make many feints and movements between here and his army," de Lucy suggested. "Many small companies, busy. To give the appearance of much activity and larger numbers."

"If Robert did not know the country so well, that might serve something. But he was part-reared here at Winchester. He will know where to send his scouts – and they would soon tell him of the true situation."

"Then we must talk, parley, delay that way," Bishop Giffard said. "A deputation, to discuss terms. At length. Until Your Grace has assembled a sufficiency of men."

"What terms could be discussed, for days? He is on our very doorstep, man! Anything that I can offer Robert will not delay him one hour. He seeks the throne!"

"This of delay," Archbishop Anselm questioned. "Must we consider only a device? Is there no agreement which we may come to, in honesty?"

"I shall not yield the crown," Henry asserted flatly. "And that, I think is all that he will want. I tell you, he would make no king for this divided realm. He is weak."

"If he is weak, Sire, then we must make play on his weakness," Bishop Gundulf said. "There must be a way."

"A vice-royalty? Over part of the kingdom?" Giffard proposed. "The principality of Cornwall?"

"Aid for his aims in Normandy," Breteuil put in. "We know that he has lost some parts to the Count of Brittany and the

Emperor. Offer him an English army, in due course, to help him retake them."

"If he takes this throne, he can have all the English armies he requires."

"May I speak?" David asked, diffidently.

"Why not?" Henry said grimly. "We are but beating the air, anyway!"

"It is said that the Duke Robert ever lacks money. They say that his treasury in Normandy is ever empty. And he has been away on this Crusade for over four years. With many men to pay. Perhaps that is in part why he has brought them here – to fill their pockets. If he could do so, and fill his own, without taking Your Highness's crown, he might be tempted."

Henry looked at him thoughtfully.

Encouraged, David went on. "Did not King William – King William the Second, I mean – buy the Duke off with money, once? So our tutor told us. When the treaty was made between them. After Your Highness's father died."

"Scarce that. It was in 1091. William gave Robert ten thousand marks, and took all Normandy in pledge. That was to help pay for the Crusade."

"And was there not a payment another time?"

"Aye – that was to *my* loss! When William got England, in our father's will, and Robert got Normandy, *I* got five thousand pieces of silver – that was all! And advice to wait! I have waited. I gave Robert three thousand of them, for lease of one-third of the Cotentin. And went to act Count there. But William took it all from me, by force of arms – which was scarce Robert's fault."

"No. But it means, does it not, that he loves money rather than land, and power? Twice he has given away his lands for silver and gold. You say that he is weak. May not this be part of his weakness?"

"Out of the mouths of . . ." Anselm began, then shook his grey head, smiling. "Your pardon young man. Forgive an *old* man. But – here is sound reasoning."

"Lord – am I to *buy* my brother?"

"Highness – in the North Tower of this castle are chests by the score, filled with gold and silver pieces. I saw them. Merest metal, lying there. You have used nothing of it, I think? Now if it would serve , or some part of it, to win you free of this trouble, to keep your crown, is not that good use for it?"

"The lord David speaks good sense," Bishop Gundulf said. "If the Duke would accept."

"He is no warrior," Northampton asserted. "This of the Crusade was not his usual. He has never been a man for war and battle. If he was offered money, much money, the certainty of it, as against the great uncertainty of fighting, slaughter . . ."

"Especially if the offer was made with dignity. And made more to his taste," Anselm said. "A thought to the future. Robert is now fifty years. He will be concerned for his old age. A pension, as well as the present moneys? It would tempt. Also perhaps ensure no further trouble."

"At least it would give us time. For talk, debate, chaffering," de Lucy nodded. "While Your Grace gathers men."

"Perhaps, yes. *I* would not wish to do this . . . chaffering," Henry said distastefully. "But if it was attempted for me . . . ?"

"I will go," Anselm volunteered. "I know Robert. Indeed we have been friendly. I will act mediator."

"Very well. A deputation, an embassage. Choose whom you will."

"May I go?" David asked.

"Why, lad? What could *you* do, in this?"

"My uncle Edgar the Atheling is there. This appeal to the Saxons. I could tell him that you are good to the Saxons. That Matilda – Maud – the Queen, ever considers their cause. That war could only hurt them. It might all help . . ."

"This young man has, I think, something of his mother's abilities. The Queen Margaret was a notable negotiator," Anselm said. "I would be glad to take him, Sire."

"As you will. We must consider this of the moneys. How much . . . ?"

*　　*　　*

The next morning, then, the deputation set out southwards, almost as though they were making for the New Forest again. Anselm had decided that the cavalcade should be impressive and dignified but not warlike. *Amour propre*, appearances, self-respect if not pride, were all likely to be involved here; and a careful and light hand needed. Especially if debate, discussion, had to be prolonged for strategic purposes. So the military manners were not those required; and apart from de Breteuil and David, practically all the members of the company were clerics, including the two bishops and most of Winchester's clergy. The quite large party was led by the King's mounted instrumentalists and a choir of singing boys, to provide sweet music and the right atmosphere. They did have a small escort of horsed soldiery however. And they sent scouts well ahead.

Instead of turning away westwards for Romsey at Otterbourne Hill, they continued due southwards to follow the Itchen valley. Some seven miles from Winchester, just past Bishop Stoke, their scouts came back to tell them that a great host was ahead of them, in the North Stoneham area, a couple of miles.

No doubt the Duke would have his own scouts out, to report their presence. They unfurled the Red Cross standard of St. George and the diocesan banners of Canterbury, Winchester and Rochester, set the choir to its best singing, and proceeded thus to meet the invaders.

Well before they saw the Normandy army, mounted patrols appeared on either flank, to escort them onwards, at a distance, their gleaming steel armour and trappings contrasting notably with the very evident non-martial aspect of the Archbishop's company. These would certainly send back information as to what was approaching and that no immediate battle was to be looked for. Presently they saw the great array of the Duke's force blocking all the Itchen's shallow vale ahead, north of Swatheling. They rode on, chanting, if a little breathlessly.

A richly-armoured party came riding out to meet them, under the banner of Normandy, David recognising the tall, stooping figure of his uncle beside the thicker-set, stocky man in the centre who was distinctly similar in build and appearance to King Henry, although obviously older. Anselm kept up the musical accompaniment until the two groups were only a few yards apart, then signed for silence. He kept his beringed hand upraised, however, and sketched the Sign of the Cross over the fellow-Normans in front.

"In the Name of the Father, the Son and the Holy Ghost, I bless you and yours, Robert fitz William," he said clearly.

A little taken aback, evidently, by this greeting, the Duke coughed. "Anselm!" he said. At close range it was to be seen that though he had features similar to those of both Henry and Rufus, in the elder brother's case these had the appearance of being somewhat blurred, were less positive, although he was in fact better-looking than the other two. But his dark, close-cropped hair was powdered with grey and there was an air of something like dissipation about him, the family corpulence of belly pronounced. "What is this . . . mummery?"

"No mummery, my lord Duke, but friendly greeting. King Henry, your royal brother, sends his welcome, as do we all. We

57

bid you welcome to England again on your return from your
noble expedition against the infidel in the Holy Land. Of which
His Grace, and my humble self, hope to hear account in due
course."

"Indeed." Robert recovered himself. "You may have to wait
for that, my good Anselm! I did not come here to tell stories!
But to teach my insolent young brother a lesson. Do not name
him king, Archbishop. How can he be? *I* am the King of
England, both by birthright and by treaty agreement. Let none
mistake."

"Henry is crowned King at Westminster, my lord Duke,
with all due coronation circumstance. He has the oaths of
allegiance of the great ones of this realm. And the kingdom's
Treasury . . ."

"As usurper, man – usurper! You of all men know it. I am the
true heir to England, the rightful suzerain."

Anselm shook his grizzled head sadly. "Heir, suzerain,
usurper, my lord Duke – here are but words, I fear. Words,
when we are faced with facts. The facts are that Henry *is* King.
He *holds* throne and kingdom. You were far away when your
brother William died. England had to have a king, at once. Or
there would have been disaster, revolt, war, chaos. Had Henry
not taken the crown then, there would have been no crown now,
other than an empty title. These are the facts – even if they are
hard. This divided realm needed a strong hand, there and then.
I am sorry."

"I think that you have become a hypocrite!" Robert said.

"I hope not that – I *pray* not that. But I have learned to face
facts. Learned it in sorrow and travail. As you know. As, I fear,
must you."

"*Must*? You say that to me, old man? I have come for my
throne, and will have it."

"My lord Robert – hear me. Even if the throne should be
yours by right, Henry will not yield it now. So you must needs
fight for it, battle against the assembled might of England. Is
that your wish? War – for it would be a long and bloody war.
Remember, you would not be fighting Saxons only, as did your
royal sire. But *Normans*. Your own kind. Are you prepared for
such a long war? Even if perchance you won the first battles.
Henry will resist to the end. If he does not beat you at the
beginning. You would have to fight up right through England,
through Wessex and Mercia and Deira and Cumbria and
Northumbria. And then still fight, for the King of Scots' sister is
Queen to Henry. Are you prepared for that?"

58

This was David's cue. He cleared his throat. "My lord Duke – I am David of Scotland. The Queen's brother." His voice was a little uncertain but strengthened as he went on. "I greet you, humbly. And you, my lord Edgar – your nephew. I bring you both the Queen's good wishes. She says to tell you that she has the Saxon folk always in her heart. She will never cease from aiding and supporting them. But King Henry also is their friend. He has already shown it, clearly. The Saxons are no longer oppressed, their lords freed from the prisons. They are the King's friends, now. That is truth. I, David, have seen it."

"A device, nephew – a stratagem to keep the quiet meantime," the Atheling said. He had a tired, querulous voice. "It will not last. Henry no more loves my Saxons than did William, I swear!"

"Why not, Uncle – if the lord Robert can do so?" David asked simply. There was a moment's silence at that. Then the Duke spoke.

"Such talk is profitless," he declared. "I have not come all this way to argue with clerics and striplings about my rights – but to *take* them. I am not dependent on the aid of a few Saxons."

"Yet the Saxons, my lord Duke, since they inhabit all the land, however lowly their state now, could of themselves deny you any lasting victory," Anselm said. "Even if you won battles, they could starve your armies behind you, whilst you fought your brother in front. And Henry will fight, be sure of that. He summons all his power, near and far – although he hopes not to use it against his own kin. In the name of Almighty God, I beseech you, consider what you do. And consider this England which you would drench with blood."

"Not I, but Henry. He is the usurper, not I. Would you have me to turn back now, empty handed? I, Robert fitz William, like some cur denied bone."

"Not empty-handed, my lord. Nor turn back. King Henry would have you to come on, to be his favoured guest, you and yours, in brotherly amity. In token whereof . . ." The Archbishop turned and waved hand.

Two of the escort, at his sign, led forward a pair of heavy pack-horses laden with wicker panniers. The soldiers bent to throw open the covers of these. Inside were iron-bound chests. In turn the lids of these were raised to reveal them filled with gold and silver pieces. There was an involuntary murmur from the company opposite.

"King Henry recognises well that your interests have suf-

59

fered in all this, my lord," the Archbishop went on. "He would show his regard and sympathy, as best he can. There are three thousand gold pieces here, and as much again in silver. He gives this, freely. Take it now. There is as much again awaiting you at Winchester, if you care to come – and to send back your armed force here. Back to their boats at Itchen-mouth!"

Robert's face was a study. He could not keep his eyes off the shining gold and silver. He actually licked his rather slack lips. But at the same time he frowned in doubt and indecision.

"If . . . if I was king all this, and more, would be mine, anyway," he said. He looked around him, at Edgar Atheling and the others, for guidance, support.

He got little, all having eyes only for those chests. Gold, vast amounts of yellow gold, can have an extraordinary effect on even resolute men, especially professional adventurers such as the Normans.

"If your lordship won the war. And survived," Anselm pointed out, mildly. "And if all was not squandered or looted by then. This is yours *now*. Moreover, King Henry suggests that a pension would be fair and convenient. A sum, perhaps five hundred gold pieces, paid each year, for the rest of your lordship's days. From the English Treasury."

That clinched the matter. Robert, essentially lazy, indolent, was not the man to resist such a comforting notion, moneys coming to him without effort until his dying day, without responsibilities, the responsibilities of a kingdom to win and rule.

"So be it," he nodded. "That is just and proper. I shall repair to Winchester further to discuss the matter with my brother."

"I applaud your decision, my lord Duke. We all do. And this host, here – it will turn back?"

"Yes. Some hundred or two will accompany me, as is suitable, the remainder will go back and await my return to Itchen-mouth. That is best . . ."

More than the choristers had something to sing about on their way back to Winchester.

4

THE MONTHS and into years that followed were full ones, as
David grew to manhood, full for all in England, an England on
the move. For Henry was something new in kings, not just a
warrior and master of strategy like his father, nor yet a tyrant
and self-indulger like his brother, but a man of ideas and vision,
something of a statesman, with vehement notions of justice; yet
strong, with little that was gentle about him, indeed much of
the family harshness, so that even the boldest, brashest and
most powerful of his lords thought twice and thrice before
countering him – and few could be more powerful, bold and
brash than some of the great Norman earls whom the Conqueror had created out of his companions-in-arms, even
though they had been but the sons of grooms and sergeants in
their native Normandy, some owning as many as two hundred
former Saxon manors scattered over England. Such men were
not easy to rule, especially with Henry seeking to raise up again
the down-trodden and dispossessed Saxons, so that all his
strength and much of his harshness was in fact necessary – even
though David mac Malcolm for one could not bring himself to
accept cruelty as a deliberate instrument of rule, as Henry
appeared to have no difficulty in doing. They remained friends,
and the King took the young man into his confidence and
sought his advice on occasion – his credit had been much
enhanced by his part in the Robert interlude – and they
remained fairly close. But there were occasions, and aspects of
policy, where they could scarcely have been further apart in
attitude. Not that Henry allowed this to deflect his chosen
course in any great degree – for after all, David was only the
Queen's young brother, landless and essentially insignificant.
In such periods of what was almost estrangement, Maud – as
she had now to be called by all, even her brother – held them
together. For Henry was devoted to his wife, her influence
greatly to the good, although even she did not always find it
easy to live in amity with one of the implacable Norman breed.
As, for instance, when Henry insisted on bringing his illegitimate daughter Sybilla over from the Cotentin, to join his Court,

61

begotten in his youth and now a pert and arrogant sixteen-year-old, cause of strife from the moment she arrived.

But Henry's virtues much outdid his failings, however heavy-handedly. He restored the Saxon laws, as to the reign of Edward the Confessor, David's and Maud's great-grand-uncle, abolishing the many penal prohibitions and extortions which had made life a misery for the subjugated race. He laboured continually to improve the quality of justice dis-pensed throughout the land – a difficult task indeed, with the feudal system giving almost unlimited judicial power to the individual lords – by instituting a great many itinerant justices, with the royal authority. He consistently supported the Church, and used the bishops as his ministers and advisers – though this was undoubtedly on account of their education rather than out of any religious enthusiasm on his own part, for he had a great respect for learning and books – indicated by his father's nickname for him of Beauclerc – and most of his baronage could not so much as write their own names. He much reduced taxation – which did much please the said barons – and encouraged merchants and traders.

When Maud in due course produced a daughter, Henry suppressed his disappointment notably, and named the child Maud also.

It was not all progress and peaceful advancement, of course. The almost inevitable revolt of the dissatisfied and warlike Norman nobles took place in the summer of 1102, led by the too-powerful Montgomery brothers, Shrewsbury, Lancaster and Pembroke, Robert de Bellême of Shrewsbury in command. The rising took place in that everlasting trouble-area, the Welsh Marches, where Gruffydd ap Cynan and his people were apt to be more than ready to join in anything which would embarrass their English overlords. Henry managed to put down this rebellion, with major Saxon but precious little Nor-man support. He exacted a terrible vengeance thereafter – but mainly on the unfortunate Welsh, rather than on the Norman earls who had instigated all, and who quietly made themselves scarce when things went wrong. David went along, to experi-ence his first real taste of war, but saw little of the actual fighting, being on detachment with Hervey's father, the Earl of Surrey, one of the few Normans actively supporting the King, capturing a troublesome castle in the Forest of Clun, when the vital battle took place twenty-five miles to the north, near Haughmond Abbey. He saw plenty of the aftermath, however, the hangings and maimings and eye-gougings, and in due course returned to Winchester sickened, further estranged from his brother-in-law than ever he had been. It took a lot of his sister's quiet persuasion – she was already being called the Good Queen Maud on account of her patience and charity – to bring him to accept Henry's point of view as perhaps forgive-able, and to recognise the special pressures and problems bear-ing upon a monarch. And Henry was, after all, a Norman of the Normans, reared in a hard school. The wonder was, Maud pointed out, that he should be so good and enlightened as he was. He had not had the advantages of being brought up by a sainted mother.

David sought to swallow his resentment, if not his aversion to savagery and cruelty, even though perpetrated in the name and cause of justice and the realm's well-being. But he did question Henry himself on why the Montgomery brothers and other Norman barons were let off so lightly, only a token part of their lands confiscated and temporary exile imposed. The King had to admit that he dared do no other, just dared not offend the Norman baronage too greatly, in which his ultimate power rested. David had to accept that. He had no option, anyway, for he was wholly dependent on Henry – unless he went back to Scotland, where Edgar evinced no signs of wanting him. Apparently his brothers already there, Alexander, Ethelred and Edmund, were sufficient problems in their various ways.

But when, a year later, Maud was delivered of another child, and a fine healthy boy this time, Henry's delight spilled over on to David, indeed on to all around. A male heir to the throne was what was required before all, for the security of the dynasty. Henry named the child William after the Conqueror but adding that he would be called The Atheling, to the astonish-ment of all. Atheling was the Saxon word meaning heir appar-ent; but it had more or less become adopted as the surname of Edmund Ironside's descendants. This using of the term as official title for a Norman prince was significant, a major ges-ture towards the Saxons and a bid for unity in the kingdom. Maud was as pleased as she was surprised, and David himself was touched. Relations improved again.

One day the following May, Henry sent for David to attend on him in his private chamber, alone. He was just back from a visit to his manor of Woodstock, which his mother had left him and of which he was fond – indeed he talked of leaving Win-chester, which he considered as far too far south for conveni-ence and security, and residing either in London or Woodstock, the New Forest not drawing him as it had done his father and brother.

"David – I have been considering sundry matters whilst I have been away," he announced. "I have come to the conclusion that you may be able to help me in one, at least, of these. More especially as I have felt for some time that you were seeming to champ somewhat on the bit, to be restless. You are a man now, to be sure, and should be given a man's part to fill."

Warily David waited, without comment.

"I have also been considering the state and situation of my daughter Sybilla," the King went on – and ignored the younger man's quick intake of breath. "She should be wed. She is a spirited piece and could well do with a husband to master her. Given a firm hand she will, I am sure, make a good wife."

"No!" David exclaimed. "Your pardon, Sire – but no! Not that, not myself! I beg you . . ."

Henry narrowed his eyes. "Are you so averse to her – my daughter? Or . . . is it marriage itself that you mislike?"

"No. Or . . . not yet. I do not . . . I would not wish to wed, as yet. Wed anyone. One day, no doubt. But not, not . . ."

"Not the Lady Sybilla?"

"No, Sire. Not the Lady Sybilla."

"You think so ill of her?"

"Say – that we have little in common. And she has no fondness for me – that I swear! An ill match, it would be, from the start."

"The sons and daughters of kings, David, cannot always choose their mates so nicely, like lesser folk."

"*You* did"

"M'mm. I was particularly fortunate. However, my candid friend, you go too fast. It is not to you that I propose to marry my daughter, landless and lacking fortune as you are. I must do better than that for my Sybilla! I look . . . further north!"

In his relief, David scarcely heeded the significant note in Henry's voice.

"Tell me of your brother Edgar," the King went on. "I saw him only those two days, at the Crown-wearing. He had never married. He must be thirty years? He has no heir but his brother, Alexander. Does he hate women, like *my* brother William did? Has he any natural children?"

David shook his head. "I do not know. I think not. I know of no children. I fear that I know Edgar little better than you do, Sire. We have been reared apart. I have never heard that he

64

mislikes women – or, or was of that sort. But I have never heard his name linked with any woman's."

"So says Maud. But in her nunnery she might not have heard. Edgar is King of Scots. It would be of great advantage to both realms, would it not, of the King of Scots was to wed the King of England's daughter? A most suitable match."

David reserved his opinion on that. Sybilla was only a bastard after all.

"If he is not of the marrying kind, then he can produce no heir. Am I right in presuming that Alexander will heir the throne after him? There are two older brothers, but they are churchmen, so not able to mount the throne?"

"Yes.' Ethelred is Abbot of Dunkeld in the Columban Church – Primate, by name. He is married already – but that is permitted in that Church. Edmund has taken holy orders – if only to escape the consequences of his much wrong-doing! Neither would be accepted as King. Alexander is heir."

"And how does Alexander view women?"

"I have heard that he is . . . not averse!"

"Ah! Yet – not married either. At twenty-six years, is it? Is this your sainted mother's doing, think you? Only one of her many sons married – and he a rebel to her Church?"

David's lips tightened. "Why should you say that? Our mother was the noblest of women . . ."

"Yes, yes – all know that! Here, then, is the situation. It would please me to wed my daughter to the King of Scots. Further to draw together our two realms. To the advantage of both. *I* prefer such closeness and harmony to this talk of Lords Paramount and threats of force. You agree? So I wish you to go to Scotland, on my behalf, David. As it were, spy out the land for me. Discover whether Edgar is willing. And, and able! I would not wish Sybilla wed to such as my own brother William! And if Edgar is not, to consider Alexander for the role. It is a somewhat delicate task, as you will perceive. Will you do it for me?"

The younger man rose from his chair to pace the floor, frowning in concentration. "There is much here to consider . . ." he temporised.

"Would you rather I summoned Edgar here, to me, as Lord Paramount of Scotland? As William did?"

"No, no. Not that. That false claim again. No – this is better. I agree. But . . ."

"Your mislike of my daughter holds you back? You would not have her to wed your brother?"

65

David could scarcely admit that this was so. "It is a delicate matter, as you say, Sire. To put this to Edgar . . ."

"I would give you a letter. To be presented to Edgar – or not – once you have ascertained his attitudes, his way of living. Discreetly. You recognise the problem I face? Only you could do this for me, my friend. No other envoy would serve. Will you do it, David? You would wish to see your brothers again, would you not?

"Very well. When do I have to go?"

"So soon as you are ready."

"May I take my friends?"

"Take whom you will . . ."

* * *

So the three young men set out on their long journey to Scotland, attended by a small escort of the royal guard, on Henry's insistence. If David was scarcely as light-hearted and carefree as the other two, at first, he fairly soon threw off most of his doubts and forebodings. He was, after all, only in his twenty-first year, and the late spring sang over the land, the larks shouted, the swallows darted, the trees burgeoned and life cried aloud to be lived, especially to young men released. For once they were their own masters, and for a quite appreciable time, yet bearing the royal authority. And there was no hurry, Henry having set no time-limit for their return, within reason. They had over four hundred miles to go, and while they had no wish to dawdle, neither did they have to push themselves or their horseflesh, even though it was the King's horses that they rode now, and could exchange these for fresh animals at any manor on their way up through England. They reckoned that forty miles a day was a fair average to keep up, but it did not matter if they covered less or more. Much depended on the terrain they traversed, the state of the roads and the quality of their entertainment *en route*, particularly casual female entertainment, a matter of some moment for young men on the loose. Consequently they tended to be selective about where they passed each night, usually avoiding the monk-run hospices of Holy Church and convenient monasteries, which travellers usually utilised, preferring small manors, especially where young women were in evidence – which quest was apt to occupy some little time most evenings. Inns and ale-houses, of course, were practically non-existent in Middle England.

It was not all a heartening and spirited spring-time jaunt

however. Large areas of land they had to cover were little better than man-made deserts, where the effects of the Conqueror's heavy hand were everywhere evidenced. It had been William's set policy, ably continued by the second William, deliberately to devastate huge tracts of territory, for one reason or another, to remove the Saxon population, to creat empty zones around key fortress castles, to punish whole districts or merely to provide warnings, or to allow his great lords to establish their own depopulated wildernesses as hunting-parks, on the New Forest model. It was eighteen years since the Conqueror had died, but the traces remained all too evident. The black of the burning had largely disappeared under green growth, but broken, deserted villages and whole towns were commonplace, farms, mills and cothouses mere shells, former cultivation-rigs growing only reeds, thistles and scrub-thorn, rivers and streams spreading into marsh, trees and gibbets bearing their skeletal fruit at every crossways. Sometimes for half-a-day the travellers rode without seeing an occupied house. This, as much as the rich manors, was the Normans' England Henry had inherited.

They went by the shortest route, by Inkpen and the Marlborough Downs and the Cotswolds to the Vale of Evesham, keeping west of the hilly spine of the land thereafter through Mercia to the Mersey and on to the Ribble. After eight days they entered Strathclyde, over the Lune, north of Lancaster — one of the Montgomery brothers' earldoms, which still showed ample signs of Henry's own strong hand, as punishment for the recent rebellion. In theory, as they crossed Lune into Cumbria, they entered Scotland, for the ancient kingdom of Strathclyde, stretching from the Clyde right down to here, had been ostensibly incorporated in the Scottish realm since 1018. In fact, Cumbria, this southern portion, was practically independent although having no other overlord than the King of Scots. It had a Scots governor, usually styled Earl of Cumbria, at Caerluel, in the north; but his sway was of the sketchiest, the position more title than fact. Prince of Strathclyde was the official title of the heir to the Scots throne; but as far as Cumbria was concerned, and Galloway also, it was mainly an honorary designation.

Skirting the great Cumbrian hills they came down to the Eden valley to Caer-luel on the tenth day out, to rest there for a couple of nights. The present Earl of Cumbria was Dolfin, David's own second-cousin, son of the late Cospatrick first Earl of Dunbar and March and brother of the young Earl Cospatrick who had been in Edgar's party at the unhappy Crown-wearing. He was an amiable, if somewhat bovine man, who was glad to see visitors. He took them hunting in the high fells and moors around the Roman Wall area by day, and by night they had no reason to complain of lack of enthusiastic feminine company. Hugo and Hervey were quite reluctant to leave.

Now they crossed Esk into Scotland proper, immediately and strangely into a different land. Cumbria had been hilly and with its own wildness; but here the hills were everywhere, sterner suddenly, the rivers swifter, foaming, the land somehow challenging, untamed. David's heart lifted to it, nevertheless, the exile returned if only temporarily. It was many years since he had seen his native land, having had to be content with his dreams of it. Now it spoke to him in no uncertain voice, even this extreme south-western corner of it. His companions, curiously enough, saw it merely as a harsh and barren country, suitable for the barbarians their friend had the misfortune to be connected with. They hoped, without conviction, that it might improve.

Until this they had kept to a fairly consistently northerly course, but now, because of the seemingly impenetrable hill-masses ahead, they must detour. They were making for Edinburgh in Lothian, which Edgar had chosen to use as his capital, instead of his father's Dunfermline; and this entailed crossing the entire grain of the land, against the lines of mountain ranges and rivers. So they swung right-handed, eastwards, up Eskdale into the tributary valley of the Ewes Water and over the watershed to the head of Teviot. Now they were into the vast area known in Scotland as The Forest, or sometimes Ettrick Forest, covering most of the land between Northumbria and Lothian, a terrain utterly different from the forests of England in that most of it was not tree-covered at all but endless hills of grass and mosses and heather. There were woodlands too, in the valleys and sometimes climbing high. Clearly it all abounded with game, deer, both red and roe, boar, hares, brown and blue, feathered game including some great birds as large as turkeys which the local folk called capercailzies, duck and wild-geese and herons in the low grounds of the lochs and rivers and marshes, and whirring grouse on the heights. But as well as these there were large herds of wild cattle, which could be dangerous as they were warned, especially the massive white bulls with the enormous curling horns. And the two nights they passed within the confines of the Forest – for travel therein was inevitably slow, with no true roads, only winding paths through valleys, often flooded, and over passes – they heard the howling of wolves. Here there was no question of seeking out choice lodging and female company, for settlements were few and far between, villages almost non-existent, and they were thankful to enjoy the modest shelter and simple fare of small Celtic Church cashels, which seemed more like rude stockaded forts with grass ramparts than monasteries.

But, at last, up Wedale and the head of the Gala Water, they won out of the northern outskirts of the Forest and could look down from the final escarpment upon the wide-spreading and fair coastal plain of Lothian, with the blue Scotwater and the hills of Fife beyond, a magnificent prospect after the days of the constriction of hills and woods. More isolated and lower hills rose like stranded whales out of this fertile plain, some quite dramatic in shape, none more so than the great crouching-lion outline, near the coast, which David remembered as being Arthur's Chair after a long-dead Celtic prince, with nearby the rugged rock of Dunedin, around which lay the small town of Edinburgh – and journey's end, they hoped.

They still had three hours' riding to reach that town, through populous country now, as fair as any they had seen. It was evening before they were able to gaze up at Dunedin's awesome, soaring rock, seen now to be crowned with the ramparts of an extensive fort, with stone buildings within. David's father, in the last years of his reign, had built something like a Norman-style castle, foreign to the Scots rath or hallhouse tradition, within the ancient Pictish fort, principally so that he might keep Lothian – and Cospatrick of Dunbar, its lord – under better control; and Edgar, with no love for the Celtic part of his heritage, had elected to reside mainly in this eagle's nest of a hold.

Unlike Winchester and most Norman-held towns, Edinburgh was not a walled city, and the travellers had no difficulty in entering, even at dusk, nor in making their way up the steep track to the fort. There was a deep ditch, drawbridge and gatehouse there, but the guard was slack and unsuspicious, allowing the riders in without hindrance or much questioning. Hugo and Hervey were censorious.

To David it all brought back a flood of sad memories. When last he had been in this place, in 1093, twelve years before, his beloved mother, already ill, had died on word being brought of the death, in Northumberland, of both the King and their eldest son, by treachery. In one grim day David had lost mother, father and brother. His Uncle Donald had seized the throne and Edgar, who had brought the evil news, had taken his two younger brothers and two sisters, and fled with them to England and into Rufus's clutches. Perhaps they would have been better to have stayed and sought the mercy of their uncle, for Donald Ban was not a savage man . . .

The household in the bare and uninviting buildings of the fortress appeared to be notably small and undistinguished, quite unlike a King's Court. There was certainly no feminine touch here. All present were strangers to David, mainly Normans, and seemed to him at first glance a dispirited lot, with nothing of the illustrious about them. After the Winchester Court it was all shabby, dull and a great surprise. The greater surprise still was that the King was not absent, as they at first assumed, but retired to his bed for the night.

The initial reaction was that perhaps the quest about Edgar's attitude to women was already answered – for it was only dusk, still hours before midnight. But no embarrassment was evinced by the castle steward, only glum looks. So, leaving his friends to refresh themselves at a less than well plenished table, David went off to his brother's bedchamber, the same room in which their mother Queen Margaret had died.

When he saw the King of Scots lying on the great bed, he was shocked. Edgar looked almost like an old man, only thirty years as he was, thin, grey-faced, hollow-eyed, his yellow hair faded, lustreless. When he sat up, staring unbelievingly at the sight of David, his shoulders were seen to be bent, his body wasted, brittle-seeming.

"Davie! Davie? – is it true?" he all but croaked. "Is it in truth yourself, Davie? A man, now. I am not dreaming . . . ?"

"It is myself, yes. But . . . you!" David went forward to the untidy bed, to clasp his brother around the slumped shoulders – and as good as winced at the frail feel of him. "Edgar – are you sick? Ill? You, you do not look well . . ."

"No, I am not well, Davie – not well. But whether I am sick, who knows? God, perhaps – or the Devil!"

"But – Edgar, you are thin, poor-seeming. And, lying here? What is wrong . . . ?"

"I am accursed – that is what is wrong, Davie."

"Accursed? But . . . ?" Helplessly, David looked at his brother.

"Accursed, yes. Rejected of God and His saints. Lost, man – lost!" Edgar gripped the other's arm and shook it. "I tell you, I am forsaken. For my sin."

"What sin? Edgar – what are you saying?"

70

"I say that I am abandoned to the Evil One. For the great sin I committed. As our mother was abandoned. God is hard, hard . . ."

"Lord – what sin did our mother ever commit? She was a saint!"

"She sinned, yes – and grieved for it. But that did not save her from God's wrath. She wed our father, after he had got rid of Ingebiorg, his first wife. And then she allowed the boy Duncan, our half-brother, to be taken as hostage by the Conqueror, in place of one of *her* sons. She never forgave herself. Nor did Almighty God. She faded away and died, His hand upon her. As do I! There is a curse upon our house, man!"

David shook his head. "This is folly, brother. You are chasing shadows. Our mother scourged herself without mercy, yes. None other did – not God, assuredly. And you – what sin have you committed to deserve this?"

"Sin of the same sort, Davie. Against our own kin. Our Uncle Donald. I, I put out his eyes and sent him to the kitchens as a scullion! Our father's brother. He had been crowned in the Stone, at Scone. Now he has died. I killed him. His blood is required of me."

David was silenced. He had not heard of Donald Ban's death; but he had been deeply shocked those years ago when he had learned what Edgar had done to their uncle, after he had unseated him. He could not deny that.

"He usurped the throne," he said at length, without conviction.

"He had more right to it than had our father – who was born out-of-wedlock. He was younger, but legitimate."

"It may be so . . . but, Edgar – that is an old story. Done with. No cause for this, this despair."

"What do you know of that? Am I not the better judge? I tell you, I *know* that God has rejected me. I have become an empty husk – no more than that."

"More than that, yes. You are King of Scots, Edgar, with a realm to rule."

His brother turned his back on him, on the bed.

David sat, at a loss, not knowing what to do or think or say. He was tired, with the long journey, and hungry. Perhaps in the morning he would be able to do better.

"Leave me now, Davie," the King muttered. "I am weary . . ."

"Yes. Tomorrow, then . . ."

At least, as he went, leaden-hearted, he already had the

71

answer to one part of the quest Henry had laid upon him. Edgar mac Malcolm was not likely to look favourably on any marriage proposal.

*   *   *

After two depressing days at Edinburgh they rode northwards again, in search of Alexander, Earl of Gowrie. Edgar had proved little or no more encouraging in the interim, a man deeply immersed in his own sorrows and apprehensions, making no more attempt to welcome and entertain his brother and visitors than he apparently did to manage the affairs of his kingdom. David had sought to explain to him Henry's desire further to link their royal houses in marriage; but Edgar had shown no least interest. Indeed his attitude was that he was as good as dead and that Alexander would soon be ruling Scotland anyway. Only the one spasm of anything like animation had come to him during those gloomy days. When, speaking of Alexander, Edgar had declared that he feared for the realm's unity when he was gone. Alex would not hold it together. He was interested only in the North, the old Alba, the ancient Celtic kingdom north of the Scotwater and Forth. For the South, for this Lothian and the Merse, Teviotdale and Strathclyde, he had no concern, never coming near it, the best and civilised part of the whole. So he, Edgar, was going to leave all the South to David. Alexander could keep Alba and be King of Scots; David should be Prince of Strathclyde – the title of the heir to the throne, which he had never given to Alexander – and rule all south of Forth. Uncertain what to make of this, David had let the matter lie, and Edgar had not referred to it again.

If the three young men had felt released on leaving Winchester two weeks before, they felt still more so to get away from the grim and distressing atmosphere of Dunedin, where all was neglect, lethargy, foreboding. Apparently, in so far as Scotland was being governed at all, other than locally by its *ri* or lesser kings, the mormaors and earls of the great provinces, it was being governed from the old Celtic capital of Scone, in Fortrenn. An able Norman churchman, Robert, was Prior of Scone, and he had been appointed Chancellor or chief minister. There was a certain convenience in this as far as the Celtic part of the kingdom was concerned, for Alexander resided mainly only a few miles to the north, at Malcolm Canmore's former summer palace of the Ward of the Stormounth; their older brother, Ethelred, Abbot of Dunkeld in the Celtic Church and

72

now Earl of Moray, lived at Forteviot to the south a short distance; their cousin Madach, Earl of Atholl, had his seat at Dunkeld, not a great deal further north; and Maldred mac Melmore, Madach's brother and one of the most useful men in the land, lived at Bothar Gask, midway between Dunkeld and the Ward. So there was something of a concentration of authority in Fortrenn, the heart of the Celtic realm; and Edgar's withdrawal and near-abdication at Edinburgh, was the less disastrous – although it was still a sorry situation.

So the travellers journeyed on north by west, crossed salt-water where the Scottish Sea became the Firth of Forth, by the ferry established by Queen Margaret. They spent the first night at David's old home of Dunfermline Palace, now in the hands only of a steward, and a sad disappointment to the returned exile who had remembered a place vastly different, all life and stir and even splendour. It was now seen to be little more than a rather bare and overgrown hallhouse attached to a stark stone tower, all echoing with emptiness. The great minster to the Holy Trinity, which Queen Margaret had erected nearby, however, was sufficiently impressive, so that Hervey and Hugo could at least find something to admire there. So far they had found Scotland just what they had expected – backward, unpolished; they did not hesitate to say so.

By riding hard and long next day, they managed to reach the Ward of the Stormounth, on the skirts of the Highland mountains, by evening, only to find that Alexander was absent. Apparently there was a great wedding at Dunkeld, where Madach, Earl of Atholl was belatedly taking a wife, at the age of fifty-five, and the prince was attending.

The Ward was a pleasant place, its memories happy ones for David, of long summer days hunting and hawking in the hills, fishing in the rivers, swimming in Loch Clunie and making great expeditions with his older brothers into the mountains, to climb and clamber and explore. It was certainly a much more desirable place to live than Dunedin's fortress, and the three friends would gladly have lingered. But there was no knowing for how long Alexander might remain away; and Dunkeld was only eight miles to the west. So the following morning they rode on into South Atholl.

Dunkeld, set dramatically within the jaws of a narrow pass where the great River Tay emerged through the Highland Line into the green leafiness of Birnam Wood, was astir with lively activity, the rath on the top of its thrusting pinnacle of rock, the Abbey directly below at the riverside, and the quite large

73

township nearby, all full of visitors and their hangers-on. The actual wedding ceremony had been two days previously, but the festivities were still very much going on, a great many of Celtic Scotland's notables having gathered for this unexpected occasion. Madach was popular, and it was not often that one of the great earls of Scotland waited until his mid-fifties to marry and then to wed a girl exactly forty years his junior – in this case, the Lady Margaret Hakonsdotter of Orkney. Although the celebrations had been going on for days, everybody seemed to be in high good spirits still – including the new fifteen-year-old Countess, a large, flaxen-haired, tomboyish creature of the true Nordic breed, with nothing of the blushing bride about her. Madach of Atholl, it seemed, was likely to pass the evening of his days less than restfully.

When they arrived, sporting contests were in progress in the level haughland of the river, near the Abbey, amidst much hilarity – racing, on horse and afoot, and swimming in the Tay, jumping, vaulting and wrestling, archery, sword-fighting, javelin-throwing, caber-tossing and stone-putting. Pipers strutted and blew, dancers demonstrated, performing bears were paraded, and food and drink was laid out in lavish profusion for all-comers.

In all the crowd and turmoil the newcomers, as well as being unnoticed, were at something of a loss as to whom to present themselves; but presently David saw one familiar face. At least, the features were sufficiently like his own, although much older-seeming, and the gingery-red hair was as he thought to remember it. He led the way over to where this individual, a tall man in his early thirties, dressed in Highland fashion, saffron kilted tunic, belted with a golden earl's belt and wearing a shoulder-plaid of vivid colours, fed lumps of cold meat to a couple of long-legged shaggy deerhounds.

"Eth!" he exclaimed. "It *is* Eth, is it not? Greetings, brother."

"Eh . . . ?" The other man looked startled, "Do I know you, friend? I am seldom called brother – seldom even called Abbot now. And not Eth but Hugh."

It was David's turn to look perplexed. "Hugh . . . ? But – you *are* Eth, are you not? Ethelred mac Malcolm?"

"To be sure. But here, in the Highlands, Ethelred is a foreign name. And Eth is Aodh or Hugh. So . . . ! But, your face is familiar . . . ?"

"It should be – since we are brothers, my lord! I am David mac Malcolm."

"God in His Heaven!" the other cried, and came forward to clasp the younger man to him. "Davie! By all the powers – Davie! Young Davie – a man grown! Sakes – I have not seen you since you were . . . when would it be? Ten years old? Or nine?"

"Nine, yes. 1093, when I was taken to England. Twelve years ago, Eth – Hugh. A long time . . ."

"But how come you here, lad? Are you released? Come home, at last?"

"Scarce that. I am not a hostage now – at least, I think not! Now that our sister is Queen of England. I am here on a mission for King Henry." He recollected the courtesies. "These, my lord, are my friends – Hugo de Morville and Hervey de Warenne. And this is the Prince Ethelred, Abbot of Dunkeld and Earl of Moray. Although it was Earl of *Fife* before, was it not?"

"Aye – but young Constantine MacDuff came of age and got his earldom back. So I was given Moray, which had been forfeited by Malsnechtan mac Lulach. I am married to Lulach's daughter, so it was thought apt." He nodded to the two young men. "Both of your names are namely – but sorely Norman!" However, he grinned as he said that. "Friends of David's are friends of mine, forby. What is your mission, lad?"

"Well . . . it is with Alexander. Henry has word for him. We have been to Dunedin and seen Edgar . . ."

"Ah. I fear that you would have little joy in that. It is a sorry pass."

"Yes. I was grieved, much grieved. He seems to be almost out of his mind. What is to be done?"

"What *can* be done? We have all tried. But he will hear nothing. He is eaten up with guilt. He has turned his face to the wall."

"He thinks himself accursed. Yet – he is the King . . ."

"He does not act the King. Never has done, in truth. Alex at least will do better, I think."

David considered his brother thoughtfully. But for this Celtic Church abbacy and primacy, which now apparently meant little or nothing, with the Roman Church triumphing, Ethelred would have been the King, not Edgar, for he was the third of the Margaretsons. Edward, Prince of Strathclyde, had been slain with his father. Edmund, the second son and black sheep, had supported their uncle, Donald Ban, paid for it by being condemned to perpetual imprisonment – but this was commuted on his taking holy orders in the Romish Church, which barred him from the succession. Edgar had been only the fourth son, as David was the sixth and youngest.

Perhaps his face showed something of these thoughts, for Ethelred clapped him on the shoulder.

"Our fates are in the hands of the good God, not for curse and evil but for the best, lad," he said. "Doubts and fears and repinings are not for princes. Alex, see you, suffers none of these! He is yonder, at the caber-tossing. Hoping to win, as always – although he will not, for there are better men than he, here. Come."

They crossed to a corner of the haugh where men vied with each other as to who could toss a tall, trimmed tree-trunk the farthest, amidst much grunting and puffing and bulging of biceps. Most of the contestants, mainly stripped to the waist above short kilts, were big burly men; but one most noticeably was not, a fair-headed, well-built but fairly lean individual, seeming almost slight compared with the others, but at second glance his wiry body seen to be toughly muscular and in excellent condition. He had sharp, almost foxy features and a notable air of concentration and determination. He was flexing his arms and knees as he stood watching one giant, who balanced his caber high, preparing to toss.

"Alex," Ethelred called. "A truce to your stick-throwing! See whom we have here."

The other barely glanced in their direction. "Wait," he jerked, and continued with his exercises whilst closely eyeing the competitor with the swaying tree.

With a groan ending in a single explosive snort, the man heaved his enormous burden up and over, and staggered back. The thing did not seem to go very far – but the wonder was that any man could actually lift it up off the ground, much less throw it for even a few feet. The earth shook to its fall.

"Ha – not so good as your last toss, Fergus," Alexander exclaimed. "I can beat that I swear!"

Another man was already unrolling a string to measure the distance from the tossing-line to the dunt in the grass made by the butt, amongst the number of small pegs which marked the limits of other throws.

Alexander, Earl of Gowrie, turned. "So it is Davie!" he said, without evident surprise or pronounced pleasure. "Grown a man, but still . . . Davie."

"Why, yes. Would you have expected otherwise, Alex? Greetings to you, brother."

"Aye – and to you. What brings you here, so far from your English friends?"

"You do, Alex. I have word for you. But it is my pleasure to see my own kin again, likewise."

"Oh, yes. To be sure." The other looked him up and down. There was some five years' difference in their ages, but the elder seemed much the senior. He nodded briefly. "Aye, then – I shall see you later." And he turned back to the caber-tossing.

"That is Alex!" Ethelred murmured, as he took David's arm and led him away. "He has time only for the business on hand, always. But he is none so ill if *you* are the business on hand! Come and eat lad. You and your friends will be hungry. And we shall find Madach . . ."

The Earl Madach, when he was found and brought, proved to be a solid stocky but amiable man, ageing but strong-bodied, son of their father's uncle. He gave no impression of being a besotted bridegroom, but made a good if undemonstrative host. He was clearly much interested to see David, and when they had eaten, took him in search of his new wife. Before they found her, they encountered his brother Maldred, Lord of Dowally, a quietly competent-seeming man, greying but of a notably alert bearing, who had been an especial friend of Queen Margaret. With him was his handsome wife, the Lady Magda, a Saxon, both of whom David remembered vaguely from childhood.

The bride, when run to earth by the riverside, watching swimmers amongst a laughing group of young men, was all glowing health, high spirits and bodily awareness, a lusty young woman, natural and uninhibited. When Madach told her that the Prince David was a sort of cousin, she kissed him' heartily – and his two companions for good measure. She was, indeed, in kinship not only by her marriage, distantly as it might be, for her father the Earl Hakon of Orkney was son to the Earl Paul, eldest son of the famous Thorfinn Raven-Feeder, whose own mother had been the Princess Donada, sister to David's own great-grandmother. Madach recited this solemnly, such descents meaning a great deal to the lineage-conscious Scots.

Thereafter, David went off with Madach and Ethelred, on a tour of the festivities, and to meet the other principal guests; but Hugo and Hervey elected to remain with the new Countess Margaret, like most of the other young men. Alexander was now involved in a pole-vaulting contest. It was obviously no

77

time to seek a conference with him on matrimonial prospects.

It was evening, and late evening at that, after the feasting up in the hall of the rock-top rath, before Alexander indicated that he was prepared to give his younger brother some private and undivided attention. That this was not to be of long duration was made clear by his distinctly reluctant leaving behind of a lady of bountiful charms and evident promise, whom he assured he would rejoin before long.

In a small chamber off the hall, the brothers considered each other assessingly. Alexander went into what was almost the attack, right away.

"You have seen Edgar, Davie?" he asked. "Our broken reed of a brother! What did he say? About me?"

David was wary. "Little – little about you. Or about anything. Save his sore hurt of mind, his fears and despair."

"Aye, we all get that. But . . . of the future? What did he say, man? He is intent on dying! What of the future? Of the realm?"

"You will be King of course. He does not question that. But . . ."

"Aye – but, Davie? But what?"

"He . . . he believes that you, Alex, are not greatly interested in the south of the kingdom. In Lothian and Strathclyde. He is concerned for these parts – which he has always held dear."

"Oh, yes. He has lived in Lothian. Takes no care for his ancient kingdom north of Forth and Clyde. These new lands in the south – they are not the *real* Scotland. I swear Edgar is more Saxon than Scot!"

"Perhaps. He believes that you are the other way. It sounds as though you are, Alex?"

"I would cherish Alba, our ancient heritage – yes. But not throw away Lothian and Strathclyde – as he has thrown away the Hebrides, to Norway." Alexander fixed his brother with those piercing eyes. "Edgar told me once that he thought to give them to *you*! Has he told you that?"

David stirred uncomfortably. "He said something to that end. But . . . he was all but wandering in his mind . . ."

"He cannot do it, man – cannot, I say! He cannot give away parts of the kingdom. He has kept me from being Prince of Strathclyde all these years, as is my right, he being unwed. As heir to the throne. Given me only Gowrie, a mere thanedom. He hates me, I think – and you he dotes on! But he cannot divide the kingdom, when he is gone. You hear?"

"Yes. But Edgar is not gone yet – that is not to be thought on,

78

either. He is only thirty. This sorrow of mind he could throw off, in time, Alex. And it can scarcely kill him. He could, and should, be King for many years still."

Alexander muttered something inaudible. "We shall see," he added. "But – take heed what I have said, Davie. I shall not see the realm divided."

"I do not wish that, either Alex. But . . . I could wish for some stake some small stake in the realm. Scotland is my land also, brother. My roots are here."

"Aye. No doubt. We shall see." The other sat back, as though anything of import was now disposed of. "What is this word you have for me? From Matilda, is it? Our sister?"

"She sends warm greetings, yes. Mary also. But the message is from King Henry. On, on a delicate matter."

"Delicate? That Norman! I never yet knew a delicate Norman! Out with it, man."

"It is about marriage, Alex. Henry has a daughter. Born out-of-wedlock, many years ago. Sybilla. She is sixteen years. He would link our two houses closer, in marriage. He thinks to marry this Sybilla to either Edgar or yourself. Edgar, it seems, is in no marrying state. So Henry sends me to you."

"Marriage! Henry would marry me to his bastard? Henry Beauclerc!"

"Yes."

"Why?"

"I tell you – to link our houses closer . . ."

"Our realms, rather! It is Scotland he wants, not Alex mac Malcolm!"

"To be sure. But is that so ill? He would have the two kingdoms close. But not as Rufus and his father would have had it, by conquest, claiming to be Lords Paramount. Henry does not claim that. But to have an end to enmity, linked by marriage not by the power of the sword, in peace. It seems to me much to be preferred."

"M'mm. You spoke of this to Edgar?"

"No. He appeared to be in no state to talk of marriage. He will not wed – that is clear. Not in the near future. Henry told me to judge for myself."

"So-o-o! My younger brother adjudges me suitable and assigns me a wife!"

"Scarce that, Alex! Henry would have his daughter to wed either the King of Scots or the heir to the King of Scots. I am but his messenger."

"Very well."

"There are advantages in the matter, surely. To have the King of England as good-father and good-brother both . . ."

"To be sure. *I* am not witless nor lost to reason, Davie."

"No – but such match could mean much to Scotland . . ."

"I have said very well. What more do you want, man?"

David stared. "You mean . . .? You mean that you agree? That you will indeed wed the Lady Sybilla? Just, just . . . so?"

"That is the object of your mission, is it not? What more need I say?"

"You, you do not wish to hear more? Of this young woman, Sybilla? Of Henry's proposals?"

"My terms for the marriage will be a matter between myself and Henry Beauclerc, Davie – spoken to by more seasoned envoy than my youngest brother! As for this Sybilla, I know nothing of her. But provided that she has two legs and what goes between them, and is the King of England's daughter, I shall wed her! I can seek my comforts and pleasures elsewhere – as no doubt does Henry!"

"Henry is devoted to our sister." David was indeed perceiving what sort of man was this brother. The pert and unmanageable Sybilla might well meet her match here. Ethelred had been right when he said that Alex had time only for the business on hand but that such business would receive his full attention and decision. He shrugged. "She, Sybilla, is . . . spirited. She is not beautiful. But she is not lacking in, in a woman's parts. Indeed she makes that plain, at times! She is French, of course. Her mother, Sybille Corbet, is sister to Renaud de Dunsterville. Henry spent his early manhood in Normandy . . ."

"No doubt. I did not suspect that Henry was a saint! I have a bastard or two of my own – and will be surprised not to have more! Which, Davie minds me – I have a lady awaiting me. I had her nicely warmed. A pity if she should cool off!" Alexander rose. "So, unless you have more of earth-shaking import for me, I shall bid you good night!"

David nodded. Apparently his mission was completed. "If there is more that you wish to hear, I can tell you tomorrow . . ."

The morrow brought no particular questioning from Alexander, only the announcement that he was for off – and not back to the Ward of the Stormounth, where David had thought to accompany him for a brief spell before setting off southwards again, but north-east to the Mearns, to another palace, the hunting-seat of Kincardine, sixty miles away. It seemed that the lady he was presently interested in was the wife of the elderly Thane of Edzell nearby. There was no suggestion that his brother and friends should join him at Kincardine. As the wedding festivities appeared to be breaking up at Dunkeld, Ethelred proposed that David and his companions should return with him to Forteviot, for so long as they might wish, before commencing the long ride south to Winchester.

This they were glad to do. Alexander did not so much as bid them goodbye, in the end.

Forteviot, the ancient Pictish capital, lay some twenty-five miles to the south, in Strathearn, near where Earn joined Tay and Tay widened to its estuary. The old palace here had been the seat of a succession of Scots kings, from Kenneth the First, MacAlpin, for two hundred years until Duncan the First, David's grandfather, had deserted it for nearby Dunsinane; so it was apt enough that it should now be the home of the most true heiress of that venerable line, Ethelred's wife, Malvina. The first Duncan had been not exactly a usurper but with less right to the throne than the offspring of Kenneth the Third – that is Gruoch, who had married MacBeth, a granddaughter. Lulach had been her son, and he had heired the throne for six months after his stepfather's, MacBeth's death, before Duncan's son Malcolm Canmore slew him, as he had slain Mac-Beth, and took the crown. This, the Lady Malvina, was Lulach's daughter and had married Ethelred.

She proved to be a gentle creature, holding no evident grievances. There were two sons, Angus and Malcolm, still only boys. It did not fail to occur to David, although he did not mention it, that if all had their hereditary rights, and primogeniture meant anything, it should be this young Angus to whom Henry should seek to marry his daughter in due course, not Alexander, since he it was who was lineal heir both of his mother's and his father's lines.

A few days at Forteviot by the Earn and they were ready for the journey south. David debated with Ethelred whether he should call again upon Edgar on the way – and was guiltily relieved when his elder brother said that he could see no point in it, at present. Edgar would not thank him, desiring only to be left alone; and there was nothing that he could do to help him, anyway. That David should feel the same way himself did not greatly assuage his conscience.

They started on the long road to Winchester, down the centre of Lowland Scotland, to cross the stripling Forth at Stirling, not going within a score of miles of Edinburgh, making for Clyde and Annan and Esk.

81

5

ANOTHER WEDDING AND a very different one, exactly a year later, with much pomp and ceremony. Henry almost seemed as though he must make up for his daughter's illegitimate birth by giving her a wedding as splendid as his own six years earlier. Again Anselm the Archbishop officiated, in Winchester Minster, and all the greatest of the land were invited. It was largely a show, to be sure, to demonstrate Henry's policy towards Scotland, his belief that there were better ways of influencing events than by drawing sword. He professed to be disappointed that the King of Scots had not come south with his brother, as invited; but probably was just as well pleased, for by all accounts Edgar would have been apt to put a damper on the proceedings, even though in somewhat better state, apparently, than he had been.

Alexander himself, strangely enough, seemed to take it all a deal less seriously than did Henry, making little or no attempt to create an impression, bringing no large train with him, wearing no splendid clothing, treating the entire affair it seemed rather cynically as something of a necessary evil which fell to be got through as expeditiously and with as little fuss as possible. Amongst all the richly-dressed Normans, the bridegroom looked like something of a poor relation. Even David was better turned-out than his brother. This could be only deliberate, for Alexander's earldom of Gowrie was far from poverty-stricken.

He even cut fine his appearance on the scene, arriving only the day before that fixed for the ceremony, to Henry's considerable offence. Alexander's first meeting with his bride, that evening, was on a par with the rest, low-key to a degree. Sybilla, resembling her sire, stocky, short-legged and plain of feature, was dressed most handsomely to display her prominent bosom, undoubtedly the aspect of which she was proudest, her rather sallow cheeks and wide mouth reddened, her small eyes sharp, lively. On her father's arm, she stared, to take in her husband-to-be's lithe manly figure, long, reddish-fair hair, keen glance and slightly twisted half-smile, and sank down in a

82

full curtsy before him, leaning forward so that he gained the benefit of her breasts, head demurely dipped but eyes upwards, bold, searching.

"Lady!" he said, and that was all, stepping forward to raise her up and to kiss her stubby-fingered, capable hand.

"My lord Alexander," she acknowledged, her French voice husky for one so young. She dropped her father's arm and turned to take the younger man's. They moved off together, as though they had known each other all their lives, David and the Queen as surprised as was Henry.

The King fingered his clean-shaven chin thoughtfully, before leading the way, with his wife, into the hall for the banquet. "Those two, I think, would bed together this night *before* the wedding!" he observed. None thought to controvert that nor to comment that neither would be apt to prove inexperienced in the business.

Next day, at noon, David, who was to act groomsman, waited with Alexander at the chancel-steps of the great minster of St. Swithin, quite close to where he had stood those seven years before at Rufus's Crown-wearing, The two brothers were isolated, today, although the cathedral was packed, target for all eyes. Not that Alexander showed any awareness of it, any nervousness or concern, as he stared about him at the architecture, the painted glass, the plenishings and decorations, dressed more or less as he had been the night before. David was considerably the more affected.

A flourish of trumpets heralded the Queen's entry, from the chapter-house doorway, with her ladies-in-waiting, the Dean coming to lead her over to one of the thronelike chairs on the right of the chancel, nearer the high altar. Maud gave her brothers a warm smile in the by-going. The sweet chanting of a large choir ushered in the celebrants' procession, Giffard, Bishop of Winchester, leading the way, gorgeously vested. After the minster's clergy Anselm himself brought up the rear, looking frail and old. He was only recently returned to Canterbury after a second exile of nearly three years, for he had withstood Henry over the question of the investiture of bishops, and returned to Normandy. His officiating today was the measure of his fondness for Queen Maud. He took up his place, with the others, before the altar.

A louder and longer fanfare turned all eyes, as the King entered, his daughter on his arm. Sybilla's person was more covered-up today; but she made up for this in the vivid colours of her apparel and the glitter of her jewellery. None would say that the Conqueror's grand-daughter would not hold all eyes at her wedding.

One pair of eyes, however, Sybilla did not hold – David mac Malcolm's. His gaze switched to and was held fast by the young woman who walked alone behind the pages who upheld the bride's train. This was quite the loveliest woman he had ever set eyes upon, a tall and willowy creature, dark-eyed, raven-haired, with fine sculptured features, carrying herself with an unselfconscious pride and grace, to make the stocky, strutting Sybilla seem like a cart-horse compared with a pure-bred Barb. She was no precocious child, this one, but a woman in her earliest twenties, splendidly built, serene of manner. David almost forget to bow as the King nodded graciously to the two brothers waiting there, and turned to lead his daughter up the steps towards the altar. Alexander and he fell in immediately behind this vision of loveliness as they moved forward in turn.

Here, then, must be the other Matilda, Countess of North-ampton and Huntingdon, wife of the lame Simon de St. Liz, Earl of Northampton, child and heiress of the late Earl of Waltheof and the Countess Judith, the Conqueror's niece, also dead, chosen today to attend on Sybilla as the only semi-royal female of the Normandy line available in England. Hers was a strange story. Her father Waltheof, or Waldeve, half-Dane, half-Saxon, son of Siward the Strong, usurping Earl of North-umbria, was like many a son of mighty men, something of a weakling. The Conqueror had married Judith, the hard and shameless daughter of his brother Lambert, Count of Lens, to Waltheof, taken Northumbria from him to put in stronger hands, and given the Mercian earldoms of Northampton and Huntingdon instead, where weakness was less of a danger to the realm. But Waltheof had plotted against William, been betrayed by his wife, and executed, saying the Lord's Prayer. This dark beauty was the offspring. The Conqueror had desired his widowed niece to marry his old campaigning friend Simon de St. Liz, then; but she had scornfully refused, because he was crippled by an old wound. So in fury William had taken the child Matilda as ward and married her to St. Liz instead, barely into her teens, he old enough to have been her grand-father; and taken the earldom of Northampton from Judith also, for St. Liz, leaving her only Huntingdon. When Judith died, Matilda heired that great heritage. Now she attended Henry's pert bastard, one of the most nobly-born heiresses in England.

It is to be feared that David paid little attention to the

wedding service which followed, thinking of all this, especially when Alexander left his side to move forward to his bride, Henry moved away to his throne and he found himself standing beside the Countess for the remainder of the ceremony. Her slight smile to him as they took up their positions behind the principals, threw him into a strange turmoil of emotion.

Alexander and Sybilla duly pronounced man and wife, the bridal party moved down through the packed nave, behind the chanting choristers, to the great west doorway of the minster, David and the Countess still side-by-side. Out in the sunlight before the cheering crowds, a horse-litter was brought forward to convey the bride to the palace, Alexander walking alongside, still behind the pacing choir. No provision appeared to have been made for the Countess, although another litter was waiting for the Queen.

"I think that we must needs walk," she commented to him, but pleasantly, unconcerned, "The singing is a joy, is it not? You will be David of Scotland?"

"Yes. I . . . I will go find you a litter, lady . . ."

"No need, my lord. I am very well afoot. It is not far. Come." She had a musical voice which had the effect of making him lose his own.

She hitched up her skirts and took his arm companionably.

"Your husband?" he got out. "My lord of Northampton – will he not be seeking you?"

"I think it unlikely, my lord. Any urgent seeking will be for wine, I should suspect!"

"Oh. I . . . , ah . . . am sorry. And – do not call me lord. For I am none. I have no single acre of land to my name, lady."

"Then lady me not either, David. I am Matilda – as was your royal sister. I am thankful for this, at least, that Simon has not changed me to Maud!"

"Yes," he said.

They walked on together through the crowded streets behind the bridal pair and singers, with their armed escort. Winchester had never seemed so fair to David.

It was not far up the hill to the palace and, arm-in-arm, their walk was over all too soon, for the man at least. He could have walked on by the hour with this companion. He saw Henry, still on horseback, who had ridden back by a different route, eyeing them with something like amusement as they entered the palace courtyard – and flushed at his knowing grin. But the Countess did not flush, nor indeed drop his arm, even gave it something of a squeeze as they passed the King.

85

"Sire," she called, "walking, they tell me, is good for the shape. I would commend it to you, cousin!" And her glance sank to his round belly.

"Ha!" he said. "Walking, heh? So long as one watches where one treads. Eh, David?"

That young man's tongue was failing him today, like his wits perhaps. He shook his head as they passed on.

He conducted the lady right to her chamber-door, so reluctant was he to part from her. There she thanked him for his escort, with easy friendliness, saying that it had done her good, not so much the walking as being squired so ably and kindly.

He went off to his room thereafter, in another quarter of the palace, in an odd mixture of delight and despair. He was not totally inexperienced with women – that was scarcely possible for one reared in the ambience of the Norman Court – and had had calf-love moonings, as well as sampling the charms of sundry, kind ladies. But never had he been attracted like this to any woman, never felt that here was the object and focus of his life and needs, the sum-total of all joy. The guilt behind that recognition was almost as strong an emotion, shame for himself and, even more sinful, a sort of hatred for Simon de St. Liz. That this abrupt awakening of admiration and need, of caring and, yes, desire, should be for another man's wife, was almost as shattering as the revelation itself.

Yet, when presently he repaired to the hall for the wedding-feast, uncertain where to seat himself, it was with a great surge of unalloyed satisfaction that he heard the Deputy Chief Butler inform him that, on the King's express commands, he was to sit at the dais-table next to the Earl and Countess of Northampton. He was surprised, but knew a warm access of affection for Henry, whatever his reasons. The dais was still unoccupied, so he stood back awaiting the usual trumpeting to usher in the royal couple, this time with the bridal pair and the principal guests. He had eyes only for the Countess Matilda, as they came in – but he knew a pang as he perceived that she was now holding her husband's arm, and unnecessarily tightly he considered, until he perceived also that the Earl Simon was already blear-eyed, and staggering with more than his twisted leg, and that the young woman was in fact all but holding him up. His emotion changed immediately to hot resentment that she should be put in so humiliating a position. Not, of course, he assured himself, that she could ever be humiliated by anything, so serene was she. David's perceptions and emotions were unusually highly developed that day.

86

When, the others seated, and with a faint smile from Henry, he went to sit down at the vacant seat at the Countess's left, her husband at her right, she greeted him with an approving nod.

"This is clever of you, Prince David," she said.

"Not I, Countess – but the King. He contrived it." He leaned over to incline his head at the Earl, who was already fumbling with the wine-flagon before him and saw him not.

"Henry did this?" she asked. "That is . . . interesting. He sees more, perhaps, than we think."

"I am much in his debt, at any rate."

"Why then, so am I," she agreed. "But I would like to see inside our thoughtful monarch's round head? Oh – I am sorry, David. *My* monarch, not yours."

"I think I feel that he is my king also – much more than my brother Edgar."

"Yes. Perhaps that is his intention."

"Eh . . . ?" He looked at her questioningly. "Why that? He is my sister's husband."

"To be sure." She did not answer him directly. "Do you never long for your own land, David? I think that *I* would."

"Yes. I often do. Sorely. But there seems to be no place for me there. I have four brothers remaining, older than myself. Edgar is . . . strange. He does not mislike me – but he does not wish me back in Scotland."

"No? And this other? Alexander, the bridegroom. How is it with him? He is your brother's heir, is he not? Although why, I have never understood, with two others older?"

"They are both churchmen, and so debarred. Although Ethelred, the oldest, is scarcely in truth a clerk by our, by your notions. He belongs to the Old Columban Church, which is very different from ours of Rome. He is married, with sons, and is Earl of Moray as well as an abbot. It *might* be possible for him to be king – I do not know. Not that he desires it, I think. But . . ." David glanced along the table towards Alexander, who sat with his new wife between Henry and Maud.

"But not if Prince Alexander has aught to do with it?" she finished for him. "A man of determination that, I would say?"

"Yes. I think – I do not know, but I have the notion that that is why Edgar does not wish me to return. I think he fears that I might side with Alex. Alex holds that Edgar does not govern Scotland well. Neglects the North. Has given away the Hebrides and the Highland West to Norway. He, Edgar, fears, I think, that Alex might unseat him from his throne . . . " He paused, to ask himself why he was talking thus to this woman, saying things which he had never actually voiced before, even to his two close friends – whom he could see sitting half-way down the hall.

"I see. And *would* you support Alexander?"

"Not against Edgar, no. I would if he was king, lawfully. But – I fear that he also would neglect part of the kingdom, the other part, the South. He has no interest in Lothian and Strathclyde, concerned only with the *old* Scotland, Alba, north of the Scottish Sea. The kingdom is divided, you see into old and new. Edgar prefers the new, Alex the old. Scotland requires heedful ruling, to cherish and advance them both."

It was the young woman's turn to eye him searchingly. "Cherish and advance! I like that," she said. "Do you wish that you had been born earlier? Older than these two. So that you could set your own hand to it, to cherish and advance?"

"I? No, no, I have no such thoughts. But . . . I would like to help. To play some small part. Instead of only playing the courtier here . . ."

"I understand that, very well." The Countess gently, unobtrusively, pushed her husband away a little, who had slumped against her shoulder, eyes closed. "I know what it is to see a heritage wasted and divided. Simon, here, has little interest in . . . cherishing! Lands or other. He is a soldier, now past soldiering – no happy state. He takes little concern for Northampton, his own earldom. But Huntingdon which is mine he ignores utterly – save for its revenues! I do what I can, but a woman, and a mother of three, cannot govern a great earldom of over nine-score manors." She spoke almost as though her husband was not present.

"You have children? *Three* children . . . ?" He sounded incredulous.

"Why, yes. I was married little more than a child. You sound surprised?"

"I . . . you do not seem . . ." He shook his head. "It is all wrong," he said, helplessly.

"Not *all* wrong, friend. I love my children. I have much to be thankful for. We none of us have all as we would wish it."

"No."

"You, now? If you do not go back to Scotland, what do you intend? To remain with Henry and your sister? Always?"

"Lord, no! There must be something that I can do, some place for me to fill. Perhaps, like my older brothers, I should have become a churchman!"

She smiled. "I think that is not for you, David."

88

"No. No – I am much interested in religion and Holy Church. Or . . . think that I am. But, but not turn monk or priest. Like Henry, I love books and learning, but I·am not of the stuff of priests."

"That would be a waste, assuredly."

"You think so?" That was almost eager. "Why?"

"As a woman I am prejudiced, perhaps. I cannot see that our good God made excellent young men to shut themselves up in monasteries and church-cells. Or young women either. Is that shameful of me? Heretical? Immodest? To speak so to you. If so, excuse it in that we are kin of a sort – or so I think."

"No, no – not that. Do not say it. I mean – I believe as do you. But – are we indeed kin?"

"Far distant. My father's father, Siward the Stout, Earl of Northumbria and of Huntingdon, had a cousin, Sybil, who married your King Duncan the First. Your own grandfather."

"M'mm. I fear not! Duncan was indeed my grandfather. But his wife, *your* grandfather's cousin, was not the mother of my father. King Malcolm was born out-of-wedlock, his mother but a tanner's daughter. I cannot claim to be your kin, then . . ."

Further conversation was restricted by a succession of toasts and speeches relative to the happy occasion. That her husband was not able to honour any of them did not appear to embarrass the Countess as much as it did David – although the Earl was not the only one so affected by the King's wine and mead. Alexander made brief but surprisingly witty reply to Henry's good wishes. Thereafter the entertainers took over.

When, suitably early, the King gave general permission for all who wished to leave the hall before himself to do so – with the required knowing glance at the happy couple – the Countess Matilda quite soon took the opportunity to sign to waiting servitors to convey her snoring lord to his chamber. Curtsying to the King and Queen, she indicated her own retirement. David was immediately on his feet to escort her – and, Henry's nod forthcoming, he led her out by the dais-door in the wake of her spouse.

"You should not leave because of me," she told him. "The night is still young."

"It is my pleasure," he assured. "This day you have given me much pleasure. I would not forego one moment of it."

"You are kind, David. I shall treasure today also."

They walked in silence for a while, across the courtyards where oxen roasted over glowing fires, for the palace-guard and the guests' servants and men-at-arms, then along the vaulted corridors of the wings beyond. At the door of the Northampton tons' chamber, they met the servitors coming out, who had carried the Earl Simon to his couch.

David grimaced, in the light of the flaring torches. "I mislike this," he exclaimed. "To leave you so. For you to have to, to go in there. It is a sin, a shame!"

"It is not so ill," she told him, quietly. "Simon will not trouble me. Not tonight. Anyway, he is long past that. He will sleep. He is not an evil man. Only disappointed – disappointed in his life. He takes ill out of being crippled – as must any man."

"And you suffer!"

"Not beyond the bearing. If I do, perhaps I deserve to. I am not blameless. Do not fret for me, David. I shall do well enough. And tomorrow I return to my children.

"Tomorrow? So soon? Where? That, that I may think of you there."

"To Thorpe. Earl's Thorpe, north of Northampton. A fair enough place. If ever you are near there, come to see me. You will be welcome, very welcome."

"It would be . . . unnecessary torture!"

She eyed him directly in the flickering light. "Perhaps you are right. For both of us. We are not of the easy sort, you and I, are we? I will close this door tonight . . . hardly!"

He could not speak.

"But close it I must, David. Now – go you back to the hall . . ."

"No – not there. I shall not go back. It would be but an empty folly, lacking you."

"Ah, but I think that you *should* go. Wiser – for my sake. That tongues should not wag – as tongues can."

"Oh. Yes – I had not thought of that. Very well, I shall go. For a little."

"Then . . . goodnight, David of Scotland. And, and a weak woman's thanks."

"Weak – you! It is I who am weak."

"I think that you are stronger than you know. And *I* am weaker than you think!" She opened the door, the snoring suddenly louder, hesitated, turned back, leaned over swiftly to brush his cheek with her lips, then slipped within and quietly closed the door behind her.

He stood for moments there, staring at the solid oak planking, fists clenched, before sighing and turning slowly away.

90

David knew, from that moment, that so far as women were concerned, his fate was sealed, whatever substitutes might fall to be contrived.

6

THE NEWS WAS delayed more than normally. For one thing it was mid-winter and no time for making four hundred mile journeys. For another Henry and his Court were wintering at Westminster, in London on the Thames, something of an innovation, and the young Earl Cospatrick of Dunbar, acting as courier and envoy, when wearily he eventually reached Winchester, had to turn and ride eighty miles eastwards. And even that was not the end, for when he arrived at Westminster, in early February the year after the wedding, it was to discover that Henry and his close associates were, in fact, presently at his private demesne of Woodstock, near Oxford, almost seventy miles further up Thames, where the King was in process of building up a menagerie of animals, the study of which interested him greatly. So the travel-worn Earl had to journey on westwards again, with his tidings.

Even at Woodstock he was balked of his quarry, for it transpired that Henry had taken his queen to see how work was progressing on the new abbey he was building at Reading, on her instigation. However, the royal party was expected back with the dusk, and Cospatrick was more than content to await them.

When, refreshed and rested somewhat, he was at last ushered into the King's presence, it was in the intimacy of a comparatively small family chamber, bright with colourful needlework hangings and tapestries, some by the Queen's own hand, and a blazing log-fire, before which David mac Malcolm played on the deerskin rugs with his nephews and niece – for, as well, as Maud's pair, they were having a visit from her sister Mary and her husband, Eustace, Count of Boulogne, with her three-year-old son. The four proud parents sat, sipping mulled wine and relaxing after their long ride in the chill wind. It made a pleasing domestic scene.

91

Cospatrick was accepted informally, almost as one of the family, for he was a cousin of the Scots present and also distantly connected to the Norman royal house. But, easy-going and personable young man as he was, he appeared ill at ease this evening. Perceiving it, Henry asked if he wished speech with him alone?

"What I have to say concerns more than yourself, Sire," he answered. "But . . . it is scarcely for saying in front of bairns."

"Ah." At that rather ominous note, the King said that they would have the children taken out meantime; and Mary, a gentle and modest creature, declared that she would take them.

Cospatrick shook his head. "You should also hear this, cousin," he said.

The Count Eustace, who was fat and lazy but amiable, said that *he* could scarcely be involved, and led the children away, to their much protesting.

"It is Edgar, I think?"David asked. "You bear tidings of Edgar?"

"Yes. I am sorry. The King died on the third day of Epiphany. At Dundee, in Angus. Died of a sickness. He had been a sick man, as you know, for long. Although seeming something bettered. I am sorry."

They were silent, the brother, two sisters and brother-in-law of the dead monarch. What was there to say? They were not unprepared for the news, any of them, even though they had been more hopeful these last months, with the word that Edgar was behaving more normally. But he had long been, as it were, largely resigned from the business of living and reigning. The end could not really shock.

"He had not gone north of the Scotwater for long," Cospatrick went on. "It is strange that he should have died, when he did go. He has been buried at Holy Trinity Minster, at Dunfermline, beside his mother and Edward."

Henry, glancing round the others, shook his head. "I too am sorry. But – perhaps he is more content now than he has been these long years." His voice changed. "And Alexander?"

"Alexander has assumed the throne, Sire. He was crowned at Scone, on the Stone. And has sent me to inform Your Grace. He gives greetings. The Queen Sybilla, your daughter also."

Henry could scarcely show his satisfaction that it had taken only eight months for his bastard daughter to mount the steps to the Scots throne. He inclined his head.

"There was no dispute, no trouble," Cospatrick went on. "None of the earls or mormaors made objection – although

Ross sent no word." The Mormaor of Ross was Murdoch, grandson of King MacBeth. "My lord Earl of Moray, Ethelred that was, bore the sword of state. And Constantine MacDuff of Fife placed the crown on the King's head."

The listeners exchanged glances. So Ethelred had not elected to assert rights of primogeniture – and Edmund could scarcely do so, as a Romish cleric. Alexander would sit fairly secure then – which was more than Edgar had done.

"He will make a good and strong King, I think," Henry said.

The Earl nodded. "For the North," he added.

There was a brief pause at the obvious reservation. Cospatrick of Dunbar was the greatest noble *south* of the Forth, lord of most of Lothian as well as the Merse and some of Teviotdale and Tweeddale.

"You have doubts, friend?" Henry asked.

"My doubts are of little import, Sire. But the doubts of certain others, in this matter, may be more telling. I have a letter here, for the Prince David." He drew a folded and sealed document from within his tunic. "More than a letter. That is the Great Seal of Scotland." And he rose, to hand over to David the paper, with the heavy beeswax disc attached by ribbon.

The younger man took it, eyed it, eyed them all. He did not break the lesser seals. "You . . . you know what this is, what it contains?" he asked, a little uncertainly.

"Yes."

"Is it from Alex?"

"No. It is from Edgar. It was written two years ago. By the Chancellor. Signed, in council, by the King, by Edgar. Left with the Chancellor, the Prior of Scone. Who was to send it to you only should the King die. It appoints you Prince of Strathclyde and ruler of all Scotland south of Forth!"

There was a gasping of breaths, then silence.

At length David found his voice. "But . . . but – how can this be? The kingdom – it cannot be split in two!"

"It already is, in many ways. This charter declares that it is for the good of the realm, the whole realm. King Edgar believed that the South would suffer, that Alexander would care little for it. We all believe that to be true. Alexander aims only northwards, to win back the Hebrides and the Highland West. To extend his rule into Moray and Ross – always he has said that. He will have no time for Lothian and the Merse, for Strathclyde and Galloway." He glanced at Henry. "Or Cumbria."

"Even so, the realm must not, cannot, be divided," David

insisted. "And Prince of Strathclyde is the title of the heir to the throne. I could be that only if Alex had no son."

Henry nodded. "Does Alexander know of this?"

"Yes. He does not approve of it. But he did not seek to keep it from you, David. Since it had the approval of the council and bore the seal of the realm."

"He will never agree to it. And if the new King does not agree, it can never be. *I* will not seek to force this, against my own brother's will."

"No, you could not do that, Davie," the Queen agreed. "Yet, and yet . . ."

"Yet this requires much thinking on," Henry completed for her.

Cospatrick agreed. "Edgar was right, in large measure. Something requires to be done. About the South. And there is Galloway, also. The Orkney earls have ruled in Galloway, for long. In name, as governors for the King of Scots. But now Orkney itself has been taken, by King Eystein Magnusson of Norway. Who now also rules the Hebrides and much of the Highland seaboard. He could grasp Galloway too – and threaten all the south-west. Scotland could be broken in pieces, as well as divided."

"I have heard that Eystein has his eye on Man, also," Henry said. "He is a dangerous young man. Rash. Worse than was his father, even – Magnus Barefoot."

"That may all be so. But I cannot name myself Prince of Strathclyde and go to take over South Scotland against my brother's royal wishes. Edgar meant well, no doubt. But . . ."

"Not that, perhaps, no," Cospatrick acceded. "Not Prince of Strathclyde. Alexander would look on that as near to rebellion. But something less. Go there as a kind of governor. For Alexander. That might serve."

"I could only do that if requested to do so by Alex, as King. And he will not do that, we may be sure. No – this charter would have been better never written. I shall give you it back unopened, cousin – and you can return it to my brother. That is best. It is all that I can do . . ."

"Oh, Davie," Mary put in. "How hard! Hard on you, when you have always wished for something to do, some part to play, in Scotland. Here is work to your hand – and you must put it away! Poor Edgar saw it, saw that you could play an important and strong part . . ."

"Yet Edgar never sent for me, whilst he yet lived! Only after his death. This charter was, I think, written out of mislike for

Alex rather than out of love for me! Or for Scotland itself, perhaps. No, I shall not . . ."

"Wait you – wait," Henry said. "Be not so hasty, David lad. There is the possibility of good in this, I think. With no open offence to my son-in-law Alexander. See you – I have been concerned about Cumbria, for long. William, my brother, took it by the sword, in 1092. Incorporated it in the realm of England, for better or worse. It has been accepted as such, since. Since your father's death, David, the three Kings of Scots, Duncan the Second, Donald and Edgar have not contested it. I have done little or nothing there, not wishing to endanger my policy of goodwill towards Scotland. I have not appointed a governor, even. It is remote and difficult country, its people all but independent. Of England, now – as they were of Scotland before. But, if Norway takes the Isle of Man, which lies off the Cumbrian coast – worse, if Eystein takes Galloway, which borders Cumbria, I must act. Act, before he may do so. I cannot delay much longer."

Henry rose, to pace back and forth before the fire.

"This charter of Edgar's, his will indeed, we hear appoints you Prince of Strathclyde. Strathclyde used to include Cumbria. You say that you will not accept the title. But suppose that I made you *Earl* of Cumbria? And sent you up there as *my* governor, of that land. With all authority to ensure its safety. From the Norsemen and others. Alexander could not object to that?"

They all eyed him, wonderingly.

"You would do that?" David demanded. "Trust me with so great a duty? So great an honour – aye, and responsibility?"

"Why not? You are of full age, now – and with sound wits. We have known for long that you were restless, in need of better employment. This would aid you, aid me, aid England – and, I think, aid Scotland too. For although you would be the English Earl of Cumbria, you would still be a prince of Scotland. At the new Caer-luel Castle you would sit on English soil – but all South Scotland would be open to you, if you so required. I think that Alexander might be well pleased to have you there – as *my* earl, and having rejected the title of Prince of Strathclyde. And it would be a warning to King Eystein. I say that it would provide an answer to much of this vexed matter."

"Davie – is that not an excellent notion?" the Queen exclaimed. "Work for you to do, at last – important work. Henry has said well. We shall miss you here, sorely, but . . ."

"It is well thought of, yes. And kind. I am flattered by the

95

King's trust. But – there is already an Earl of Cumbria – your brother Dolfin, Cospatrick. At Caer-luel."

"Yes. But in name only. I think that need not cause difficulty. Dolfin cares nothing for titles and positions. So long as he can hunt and wench and eat and drink, he is content. My father put him there – but he has never sought to *rule* Cumbria."

"He is an earl of Scotland," Henry pointed out. "Not of England. I have left him at Caer-luel, these years, since he came back after William's death. He has done no harm, and represented some authority. But with Cumbria now in England, I can and should appoint a new earl. No doubt Dolfin can be suitably compensated."

"I shall speak with him," Cospatrick nodded. "I foresee no trouble."

"Excellent! Then, out of much difficulty, much good may come. And we can look for great things from my new Earl of Cumbria!"

David considered his brother-in-law. He recognised very well that the great things looked for were calculated to be for England's benefit rather than Scotland's, that this would be a shrewd move to consolidate the English grip on the former Scots province, and serve as warning to Norway, and all others, that Henry was watching his North-West. Any advantage to Alexander would be purely incidental. Nevertheless, he rose and handed back the paper he held, to Cospatrick, seal still significantly unbroken.

In the game of statecraft he too, perhaps, could learn to play a part.

7

IT WAS MID-APRIL when David rode north again, and in very different style from heretofore. Again he had his two favourite friends with him, but now they were joined by quite a large group of other young Normans, to form the officer-corps of the Cumbrian army which the new Earl was to build up. As well as these sprigs of the noble and knightly class, there was a band of some three hundred men-at-arms, mainly Norman likewise, tough veterans these, destined to train and form the backbone of the local Cumbrian force. Henry was not looking for war and armed conflict, but recognised the wisdom of demonstrating that he was prepared for it. So they made a very martial company – and David had some difficulty, on the long ride, in preventing some of them from acting the part too enthusiastically.

For the first time, he was really aware of the heady experience of wielding almost unfettered power. He wore a golden earl's belt – which, under the King, gave him unquestioned authority as well as rank. He was the Crown's lieutenant and representative, also, so that his word was law. And he had immediate command over this large and effective body of armed and experienced men, who would carry out his every order, even whim. It was a strange and exciting situation for a young man in his early twenties who hitherto, however illustrious his background, had wielded no personal power whatsoever. Time and again he was tempted to demonstrate this new-found potency and authority – but managed to restrain himself, deliberately seeking not to allow any change in his attitudes and behaviour to become evident. Nevertheless he was honest enough with himself to recognise that there *was* a change, that he was not exactly the same person, in some respects. Power, authority and responsibility do alter any man, inevitably. David mac Malcolm had at least been near enough, all his life, to those in that position, to observe and heed the dangers and aloneness, as well as the elations and opportunities.

Yet, on the fourth evening out from London, he found himself faced with a test of his resolve and authority both, unpalatable as it was urgent. They were spending the night at the manor of Great Stoughton on the Kym, actually one of the Huntingdon manors belonging to Earl Simon and the Countess Matilda although still occupied by its Saxon tenants; and after eating in the somewhat decrepit hall, David felt the need to stretch his legs after a long day in the saddle. He went walking, with three or four of his closer friends, Robert de Brus, son of the Lord of Cleveland, and Walter fitz Alan, son of the Lord of Oswestry, as well as Hugo and Hervey. Strolling through the woodland, which was an outlying portion of the Forest of Kymbolton, they became aware of a hubbub some distance to their right, men's shouts and women's screams, masked by the trees. As these continued, David turned, to lead the way, hurrying through the copsewood towards the noise.

They came into a clearing, where there was a small hamlet of clay-and-timber hutments, thatched with reed-straw, evidently one of the many charcoal-burners' communities on which the iron-workers everywhere depended. The place was in turmoil, with about a score of the mainly fair-haired Saxon men and women grouped round about one of the cothouses, exclaiming and gesticulating, whilst children cried and dogs barked. They were being kept at bay before the open doorway of one of the hovels by two armed Norman troopers with drawn swords, who grinned and feinted and challenged. None of the villagers were armed. All were so preoccupied with what they were doing that only the dogs noticed the newcomers' arrival.

Pushing forward through the throng, David and his companions confronted the contestants – and at sight of the young nobles in their richer clothing, the shouting died away. The two soldiers looked alarmed and suddenly guilty, dropping the points of their swords.

"What is to do here?" David demanded. "Put away those swords."

There was no answer from the pair; but an answer of sorts came from within the hovel, a moaning sound.

Thrusting past the hesitant pair at the door, David strode within. There he found three people, two more Norman soldiers, one standing watching, dagger drawn, eager, the other on the earthen floor– or rather, on top of a young girl, sufficient of whose clothing had been torn off to reveal that she could be no more than twelve or thirteen years.

Stooping, to take the busy rapist by the ear, David twisted viciously, pulling the cursing, spluttering man off his victim. Handing him over to his friends, he then sought to raise up the gibbering, shocked child, attempting to comfort and soothe, and in some measure rearrange her disordered clothing. But the girl cringed away from him, sobbing. Whipping off his short riding-cloak, worn to counter the chill of the April evening, he wrapped it around her.

"Take these, these animals back to the hall," he ordered, having difficulty with his speech. "I shall deal with them later." Then he led the trembling child out.

The parents rushed forward to claim her, and David found himself almost afraid to meet their agonised and accusing eyes. He said, haltingly, that he was sorry, ashamed, that the evil men would be punished. He offered the couple a silver piece, and when they rejected it, insisted that they take it – although recognising that there might be little enough that such folk could do with it. Then, finding that the little community wanted nothing to do with him, he turned unhappily away, leaving the cloak with the girl.

Back at the camp beside the hall, he commanded an immediate assembly of all the company. As the men, grumbling, were being gathered in, he demanded whose soldiers were the four involved, and was told that they were in Drogo de Limesay's command. He ordered young Limesay and the four to be brought and placed in the midst.

When all who could be found were present, David raised his hand and spoke. "I gave clear and strict orders to you all, when we set out on this enterprise, that there was to be no indiscipline in my command, no pillaging, no ravishing, no savagery used against the people of the land. They are our fellow-subjects of King Henry. This order has today been grievously disobeyed. It is the plain duty of every officer to see that his commander's orders are carried out. Therefore you, Drogo de Limesay, are not guiltless in this matter." He forced himself to frown heavily at Limesay, a cheerful and uncomplicated character whom he liked very well, and who looked bewildered.

"As for these four men," he went on, "they have disgraced my name and command. They drew steel on harmless and peaceable people, in order to wreak their evil desires on a girl young enough to be the daughter of any of them. These are not callow youths but grown men, veteran soldiers. Chosen for this venture and duty of training my Cumbrian levies. They may have behaved so in Normandy, but here they obey my orders and act like soldiers of a Christian king. I know that men need women on occasion – we all do. But the women shall be willing. Do your hear – willing! Cold steel is no proof of manhood. If you must thrust with that before you thrust with the other, you are not worth the name of men! You will remember that, all of you."

David drew a long and rather uneven breath. "These must be punished. I could, perhaps should, hang them. But I need trained soldiers. There is no need for trial, for I myself caught them in the act. They shall be whipped – and you shall all witness it. Twenty lashes each of an oxen-whip for the two who were inside the hut. Ten each for the two who waited their turn outside, with drawn swords. And, and you, Drogo de Limesay, shall do the whipping."

"No, David – no, my lord Earl!" that young man cried. "Not

me, I pray you! I cannot do it. It is not suitable. For one nobly born . . . !"

"You will do so, I say. For all to see. These are your men. You have responsibility for their behaviour. And you will not be gentle about it. For each too light lash, an extra one will be required!"

So the four culprits were tied to palings of the hall farmery, their tunics removed, and a long hide whip, for use with a team of plough-oxen, produced. Young Limesay, who was not very efficient at wielding the thing, was ordered to practise on the trunk of a nearby tree, before all; then reluctantly started upon his victims. Even so he remained inexpert, and probably the resultant floggings were less than usually effective. Nevertheless they were sufficient to change the men's white backs quite quickly into an aspect of raw red meat – although only one of the sufferers called out during the prolonged process. David himself hated every moment of it quite as much as did Limesay, but forced himself to watch every stroke, gritting his teeth as each lash struck. He did not, however, claim that any of the blows were too feeble and must be repeated.

When at last the sixty lashes had cracked out and the bleeding victims sagged against their palings, David gazed round at the silent, watching throng.

"Let us all remember this," he said. "It is not pretty – but nor is rape and oppression. Worse than this will befall the next offenders. I shall reward good service – and punish disobedience. And see that all under me do likewise. Now, Drogo de Limesay, you will take these four, as they are now, and display them to those folk in the charcoal-burners' village. As sign of the Earl of Cumbria's justice . . ."

During the rest of the journey northwards there were no further outbreaks of indiscipline. And the young Norman lordlings and knights tended to eye David mac Malcolm rather differently also, with more deference, even Hugo de Morville and Hervey de Warenne – although that young man himself was far from doing so. It seemed to him a strange commentary on the nature of men that an act of counter-savagery not only should be necessary to enforce regard for justice, but that it should enhance the regard of others for the perpetrator.

A large party travels more slowly than a small and it took almost two weeks to reach Caer-luel on the northern edge of Cumbria. There the Earl Dolfin was waiting for them, and with no sort of ill-will. Cospatrick had been to see him on his way home to Scotland; and his brother was content, indeed seemed almost thankful, to relinquish any responsibility he had felt for the province to his second-cousin David. He asked only that he be allowed to retire to the family's lordship of Allerdale, in the fells to the east, where his sister, Ethelreda, formerly Queen to Duncan the Second, dwelt with her son William – and where the hunting was the best in all Cumbria. David, who had assumed that Dolfin would return to Scotland, to one of the Dunbar and March properties, saw no objection to this however, and agreed. In fact, after he had talked for a while, that evening, with his cousin, he came to the conclusion that to have him nearby might be a useful development. Dolfin was clearly popular with the local Cumbrian notables, and this could help the new administration. Also he might prove a valuable adviser. For although lazy and pleasure-loving, he was no fool, and knew the situation here better than anyone, having been Earl of Cumbria for a score of years. Likewise, as brother of the former Queen, he might serve as some link with that faction in Scotland who distrusted the Margaretsons. And these were strong in Galloway, apparently.

Indeed it was on the subject of Galloway that David found Dolfin especially informative, for he himself was really very ignorant about that great province of South-West Scotland, so all-but-detached from the rest as to look upon itself as practically an independent entity, in Strathclyde but scarcely of it – yet Cumbria's close neighbour. Although entirely Celtic as to population, and formerly having its own Celtic lords, it had been for long under the sway of the Norse Earls of Orkney – for its almost peninsular situation, and extraordinarily lengthy and indented coastline, made it very vulnerable to assault by sea; and the Vikings had for generations taken advantage of the fact. But now that the far-distant Orcades themselves were no longer independent, taken over by Eystein Magnusson of Norway, and with much internal feuding between the Earls Hakon and Magnus, grandsons of the mighty Thorfinn, the Orkney grip on Galloway had slackened. In the troubled state of Scotland since Malcolm Canmore's death, there had been little attempt to assert more than nominal sovereignty; certainly no authoritative control. Alexander's eyes were turned northwards meantime, not south-westwards. As a result the province was in a state of near-anarchy and unrest. Eystein was rumoured to have his acquisitive eyes on it, along with the Kingdom of Man. If he took it, since, with his longships he already dominated the West Highland seaboard, he could probably annexe all West Scotland.

This, Dolfin explained to David. He admitted that he personally had done nothing about it, had had no orders to do so and had been disinclined to act on his own – even though anarchy made a bad neighbour. Not that he could see what he could have done, anyway. He had no army, and the Cumbrian lords certainly would not have thanked him for seeking to embroil them in Galloway's affairs.

David asked who was wielding such rule and authority as there was in Galloway? It was a large province, almost a principality in itself. Surely it must have some government, even if ineffective?

His cousin admitted that there were two claimants to authority – but unfortunately they were more concerned with fighting each other than with ruling the province or keeping any sort of order. One was the young Earl Hakon Claw, second son of Earl Hakon of Orkney – whom David had met at Dunkeld, father of Madach of Atholl's bride. This character, in name Governor of Galloway, was little more than a youth, and though shaping up as a typical Viking sea-rover, was all but useless as a ruler. Dolfin looked distinctly apologetic as he said that, well recognising that he himself was no ruler, although no raider and plunderer either. But Hakon Claw, he indicated, was the very negation of all law and order. The other would-be overlord, he went on, was one Fergus of Carrick, a descendant of the old Celtic Lords of Galloway, dispossessed by the Norsemen and Orkneymen, also a warrior but a more able man, administering his own inherited territories in the hill-country to the north-east well enough – although he had a heavy hand and a name for cruelty. But he had no hold in the low country, although he raided it at will. There were other, many other, lesser lords and brigands let loose in that unhappy land, of course; but these two were the greatest, and could field most men – especially as Fergus had a kinsman, Dunegal, Lord of Nithsdale, who frequently joined him in his raiding activities, with large forces. Combined they could allegedly put five thousand men in the field.

David listened and pondered. He asked, also, about the situation on Man.

There Dolfin could scarcely be so well informed. But there was quite a lot of coming and going between the island kingdom and the Cumbrian coast, and he knew at least the bare bones of the situation. Godfrey Crovan, the warlike King of Dublin and Man, had died a dozen years before, pirate from Islay, son of a pirate from Iceland, who had seized the island in 1075. His

102

eldest son, Logmann, was worse even than his predecessor, emasculating and putting out the eyes of his own next brother when he rebelled against his savageries. He had died young, fortunately, and in 1103 was succeeded by his younger brother, Olaf the Morsel. Olaf was still only a youth, of a peaceable disposition; and therefore represented an open invitation to all adventurers and raiders, especially Norsemen. It seemed to be only a question of time before Eystein sought to take Man over. Only fear of the Irish had probably prevented it so far – the Norse-Irish, for Man was linked with the Viking kingdom of Dublin. Now it was being suggested that Eystein had his eyes on that likewise, for he already had taken over much of Ulster.

If he had not recognised it from the first, David perceived that his new role as Earl of Cumbria was unlikely to be a bed of roses, and Dolfin's relief at being superseded entirely understandable. Fortunately there seemed to be little of trouble brewing internally in Cumbria itself, its local lords often quarrelling amongst themselves but none apt to have larger ambitions. The strongest man there was Richard d'Avranches, son of Hugo, Earl of Chester; but he represented little threat, not only being a Norman but Henry's friend, indeed kinsman, grandson of Emma, the Conqueror's half-sister. Henry had told David that he ought to be a useful lieutenant.

As for the area to the east, Northumbria and Durham, these parts were meantime peaceful and under fairly strict rule, posing little threat to Cumbria. Ivo de Vesci was acting earl in Northumbria, at Alnwick, and controlling that province adequately. Whilst further south, Henry had come to terms with the scoundrelly but able Flambard, had re-established him as Bishop of Durham, and he was now managing the all but princely see effectually if less than kindly. Any trouble, therefore, was to be looked for from north and west, from Galloway, the Western Sea, or Man.

Henry's insistence on military preparedness and the need to build up a Cumbrian army, was now to be seen in its true light. David was to be his brother-in-law's answer to Eystein rather than to Alexander.

*   *   *

The weeks that followed were the most busy and exacting of David's life to date, new experiences, new situations, new decisions to be made every day, and on which no previous experience assisted. One of the very first decisions was not to settle in at the grim stone castle of Caer-luel, which Rufus had ordered to be built when he grasped the province seventeen years before, and still was not fully completed. One look at its stark and gaunt lines, its general air of oppressive and uncompromising discomfort, and he declared that this was no place for him. It might serve well enough as fortress, in time of war, but was not for honest living in. A company of young men were not, of course, over-concerned with bodily comfort and delicate living; but David had an eye for beauty and the graces of life, and saw no point in accepting harsh conditions when not necessary. Dolfin – who was no soldier either, to be sure – had lodged in the monastery of St. Nicholas, as had his uncle before him. David settled there also, Prior Ulfwin well content to accommodate him. It was a Benedictine establishment, and not over-strict in its rule. Brother John, David's former tutor and now the chaplain, an enthusiastic adherent of the Cluniac discipline, saw an inspiriting work of reformation ahead of him. There was no room here for all the young Normans, and some must needs bestow themselves in the castle and elsewhere.

Although Henry's commands made it inevitable that military preparedness must be their first priority, David himself did not devote much of his time to soldierly activities. He was trained in knightly practices, as were they all; but he was no dedicated warrior. And he had brought plenty of trained soldiers with him. He left to them the recruiting, training, and marshalling of the men for his new army. Nevertheless these men had to be obtained, in the first place, from the levies, lands, tenants and serfs of the local Cumbrian lords and land-holders; so David had more than sufficient to do in going round and making himself known to these lordly ones, seeking their co-operation rather than heavily acting the viceroy. They represented a great mixture, Normans, Saxons and Celts, both Scots and Welsh, and by no means all rejoicing to see the new Earl, nor anxious to be involved in his regime or in any way interfered with in their hitherto more or less independent affairs. However, with persuasion and tact rather than any sword-rattling, he managed to get most of them to agree to work with him. He found Richard d'Avranches in especial capable and helpful, and bound him and the local Norman element closer to his cause by appointing him his official deputy with the title of viscount, with particular responsibility for the southern part of the province down to the Lancaster border.

All the time, as the summer advanced, they awaited word of the Norsemen. There were plenty of reports of the young Earl

Hakon Claw's typical activities from Galloway – even one or two minor raids on Cumbrian coastal districts, hit-and-run affairs which were all but impossible to prevent however much they might call for punishment; but on the wider scene, of major assault and invasion, there was no word. The dreaded Eystein presumably was engaged elsewhere. If some of David's hot-bloooded lieutenants were disappointed in this, spoiling for a fight and somewhat critical of his refusal to let them loose on a retaliatory expedition against Hakon Claw, he himself was thankful for the breathing-space. His forces were growing fairly satisfactorily, so that by August he had some three thousand men under arms; but they were only part-trained and quite unblooded yet, in no state to take on Viking hordes or even the fierce Galloway kerns, acknowledged to be amongst the toughest fighters in Christendom.

Then, at the beginning of September, a messenger arrived from King Henry, with a letter. This informed that there had been serious dynastic trouble in Norway – for which the saints be praised! – which had had the happy effect of clipping some-what the intolerable Eystein's wings for the time-being. When Magnus Barefoot had died in battle in Ireland, he had left three sons – innumerable more, no doubt, but these three especial in that though they were all by different mothers, each of the ladies believed herself to have been Magnus's lawful wife. These were Eystein, Sigurd and Olaf. More uncomfortable still, the first two were sons of sisters, daughters of the Earl of Saxi. Eystein was the eldest by one year; but Sigurd Half-Deacon was the child of the elder sister. To add to the confusion dynastically, Olaf, much the youngest, was nevertheless the son of the true wife – or at least the lady recognised as such by Holy Church. Since 1103, when the potent Magnus died, this situation had been, as it were, in the simmer, with Eystein, now twenty years, acting King of Norway and his half-brothers lying fairly low. Now conflict had arisen, exacerbated by Eystein's predilection for overseas adventuring, so that he was seldom at home, and Norse affairs neglected. The supporters of both Sigurd and Olaf had risen in arms and there had been much warfare. Now an uneasy compromise had been reached. The kingdom was to be divided between all three, Sigurd to have the northern half, Olaf the southern and Eystein all the outlying domains and conquered territories, such as Iceland, the Orkneys, the Hebrides and Ulster. This situation was unlikely to be stable for long; but it accounted for Eystein's lack of aggressive activity that year. However, it might well imply

105

an even increased threat hereafter, when the campaigning season opened again next year, or later, with Eystein possibly more eager than ever for overseas conquests to wipe out his humiliation and increase his dominions. So the need to build up forces in Cumbria was far from lessened. Thus Henry's letter.

He added a postscript which he thought might interest his brother-in-law. The lame Simon de St. Liz of Northampton, of all things, had been bitten belatedly by religion and had gone on the new Crusade. Was it not said that there was no fool like an old fool?

David was indeed interested. In fact his heart sang at the news. At his prayers, at which he was fairly assiduous, he had subsequently to ask for strength not to hope that the Earl Simon should meet with a glorious but untimely death in this most excellent of causes. He did permit himself to write a letter, however, to the Countess Matilda, at Earl's Thorpe – a letter which he wrote and rewrote many times – saying that he had heard of this situation and rejoiced that her husband was thus so notably employed, and wishing for the happiest outcome possible for all concerned. He sent his admiration to the lady and his undying devotion.

Henry's news meant no slackening in the great task of recruitment and military training; but it did give David time and opportunity to seek to get to closer grips with the more local situation – since autumn and winter storms were likely to rule out any major high-seas adventures on the part of even Viking invaders. He decided that it was time to do something positive about Galloway. But before he did so, he wrote another letter, this time to his brother Alexander. There had been a notable and perhaps ominous silence from the King of Scots regarding this Cumbrian appointment. Alex was no correspondent, but some word or reaction might have been looked for. Cospatrick, who paid them a visit that September, was unable to inform as to the Scots attitude. Lothian, the Merse and Teviotdale welcomed the arrival of David, and a stronger hand at Caer-luel, as adding to their security; but what Stirling, which Alexander was making his chief seat of government these days, might think about it, he had no idea or information. He kept away from the place, by preference; and the King tended to leave the South severely alone.

David wrote, therefore, telling his brother of his own position, explaining how he had rejected Edgar's division of the kingdom, and assuring that he had no thought of claiming any form of rule in Southern Scotland for himself. But he did say that he proposed to do something about Galloway, not in any sort of take-over of the province but merely to try to restore order therein, for Cumbria was suffering. He included the information on Norway which Henry had sent, in case Alexander had not heard of it, adding that it might be a good opportunity for his brother to reassert his authority in the West Highlands. He wished Alex very well and hoped that an heir to the throne might be on the way.

Duty done, he prepared for his first major venture in the sphere of rule and governance.

*   *   *

On a crisp golden day of early October, David crossed Eden and Esk into Scotland proper, with a small group of his associates and an escort of no more than fifty men – to show that this was no aggressive expedition – and flying the dragon banner of Cumbria, so similar to that of Wales. They rode due westwards along the Solway plain, the marshy coastal flats on their left, the hills beginning their rise to the right. They splashed across the mouth of the Annan, and on towards the estuary of the Nith, both great rivers coming down by wide straths out of the vast hill mass of Southern Scotland. This country was largely deserted, near the coast, although fertile, showing all the grim signs of raiding and devastation, burnt homesteads, cultivation gone back, abandoned townships, the wilderness taking over. Although the Solway Firth was notoriously shallow, the tidal sands extensive and navigation difficult, the Vikings could sail their shallow-draught longships up the river estuaries and fan out on foot from there. But they were never fond of walking or riding, and seldom went far from their vessels. So the local folk had retired from the seaboard and river mouths up the straths and valleys into the hills. In consequence, David's party scarcely saw a living soul all the way to Dumfries, which lay at the foot of Nithsdale, twenty-five miles from the Esk. And there they found the worst ruin of all, quite a large town in blackened desolation, its stockaded defences unavailing against the Norsemen's attacks. Bodies lay or hung everywhere, but these dead were not new, mainly skeletal now. Semi-wild swine rooted and scavenged, but apart from the equally busy birds on like business, that was the only sign of life. For those interested, it was possible usually to tell the men's remains from the women's and children's; for these tended to be headless, the heads being detached and hanging by their long hair in serried rows all around the township's pallisading – typical Viking touch.

After crossing Nith by a wide ford, the party left the coastal belt to proceed up Nithsdale, or Strathnith, some little way, before branching off westwards again over the higher ground, making now for the next valley-system, that of the Water of Urr. And soon they were aware of people, furtive folk who scuttled and hid and watched from cover, cattle hurriedly driven off, only the dogs left to bark at the travellers. Whoever was nominally lord here, it was fear that reigned. Most of the Normans were used to this sort of thing; but David mac Malcolm at least was sickened at heart. And this was in his brother's kingdom. Yet his own father, he knew, had enjoyed nothing better than creating just this sort of devastation.

They were some way up into the higher ground of the Dunscore hills, and the well-bred Norman horses, of Barbary stock mainly, making heavy going of the rough wet terrain, when they became aware that they were being followed. Every now and again they caught glimpses of a mounted company, up to a mile back, which did not seem to draw any nearer but which definitely grew in size. Some of David's colleagues were for turning back to challenge these people before they grew any stronger, but he said no. It was *their* country, and any initiative must come from them. As a peaceful traveller he was not going to challenge anyone.

In time, however, the shadowing force grew bolder and came on apace, presumably feeling themselves to be sufficiently reinforced, or perhaps now joined by someone in authority. When they were only a quarter-mile or so behind, David drew reign to await them, his armoured horsemen carefully non-aggresive as to stance but ready to close in on a signal, for immediate action, swords and maces loosened but not drawn, lances to hand.

The newcomers, when they drew close, proved to be a fierce and distinctly ragged crew, mounted on shaggy garrons but bristling with arms, the typical round Celtic shields, or targes, slung over left arms, perhaps three hundred strong. Their obvious leader, a youngish man, equally wild-looking but better clad in long ponyskin sleeveless jerkin over saffron shirt and short kilt above bare knees and thong-bound calves, carried a great two-handed sword across his thighs. He was red-haired, foxy-looking, keen-eyed.

"Who are you who rides so bold and unbidden over my lands?" he demanded. He spoke in the soft, sibilant Gaelic tongue, but managed to make his question sound sufficiently menacing nevertheless.

It was long since David had spoken Gaelic but he knew it well enough. His father, whose native language it was, had nevertheless discouraged its use; but oddly enough his mother, the Saxon Margaret, had made all her children learn it, since it was the language of the common people and used by their household servants.

"I am David mac Malcolm of Scotland, friend," he said. "Earl of Cumbria for Henry of England. But it is as brother of the King of Scots that I ride through Strathnith."

The other nodded. "I thought that it might be something such," he admitted. "I have heard of the Earl of Cumbria. I am Dunegal mac Murdoch of Strathnith."

"Ah, my lord," David acknowledged, and kneed his horse forward closer to the other's garron, both hands out to grasp the man's forearms in friendly fashion. "Your fame is known to me also. I salute you. I had thought to visit you. After I had seen the Lord Fergus of Carrick."

"Fergus? You ride to see Fergus? He is in cousin-ship to me."

"So I understand. You will, then, be able to direct me, friend? We have heard that he has many houses or strongholds. We are making for Lochinvar, where it is thought he might be . . ."

"No. He is at Kenmure. I saw him there but four days back. What is your business with Fergus, my lord David?"

It was as well that none of David's Norman friends understood the Gaelic, or they would have taken ill out of such a blunt demand to Henry's viceroy. But their leader showed no resentment.

"I seek to discuss with him what may be done about the Earl Hakon Claw of Orkney and his misdeeds," he explained.

"Ha! That jackal! That Norse pirate! I can tell you what should be done with him, David mac Malcolm! I . . ."

"Yes – but it is not *being* done, is it? He must be shown the error of his ways, I think. His sister is wed to my own cousin, Madach of Atholl . . ."

"More to be pitied him, then! What do you intend?"

"I intend to confer with Fergus. He is at . . . Kenmore, did you say? Where is that?"

"Kenmure. It is at the head of Loch Ken. Yonder, fifteen miles." He pointed westwards. "*I* shall take you there."

"You are kind. That will serve me very well. For your advice will be valuable. In the matter of Hakon Claw. Fifteen more miles is less than we had expected to have to go . . ."

So the Lord of Nithsdale dismissed some two-thirds of his company back whence they had come – but still retained about twice David's numbers, just to show what was what in Strathnith. He mentioned that the numbers were necessary for the visitor's protection, the Lord Fergus being a fierce man, his lands not to be encroached upon with impunity.

They rode on, the Normans and the Galwegians tending to look askance. Over the high moorlands and bare hills, with the local garrons making better going than the taller and heavier horses of the visitors, they came at length to the hidden valley of the Ken, a green and pleasant oasis in that lofty wilderness, the long and very narrow Loch Ken filling its vale for miles, quite populous country suddenly. Near the head of the loch, at the far, western side, they could discern what looked almost like a Norman stone castle crowning a height above the water. Dunegal declared, almost proudly, that the potent and mighty Fergus, his cousin, had built a hold there as good as any Frenchman's keep.

David was intrigued, for the Scots did not go in for stone castles, any more than did the Saxons and Welsh – they were a Norman conception – the native strongholds being timber raths or hallhouses set within ramparts, palisades and ditches. On their way to that castle, round the head of the loch, they passed another establishment within ramparts; but this was a cashel, a monastery of the Celtic Church, unlikely as it seemed to those used to Romish abbeys, a cluster of simple timber-and-thatch huts, large and small, within the earthen banks and palisade. This was the Cashel of St. John, Dunegal revealed, under the famous Abbot Gillicolm, uncle of Fergus.

At this information, David insisted on pausing to pay his respects to the man of God – of whom, in his ignorance, he had not heard. However, monks of the Columban Church, in their simple dark-brown, leather-girdled habits with forehead instead of crown tonsures, declared that their Abbot was presently dining up at his nephew's rath of Kenmure. So on the travellers rode, southwards now, in the evening shadows.

From Dunegal's description and constant references to the mighty power, if not downright ferocity of this Fergus, David had expected all the way to be challenged, if not assailed by his armed minions. But nothing of the sort had materialised – and still did not. Near the castle on its hilltop site they had to pass through quite a large township of hutments and hovels, where plenty of armed kerns were in evidence; but though these eyed the armoured knights sullenly there was no actual threatening gestures. Perhaps they imagined David's party to be Dunegal's captives.

Their approach had not passed unnoticed, however, for when they had climbed the winding track which corkscrewed round the hillock to the summit they found quite a sizeable company awaiting them in the level forecourt under the soaring, harsh stone-walls of the square keep. This was a very similar, if somewhat smaller, building to Rufus's castle of Caer-luel – and as new, by the look of it.

David was surprised. But much greater was his surprise at the appearance of the central figure of the group awaiting them. Two men stood slightly apart here, one older and dressed exactly as had been the monks of the Cashel of St. John, save that his tonsured long hair was grey – presumably the Abbot Gillicolm. But the other was young, pale-faced, slightly-built and dressed as might be any Norman, no older than David himself and of much the same physical stature.

David stared at this individual, scanning his good-looking features, and then exclaimed. "Sweenie!" he cried. "On my soul – Sweenie Mac Sween! You!"

Hugo and Hervey were gasping the same name.

"David mac Malcolm – grown a man, a God's name! Like Hervey here, and Hugo de Morville!" the other jerked, and came hastening forward. "You three! God be good – Davie himself!"

David leapt down from his horse, to reach out and embrace the speaker, Hugo and Hervey doing the same, whilst the other Normans stared, astonished. "Sweenie – here's a joy! Who would have thought . . .? How long is it? Eight years? Nine? Since you left Romsey Abbey . . .?

"Nearer ten, *a graidh*. Aye, then. 1098. And we were all laddies. Now . . .!"

"Laddies no more. Hostages no more. But – you? Do you live here? Or but visit . . .?

"I live here, in the main, yes. Since most of my other houses are . . . in other hands! Do you like the castle I have built? It is not finished yet. But when it is done it will be as good as any of your Norman holds. Eh, Hugo? Hervey? Have your sires better?"

"*You* built it . . .?"

"Aye. But I forget the civilities. Here meet my uncle, the good Abbot Gillicolm mac Malcolm of St. John."

111

David bowed to the older man. "I greet you warmly, my lord Abbot, and seek your blessing," he said.

"My poor blessing you have, my son. But lord me not. We do not lord our abbots in Scotland. I am but a humble servant of God – and leave the lording to my nephew here!" But the Abbot smiled as he said it.

David nodded. He should have remembered that. He turned back to the younger man. "Sweenie – can it be that you are the son of the Lord Fergus?"

"Son? Scarce that. I *am* Fergus. Do you not remember? Fergus mac Suibhne. Your old fellow-pupil and hostage."

"But . . . but . . . ! You were never anything but Sweenie! Sweenie Mac Sween."

"To the Normans, yes. My name was uncouth, impossible for them. Sween was as much as they could get their miserable tongues round!" The young man glanced at the watching Normans, grinning. "So Sween I was – my father's name, mispronounced. I am Fergus mac Suibhne mac Malcolm, mac Gilliciaran – name enough for any man!"

"Saints above! So *you* are the mighty Lord Fergus of Carrick, Sweenie! Who would have believed that? I ever thought that your father was some Viking! I have come this long road from Caer-luel in fear and trembling, seeking Sweenie Mac Sween!"

"Caer-luel? Then you . . .?"

"Yes. I too am transformed, Sweenie . . . my Lord Fergus. You see before you the lord Earl of Cumbria, no less, Henry Beauclerc's Viceroy of the North-West!"

"Ha! So that is it? I heard that poor Dolfin was put out to grass. That the new governor was some kin of the King of Scots. But – who would have thought that it would be our gentle Davie!" He grimaced, comically enough. "Forgive me. Perhaps you are none so gentle now? Like myself!"

"I would hope to be – when permitted!" David's glance flickered around his watching companions.

"To be sure." Fergus clapped him on the shoulder. "Well, my lord Earl – enough of this. Standing here. We were at meat when we heard that the visitors who had been crossing my lands all day, unbidden, under Cousin Dunegal, were approaching my house. So you are well come. Inside with you – yonder, into the hall. All of you. Your men and beasts will be attended to."

So, after much dismounting and rough-and-ready washing, they were led into, not the great square keep but into a long hallhouse, of timber and plaster erection, lean-to against one of the courtyard walls, with other subsidiary building – a deal more comfortable than the stark stone chambers of the donjon-tower itself; while the escort was shown into another and still larger hall across the yard, Strathnith men and Norman soldiers both. No one seemed to be concerned about the extra food situation.

The lordly ones had no reason to complain, at any rate; and after a more than adequate repast in the seemingly bachelor establishment, over the ale-beakers, Fergus asked what brought Henry's Earl of Cumbria into Scotland seeking the Lord of Carrick?

"I came to see what sort of man he was," David admitted. "I had heard that he was strong. Even with a name for . . . harshness. I desired to seek out his strength. And, if it was sufficient, propose an alliance. Should he be not too ill a creature! Cumbria and Fergus – against the Earl Hakon Claw."

"Ha!" That was all the other said.

"My lord David finds the Orkneyman less than to his taste," Hugo de Morville commented.

"As do all half-honest men," Fergus agreed.

"He has been raiding the Cumbrian coasts," Hervey added. "We were for teaching him a lesson. But David – he is still sufficiently gentle to look askance at bloodshed! Or perhaps he thought that *you* might do the shedding for him!" The strong Galloway ale, on top of good feeding, had them distinctly relaxed.

David showed no offence. "I thought that we might perhaps act together. You suffer from Hakon Claw still more than does Cumbria. He never goes far from our coasts, from his longships, so he is hard to catch red-handed. *I* have no authority, as England's Earl of Cumbria, to go warring on Scottish soil. But if you went warring, a native lord, against these Orkney brigands I could support you."

"Ah, yes. But . . . the Orkney brigands are led by a man who is, in name at least, Governor of Galloway."

"I had not forgotten. But Hakon Claw was appointed by his father, Earl Hakon Paulsson of Orkney. And Orkney is now taken over by Norway. The King of Scots cannot have a subject of the Kings of Norway governing a Scots province. So . . ."

"Very well so. I do not contest that. What, then, do you propose?"

"That you call upon me, as brother of your King, to aid you expel Hakon Claw from Galloway. How many men can you raise?"

113

"Four thousand in two weeks. Another thousand a week later. And you?"

"I cannot do as well. As yet. Two thousand will be as many as I can field this season. But three hundred will be trained Norman cavalry."

"To fight on rough and broken country where Norman cavalry is at least advantage."

"It is my hope that there should be no real fighting."

"Eh?"

Hervey de Warenne hooted and slapped the table. "I told you, Sweenie – Davie has not changed with wearing an earl's belt!"

"A show of strength and the threat of greater force," David went on, quietly. "Threat of the King of England and the King of Scots, both, moving in. Not just Fergus of Carrick and the Earl of Cumbria. I believe that Cospatrick of Dunbar, with at least a token force would join us. How many men has Hakon Claw?"

"His own Orkney Vikings, no more than twelve hundred. But Galloway levies amany. Perhaps six thousand. More."

"How reliable are they? Will they fight for him? Against their own folk and the King of Scots' brother?"

"If they think Hakon Claw will win, yes!"

"Then we must convince them otherwise. They must be led to believe, beyond all doubt, that Hakon Claw's days are numbered in Galloway. That you Fergus, will be the next Lord of Galloway. And their chiefs to know whom to support."

The other raised his brows but said nothing.

"I will seek to bring Man into this. If only in a gesture . . ."

"You will gain nothing there. Olaf Morsel is still but a youth – and a timorous one. He will not go hosting."

"Not himself, no. But there are stout men on Man, warriors. And they fear attack by Eystein of Norway – as does all the West. Eystein has boasted that he will rule from Iceland to Dublin. And he would use Galloway as his base, in the south. Man would be glad to see Hakon Claw and all Orkneymen and Norsemen out of Galloway, I swear. A fleet of Manx longships lying in the Solway Firth, with not so much as a sword drawn, might work wonders."

"Would they do that? For you?"

"Not for me – for themselves. Will you do it?"

"Oh, yes – I will do it. Since I have been itching to do something of the sort for long. Whether the rest do, or no, is your concern, Earl Davie! When do we march?"

It was as easy as that. David had set out from Caer-luel anticipating having to work hard and long to gain agreement for his project. He leaned back relieved. Details could be worked out later.

*   *   *

Five weeks later, on the Eve of St. Clement, a chill day of late November, almost too late for practical campaigning, David's Cumbrian force met Fergus and his Galwegians at Dumfries. Fergus was better than his word, he and Dunegal between them producing well over five thousand men, a fierce-looking horde, well-armed if unruly and certainly with no appearance of being the scrapings of any barrel. For his part David also had improved on his predictions, for with the Earl Cospatrick of Dunbar and March, who had gladly joined in the venture with four hundred Border moss-troopers, he had brought three thousand. Dolfin had come along too, less enthusiastic than his brother, and though little acquisition militarily, adherence had its own value for he was popular with the Cumbrians. So the combined force made a quite impressive army of over eight thousand.

But combined force was perhaps scarcely the phrase to apply. Even that first night at Dumfries, trouble broke out, Galloway kerns fighting with Borderers and Cumbrians, Normans assailed by all and sundry, and the unfortunate locals of Dumfries anyone's prey. Fergus did not seem to be greatly perturbed at this, possibly because his people were greatly in the majority, but also, clearly, because this was normal campaigning behaviour, mere high spirits unavoidable in a host of fighting-men of any worth. David however was much concerned, angered, and insisted on order being restored and maintained, using his chain-mailed and mounted Norman knights to exert heavy-handed discipline, and reproaching Fergus for his attitude. To mollify his boyhood friend rather than out of any sense of duty apparently, the Lord of Carrick thereafter summarily hanged a dozen of his Gallowaymen, selected evidently at random, hoisting the corpses at various corners of the unhappy town where the cowering inhabitants would be apt to see them by the light of their flaming hovels. Almost as upset by this as he was by the rioting and looting itself, David urged no further punishment, and meted out none himself, other than that inflicted by the flats of Norman swords. It all made for a disturbed night.

By morning David had changed his plans. The army must be divided, he decided. Fortunately this would be effective enough strategically; and there were two routes to their goal at Kirk Cuthbert's Town, on the Dee estuary, where Hakon Claw had his headquarters – that is, north-about and south-about around the mountain-mass of Criffel. The larger force, under Fergus, would advance by the Urr and Carlingwark Loch to the Dee valley, whilst David would take the Cumbrians, men of Teviotdale and the Merse and the cavalry, by the Solway coast. They would keep in close touch, for the two hosts would never be more than a dozen miles apart, although high ground would separate them. Hakon Claw would no doubt be informed of the approach of both armies. It would be interesting to see his reactions.

Fergus had no objections. In fact, David had the impression that he might even be relieved, to have any restrictions on his command and people's behaviour removed. It was only about thirty-five miles to Kirk Cuthbert's Town, by both routes. They allowed themselves three days – for non-mounted hosts could not move much faster, in large numbers, however galling this might be for the horsed men. Besides, timing was of the essence in David's planning. Olaf Morsel of Man – or at least that youth's advisers – had agreed to make a demonstration, as far as they were concerned. Which meant that Hakon's longships should not actually put to sea to give battle. The Manxmen would show themselves off the mouth of St. Cuthbert's Bay and seem to threaten – but that was all. That was to be in three days time. So the Orkneymen must by then be so concerned over the near approach of the land armies that they would not risk dividing their forces and sending out their longships. David had to time this exactly, or the Orkneymen might sally out, and the Manxmen turn for home, with nothing achieved.

So his mixed company marched south-eastwards, skirting the high ground, towards the Solway shore with all its deep indentations and shallow tidal bays. It was difficult country, with much marshland, mud and scrub forest, and practically empty, with everywhere signs of Norse raiding from the sea. The various sections of the force, Normans, Cumbrians and Borderers, kept well separate, and camped those two nights almost a mile apart. There were no occupied villages or town-ships to tempt looters and ravishers. David was learning the lessons of command; strategy was not all.

They glimpsed the Manx fleet on the evening of the second

116

day, as the grey November dusk was falling – or at least an assembly of about forty longships and birlinns heading north by east, perhaps three miles offshore. No identifications were possible, at that range and light; but the vessels seemed to be in no hurry, and were probably the Manxmen.

That evening later, when they were camped on the blunt peninsula of Dundrennan, between Auchencairn and St. Cuthbert's Bay, the first messenger arrived from Fergus – although David had sent three northwards. He informed cheerfully that all was going well with the Carrick-Strathnith array. Indeed very well, for they had had two skirmishes with the enemy and beaten them soundly both times. In token whereof the Lord Fergus sent his old friend a golden Norse-type bracelet, of snakes eating each other's tails – still encrusted with blood where it had been hacked off the victim's forearm – indicative of the quality of the defeated. They were making excellent progress, likewise, and were considerably further ahead than anticipated – which, of course, was not the objective either. David fretted somewhat.

Next forenoon the southern force had their first sighting of the enemy, a small mounted party, which made off westwards at speed when they saw how large a host there was. The Norman cavalry, spoiling for action, would have given chase, but David said no. They *wanted* the news of their presence to reach Hakon Claw. Why interfere with his couriers?

Presently from another and lesser headland they saw the fleet of ships rowing up and down at the mouth of St. Cuthbert's Bay. It seemed that all was going according to plan.

St Cuthbert's Bay runs inland for about seven miles, to merge into the estuary of the Dee. David's force now turned inland, well back from the salt water. They were about halfway towards Kirk Cuthbert's Town, still with no appearance of the Orkneymen, other than an occasional watching mounted figure, when David realised that all was *not*, in fact, going according to plan. There was a chill north-easterly breeze, and on it, distant but clear, was borne the sounds of battle, large-scale clash.

It could only be Fergus and Dunegal arrived too soon and engaging or being engaged by Hakon Claw on their own, which was folly. A pitched battle was what David sought to avoid. One of the guides Fergus had lent him declared that the fighting sounded as though it must be coming from the Dunrod area, the valley of the Dunrod Burn, some three miles away. David considered sending a swift mounted party to go and bring him word of the situation, then decided to save time by going himself. Leaving the Earl Cospatrick in command, with orders to bring on the force at best speed, he rode off with a few companions.

It was good to be riding fast and free after days of footmen's-pace dawdling, however dire the emergency. Over a series of low grassy ridges, with scrub and bog in the intervening shallow hollows, they went, the noise of conflict growing ever louder and more sustained, the ring and clash of steel and the shouts and yells and screams of men, a human storm which was almost the more tangible for being unseen.

Presently they topped a higher ridge to overlook a wider, truer valley beyond, with more major hills rising behind – these having acted as back-cloth to project the sounds of the battle southwards. From the ridge, all was apparent. The valley-floor was an indescribable chaos of struggling, bawling, groaning men in their thousands, and flashing, flailing steel. There was no recognisable front line, only two noticeably denser, more concentrated groupings in the midst, a fair way apart, undoubtedly the respective leadership parties. There were no standards or banners, no command-posts, no vanguards or rearguards, only countless individual hand-to-hand conflicts, of large groups and small, men battling it out without regard to any other tactics than skill with weapons, brute strength, untiring muscles and sheer blood-lust – and courage.

"A rabble!" Hugo de Morville exclaimed disgustedly. "A barbarous mêlée, no more!" Such elemental battering ran counter to all Norman notions of warfare.

"How can they even tell who is winning?" Hervey demanded. "Until a sufficient number of one side flees? Or until only a few are left alive and heads counted?"

David was not concerned with that aspect of the battle so much as that the leadership could not be picked out nor reached. "A plague on Fergus!" he muttered. "I want to talk with Hakon Claw. How can I, in this broil? He will not so much as perceive us!"

"If we rode down? Even so few of us. A charge. We might do something. Hearten Fergus," Hugo suggested. "At least make our presence known to Hakon Claw."

"No. We would but be lost in the strife. This nine of us would make no difference. We would be fighting for our lives. Never win near to Hakon. And Fergus needs no heartening, I vow!"

"What can we do then?"

"We can only wait. And hope that Cospatrick comes up

118

quickly. Our host drawn up here would surely give even Hakon Claw pause." David sent a young knight back to hasten on the following force, if that was possible.

To sit their horses on the ridge and watch that bloody strife was an extraordinary experience, frustrating as it was exciting for spirited young men, with every instinct urging them to take part, to move forcefully to the aid of their friends. It was galling, too, not to be able to tell, as Hervey predicted, even which side was in the ascendant. The ebb and flow of the struggle was no more consistent or informative, seen from up here, than the swirlings in a cauldron. All that could be seen was that while the Orkneymen were constantly being reinforced from the west, from the Kirk Cuthbert's Town direction, although not in any large numbers, the attacking host was not, Fergus evidently having thrown in his full strength from the first. Not that there was any impression given of him being forced back or overwhelmed.

The waiting seemed endless, although it cannot have been much more than half-an-hour before their own army hove in sight, for they had left it only three miles back. But at last something might be achieved, and hopefully, not too late, with the battle appearing to be no more certainly decided than when first they viewed it, however many men had died meantime.

David and his companions spurred back to their force, to shout orders. The entire host was to form up along this ridge, by troops and companies and squadrons, spread out lengthwise to give the appearance of greater numbers still. All Norman cavalry to ride back and forth before the ranks with banners. That, and great sustained shouting. And a large white flag, brought for the purpose, to be unwrapped and hoisted in the centre, above all.

This maneouvre proceeding, it was difficult at first to assess the effect on the struggling masses below. However preoccupied with their grim activities, even the most dedicated fighters must glance up sometimes, surely? Especially the leaders. And the rhythmic shouting from thousands of fresh throats must surely penetrate the hubbub?

"If Fergus would but draw back a little, disengage . . ."

"How can he?"

"Fling our whole array down upon them, Davie. Sweep all of the field, friend and foe alike!" Hervey urged. "Our fresh forces will finish off this unseemly affray."

"No, I say! That is not the way. I want Hakon Claw face to

face. Talking. Not half-beaten, and escaping back to his ships. Where we cannot follow. All to be done again . . ."

At length there was some change visible, some indication that the newcomers had been noticed and their presence having some effect. The fighting went on, but some vigour appeared to go out of it, especially around the leadership groupings.

"The Orkneymen have seen the light at last!" Cospatrick said. "What will Hakon Claw do now?"

"He cannot fail to see this white flag. Let us take it nearer to him, so that he can have no doubts. Hugo – ride round and down. Try to get Fergus to halt his fighting . . ."

David and most of his notables rode some way on down the slope, under the flag-of-truce, leaving the army drawn up on the ridge. Halting some six hundred yards from the edge of the fighting, David ordered his trumpeter to blow a prolonged summons.

Strangely, it seemed as though that trumpet had a real effect on the combatants. Possibly it was Fergus whom it affected most, forcibly reminding him of the agreed strategy. There was a recognisable further slackening of the fighting, which spread over the entire field.

David ordered another and still more peremptory blast. They moved still closer to the arena.

At last the desired result was produced. Out of much stir and commotion amongst the throng to the west, now seen to be a mixture of Orkneymen and Galwegians, notably different in their garb, a group began to push through from the centre, in the direction of the waiting party under the white flag. As these drew nearer, through the seething, panting, bleeding press, they were clearly all Vikings save for two, big men with long shaggy fair hair and beards, wearing winged and bulls'-horned helmets, leather tunics with metal scales as armour, and thong-tied breeches. Some were bleeding and battered, but all looked arrogantly assured. Different were the pair of local chiefs with them, darker, slighter, more wiry, in saffron kilts and sleeveless calf-skin jerkins, seeming a deal less confident. The central figure was a young giant of a man with hot blue eyes, no beard but with thin, down-turning moustaches, both forearms almost half-hidden under golden snake-bracelets. He had a slashed cheek, but grinned as he came.

"Earl Hakon Hakonsson?" David called, as they drew near. "I am your kinsman, David mac Malcolm of Scotland, Earl of Cumbria. Greetings!" The relationship was very distant; their great-great-grandmothers had been sisters.

"David? Henry's hound dog!" the other shouted back.
"What seek you in my Galloway? With such host? If it is
robbers and rogues you seek, there they are to your hand!" And
he pointed towards Fergus's people.

"Not *your* Galloway, friend. My brother Alexander's Galloway. And the Lord Fergus, there, is its new governor."

"Who says so, to Hakon Claw of Orkney?"

"*I* say so, cousin. And I speak for King Alexander and King
Henry both. No Orkneyman, under Norway, may any more
rule in Galloway, Strathclyde or Cumbria."

"Large words for so puny a man! But *only* words, David mac
Malcolm!"

"I prefer words – and they can be sharper than swords, see
you. But – I have swords also."

"I care not for your swords any more than for your words,
man! Here I rule. Here I stay."

"We shall see. I fear that I have credited you with more
nimble wits than you possess, friend. The Lord Fergus said as
much. But I believed otherwise." David shrugged. He turned
towards his companions. "Here is the Earl Cospatrick of Dunbar. And his brother the Earl Dolfin, whom you know. And
this is the Viscount d'Avranches. And Hervey de Warenne, son
to the Earl of Surrey. And others equally illustrious. King Olaf
of Man could not be with us, but he has sent his fleet. It lies off
your bay of St. Cuthbert – as perhaps has been reported to
you?"

The other said nothing.

"These friends of yours," David gestured towards the two
native chiefs. "They will no longer be able to support you. Now
that you are no more governor here. They are subjects of the
King of Scots and must needs support his representative. You
agree, my friends?"

When neither of the pair answered him, however uneasy
they looked, he changed his tone of voice suddenly, dramatically.

"Names?" he all but snapped.

"Colin of Dunrod, my lord," the elder said quickly.

"Murdoch of Borgue."

"And some of these men fighting are yours'?"

They nodded.

"Then withdraw them. Withdraw them all. Now. Under
pain of treason."

It was the moment of truth, of decision. The chieftains eyed
each other, looked at Hakon Claw and then back to David.

Fergus helped by choosing this moment to come striding over, limping, looking grim, Hugo with him.

"Do you know these two, my lord?" David called, to him. "Dunrod and Borgue?"

"I know them. And will know them better before I am done! Turncoats! Traitors!"

"No! No!" They cried that, as one.

"So long as the Earl Hakon was governor . . ." Dunrod pointed out, urgently.

"What else could we do?" the younger man asked, almost pleaded.

"Snivelling curs!" Hakon Claw roared. "White livered rats!"

"Not so, my lord Earl, but loyal subjects of my brother the King," David observed mildly. "Or will be hereafter, pray God!"

"Yes, yes, my good lord Prince . . ."

The die was cast, and all knew it, decision crystallised – and on the face of it decision made by the least important, least influential there. The Orkneymen could not prevail now, could not stand out in the face of the overwhelming forces David had marshalled against them. It only remained to seek to make capitulation easier for Hakon Claw to swallow, make the draught more tolerable before all, Viking pride acknowledged.

"My royal brother and good-brother will no doubt consider some suitable compensation in view of your . . . retirement, my lord Hakon," David said. "I shall so advise when I report your excellent acceptance of the change of governorship. Some recompence for loss sustained."

Fergus snorted and Hakon Claw glowered. But no other comment was made.

"No doubt you will wish to retire to your own Orkney Isles? How soon can you leave?"

"Leave . . . ?"

"Leave Galloway, yes. We do not wish for trouble between your people and mine. Or the Lord Fergus's. Nor yet the folk of Kirk Cuthbert's Town. Nor the Manxmen. It would be unfortunate if there was any paying off of old scores. As might well be. Do you not agree? With so large a combined host as I command, I cannot promise to protect you and your ships from attack. From those who might esteem themselves as having debts to settle! Your raidings here, in Cumbria, in Man, even over in Ireland, have made you many unfriends, I fear. The sooner your longships are at sea, the better, I think."

"I am not afraid of your rabble, Earl David."

"Perhaps not. But *I* am. Knowing their temper. The Manx fleet will not enter St. Cuthbert's Bay until I signal them. I can order them to let your ships through, unharmed. Today. But if they were to come ashore tonight."

"I have a strong fort at Kirk Cuthbert's Town."

"You cannot take your ships into your fort, my lord. You will not wish them to be burned? Or sunk?"

Hakon Claw looked away. "So be it," he said, at last.

"Tonight, then."

"Tonight."

"The weather is none so ill. For your voyage."

"I care not for weather. Any more than for your threats."

"To be sure. All know of the Vikings' powers at sea . . ."

So it was accepted. The Orkneymen and Fergus's people began their disengagement – not without some further scuffling – and withdrew their dead and wounded. The leaders returned to their own hosts. David sat waiting, up on the ridge, until Hakon Claw led his Vikings back to the town and haven. The local forces who had started the day with them seemed to melt away.

Fergus came back, after seeing to his own folk. "You have a tongue in you, Davie," he said. "You had that Orkneyman roped and tied. After I had hobbled him for you!"

"Had you left it to my talking he would still have gone, I think. And you would have saved the lives of many men, Fergus. How many have you lost?"

"No great number. No more than I can afford. Someone has to do the fighting, see you."

"That I question. I say show your strength. Be prepared to fight – but only if you must. Sharp wits will often serve better than sharp steel!"

"Are these men's words? Or women's?"

"Does it matter? So long as you gain your ends. And at less cost. I care not which. But, indeed, they were a woman's words to me. My mother's. Her wits won more victories for my father than ever did his over-ready sword! She taught me much."

Fergus inclined his dark head. "I cannot dispute with Margaret the Queen!" he acceded.

8

DAVID APPROACHED DUNBAR CASTLE, in Lothian, somewhat doubtfully, uncertain of his reception. Not from Cospatrick, of course – he would make him welcome enough. It was Alexander's attitude which could be in doubt, this summons a questionable joy. Cospatrick had sent a messenger to Caer-luel merely saying that King Alexander desired his brother's attendance at Dunbar on Scarce Thursday. No details, no indications or warnings.

David recognised only too well that he had taken chances in his move against Hakon Claw in November, used Alexander's name and authority without proper permission, acted in what his brother might construe as a high-handed fashion. The fact that the thing had needed to be done, and that Alexander himself was doing nothing about it, did not mean that the venture, however successful in the event, might not be frowned upon by the King of Scots. Especially when he might feel that his young brother was indeed seeking to exercise the functions of Prince of Strathclyde, as bequeathed to him by the late Edgar against Alexander's wishes.

But when they came to meet, in the curious sea-girt stronghold on its rocks-top site, Alexander revealed no trace of resentment nor displeasure. He was not an affectionate man by nature, nor demonstrative in any way save when angered. But he seemed to be in good enough spirits this fine April evening, although David thought, looking a deal older than when they had last seen each other four years before, at the wedding. Perhaps marriage did not agree with him.

"So, brother, it is good to see you," the King said, proffering a quick self-conscious embrace. "Man, you look well. Being Henry's watch-dog in the North suits you, it seems."

"I am glad to have work to do, yes." David was wary still. "I am kept engaged. And you my lord King?"

"I do not ail. But . . . I feel twice my years! Who would be a king, Davie?"

"*You* would, Alex, I think! Despite the burden."

"Perhaps. Yet it is a thankless task. Sometimes I could wish . . ." He shrugged, leaving that unfinished.

124

"And the Lady Sybilla? The Queen?"

"She is well enough, I believe."

"You believe . . . ?"

"I see little of her. She finds her own . . . amusements. At the Ward. I have lent her the Ward of the Stormounth. She keeps her own Court there. For a bastard, she has large notions!"

"And no children? No heir?"

"No heir. But, see you, I did not come here to talk about Sybilla." They stood on one of the many bridges of red masonry which linked together the stark rocks, rising from the swirling tides, on which that strange castle was built. "I have a deal more serious matter in mind."

David waited.

"I need your help, Davie. You have proved yourself to be a man of some wits. And this business requires wits. Careful handling."

Surprised, he looked at his brother. "Not . . . Galloway?"

"No, no – Galloway can wait. It is our father, Davie – his body. See you, it is time that he was brought home. To Scotland. From that Tynemouth. Unsuitable that he should lie there, little regarded. Too long it has been. Now Holy Trinity Minster is near finished. Our mother's great church, at Dunfermline. Edgar carried on the work. As have I. It is near done – a noble monument. I thought to mark its completion by bringing back our father's body from its poor grave at Tynemouth, and placing it beside our mother's, before the high altar she erected. This I would do."

Still more surprised, that this headstrong, down-to-earth brother should be concerned for such a thing, David nodded.

"An excellent project," he agreed. "What can I do to help?"

"It is difficult. These churchmen – a plague on them all! You know that I am having trouble with Turgot? Our mother's friend and confessor, who was Prior of Durham. Whom I made Bishop of St. Andrew's when I gained the throne. He is proving obdurate."

"That I can believe. For he was ever a determined man. But what has this to do with our father's body?"

"He says that once given Christian burial, the body cannot be exhumed without the authority of Holy Church. And since our father is buried, where he fell, at Tynemouth, in the See of Durham, authority to exhume may only be given by the Bishop of Durham. And I am at odds with that man, Flambard!"

"Ah!" So it was Ranulf Flambard again, Rufus's one-time

125

minion and hater of things Scots. "I also know Flambard. He will not give permission for the exhumation?"

"No. Or he says that, in the case of a king, it should be given by his superior, the new Archbishop of York. And I will not go seeking *his* permission either! For he claims spiritual rule over Scotland, in his arrogance – which I will not have. To go to this Thomas the Second and ask his permission, would be as good as admitting his false claim. Turgot could resolve this coil, but will not. For he supports the Archbishop's claim to rule the Church in Scotland. He says that *he*, as Bishop of St. Andrews, is the Archbishop's representative. I will not have it! *I* appointed him, not York. Or Durham."

David stroked his chin. "Yes, I see the difficulty."

"I could take an army and go dig up our father's body and bring it home. No doubt the Columban Church would give all necessary authority to do so, and gladly. Our brother Ethelred is still Primate, in name at least. But that would undermine the position of the Roman Church here, which our mother did so much to build up. And which Edgar and I have sustained. To spurn the authority of the only Romish bishop in Scotland, Turgot, and use that of the Old Church, would undo all that has been achieved – when already I am in difficulties with Turgot. To march would end all . . ."

"Yes. To be sure it would! And Henry would not like it. He is no churchman, and does not love Flambard. But to march into his realm, uninvited . . ."

"I know it, man. I know it. But I have set my heart on this."

"What do you wish from me, Alex?"

"That you use your wits, in this. I need help. You are Henry's friend, his viceroy in the North-West. Go to this Flambard. I am told that *he*, in fact, makes all the larger decisions for the new Archbishop. He is the true power there. As Earl of Cumbria, you have authority in the North . . ."

"Not over Northumbria. Nor over Holy Church, brother."

"No. But you are in a stronger position than am I. And Malcolm was *your* father, also. Will you do it, Davie?"

"What can I do, and say, that has not been thought of? Our good mother scarcely considered this, I think, when she sought to turn Scotland to the Roman Church!"

"Henry does not love Flambard, you say. Can you not play on that? You, Henry's right hand."

"I am scarcely that . . ."

"You acted it, when you invaded Galloway! And acted mine too, from what I hear!"

David smoothed his lips. "Something had to be done there, Alex. That Hakon Claw was ruining the province. And raiding Cumbria. I acted with Fergus of Carrick . . ."

"I know what you did, man – for whatever reason you did it. And I am glad to see the last of that Hakon Hakonsson. I should have dealt with him myself – but I have had over much else to do." He sighed. "I sent him one hundred gold pieces, to Orkney, as you asked in your letter. I hope that I did not waste it!"

"Henry also sent gold. Even so, it was a cheap victory, I say."

"No doubt. See you – if you use your wits as nimbly with Flambard of Durham as with Hakon Claw, I will have the more cause to be grateful!"

"Very well, I shall try. But I can promise nothing, Alex. And . . . you will confirm Fergus of Carrick as Lord of Galloway?"

"It is as good as done, Davie – when you bring me Flambard's authority to exhume at Tynemouth!"

*   *   *

So the next morning the brothers parted, Alexander to ride north through Lothian to Stirling and the burdens of kingship, David southwards for Durham. As well as his pair of close Norman friends, he had the company of their host Cospatrick also, a young man always ready for stir and movement. His father, the first Earl Cospatrick, had been slain alongside Malcolm Canmore at the Tynemouth disaster in 1093 – although he had been buried with more ceremony, in Durham Cathedral itself, because of his close association with the then bishop; he would call it a pilgrimage to his father's grave.

With good horseflesh, nobody to delay them and the coastal route in dry condition for travel, they made excellent time, crossing Tweed at Berwick and getting to Waren on Budle Bay, within sight of Bamburgh Castle, that first night. Two of the little party had interests here, for Waren was a new name, a local Anglian version of Warenne, a manor of William de Warenne, Earl of Surrey, Hervey's father. They stayed the night with the Earl's steward. And Cospatrick could look across at the great castle of Bamburgh, the strongest north of Tees, which he claimed should be his own, his father having been Earl of Northumbria until the Conqueror ousted him, when Malcolm Canmore had given him, his cousin, Dunbar.

Next day they were able to reach Tynemouth Monastery

itself, a small and modest establishment above a fine mile-long sandy beach, in the graveyard of which, amongst the unmarked tombs of generations of monks – for the place had been founded as early as 627 by the Celtic Church – a rough upright stone marked the resting-place of Malcolm the Third, King of Scots, treacherously killed by Moubray, Rufus's Earl of Northumbria. David had never loved greatly his harsh and irascible sire; as he stood at the graveside and said a brief prayer, his thoughts were more with his beloved mother.

Across Tyne by the ferry of another and larger priory, Jarrow, and turning inland now, by noon the following day they were at Durham, in its dramatic valley, cathedral and castle-palace crowning the whaleback ridge which rose above the coiling river in the midst. The Bishop was out hawking when they arrived; but it was evident that he lived in princely style here. After he had escaped from prison and fled to Normandy, Henry had rather weakly forgiven Flambard and allowed him to return to this See of Durham, which Rufus had bestowed on him in 1090 – on the theory that it required a strong hand to hold it together against the dominance of York; but as much as anything to appease Canterbury, always looking for means to hold York down, and esteeming Flambard, no doubt rightly, as a satisfactory thorn-in-the-flesh for the rival archbishop.

When the Bishop eventually came riding into the palace courtyard amidst much shouting, baying of hounds and feminine laughter – he was particularly notorious for his concubines – David was struck by how gross and heavy the man had become. It was, of course, ten years since he had seen him, and he was now well into middle years. Even so, the change was extraordinary, the body huge, swollen, shapeless in rolls of flesh, the features even lost in fat. Yet when he came close, to greet his visitors, they could see that the little piglike eyes, half-hidden as they were, gleamed as quick and shrewd as ever they had done.

Flambard could scarcely have been glad to see them, but he played the host adequately, genially, making much of David as Earl of Cumbria and giving no impression of past unpleasantries. He introduced his two current ladies openly as his daughters-in-God – and hinted, chuckling, that his principal guest might possibly enjoy the hospitality of one of them, the choice being his.

David, however, found difficulty in gaining private speech with the man. It was not until the rich feasting was over and many of the company were so drunken as to be beyond hearing or comprehension, that he and his friends got the Bishop's attention approximately to themselves. Flambard, admittedly, showed no least signs of the amount of liquor he had consumed.

"I have come to see you on a matter of some import, my lord," David began. "For your ear alone."

"You have my respectful attention, my lord Earl. But drink up, my friends – the night is young. If it is in my power to aid you, I am yours to command."

"I am glad of that, Bishop. I am anxious, you see, that my father, King Malcolm's body, should be uplifted from Tynemouth where he is presently buried, and given final and decent resting-place beside my mother in her new minster of the Holy Trinity at Dunfermline, now nearing completion."

"A most admirable and filial desire, my son. None could do other than commend it."

"Yes. But it appears that an authority for exhumation is required."

"To be sure. But that should present no difficulties. My lord Archbishop Thomas of York will be pleased to grant it, I have no doubt."

"Need the Archbishop be troubled? *You* could grant it, my lord, could you not? Indeed, if any priest may bury, may not any priest unbury?"

"Ah, scarcely that, my good young friend. Because a priest has enjoined the soul to rest in peace, it requires a greater priest to disturb that rest. In the case of a king, an archbishop would be suitable."

"Suitable, perhaps – but not essential, I think. The bishop of the see has fullest authority within his see, has he not? Tynemouth is in your see."

Flambard sipped his wine. "In this matter I would prefer to consult my archbishop, my lord," he said.

"As *I* would prefer otherwise – and for sufficient reason." David spoke conversationally, quietly. "Your archbishop claims archiepiscopal jurisdiction over Scotland. Which all Scots deny. *His* authority therefore is not acceptable in this matter."

There was a considerable pause, now that the issue was out in the open "I fear that I am helpless in this situation," Flambard said, at length.

"I think that you do yourself injustice," David returned, though mildly enough. "You could give me the authority. And inform the Archbishop later, for ratification of your act – if you felt that was necessary. By which time my father would be on his way home to Scotland. Or you could refer the matter to the Prior at Tynemouth, leaving him to give me the authority. Which again could be refuted later, if advisable. Neither way would your name and repute suffer."

"These would be deceits, dissembling, my lord Earl!" Flambard sounded shocked. "You would not have me, a prince of Holy Church, to countenance deceit, deception in matters of religion!"

David eyed him directly. "I suggest, Bishop Flambard, that you are practising deception every day, in your office! For less worthy causes than that of a son wishing his father's body to rest beside his mother's. Princes, not only of the Church, have to dissemble frequently, in the process of rule. King Henry, now, my brother-in-law, must dissemble that he does not know that all is not well in the See of Durham, that parishes are empty, churches priestless, their revenues unaccounted for. Is it not so?"

David's companions held their breaths at that, afraid that their friend had this time let his tongue run away with him.

It was impossible to tell whether the Bishop's expression changed, so formless were his fleshy features. Nor did his voice betray him, for he did not speak.

Far from resiling, David went on, however calm his tones. "And I, as Earl of Cumbria, have likewise to dissemble. In that I do not report to Henry and to Canterbury that Cumbria is all but a heathen province, a Godless desert – although it also is in Durham's see. That few churches are manned, tithes and revenues swallowed up, and there has not been an episcopal visitation in ten years, I am told."

"I lack men, my lord – priests, deacons, monks. In especial senior clergy."

"But not money, gold to hire them?" David gestured at all the luxury around them, greater than he had seen at Henry's or even Rufus's Court.

"A see such as Durham involves great expenses. You cannot conceive how much falls to be spent in maintaining the dignity of Holy Church in this, the largest diocese in England. Nor the problems . . ."

"Your revenues are insufficient, Bishop? Despite all?"

"Greatly so. I must support York also, with moneys. Durham is York's greatest support. At times I know not where to turn for gold."

"You say so? Then perhaps, who knows, I might be able to

help in some small way. No large aid, I concede, But . . ." David paused.

"Yes, my lord Earl?"

"It is the matter of Coldingham, in the Merse. My brother, King Edgar of Scots, left the church of St. Mary, Coldingham, with ten farmsteads, to Durham, In gratitude for Turgot the Prior's ministrations towards our mother . . ."

"This I know. Turgot has informed me. But I have received not a penny."

"King Alexander has withheld payment. On account of this . . . dispute. About spiritual jurisdiction and York. But – I think that I might persuade him otherwise."

"How much worth is this Coldingham?"

"That I do not know. But the Merse holds some of the best land in Scotland. My cousin, the Earl of Dunbar here, perhaps can tell you. Coldingham is in his earldom."

"They are rich farms, my lord Bishop," Cospatrick said. "And the church's own manor is a fair one. It was once an important abbey of the Celtic Church. The revenues will be of no little substance."

There followed a pregnant silence.

"How can your lordship be sure of King Alexander's agreement?" Flambard asked, at length. "To this withheld payment."

"King Malcolm was his father also, Bishop," David reminded. "I have little doubt as to his approval."

"I see. The Archbishop Thomas is . . . indisposed, at the present. At York. It would be a pity to trouble him over this matter. How soon would your lordship wish to raise the body of your royal father?"

David hesitated only for a moment. "At once. As soon as may be."

"Then, my lord, go tell Prior Eadric at Tynemouth that you have seen me, and that he may exhume."

"Ye-e-es. Will that be sufficient? No writings?"

"No writings. He is a Saxon. He will do what he is told." That was scornful.

"My mother was a Saxon, Bishop Flambard. I would wish this Eadric to come to no hurt thereafter. You will mind it?"

"He will be well enough."

"Then we are agreed. One last matter. Send you priests to me, at Caer-luel. I shall see that they find parishes in Cumbria. And are paid. Then I shall dissemble the less!"

They eyed each other.

*   *   *

131

Flambard was right in one respect, at least. Prior Eadric of Tynemouth, when they returned and announced that his bishop had given permission for the exhumation, made no objection, demanded no written warrant.

It was a harrowing and unchancy business, unpleasant to a degree. The Prior provided two burly lay-brothers, who went to work with spade and mattock, beneath the upright monolith bearing the roughly-inscribed legend MALCOLM. The King had been buried just as he was when dragged out of the river, in campaigning garb and chain-mail shirt, and had lain so for eighteen years. David had purchased from Flambard some blankets and a large and handsome cloth-of-gold bedcover to wrap the body in; also two pack-horses to carry a litter.

Fortunately the soil was sandy, near the beach, and this helped, both in the disinterring process and because of its dryness, in preserving the corpse from putrescence and, at this stage, liquefaction. Even so, when the remains were reached, part covered in the relics of a cloak, it was a gruesome sight, mainly skeletal but with semi-mummified flesh and sinew adhering, the more incongruous for the rusty chain-mail over the empty rib-cage and the leather accoutrements. At least there was no strong smell, as they had feared. Nor was there any doubt about identification; the great skull, with patches of grey hair still clinging, could be only that of Malcolm Canmore, Big Head. The huge cavernous eye-sockets seemed to stare at them accusingly.

Muttering a prayer, David hurriedly had the remains wrapped up in the covers he had brought, hiding all under cloth-of-gold. In the horse-litter it looked less dire.

Nevertheless, on the long ride northwards thereafter, slowed as they were by the pack-horses, the young men never ceased to be aware of the burden they escorted. The success of their mission could not make it other than a gloomy journey.

It took them five days to reach Stirling – only to discover that Alexander had gone to Invergowrie, on the verge of Angus. When he had been Earl of Gowrie this had been his favourite house; and it remained so even though he made Stirling, with its mighty fortress above the first bridgeable reach of Forth, his capital.

Reluctant to make a further lengthy journey with the corpse, and then to have to take it back to Dunfermline – he had a notion that the remains were indeed beginning to smell – David sent Cospatrick on, at his fastest, to Invergowrie, whilst he and the others next day proceeded on eastwards, at a slower pace, along the north side of the Forth estuary, through Fothrif, to his father's capital and his old home at Dunfermline. He thankfully deposited his strange burden before the high altar of the great minster on the hilltop there.

They had less long wait than he had feared. Alexander was no laggard when his interest was aroused. He arrived, with a weary Cospatrick, the very next evening, having been ferried over Tay and ridden hard across Fife.

"Davie – you have done it!" he cried, coming to embrace his brother, a deal more warmly than the last time. "You have the body upraised and here, man? This 'fore God, I had never expected. It is a wonder! I looked only for a paper, a written warrant to exhume. How did you achieve it? Cospatrick has told me some of it, but . . ."

David explained as they walked to the minster from the little palace on the rock, informing that he had pledged the Coldingham revenues.

They stood beside their father's body, still in its cloth-of-gold shroud, silent. David had advised his brother not to look beneath. Nearby was a slab of Iona marble in the flagstones of the floor, just in front of the altar, beneath which lay the body of Queen Margaret, with on her right that of her eldest son, Edward, and on her left the late Edgar.

"Together again, at last," Alexander said, at length. "I shall have a leaden coffin wrought." He paused. "There is but one difficulty. As you see, the building is scarce finished. I had thought that it could be months yet before we obtained the body. I planned that there would be a great celebration, to mark the completion of our mother's dream, the first great stone minster in Scotland. And to inter her husband at her side. Many present. It is a dream I have had. But now . . . ? This, this cannot be delayed. Burial . . ."

"No. But it need not be spoiled. Your dream, Alex. A temporary burial here, now. Simple. Just a priest and ourselves. Then, when you have the coffin made and the building finished, your great ceremony. One more uplifting will make no difference. Then the final committal. Until, until Resurrection Day!"

"Yes. Yes – that is it. The best way. We shall do as you say . . ."

So the next forenoon, before the two brothers and a handful of others, Malcolm's remains were placed by the Prior of Dunfermline in a space scooped out beneath the flagstones near the others, in the briefest of services. When it was over, Alexander

133

announced that he would in fact build a stone-lined crypt under the chancel here, instead of these graves, where all the family, their dynasty, could be buried.

For so young a man – he was only twenty-eight years – his mind seemed to be greatly concerned with death and burial.

Before David and his friends left for Caer-luel, the King announced that he confirmed Fergus of Carrick as Lord of Galloway. Not only that, but that David should hereafter be entitled to exercise rule and sway, subject to the King's control, over Strathclyde and the parts of Scotland south of Forth and the Scotwater. He was not making him Prince of Strathclyde, nor yet governor – which would be unsuitable in a joint-subject of the King of England. But he could act in vice-regal fashion, with the title of an earl of Scotland.

It was curiously vague and not entirely satisfactory position – but clearly it represented a considerable gesture on Alexander's part. David, uncertain what might be implied, decided to take it meantime as a compliment of sorts.

9

DAVID HAD NO call to act for his brother, vice-regally or otherwise, before, unexpectedly, he saw him again. The following May, two messengers reached Caer-luel, each from a king. Henry announced that his patience with the Welsh princes and their revolts was finally exhausted and that he was going to lead a great army against them. David was commanded to muster and bring as many men as he could, to join the Marcher Earl of Chester, to threaten the Welsh north flank. This by the Feast of St. Barnabas at the latest. The word from Alexander was in the same vein, that Henry had besought him, for kin and friendship's sake, to send a Scots force to aid against the rebellious Welsh, so that their incessant risings might be put down once and for all. Alexander would have thought twice of acceding. But he was having difficulty with his new Bishop Turgot of St. Andrews, who was inclined to look to his old master, the

134

Archbishop of York, as his ecclesiastical superior – which the King of Scots would nowise admit. He wanted Henry's sympathetic aid in this matter, to bring pressure to bear on York, through Canterbury, to relinquish ideas of hegemony over Scotland. He therefore felt that some such gesture as this might be valuable – and at the same time, any warlike adventure, especially one which would not involve his own realm, suited his temperament. So he would comply, and come south, leading his own army. He thought it likely that his brother would also be involved. They could march together.

By now David could raise fully five thousand armed and trained men, given a week or so of notice; so that, when the Scots force of some eight thousand arrived in due course, they made quite a major army. Alexander had most of his Scots earls with him – Fife, Angus, Strathearn, Atholl and the Mearns. Mar and the North remained hostile. Eth, or Ethelred of Moray was left in charge in Scotland.

Headed by this resounding company the combined legion moved down through Cumbria.

They debated why Henry, no warrior, should have decided to go to war against the Welsh at this stage. In Cumbria they had not heard that Wales was any more restless than usual. A proud small people, the Welsh were perpetually up in arms, somewhere, against their Norman overlords – and the so-called Marcher Earls especially were apt to oppress them grievously. David felt considerable sympathy for them, in fact, and knew some discomfort at proceeding against them in arms. But he was in no position to reject Henry's command – and the first time that the King had sought the use of the new Cumbrian command. Alexander evidently felt no such qualms. It took the joint force nine days to reach Chester, only one day short of the given date, going by Kentdale and Lunedale and crossing out of Cumbria at Ribchester in Amounderness. Hugh d'Avranches, Earl of Chester, Richard the Viscount's uncle, son of Emma, the Conqueror's half-sister, was an old campaigner and clearly not prepared to put himself in any subordinate position to the royal Scots brothers. This suited David well enough; but Alexander, of course, as a monarch, could not place himself under the command of any man. So it had to be a joint command, never a satisfactory arrangement; although in fact, the veteran Norman earl would make most of the decisions. His own force of some seven thousand brought the total up almost to twenty thousand, a mighty army.

Chester told them of the strategy worked out. They would

close in on the Welsh from three sides. Henry himself, with two large hosts, would approach the Welsh marches centrally, from Gloucester and Hereford, making directly for Powys, where Gruffydd ap Cynan, Prince of Gwynedd, had his headquarters, in the Upper Severn valley. They themselves would move down on a wide front on Gwynedd, the northern province of Wales. While Richard de Clare, Earl of Cornwall, would lead another mixed force, of Cornishmen and South Country Saxons, up through South Wales, where little opposition was expected – indeed it was likely that many of the southern Welsh would join him, for they were at odds with the rest of their barbarous countrymen. The aim was to compress Gruffydd and his chieftains into an ever contracting area between Powys and the sea. Large numbers were necessary for such a manoeuvre, that the Welsh forces would find no gaps or weak points to break out through – hence this great concentration of men. The tribesmen would move back into their central mountain fastnesses, of course – they always did – but very large numbers could not subsist in those barren heights for long. Henry hoped either to root them out or starve them out.

When David asked why Henry, a peaceable monarch in most respects, should elect to make this great effort, and choose this time to do so, he was told that there was more to this than Gruffydd ap Cynan, who was more or less always in a state of rebellion. It was another move to limit the power and ambitions of the Montgomery brothers, the dangerously mighty Earls of Shrewsbury, Pembroke and Lancaster, who were the most intractable of Henry's nobles. Although Norman's themselves, they would sometimes take part in the Welsh revolts, use them for their own ends. There was even talk that Robert de Bellême, Earl of Shrewsbury, the most arrogant of the trio, saw himself as a possible King of an independent Wales. This show of strength was Henry's answer.

So they carried on southwards, in mighty strength but at a direly slow pace inevitably, Normans, Scots, Cumbrians and Saxons, to cross into Gwynedd at Trevalyn, push through Denbigh and cross Dee at Llangollen. Here they reformed, to change order of march, spreading out as it were in line abreast, to advance across country in a swathe twenty miles and more in width, using every road and track and valley through the ever-rising hill-country.

Word had awaited them at Llangollen that Henry had in fact reached the Severn at Powys and had commenced his advance towards the sea, so far without any major clash. The Cornish force was coming up fast from the south. So that they now had Gruffydd's people squeezed into an area perhaps forty miles by thirty. It but remained to tighten and tighten the ring of steel until they had them helpless. There must be no break-outs. Nothing was mentioned about the Montgomery Marcher Earls.

David for one was thankful to be separated from the main northern army. The treatment of the local populace by much of the soldiery, since they crossed into Gwynedd, sickened him, the Norman leadership showing little concern to check it, looting, assault, rape and arson. He had protested, but achieved little improvement. The Scots were not a great deal better, Alexander fairly heedless. It appeared to be accepted that this was how armies behaved on the march, and that good fighting could not be expected without its due rewards. Keeping his own Cumbrian levies under control was not easy, in the circumstances. Away from the others it was less difficult.

The Cumbrian contingent's position in the long line of the advance was left of centre, with Alexander on the left again and most of Chester's force stretching away westwards towards the sea. They were now climbing steadily through the Berwyn Mountains, south by east, difficult country in which to maintain any sort of line. They saw little of any enemy, only the occasional distant glimpse of a scouting party, evidence that they were being kept under observation. There was not any large population in these hills, and such small villages and townships as there were, in every case were abandoned before the invaders reached them, sad scenes in a peaceful upland region.

When, in time, they reached the long twisting and major valley of the River Dovey without real incident, word came back from Chester to say that Gruffydds's forces were drawing back on the Plynlimon area of lofty mountains, about a dozen miles to the south of David's position. This was one of the principal Welsh redoubts or mountain strongpoints. The entire northern line-abreast was to swing more to the south-eastwards, in consequence, out of the Dovey valley which ran north-east and south-west.

This new direction, as it were against the grain of the land, brought David's contingent into a welter of hills, wooded on the lower slopes, sheep-strewn above. Soon they came upon signs of quite a large force having passed this way recently, carcases of sheep and cattle, blackened embers of fires, discarded rawhide brogans, human excrement. This sight stirred the weary marchers into hope of action at last – although it affected David otherwise.

This trail led him, presently, into another quite broad and very lonely valley, that of the River Twymyn, clearly a major tributory of the Dovey. It seemed to probe ahead into the still higher hills for a long way, due southwards. With detachments stretching out for miles up and down the slopes on each flank, David followed the axis of this well-defined vale, in the wake of what could only be a retiring Welsh force heading for the Plynlimon redoubt.

He was less than eager to catch up, however keen most of his force. He had no quarrel with the Welsh, another Celtic people, certainly no ambition to be the first of the northern army to come to blows with them.

It was on the second day in that long and sylvan valley of the Twymyn that David's attitude suffered a change. After a pleasant widening of the vale, two tall, steep hills to north and south thrust forward shoulders, abruptly to narrow all to a deep trough, with almost cliff-like rocky sides instead of the grassy, tree-grown slopes, the river itself becoming a foaming white torrent after a great right-angled bend to the west. And just before the mouth of this chasm, still in the green heart of the valley, sheltered as in the lap of the wild mountains, they came upon the new monastery of Pennant-Bachwy, a remote, challenging and yet peaceful spot indeed – but at present in no peaceful state. The retreating Welsh had passed this way the previous evening – but failed to pass. And they had left their mark. Inside and out was devastation, church and monastic buildings desecrated and damaged, the well filled with slaughtered farm-stock, new-planted orchards and growing crops destroyed, even the hives for honey and wax burned. None of the score or so of monks and lay-brothers was actually injured, but all had been roughly handled, mocked and their habits slashed and torn.

David, deeply outraged, demanded why, why? Prior Ralph, a youngish man of fine features and stalwart build, shook his head sorrowfully. It was hard, hard, he admitted – when the establishment was beginning to take the shape that they had worked for. Perhaps it was God's way of testing their sincerity? These unfortunate Welshmen had done it out of a mistaken hatred he said. They were not really to blame. They thought that he and his monks were Normans, the hated Normans who oppressed them. They were not. They were Frenchmen, yes – from Tiron, near Chartres in the Forest of Perche. But not

Normans. No enemies of the Welsh but their friends. They grieved at what the Normans did to the Welsh. But . . .

"Tiron?" David said. "The famous Tiron, in Eure-et-loir? Where the noble Bernard of St. Cyprian rules?"

"The same, my lord. Bernard, our beloved master-under-God, sent us here. Two years ago. At the request of Prince Gruffydd. And now, now . . ."

"Gruffydd asked for you to come? From Tiron? Yet his people do this?"

"They were not Gwynedd or Powys men, lord. They had marched north from Ceredigion, and now were turning back. They knew us not, did not believe us when we said that we were not Normans. To them all French are Normans. But – God teach us, help us not to blame them. Their error was unintentional . . ."

"You are generous, Sir Prior. And forgiving. I think that *I* could not aspire to such nobility. In the face of ill-usage such as this. It is noble indeed."

"It is but our faith, my friend. The teaching of the blessed Bernard. We so strive to carry out the precepts of our Lord Christ, however feebly. We should not name it forgiveness, for that implies sin, offence, on the part of the other, of judgment. Who are we to judge? Only God can do that. Our part is surely acceptance, understanding, concern."

"I am greatly admiring, Brother Ralph. I have heard much good of the Tironensian Order. This is the first I have seen of it . . ."

They camped for the night at the ravaged monastery, and David set his men to work to help the monks repair what they could. But nothing would undo most of the damage.

The Prior told them that the Welsh force responsible, perhaps six hundred strong, was heading south into the great mountain fastness of Clywedog, between Pennant and Llanidloes, under mighty Plynlimon, where the River Severn rose amongst a cluster of small lakes. This was Gruffydd's stronghold area and all but impregnable, so difficult were the approaches, it was said.

David was in doubt as to what to do. His instructions were to press on, to confine the enemy ever more closely, and bring them to battle if possible. But he could see the mass of Plynlimon and its neighbours towering ahead, half-right. It could not be more than ten or twelve miles further. Therefore he could well be catching up with the main enemy defensive strength in half-a-day's march. It was no part of his duty, any more than his desire, to make a single-handed assault on Gruffydd's redoubt. Yet, as far as he could gauge, his was the command nearest to the enemy, so far. Probably Chester himself would mount an assault on Plynlimon from the west, from the River Rheidol side; but that would not be likely for some time yet. And where was Henry?

He sent couriers east and west to inform Chester and Alexander of his situation – but did not ask for instructions.

That night, before taking his rest, he had a long talk with Prior Ralph about the Tironensian creed and rules, so much admired by the discerning. Bernard, former Cluniac Abbot of St. Cyprian of Poitiers, of a noble Burgundian family, was a reformer of the reformed. The Cluniac reforms had been a great step forward, forty to fifty years ago, in countering the laxity which had crept into the monastic orders – David's mother had been a great admirer. But abuses and faults and weaknesses had come even therein, with the years, and Bernard had set up his new Order at Tiron-in-the-Forest, in 1109. And in only these four years had made a remarkable impact – enmity as well as praise and emulation, to be sure. David had not heard that there was any Tironensian house established in England; to find one in deepest Wales was the greater surprise – and shed a new light on Prince Gruffydd, the inveterate rebel. The Tironensian teaching was, according to Prior Ralph, a return to the basic virtues of humility, austerity, discipline, forgiveness and acceptance of chastening. In addition there were doctrinal reforms. The theory of the Immaculate Conception was rejected; the persecution of the Jews – popular in these crusading days – condemned; the subtleties and dialectics of much advanced Christian scholarship refuted. And so on. David was much impressed, most of it coinciding with his own ideas – and of course his mother's teachings.

In the morning, he decided that he would move on southwards for some way, at least, to try to ascertain strengths and numbers and positions of the enemy. He wished Prior Ralph and his monks very well and hoped that he would be able to see them again, possibly quite soon. He would, for himself, endeavour to practise forgiveness, as far as he could – but it was not simple for a man bearing rule and authority, especially the commander of an army.

About five miles south of Pennant-Bachwy, on rapidly-rising ground now, and the side valley of Glyntrefnant coming in on the east, they learned something of what was meant by Gruffydd's redoubt area. The country grew wilder, more savage, with naked rock, cliffs and harsh screes predominating. And water everywhere, cataracts and falls, dark pools and tarns, lakes innumerable amidst treacherous bogs. It was, in fact, a great amphitheatre, a wide basin of the mountains, a sump of waters draining from the heights all around, out of which the infant Severn rose. And it was rimmed by rock walls on every hand, as far as could be discerned, the only access by the narrow river gorges and chasms, where half-a-dozen determined men could hold up a thousand. And that these gorges and ravines were manned was evident. It would be a bold commander indeed who assaulted that natural fortress, under any circumstances.

David sent out scouting parties to prospect as much of the area as they could. All came back with the same story. The place was impregnable.

Thoughtful, yet in some measure reassured, David turned back. Somehow he did not think that Henry was the man to be prepared for most bloody battle here. He would return to Pennant-Bachwy and send Henry and the others a full report from there. In fact, he might even go and try to see Henry himself – after all he could not be more than fifteen or twenty miles away.

But at the monastery that evening, they found disaster. A party of Chester's Normans, straying from their route, had come that way after David's people had left; and decided that a half-sacked monastery of foreigners was something not to be considered. They had completed, with greater thoroughness, what the Welshmen had left undone, with a callous savagery unequalled, even slaying one of the lay-brothers who, less disciplined than the monks themselves, had protested. They had taken all the remaining church furniture and the simple plenishings of the dormitory and refectory, even the rough blankets, and set them on fire in the chapel itself, and thrown the body of the lay-brother on top, forcing the others to watch. They had moved on south-eastwards.

David was at a loss for words. What was there to be said? He blamed himself for not having left a guard. How could he have guessed?

But if words were totally inadequate, there was something that he could *do*, at least. On impulse, he told Prior Ralph that he and his remaining people were now in his, David's care and protection. He would, if they would come, take them back to Caer-luel with him and give them lands for a new monastery.

In Cumbria or in Scotland. He would see, too, that they had all that they required, moneys too, to replace in some measure what they had lost. It would not be the same, but perhaps, in time, they might serve their Order even better.

It was Brother Ralph's turn to be at a loss for words, too overcome with emotion to speak.

Leaving the Viscount Richard in command at Pennant-Bachwy, next morning, with only a few friends and a small escort, David rode eastwards. Whether he would come up with the offending Norman force, which had allegedly gone this way, he did not know – he almost hoped not, fearing what he might be inclined to do in retribution, whatever Bernard's teachings. His objectives were otherwise – first to find Alexander, and then Henry.

All the way, around the skirts of the hills, they were passing groups and sections of their own and the Scots force, these advancing more slowly over country less easy than the Twymyn valley. After some eight miles they found the King of Scots in another but lesser valley, almost parallel with their own, and in excellent spirits. The day before, he had come across and soundly defeated a Welsh contingent – not a very large one, it transpired. He and his people were eating well, with large numbers of cattle and sheep on all the upland pastures for the taking, and almost a holiday atmosphere prevailed. Alexander was not greatly interested in the Pennant monastery situation, but became adequately concerned when he heard David's description of the Clywedog stronghold area. He agreed entirely that open and straightforward assault was not to be considered. Whether a starvation policy was practical sounded doubtful. After all, with all the cattle and sheep available in these foothills, the Welsh could drive flocks into this redoubt area to be slaughtered as necessary.

Alexander decided to accompany his brother to discuss the position with Henry. Latest reports put him still at Mur-Castell in the upper Severn valley between Llandinan and Llanidloes, about a dozen miles almost due southwards. He did not appear to be advancing.

It took them well into the evening to reach this Mur-Castell, one of Gruffydd's own houses, the nearest to his mountain fastness, itself something of an eagle's-nest of a place. Here they found little of the atmosphere of an armed camp, rather that of a relaxed celebration and carefree ease. Henry gave the impression of being more or less established here, his troops comfortably settled in the June sunshine.

They were greeted warmly, their brother-in-law revealing no
evident embarrassment at their meeting with the lady who was
most clearly sharing his campaigning couch, a nubile young
person of very obvious charms. Jovial, untroubled, Henry
seemed to find the problems and anxieties of war far from
pressing. Indeed, his first explicit remarks to David were
such as to remove thoughts of war from that young man
also.

"I have news for you – which I think will perhaps cause you
to weep no tears, David. Although you might conceivably lose a
little sleep! Simon de St. Liz is dead."

"St. Liz! Earl Simon – dead?" David's voice went husky. He
swallowed. "Matilda's . . . husband?"

"The same. I see that you take the point, without delay!"

"He . . . he took the Cross. Went on Crusade . . .?"

"Yes, the more fool him! An old man, and crippled. Worse,
he went twice. First, two years ago. He reached the Holy Land,
took fever, and was brought home to be nursed by his long-
suffering wife. But he was off again – God knows why! Think
you that he found little to detain him at home, little family joy? I
have heard, but recently, that he died at Charté. So – now I am
three earls short in this realm of mine."

"Three . . .?"

"To be sure. Northampton, Huntingdon and Northumbria.
Matilda claims Northumbria in right of her father, the unfortunate Waltheof."

"M'mm. Cospatrick would claim Northumbria before
Waltheof."

"No doubt. But Waltheof's was a Norman earldom, Cospatrick's only a Saxon!"

David was not really concerned at that moment to argue
Cospatrick's claims. His head was in a whirl, although he
sought not to show it. Matilda! A free woman . . . !

Henry eyed him keenly, knowingly, grinning. "We must see
that my great-niece is well protected from adventurers, eh
David? With all those earldoms. She will be the target for many
a drawn bow!"

"Yes."

"Ambitious men will be round her like flies! I shall have to
give her good advice . . ."

Only a king might interrupt a king, and Alexander, impatient, did just that. "We came here to debate war strategy,
not widows!" he said. "What do we do? We marched far, to aid
you. And now find you . . . scarcely warlike!"

143

"What would you have, cousin? Marching to and fro? Trumpets sounding? Banners awave? Shall I stage a tournament?"

Alexander scowled. "I did not come all this way from Scotland for tournaments and show. You asked for an army. To do what? Fight, whilst you feast?"

Henry looked at David "I think that your royal brother must be hungry!" he suggested. "They say that a hungry man is an angry man. Come and eat . . ."

"I shall eat the better knowing what Your Grace plans for this campaign – if such it is!"

"Very well. Campaign it is – but not, I hope, a slaughter. If I seem to be waging war against Gruffydd ap Cynan, that is well. But my main foe is not the Welshman, but Robert de Bellême of Shrewsbury and his brothers of Pembroke and Lancaster. These are the true dangers to my realm, not the Welsh. But I do not seek to launch civil war upon England. From civil war, none gain. Norman fighting Norman is a sorry spectacle. So I *seem* to proceed against my Welsh rebels – which none may object to. But in doing so, I bring overwhelming strength to bear all around the real enemy."

"So we are not here to fight the Welsh? But the Montgomery brothers?"

"I hope to fight neither, man! See you, I have over sixty thousand men in arms, and marshalled around and between the Montgomery brothers' power – who, I think, cannot muster ten thousand, without Welsh aid. Seeming to threaten Gruffydd – but ready to turn elsewhere. We are but thirty miles here, from de Bellême's Shrewsbury. I have another army sitting at Ludlow, between him and Pembroke – which has Richard de Clare and his Cornishmen behind them. Your own and Chester's forces cut off Lancaster, should he think to move. We have the Montgomerys hamstrung!"

The other two stared at him, as the size and complexity of this planning dawned upon them. David, in especial, was admiring.

"And the Welsh?" Alexander demanded.

"The Welsh we must handle delicately. They are surrounded, rather than divided. They have, as I knew they would, withdrawn into their mountain hold yonder. We cannot prise them out, save at great cost. It is a place scarcely assailable."

"Yes – so I judged," David agreed. "I went forward, from Pennant, to inspect what I could of it. I perceived no way of

144

gaining entry, without enormous losses. That is what I came to tell you."

"I have been forward also – and came to the same conclusion. So – I have summoned Gruffydd to meet me. To talk terms. But he is stubborn. He will not. Will not come out. Nor speak with me."

"Perhaps he does not trust you!" Alexander said cynically.

"Perhaps. I think he believes that to come to me would have him seem to accept me as overlord. Yet I cannot go to him, in his fastness."

"You might wait here for long. Before he starves."

"True – although there is time enough. I am sufficiently comfortable here – more so than he will be. And the longer we sit thus, the more troubled will be the Montgomerys. But, see you – your coming is apt. For I had thought to send to you. It may be that *you* could achieve what I cannot. Gruffydd may talk with you where he would not with me. Fellow-Celts. The King of Scots and his brother. No Normans."

"And what would we have to say to him?" Alexander wondered.

"Sufficient for any reasonable man. But – come to table. I shall tell you as you eat and drink . . ."

Thereafter they learned that Henry was indeed prepared to be reasonable towards the Welsh. His terms were almost generous. In return for an undertaking to indulge in no more risings and revolts, the King would repeal much of the crushing taxation and onerous forest laws which had been in force in Wales since the Conqueror's time. He would promise to curb the Marcher Earl's powers – one of the principal causes of revolt – and be glad to do so, since the Montgomery brothers were typical of that arrogant breed. He would release all prisoners and hostages held on account of rebellion – as distinct from civil felonies. And he would accept Gruffydd's status as that of independent prince in all save the renewal of the coronation oath of fealty – which he had already taken – on some date to be mutually chosen. There was surely little here that Gruffydd would find impossible to swallow? With the understanding, of course, that the Welsh would no longer allow themselves to be used by the Montgomerys as sticks with which to beat the King.

The Scots brothers could find no real fault with all of this, and agreed to attempt a meeting with the Prince of Gwynedd, and to try to persuade him. David said that surely they might be hopeful, for had not Gruffydd shown himself to be a God-

145

fearing and upright man, by bringing a Tironensian monastery to his domains? When there was none such even in England?

Henry reserved judgment on that.

David went on to tell them of the shameful happenings at Pennant-Bachwy – and was distressed, almost angered, at the lack of response and concern evinced by his royal hearers. Almost defiantly he announced that he was going to take the maltreated monks back with him to the North, there to found a new monastery or abbey, where the noble Bernard's precepts could be practised in peace and security.

His brother and brother-in-law took that less than seriously, Alexander indicating that David would get over it, and not to let his soft heart rule his quite sound wits; and Henry suggesting that he would require a lot more riches than he could deploy at present before he started to endow abbeys. Perhaps, of course, he had a notion to *marry* riches?

David hotly denied this, asserting however that he would find a way.

Henry said, bring him back an accommodation with Gruffydd ap Cynan, and he would have a sufficiency to found his monastery – that he promised.

*   *   *

Of all things, it was the Prior Ralph who acted the essential go-between, volunteering for the task whenever he heard of the project, insisting no doubt accurately, that he was the best man to go to convince Gruffydd that he should meet the Prince David and the King of Scots. As a single, simple wandering friar he would get through the Welsh lines and defences at the Clywedog gorges. Gruffydd would listen to him.·

So they let him go, astonished at his courage and resolution, in view of the injuries done to him and his. He refused a horse or any sort of escort, probably wisely.

He returned in two days time. Gruffydd, King of Wales, sent his greeting: and was prepared to grant audience to Alexander, King of Scots, and David, Prince of Strathclyde, at noon of the following day, the Eve of St. Barnabas, at Dylife, midway between Pennant-Bachwy and his redoubt area. Each side would bring no more than a score of men as escort. Ralph said that he had not been too difficult to persuade, once he reached him, the problem having been to get past his lieutenants.

The Welshman's message certainly did not sound like that of a desperate fugitive. David was encouraged, but Alexander disturbed over the phrasing, this of the man granting audience

– an intolerable arrogance – Gruffydd presuming to call himself *King* of Wales, and David *Prince* of Strathclyde. His brother saw these matters as unimportant, mere mis-translations in terminology from the Welsh language, no doubt.

Next morning the small party climbed the steep track up the narrow gorge to the sharp bend of the Tywmyn, where they had to pass a notable waterfall thundering down in foam and spray. Above this they came, after a couple of miles, to the abandoned upland homestead of hutments, called Dylife, the prior leading them. There they found the Welsh group already in position and waiting, looking wary, suspicious, dark and wiry men, roughly garbed. Gruffydd ap Cynan stood out as much the oldest, now in his early fifties, greying but still lithe, with a broad brow, large nose and sensitive mouth. He wore the golden circlet of kingship around those brows.

Saluting with upraised hand, Brother Ralph called, "Highness – here is His Grace Alexander, King of Scots, and my lord David of Cumbria, come to speak with you."

Alexander frowned. He would have preferred the Welshman to be introduced to *him*, as monarch.

"Alexander mac Malcolm and David mac Malcolm – greetings," the other said. "I am Gruffydd ap Cynan. I can hardly give you welcome, since you appear in my realm in armed force. But I greet you, at least, as namely." He had his people's pleasing, soft, sing-song intonation.

It was unfortunate that protocol required that David should let Alexander speak first.

"We are here, sir, at the request of the lawful sovereign lord of this realm," his brother said. "Not otherwise."

"Ha! Do I hear aright? Have you then, Alexander mac Malcolm, become a vassal of Henry fitz William, Highness?"

"Not so – by God, I have not! He is but my good-brother . . ."

"My lord Gruffydd," David put in, a little hurriedly. "We come on a mission of goodwill. We know of your prowess, and admire. I have long wished to know you. In especial, since I learned of your bringing of the Tironensians to Wales. A noble gesture." He hoped that did not sound as though coming in too much of a rush.

The older man eyed them both thoughtfully. "Two voices," he said quietly. "Do they speak the same message?"

"We bring you Henry's terms," Alexander declared flatly.

"Suggestions," David amended. "Which we believe reasonable – or we would not have brought them."

147

"I am glad that we are to be reasonable!"

"Yes. Henry Beauclerc is not like his brother William. Nor yet such as his father. He is a man of honest purpose."

"And for me, and Wales, my lords, he honestly purposes – what?"

"Must we sit ahorse and discuss this like strangers passing on the road!" Alexander asked.

"First I must know if there is anything to discuss, Your Grace."

"Would we come, otherwise, man?"

"There are five heads, Prince Gruffydd," David said. "King Henry offers these. That he will repeal the excessive taxation and forest laws, as respects Wales. He will curb the Marcher Earls in their inroads upon your land. He will release all prisoners and hostages held for rebellion. He will accept your status as independent prince in all save a renewal of your coronation oath, at some future date to be chosen."

"And the fifth?

"The fifth is that you will undertake to make no further armed uprisings against his peace, on or beyond the Welsh Marches. That is all."

"Why should I agree to this?"

"Because it is to your advantage," Alexander asserted. "And Henry and I have sixty thousand men surrounding you!"

"Ah. Yet with all these, Henry Beauclerc still deems it prudent to offer me these reasonable terms? Why, think you, my lords?"

"Because he is a reasonable man, and would avoid bloodshed," David declared.

"I think it is rather that he knows that he cannot defeat me, or even reach me! Is it not so? That would be reasonable, also!"

"Yet you yourself are a reasonable man, Prior Ralph assures us – and cannot desire unnecessary bloodshed."

"I do not know about the Scots, my friend, but we Welsh value our freedom higher than our blood."

"What freedom is lacking from these terms? You have already taken the coronation fealty oath."

"What surety have I that the Norman will keep his word?"

"We have a paper here, listing these heads, with his signature and royal seal. For you also to sign. Two, each the same."

"A Norman signature can be swiftly forgotten."

"Not if it has the signatures of the King of Scots and the Queen's brother as witnesses."

"Ah – yes." Inclining his grey head, Gruffydd accepted that. "May I see the paper?"

Both copies of Henry's document were handed over, Ralph taking them, and David suggesting that the Welshman might wish to consider the thing privately for a little. They would wait by the riverside.

This they did.

"I think that he will sign," David said.

"As well he might! He deserves less generous terms. He is too stiff-necked by half, that Welsh princeling! And you are over-gentle, Davie."

"And you are no negotiator, my royal brother! But then, you never were."

"I do not play with words, as you do. I deal in facts, plain truth, not honeyed half-truths and niceties."

"Yet Holy Writ says that a soft answer may turn away wrath. And wrath is no aid to negotiations, Alex."

Presently Gruffydd came over to them. "I am prepared to sign this," he said, without preamble. "But only if you will add these words. 'We undersigned, pledge our honour, and that of our sister the Queen of England, that these terms will be carried out, and swiftly.' Will you do so?"

"You are presumptuous, sir!"

"I think not, my lord King – only careful. I have good reason not to trust Normans."

"I will write and sign that," David said. "The Queen would not disagree I think. *I* trust Henry."

Alexander shrugged.

So the words were written in, on both copies, by Prior Ralph, the signatures appended, that of Ralph added, as witness, for good measure. The thing was done.

David had brought a flagon of wine, and they pledged good faith with this, neither Gruffydd nor Alexander desirous of lingering. As treaty-making went, it was expeditious, at least.

Such little time had all this taken that the brothers decided that they might as well make the direct journey to Mur-Castell there and then, to acquaint Henry with the satisfactory outcome. Prior Ralph offering to act as guide. By using the side-valley of Glyntrefnant, and then the climbing cattle-road by Cerist, they could reach Mur-Castell before nightfall.

Henry was pleased, as well he might be. It had all worked out as he had hoped and planned. He could now turn his full attention on the Montgomerys. .

Asked by Alexander what he intended there, he said that he

149

would move his present army back nearer to Shrewsbury, then summon Robert de Bellême to his presence. With the other armies disposed all around him and between him and his brothers, also the word – which Henry would ensure that he received expeditiously – that peace was made with Gruffydd, Bellême would have no choice. And once he had him before him, face to face and alone, the King was satisfied that he had the situation mastered. So all that was necessary was for the allied armies to remain in approximately their present positions for a few days more, until he had taught the Earl of Shrewsbury his lesson – and then all could return home, with his grateful thanks.

Henry turned to David. "To you I made a promise of sorts. I think that I can aspire to deal with Robert of Shrewsbury without your valuable help! You have a few days, therefore, which might profitably be filled in. I suggest that Northampton is not too far distant from here for an active young man to reach, and return, in shall we say five days time? By Radnor Forest, Leominster, Worcester and Stratford. To convey my royal regrets to the sorrowing Countess Matilda on the death of her husband. And to ask her, in my name, what arrangements she might wish to make for her future protection and the disposition of her earldoms – as is my duty."

David drew breath, began to speak, and then thought better of it.

"We shall see if you make as agile an envoy with women as you do with men," Henry added. "There are three children whose interests concern me!"

10

IT MADE A longer journey than Henry had suggested, full one hundred and thirty miles, much of it across the very spine of England, not a lofty barrier by Scottish standards but a delaying factor nevertheless. David did not desire any companions with him on this occasion, even his two closest friends; but since it was inconceivable that such as he should travel the land alone, he selected only some half-dozen of his best horsemen as sufficient escort, together with one of Henry's Mercians as guide. By riding hard and long, they covered the distance in two taxing days.

There was a powerful, typically Norman castle at Northampton, but Matilda had indicated that she did not normally live therein but at Earl's Thorpe some way to the north of the town. This proved to be a pleasant, rambling Saxon manor-house set amongst old orchards on the edge of Thorpe Chase. In the pleasance thereof, beside an ornamental pond, almost a lake, over which the swallows swooped, David found the Countess that warm June evening.

She sat by the waterside watching three children at play in the shallows, sailing toy-boats, and with a young waiting-woman stitching needlework nearby. She was simply and lightly dressed, very different from the fine clothing she had worn when last he saw her. But she was no less lovely, heart-catchingly so indeed, as she sat idly there, looking out across the water as though her mind might be far away.

When the rising of the two tall deerhounds caused her to notice his approach, she turned to watch him casually – until suddenly he saw recognition strike her and she started up to her feet, hand to her lips. She took two or three steps towards him, then obviously restrained herself and paused. But a hand came out, nevertheless.

David also had to restrain himself from actually running to her. He came on, almost stiffly.

Wordless they eyed each other for long moments.

"David!" she got out, at last. "It is you – truly you? I do not dream . . . ?"

"No dream," he said, deep-voiced. "Unless I too dream. How beautiful you are!"

"It is beyond belief. I was thinking of you. Just now. Wondering. Wondering where you might be. What you were doing. Whether, whether . . . and here you are, before me. Almost, almost a miracle!"

"The miracle is that you should think of me, at all."

"I do. I . . ." She stopped, glancing around, as though recollecting that they were not alone.

He took that outstretched hand and raised it to his lips. "It has been long, long," he said.

"Yes. Too long. But . . ."

The three children had come up out of the water, to eye them interestedly. Their mother turned to beckon them closer.

"Come," she said. "Come and greet the Prince David of Scotland, brother to the Queen. Your kinsman, at some removes. This is Simon. And this is Waltheof. And here is Matilda, the baby, five years only. Waltheof is eight, Simon ten."

"Are you truly a prince?" the eldest asked, a sturdy, solemn-faced boy.

"In that my father was King of Scots, yes, Simon. But I am usually called Earl of Cumbria, these days."

"Is Cumbria yours, then? It is not in Scotland."

"No. Cumbria is not mine. I do not *own* it. I only govern it for King Henry. So I am earl only in that I am the King's viceroy there."

"I shall be Earl of Northampton when I am older. And I shall *own* it. And much else."

"Hush, Sim – that is no way to speak," his mother reproved. "What you own or do not own is not the important matter. It is what you *do* that matters – what you do with your life."

"I shall do lots of things. I shall kill Infidels and Moors and Saracens. I shall kill deer too, many deer . . ."

"There speaks a young man much in need of a father's hand!" the Countess said. "Waltheof is less . . . vainglorious."

David stooped. "And what will *you* do, Waltheof?"

"I shall breed pigeons," the younger boy announced. "The kind with the big tails that stick up."

"Ah – there is a noble ambition! More useful than killing, perhaps, Simon." David picked up the little girl, to sit in the crook of his arm. "And this one? I need not ask. She will grow up to be a beautiful lady like her mother, and rejoice all who set eyes on her!"

The Countess smiled. "I cannot tell my daughter to believe you, my lord. What shall I say?" She turned to the other young woman. "Editha – I leave these small problems of mine with you. I must see to the Earl David's refreshment and welcome. It is almost their bedtime . . ."

As they walked back to the house, she asked, "How come you? Where from? For how long? I can scarce accept that you are really here!"

"In a sense, my dear, I come from Henry. On the Welsh Marches, where I have been aiding him in some measure. He *suggested* that I should come – although, God knows, every mile that I rode south from Caer-luel the thought was never out of my mind that I was drawing nearer to you, how to contrive to see you ever my last thought at night and my first in the

152

morning. Then *he* proposed it! I had to hold myself in from embracing him! He said, to bring you his regrets over the death of your husband, as monarch and kinsman. And to discover what protection you required."

"Protection? Do I require protection?"

"That is what he said. I think that he meant protection from adventurers, men who would seek to gain your trust and person for their own ends, your earldoms and lands and wealth . . ."

"And he sent you!"

"Yes. But . . . not in that way! Nothing of that. He knows that I greatly esteem you. And I am the Queen's brother, so that I could decently carry his message to his grand-niece – if that is what you are . . ."

"I care not why Henry sent you – only that you are come!" she exclaimed and took his arm.

He pressed it to him, not unmindful of that other time when she had done the same, when first they had met at Alexander's wedding procession. His heart was too full for words.

But at the door of the house, he paused. "Matilda," he said, "I have not spoken of the Earl Simon's death, myself. Of your husband. Said that I am sorry. I should have said it first of all . . ."

"But did not – because you are an honest man! You are not sorry, are you, David? Any more than, in truth, am I! Let us be honest with each other, always. I cannot grieve for Simon. I never loved him, nor he me. I was the provider of his wealth and earldom, the mother of his children – that is all. He was an old, soured and crippled man, who *wanted* to die. That is why he went on the Crusade, not, I think, out of conviction. He was a soldier who could no longer soldier. Many Normans are like Simon. I cannot grieve for him. Now he is free of his troubles. And, and so am I! Free!"

He took her hand and all but ran into the house with her. There they came into each other's arms without hesitation or delay. But, after only a few moments, almost breathless, Matilda stirred in his embrace, and freeing a hand, pointed wordless to a doorway. Along the passage to this she led him, and within, into a small sewing-room as it proved to be. She shut the door behind them.

"Oh, David – my dear, my love, heart of my heart!" she said.

He dispensed with words altogether.

When at length, the first urgency of their emotions not over but under control, they found their voices again, still holding each other fast, she peered up into his eyes.

153

"David, David – what must you think of me?" she exclaimed, breathlessly. "Not only an unnatural widow who does not mourn her children's father, but, but a shameless woman who throws herself at the head of a younger man . . . !"

"I say that you are the best and truest, as well as the fairest and most lovely woman in all this, or any land! That I rejoice, rejoice . . ." He shook his head. "What can I say? No words, no words. I have longed, dreamed, prayed for this, for your regard – I scarce dared to hope for your love. And for your freedom, so that I might express *my* love for you. And now – this! I can say nothing of it, nothing. Dumb as an ox, as any brute-beast . . . !"

"Hush! You do . . . very well. Words are not all . . ."

He agreed with that, at least, and proceeded to demonstrate his agreement with her entire co-operation. In this matter they were starvelings both.

Nevertheless, presently, Matilda returned to her theme, or another aspect of it. "This is joy, my dear, delight, and I praise God for it – even though I behave like a lost and abandoned woman. Yet – I feel *found*, not lost, never lost! But – have you thought it out, David? Truly considered? What it means or could mean? This of love, between you and me? I am older than you. Much, I fear – no fresh young girl. Born in 1078 and married at the age of twelve – thirty-five years old. That leaves me but five or seven years of child-bearing ahead of me. And I have three young children to cherish. Have you thought, David? Considered what this means?"

"I care not . . ."

"But you must care, since I do! What do you want of me, David? I have to ask it. I cannot believe that it is only my earldoms and my lands. It may not even be marriage that you seek? Only my body. Even that, I think, I might give you. But if marriage, see you – marriage between us could be costly. For you!"

"Costly? What think you I am? I want you, for always. Here and hereafter. Mine, to love and cherish and care for – aye, and you to love and cherish me, companion, help-meet. Your earldoms and lands you may give to your children – for these I care not. You I want, your love and adorable self, to be the joy of my life."

She moistened her lips to match her eyes – which called for redress.

All too soon the children were brought in, for bed, and Matilda bethought her of her hostess's duties. Emotion had to be relegated meantime.

Although so great a lady, the Countess lived simply, with little of an entourage and household, so there was not much difficulty in having private converse, after the meal, as so often was the case in castle halls and large companies. Matilda had a private apartment near the children's bedchambers. There she took David. But first she led him quietly into the boys' and the girl's rooms, to see that they were all asleep. Clearly she was much more concerned with, and close to, her offspring than was usual in women of her rank and station.

When they were alone, he told her about his life in Cumbria, about his peculiar relationship with Alexander, and about Henry's elaborate campaign in Wales and the Marches. He warmed to his theme when he came to tell her of the Pennant-Bachwy monastery and the Tironensians, dwelling on the Order's virtues and the noble way its representatives had upheld its high ideals in the face of shameful persecution; but confessing that perhaps he had been a little rash in promising them a new monastery under his own protection, in the North.

Matilda would not hear of this, declaring that it was a splendid project, typical of him and worthy of all support. *Her* support, especially, she insisted. She would help in any way she could. What was the use of all the wealth and lands she had inherited and which were meantime her own again, if she could not use some part in such excellent cause? He must promise to call on her resources, as necessary.

Grateful and encouraged as he was by this, her declaration had the effect, nevertheless, of sobering them somewhat, bringing the problems of her special and involved situation uppermost in their minds again.

"Did you tell Henry of this decision of yours, David?" she asked. "What did he say?"

He hesitated. He was not going to tell her that Henry had as good as hinted that if he played his cards aright with the Countess Matilda he need not worry about finding the wherewithal to establish his monastery.

"He declared that I was . . . ambitious," he told her.

"Ambitious? But he did not say nay? And sent you to me!"

"Not, not for that."

"He sent *you*, nevertheless." She paused. "We have to consider this, David, heedfully. Not only this of the monastery. But Henry's attitude. For you, in especial. Henry is your friend and your sister's husband. But he is wily and devious – and he is King of England, with a realm to rule. In that game of kings we could find ourselves little more than pawns! You, a king's son, must know that. I am, in some fashion, in his hands. Because of my earldoms – Northampton, Huntingdon and the claim, in my name, to great Northumbria, once my father's. No earldoms may change hands without royal permission. And no Countess in her own right may marry without the King's agreement."

He nodded. "It is the same in Scotland."

"Think you, then, is Henry pushing you in my direction? And if so – why?"

David rubbed his chin. "It may just possibly be so. I do not know. But if so indeed, should we not rejoice? Myself, at least."

"*I* rejoice, yes – whatever his reasons. Since you are more precious to me than any lands or titles. But you, David – you must consider Henry's design in this, and your own interest. I insist upon it, my love. For you are a prince of Scotland. And my earldoms and lands are English."

"You are saying that Henry may seek to have me holding English earldoms? For reasons of his own? Against Scotland?"

"I do not know. But I wonder. Not necessarily *against* Scotland, but to bind Scotland to him in some measure. Scotland is always a great concern of English kings, is it not? He has married a Scots wife. He has wed his daughter to the King of Scots. Might not this be something of the same?"

"If it is, lass, need I fret? If Henry loves Scotland and the Scots sufficiently to do all this, need we be wary? Better than invading our land with armies, as his father and Rufus did."

"You may be right. It may be nothing to Scotland's hurt. Or yours. But – I would not like to see Henry shackling you to him with *my* earldoms!"

"I am warned, at least! But Henry may be acting only my good friend – and yours."

"True. I hope so. For I would be sorrowful indeed if you decided, out of all this, that the risk was too great, and rejected me!"

That called for some further demonstration to the contrary, of course, and for a while discussion lapsed.

But presently the woman found another cause for demur, not exactly pushing him away but sitting up and restraining him somewhat. This time she laughed, if unsteadily.

"David mac Malcolm," she declared, "am I not of all women the most foolish? Here have I been discussing marriage and the disposal of my earldoms – not to speak of behaving in this shameless fashion. And in fact, I do not know that you *intend* to marry me! At least, you have not asked me yet!"

"Eh? Lord!" he said. And again, "Lord! Is it . . . can it be . . . ? Save us – it is true! I have not said it, no. Not in words. Forgive me, my heart. How could I have forgotten? All this talk, assumption. It is beyond belief." He slid down from the settle on which they sat, to his knees, to take her hand "Lady, fairest of women, kindest, truest – I humbly seek this hand in marriage. Seek to be your husband and help-meet and proud companion all the days of my life. Seek the haven of your love, the warmth of your arms, the bliss of your body, and your leal companionship on the journey of our lives. Will you wed me, Matilda?"

Swallowing, wordless, she shook her head – but even a stupid man would scarcely have taken that as a negative.

It was enough eloquence for one evening, however belated.

Later still, when she saw him yawning – for he had ridden seventy miles that day – she declared that it was time that he sought his couch. She said it a little uncertainly. Taking up one of the cluster of already-lit lanterns, she took his hand to lead the way along the corridor to his room. At its door she paused.

"My heart," she said. "We say good night here?" That was a question.

He eyed her in the wavering lamplight. "You would . . . say otherwise?"

"I might. I, I am a weak woman."

"That is not how I would name you, my dear. But – I thank you for saying it."

"But . . . ?"

"*I* am weak, also. And, and sorely tempted. Not by you, lass, but by the nature of me, in me. Yet . . . with you, for you, I desire more than the body's desire. I am but a sore saint, God help me! But with you I seek to show only the best part of me. We have awaited each other for long. We shall wait a little longer, shall we not? If I can! Now that I have the promise of joy."

She did not speak.

He reached out to her. "You understand me, my love? You are not . . . hurt?"

"How could I be hurt, David? When you pay me so true a compliment. I am proud. The true, the best part of *me*, rejoices. The unworthy part will need to lean upon your strength, always. I thank you, my sore saint!" She drew away from him abruptly, thrust the lantern at him, and hurried off along the passage.

157

He looked after her, features working, a man torn and no saint indeed.

The travellers left again mid-day, on fresh horses from the Countess's well-filled stables, the parting controlled, low key, almost formal, in front of the children and the others.

"Tell Henry Beauclerc that I thank him. And that I know my own mind," she said. "He will not concede me Northumbria, I think. And Sim must be Earl of Northampton, in due course. But *you* are Earl of Huntingdon, in my eyes, from this day on. And master of all my substance, as my person. Tell him so, David. And rejoice me by endowing your monastery as first charge on it all. Make it an abbey, indeed."

He shook his head and rode away, not daring to look back.

11

THAT DAVID SHOULD be riding through the great Forest of Ettrick, in South Scotland, a few weeks later, prospecting for the site of an abbey, certainly was something that he could not have foreseen. Yet that was the way it had worked out. Henry had been graciously pleased to indicate his concurrence with the Countess Matilda's ideas as to her future and the disposal of her earldoms and wealth – as well he might since so he himself had planned it – and had, in the end, actually encouraged David in his monastic venture, just why uncertain, although that man would have a reason. So, on the dispersal of the allied armies, after a satisfactory confrontation with Robert de Bellême of Shrewsbury, David and Alexander had set off on their long journey northwards again, laden with thanks, goodwill and gifts, and taking with them the Prior Ralph and his dozen surviving colleagues. And at this stage Alexander had announced that he wished to be associated with the enterprise. In the name of their sainted mother. Let it be a joint venture. He would donate the necessary lands and charters and privileges, and David could pay for the work of building and equipping. It transpired that he was rather suspicious of Henry's support for the project, and argued that if it was good for the King of England to involve himself, then it was good for the King of Scots. Moreover, the monastery should undoubtedly be sited in Scotland, otherwise Henry would almost certainly claim much of the credit, and perhaps even take it over at some stage. As to exactly where, was a matter for discussion and selection, but he suggested somewhere in the Forest of Ettrick, which was royal property, a vast hunting demesne, almost empty, unpopulated, and might benefit greatly from such an establishment, a civilising influence as well as a useful place to lodge in on hunting trips, badly required. If David was a little doubtful as to the piety and disinterest behind all this, he had nevertheless recognised certain advantages. The cost of the exercise was beginning to weigh on his mind. He was loth to delve too deeply into Matilda's wealth before they were even wed; and he had insufficient of his own to purchase much land as well as pay for the construction. So the offer of royal land was not to be dismissed lightly. Moreover Prior Ralph indicated a distinct preference for a remote site – as at Pennant-Bachwy – the Tironensians being concerned to keep themselves from becoming contaminated by worldly preoccupations, the great danger in monastic Orders. And it was true that the establishment would best be sited in Scotland; he had promised his protection, and he was only in Cumbria on Henry's orders and sufferance and might easily be moved away. Galloway was too unsettled, exposed to invasion and war, whilst the Ettrick Forest area was almost an upland sanctuary, and fairly readily accessible from Caer-luel, up the Annan and Esk rivers.

When they had reached Caer-luel they had discovered all to be well. Fergus in Galloway, was exercising a strong hand, and this was having its effect on trouble-makers in Cumbria, so that the two provinces were more peaceable than had been the case in living memory. Alexander had left David there, and pressed on for Stirling with his host, wondering what *he* would find on his return home.

So here David was, with a small party, ranging the Forest area. It was a huge territory, covering perhaps nine hundred square miles, comprising the upland watersheds of the Ettrick, Yarrow, Teviot and Annan Waters, much of it not forested at all in the sense of being tree-grown, but consisting of many ranges of lonely green hills. There were great woodlands, of pine, oak, birch and hazel, of course, mainly in the deep valleys, but there was also much high moorland and waste, bog and water-meadow, with only here and there patches of cultivation and recognisable pasture, and comparatively few settlements.

The terrain was alive with game and beasts and birds of prey, deer, wolves, boar as well as lesser creatures, and notable for the herds of wild white cattle, the bulls whereof were exceedingly fierce and much prized for their great curling horns as trophies, drinking-horns and the like.

The party had come up long Annandale for almost thirty miles, and from its fair head had turned north-eastwards, up the Moffat Water, to climb into the empty hills, exploring each possible side-valley, considering every prospect. The Prior had a shrewd eye as well as boundless faith, and a clear idea of what he was looking for. Remoteness he wanted, yes – but no barren wilderness. His Order's monasteries had to be more or less self-supporting as well as able to send back annual tribute to the mother-abbey at Tiron; so they required arable or cultivatable land for crops, orchards and gardens, grazing land for sheep and cattle, bogs for peat, water-power for mills, oak-woods for tanneries and other timber for fuel, quarried stone and wood for building and so on. Not every valley offered all these, although the territory generally was hopeful.

Probing eastwards, by a small deserted Celtic cashel under Bodesbeck Law, too constricted for Ralph's purposes, and passing a magnificent and dramatic waterfall near a Pictish fort which had once guarded the very summit of the pass from the Moffat Water over to the Yarrow, they came at length down to a great loch, much larger than any they had seen so far, indeed two lochs really, separated only by a narrow neck of land, the whole length being almost five miles, by about half-a-mile across. Here the Prior thought that he had found that for which he sought. The hills drew well back and there was level ground around the shores, particularly at the head and foot, marshy admittedly but which, he asserted, could be drained, as they had had to drain Pennant-Bachwy. There were woods of oak and ash and pine, and workable sandstone in plenty. And there was the site of another abandoned Celtic monastery, small and simple, but with the tradition of Christian worship, according to a shepherd whose cothouse they found nearby, dedicated to the Blessed Virgin. But the shepherd also told them that the place's looks were deceitful. This was high summer and all looked very fair. But when the winter snows melted on the hills, the two lochs swelled to twice their present size and all the level land around was flooded for months, with even the little cashel becoming an island. That is why his own cottage was built well up on the hillside. No amount of digging would alter that.

So, sadly, they moved on.

160

Now they were following an ever deepening valley, really a mountain defile, whose river, the Yarrow, rising in the loch, rapidly developed into a noble, rushing stream, rich in salmon and trout they were assured. Prior Ralph admired the beauty of this vale, the wooded lower slopes and the noble hills that flanked it, a positive sea of green hills. But in mile after mile there was no major broadening, no hub of substantial side-glens sufficient to site and maintain the sort of establishment he visualised. It was not until, some fifteen miles down, the river joined another of similar size coming in from a more southerly direction, the Ettrick itself, that the joint valleys suddenly opened out to a great green basin in the hills, wide and fair with, a few miles ahead, a still further widening, where the combined river met the Tweed. The Prior exclaimed joyfully that this was the most beautiful place that he had seen in all his days. Could he, of a mercy, have this? Could he settle here and build his monastery to the glory of God in this God-given loveliness, this quiet, sylvan heaven-on-earth?

David had never been here before. There was a small township called Shiel Kirk, with one more abandoned Celtic Church cashel, and an all-but-abandoned royal hunting-lodge, unused since MacBeth's time. This presumably was the poor accommodation which Alexander had deplored and which he foresaw a monastery as usefully replacing. The folk here were herders and hunters and foresters, who moved up into this upland paradise for the summer months to take advantage of the rich but brief growth of the high pastures, returning to lower lands down Tweedside for the autumn and winter – hence its name of Shiel Kirk, the cashel of the summer shielings. It was all royal land, however neglected. If it so pleased Prior Ralph, here surely the quest could end. In the name of the King of Scots, David told the monk that all the land between Ettrick and Yarrow and Tweed, with all the nearside hill-slopes, was his – or, at least, the Tironensian Order's – to God's glory and in memory of the blessed Queen Margaret, for the erection of a monastery to replace Pennant-Bachwy. Tears in his eyes and kissing David's hand, the man thanked him, thanked his Creator and all saints, and vowed that he would build here no monastery but a great Abbey which would attempt to do justice to this lovely sanctuary in the mountains and the great heart which had inspired it all.

Almost as moved as the other, David gripped the monk's shoulder – although he realised ruefully that an abbey would take a deal more money to construct than any mere monastery.

161

But far be it from him to spoil so splendid a conception, with doubts.

So they turned back for Caer-luel. But before they left, David arranged for teams of the herdsmen and foresters to quarry and cart stone and fell timber in readiness for the monkish builders. Ralph assured them that he would be back, to start work, within the month, God willing.

David found a distinct trepidation growing on him on that return journey. Had he, in fact, bitten off more than he could chew? Had he been something of a fool in all this? Was it for such as himself, a young man not yet of thirty years, of no fortune however high-born, hopefully to wed a rich wife, to endow a great religious house? There was no single Romish Church abbey in all Scotland, only a priory at Coldingham founded by Edgar. There were Celtic Church abbeys in plenty; but these were a totally different conception, in the main mere humble settlements of huts of wood and thatch within stone-and-turf enclosures. The Columbans did not go in for stone churches, expensive or otherwise. David knew something of what it had cost his mother to build the great stone minster at Dunfermline, the first of its kind in Scotland – and that was only a large church, not an abbey. This Ralph was an enthusiast; nothing more certain than that he would be content with nothing but the best and finest. What had he let himself in for?

A week or two later, at Caer-luel, with the Prior and his colleagues deep in plans, drawings, dimensions and calculations, David was little reassured. But he kept his doubts to himself as he watched and listened. He wrote letters to Matilda, of course, and told her something of what was to do – but he tried to prevent his fears from showing through in these also. Ruling Cumbria had become considerably easier since Hakon Claw and the Norsemen had been expelled and Fergus made Lord of Galloway. David's reputation had been enhanced even by the Welsh expedition, however undeservedly, and the Cumbrians now accepted his authority without much demur; also the Viscount d'Avranches made an able lieutenant, if, like Fergus, somewhat heavy-handed in his methods. So David was not over-taxed for time and was able to turn some of his attention to South Scotland and Strathclyde, as Alexander had suggested. That great area certainly needed attention, for it had been neglected for years; and as is apt to happen in such circumstances, petty tyrants had sprung up, oppression and violence were rife, and the King's peace and laws set at naught. Lothian, the Merse and Teviotdale were well enough, under

Cospatrick of Dunbar's control; but the rest was no-man's-land – or any-man's-land. It was Cospatrick's warning that the new abbey-builders at Shiel Kirk might be at some risk, which caused David to accept some responsibilities in the matter, if his proffered protection was to mean anything.

So he began to make his presence known and felt in the great territory between Cumbria and Northumbria and the Scottish Sea. He visited and warned a number of the local lords and chiefs, burned a few robbers' camps in the Forest area – which was notorious for sheltering broken men – hanged two or three proven murderers and ravishers, as example, and let it be known that the King of Scots' writ would run from now on and that the holy brothers of Shiel Kirk in especial were to be aided and not harassed. He did not effect any lightening pacification, but improvement commenced – and there were no complaints from Prior Ralph.

So passed that summer and harvest-time. There was no news from Alexander, who was not much of a correspondent. But Henry sent word that the threat from Eystein of Norway had receded meantime, for he was at war again with his own half-brothers, Sigurd Half Deacon and Olaf Magnusson, over the division of Norway itself. Henry also informed that he had seen Matilda, given his official royal approval to their marriage, and made it his decision that the wedding should take place immediately after the Yuletide celebrations and before Lent, when he would be free to attend and would give away the bride, as was suitable. He suggested the Feast of St. Valentine would be apt.

David might have felt a little piqued that his brother-in-law appeared to be deciding on matters which were normally the bride's and bridegroom's concern; but then of course, it was not any normal wedding, and could not take place *without* the King's authority. Anyway, he was so delighted that it had got so far, and that he had only some five months more to wait, that he would have swallowed more than this. But it did reinforce Matilda's warning that Henry, might seek to use them as pawns in his own games.

Less speedily delivered than by the royal courier, Matilda herself wrote also, giving the same news but adding that she sought to have his, David's, agreement and concurrence gained before the King made any final decision. But Henry had said that this was not necessary, that David was sufficiently fortunate in getting the greatest heiress in England to wife and the earldom of Huntingdon confirmed. He, the King, would decide

163

the wedding-date since, as his ward and kinswoman, he must be present. She was unhappy about this, but overjoyed in all else, counting the days. Once they were wed, Henry could not unwed them, and they might take a stronger line. For the rest, she was at once the happiest and most impatient woman in the land. Hasten the Feast of St. Valentine – and might all heaven and its angels, as well as that saint, look after him, for her, until she had him safe in her arms.

David paid another visit to Shiel Kirk at the tail-end of autumn, in early November, before the winter snows and rising rivers made travel through the hills difficult. He was surprised at how well the work of construction was going, cheered at progress but alarmed at the ambitious scale of the establishment, the scope of which seemed to grow each time he saw the revised plans. Far be it from him to say so, however. The monks inevitably had to concentrate initially on living and working quarters, with only a makeshift chapel of timber and thatch. But the foundations of the great church were laid down and something of its dimensions could be visualised. To David it seemed enormous, if anything larger than Holy Trinity at Dunfermline, and he did permit himself to wonder, aloud, where the congregation to fill this vast edifice was to be drawn from? Prior Ralph assured him that God would provide – David praying for a like faith – and besides, it was not so large as it seemed, foundations always giving an enhanced impression of size. By the time that the lofty and groined vaulting was added, sixty-seven feet high, with the one hundred and twenty foot tower at the crossing and the two lesser towers of ninety feet each at the west end flanking the great rose window, plus the clerestoreys, the pillars – twenty-four of them – the aisles and side-chapels, flying buttresses and the rest, the building would require every inch of its length and breadth dimensions. Even the niches for the carved figures of saints inside and out, demanded space and height if they were not to appear huddled and oppressive. The payer for all this glory-to-be in stone groaned shamefully in spirit and hurried off to inspect the mill and tannery being constructed at the riverside, more in line with his preoccupations and his purse.

David was, nevertheless, interested to learn that many of the local helpers, normally only at Shiel Kirk for the summer months, had elected to stay on over the winter, in order that the good work should not be interrupted. This the monks looked upon as a notable advance and an excellent omen for the future. Fortunately David had brought sufficient funds with him to pay for this – as much as he could spare meantime, for he had large expenses looming ahead for the wedding, a suitable entourage to take down to Northampton, fine clothing, gifts and so on. To marry a prominent heiress was no doubt an enviable situation to contemplate, but as others had discovered the preliminary stages were direly taxing. His position as ruler of Cumbria did not bring him in any large revenue personally – although he might have made it do so had he chosen, as did so many governors; and he had no personal fortune whatsoever. His Norman colleagues, used to living off the land wherever they were as a matter of course, could not understand his attitude, and were apt to be a little resentful that he did not allow *them* a free hand in wealth-gathering either, one of the few rifts in an otherwise fairly harmonious administration. It was quite common custom for them to curse the late Queen Margaret of Scots, who was held to be responsible for most of her son's less-than-practical notions.

David blamed himself for his growing concern with matters of riches, gold, and sordid gain. Always he had despised men so preoccupied, such as Ranulf Flambard. He spoke to his chaplain and former tutor, John the Benedictine, about it, and gained little help. John quoted scripture with great authority – take no thought for the morrow; trust not in uncertain riches but in the living God; in the house of the righteous is much treasure but in the revenues of the wicked is trouble; and so on, little of which appeared to David noticeably to apply to his present dilemma. Was he deplorably lacking in faith?

12

THE WEDDING TOOK place, as Henry had ordained, on the Feast of St. Valentine, 14th February 1114, a few days before the beginning of Lent, in the presence of a great and distinguished company, the Castle of Northampton and the Priory of St. Andrew nearby, taken over entirely for the occasion, Henry personally stage-managing all and turning the proceedings into a major state event. Indeed the bridegroom came to feel himself to be a mere incidental, not much more than one cog-in-the-wheel of an elaborate ceremonial machine, set in motion presumably to advance the King of England's policies and influence, in especial to tighten his grip on his Norman baronage. This, in fact, was the principal problem of Henry's reign, the Montgomery brothers being only the tip of an iceberg. By and large the Norman earls, barons and landholders did not approve of Henry Beauclerc. He was insufficiently a warrior for them, too fond of the Saxons, over-concerned with laws and statutes and writings, as his by-name implied, a man who should have been a churchman not a monarch, they held. So constantly the King was at pains to demonstrate to his fellow-Normans that the pen could be quite as effective as the sword, and that his grip on his realm was firm enough to keep them all in their places. The present occasion was undoubtedly in that tradition. All the most important Normans were invited, indeed commanded, to attend the ceremony, to perceive how the Scots could be tamed and made useful more successfully than by battle, how rich and powerful earldoms could be placed in non-Norman hands, and how what the Crown had granted the Crown could take away. The lessons would be clear to all but the blind.

Unfortunately, at the last moment, the King of Scots sent word that he was unable to attend. There had been a rising of Northerners, the men of Moray and Ross, led by MacBeth's and Lulach's descendants, and Alexander could by no means leave Scotland meantime; but he sent his elder brother Ethelred, Abbot of Dunkeld and titular Earl of Moray, as deputy, bearing gifts, along with the Earls Madach of Atholl and Cospatrick of Dunbar, with sundry other Scots notables. Henry was displeased.

David's longing was to see Matilda, naturally, and alone; but this appeared to be no part of the programme, indeed practically an impossibility in the circumstances, with Northampton and vicinity crowded out, and the King having requisitioned Earl's Thorpe Manor for himself and his family – where Matilda herself was still domiciled. The bridegroom and his party, comparative late-comers owing to the difficulties of travel from Cumbria in winter conditions, were allotted cramped quarters in the castle. His only meetings with his bride prior to the nuptials were very much in public or in the presence of Henry, Maud and others including Matilda's sister Alicia, from Normandy. The happy couple could only exchange a few platitudes, eye each other in fond exasperation and seek to possess their souls in patience.

David was glad, at least, to see his brother Ethelred, or Hugh, who was allocated quarters near his own in the castle. He told him that the rising in Scotland had been a serious one, and that the rebels had got as far south as Invergowrie, where Alexander had been residing – with one of his mistresses, it was added – his favourite house. They had almost trapped him, but he had managed to escape and reach Stirling, where he had raised a force sufficient to put the Northerners to flight, had pursued them back to Moray and finally defeated them near the mouth of Spey. But the North was still restive and Alex dared not absent himself. He sent his good wishes by himself, Eth, because he had wanted to be rid of him meantime, and to some extent their cousin Madach of Atholl too; Alex was in process of creating a new Romish bishopric and diocese at Dunkeld, only the second in Scotland after St. Andrews – and this of course would put the final end to his own Celtic Church abbacy there and nominal primacy – which was one of the reasons for the revolt of the Northerners, who were hot against the Roman Church. Turgot, Bishop of St. Andrews, was still at odds with Alex over the asserted supremacy of the Archbishop of York – indeed he had now left Scotland altogether and retired to his old monastery of Wearmouth in Northumbria – and this of a new bishopric at Dunkeld was Alex's answer.

The bridegroom, with his mind tending to be on other things, did not commit himself to taking sides in this matter.

The day before the wedding, Henry produced a preliminary ceremony, with its own significance. In this also David had his part to play, however passive a role was planned for him, Matilda likewise. A banquet for hundreds was prepared, at the bride's expense, in the distinctly gaunt hall of Northampton Castle, and here, before the feasting started, with Matilda seated on his right hand between himself and the Queen, and David on his left, the King rose to his feet – as so must everyone else. When a trumpeter had gained him silence, he spoke.

"Your Grace, Countess and my friends all – hear you. Tomorrow, to our joy – and, may I say, her own! – the Countess Matilda of Northampton and Huntingdon will wed Your Grace's royal brother, David of Scotland, my Earl of Cumbria, a match which will, God willing, enrich us all and draw still closer our two kingdoms. In this happy circumstance, the Countess has dutifully placed her two earldoms in my hands, as is proper, but prays that I dispose and destine them in the following fashion – and this, after due consideration, I have decided to do. Simon de St. Liz, her elder son, to be Earl of Northampton in the room of his late father – but not to exercise the powers and duties of that rank and title until he comes of due age. And David of Scotland to be Earl of Huntingdon, not in the Countess's right but in full and entire possession, now and for all time, together with all its manors, lands, jurisdictions, pertinents and servitures – a great inheritance. This she wishes to be done today, while yet she is unwed to him, that there can be no doubt but that the earldom is his in entirety, not by marriage but in free gift. This it is my pleasure to agree."

There was a stirring amongst the company. David turned to gaze at Matilda much moved, mind in a whirl at what this implied.

Henry went on. "I, and only I, can invest any man as earl. Before I so do, I have something other to do." He turned to two officers who had come to stand behind his throne-like chair, and from one of them took a sword. "Kneel, David mac Malcolm," he commanded.

So there on the dais, in front of all that great company, David sank to his knees and Henry tapped each shoulder with the sword-blade.

"David of Scotland, as myself knight, I dub you knight," the King intoned. "Take your vows hereafter, I charge you, and be you good and true knight until your life's end. Arise, Sir David!"

The new knight stood, amidst applause, and Henry turned to the other officer, to take from him a most splendid and heavy belt of gleaming gold, much more handsome than that with which he had been invested as titular Earl of Cumbria. This he raised, its weight obvious, to place over David's head and shoulder. Then he handed him a small bag of Huntingdon soil.

"I hereby invest you in the earldom of Huntingdon, in this my realm of England," the King said. "Hold it well to my sure support, Sir David, Earl of Huntingdon. It is mine as well as yours. Moreover, I do likewise charge you with the care, oversight and control of the earldom of Northampton, for the child, Simon de St. Liz, whose guardian you will become tomorrow, yours to rule until he comes of age. This also at the behest of the Countess Matilda. Cherish it to his weal, and mine, I charge you as your liege lord. As well as you have cherished my province of Cumbria." And he held out his two hands, palms together, for David to take between his own in the gesture of fealty.

168

It flashed through the younger man's mind just what was the significance of what was here involved, apart from the enormous compliment paid to him in giving him control of both earldoms which, taken with that of Cumbria's governorship, made him at one stroke probably the most powerful noble in England. Fealty. Fealty – that was the price, fealty which he had hitherto paid only to the King of Scots. He had had to swear no fealty for Cumbria, which was not his, he being only viceroy, the style of earl but titular. But this . . .

Bowing slightly, he enclosed Henry's hands within his own. "Sire, I thank you," he said. "I David of Scotland, remaining a leal subject of the King of Scots, as is my bounden duty, hereby pay fealty to you for these English fiefs of Huntingdon and Northampton. God save Your Grace."

There was prolonged silence in that hall as men considered that and what it meant.

David looked up, to find Henry's narrowed eyes directly searching his own, for once cold, hostile, assessing. There was no doubting what *he* considered it to mean. Face to face they stared.

Then the King withdrew his hands and half-shrugged, smiling faintly. "So be it," he said. Turning, he sat down without further word.

As the murmuring swelled in the hall, David moved behind the King's chair and that of the Countess, to the Queen's where he bowed. His sister was looking anxious. He touched her shoulder briefly. Then he turned to Matilda, who still stood, and taking her hand, raised it to his lips, holding it there for moments. They did not speak, save with their eyes, but those were sufficiently eloquent. Then he went back to his place, removing the heavy golden belt, to place it on the table. All resumed their seats.

Henry, usually all but loquacious, appeared to find words in short supply, for he stared straight ahead of him while the meal was being served, his shoulders slightly turned towards his brother-in-law. David took the opportunity to chat to Matilda's sister, Alicia, Countess of Leicester, who had been married at an early age to Ralph de Toelni, given that English earldom but who spent most of his time on great estates in Normandy. She had come over for her sister's wedding, a plump and matronly creature, very different from Matilda. She failed to disguise her present nervousness.

However, as the banquet wore on, Henry gradually relaxed, and at least ceased to show his displeasure without being

169

actually affable. David for his part expressed his deep appreciation of all the honour done to him and assured him that his gratitude would be reflected in his actions. They left it at that, nothing more being said about fealty.

It was a long evening, with elaborate and varied entertainment after the eating – and none might retire before the King. So it was late when, at last, a move was made, and David could at last snatch a few words with his bride-to-be as he escorted her to her horse-litter, which was to take her back, with the royal party, to Earl's Thorpe.

"Matilda, how can I thank you?" he said, as they moved down the vaulted corridor behind the King and Queen. "You are kind, beyond all telling. What can I say? This of Huntingdon. It was not necessary . . ."

"Do not say anything, my love - beyond what you said to Henry! About your Scots loyalty coming first. Serving him warning. That was good, splendid!"

"He was displeased."

"To be sure he was. But it fell to be said, if you were not to be held in his two hands always. You did it excellently well. I did not know of the knighthood . . ."

"Nor I. It must all have made me to sound ungrateful. Yet . . ."

"It had to be said – and said before all. I desire my husband to be a free man, no more tied to Henry than to my own woman's skirts!"

"You are good. You understand it so well . . ."

That was all that they had time for before they reached the courtyard doorway and the waiting horses. David would have escorted her all the way to Earl's Thorpe, but there was no point in that, with the royal cavalcade, plus a troop of Norman cavalry in attendance. Henry took charge of Matilda, making the inevitable remarks about her requiring to get to her bed in good time for the last undisturbed night's sleep that she was likely to enjoy for some time. Somebody had to say it.

The service was held next noon in St. Peter's, the largest church in Northampton – St. Sepulchre's was to be larger but it was not completed yet, having only been founded by the reformed Earl Simon on his return from his first Crusade, copying the round design he had seen at the Church of the Holy Sepulchre at Jerusalem. Even so, by no means all the notables and guests could squeeze in, and the place was uncomfortably crowded – but at least this served to heat up the atmosphere within, for it was a cold day with bitter north-east winds sweeping in off the fens.

David, with Ethelred as groomsman, took up his position at the chancel-steps in good time, with the church almost shaking to the clamour of the bells. He was dressed in his finest, but even so was much outshone by many of the guests. They had a long wait while the bells clashed and jangled above them, David assuring himself and his brother that this would be Henry's doing, not Matilda's, that she would never cause such delay to others, Eth grinning and declaring that his young brother would have to learn about women.

It was a relief when the bells stopped and into the quivering hush a fanfare of trumpets signalled the approach of the bride – although it was for her royal escort rather than herself that the flourish was sounded, undoubtedly. Three processions entered the church simultaneously. The King with Matilda on his arm moved in from the west door up the centre of the nave, the standing congregation moving aside to give them passage. The Queen and her ladies, with members of the royal family and Matilda's children, came in by the south transept, to proceed to their places at the choir stalls. And the officiating clergy, Bishop Maurice of London and Bishop Roger of Salisbury, with their supporters, from the north transept, turning into the chancel and up to the high altar. All thereafter turned to watch the progress of the bride and her monarch up the length of the church, with a choir of singing boys chanting behind them – all except David and his brother, that is, who gazed straight ahead of them, at the chancel-steps.

At last Matilda was at her groom's side and he could look at her. She was quite breath-takingly beautiful, tall and slender, a mature and assured women of poise and character, her dark hair in two long plaits hanging before her to below her waist, pearl-seeded head-veil held in place by a gemmed circlet, gowned to perfection in cloth-of-silver, furred at neck and wide sleeves with sable, this also sewn with pearls which gleamed warmly as she moved – Scots pearls, these, from the River Tay, sent south by David as *his* gift, purchased from Alexander who was reputed to have the finest collection of pearls in all Christendom. Beside her Henry, now nearing fifty, short-legged and growing paunchy, despite – or perhaps partly because of – his over-richness of dress in cloth-of-gold and embroidery, looked fussy and ostentatious. She reached out to take David's hand.

The singing over, the bridal party moved up towards the

altar where the bishops awaited them, and the service commenced.

It is undoubtedly no unusual state of affairs for the bridegroom, even one fairly religiously-inclined, to go through the nuptial ceremony with scarcely any awareness of what is done and said; as well that the marriage is none the less valid. David knew the service well enough and went through the required motions without any obvious faults and hesitations; nevertheless, it was as though it was all happening to somebody else, and he was only remotely involved. He was, at one stage, dimly aware of Henry, having done his part in handing over the bride, retiring to his seat beside the Queen; and of Ethelred handing over the ring for him to place on Matilda's finger. But otherwise the significance of what was happening largely failed to penetrate. All that he was intensely aware of was that Matilda was there by his side, just the two of them standing close, in the sight of God, the rest mattering little – and that she looked radiantly happy. Perhaps that was enough.

It was when he found himself kneeling to receive the Elements of the nuptial mass that it dawned upon him that they were now one, man and wife, joined together for all time, and that none could put them asunder – and he all but choked at the surge of emotion this blinding recognition generated within him. He turned to Matilda and found her to be considering him intently, almost anxiously. Her lips moved soundlessly. He nodded, and her eyes lightened.

The final benediction given, the trumpets blared again, this time a prolonged, triumphant paean. The King and Queen moved out first, by the south transept. Waiting until they were gone, the bridal couple, arm-in-arm, proceeded down the length of the building to the west door, through the smiling but critical throng, and out into the cold February afternoon, where further crowds awaited them. Matilda's chief steward and a servant came up, with a fur cloak for her, and with leather bags filled with coins, and from these the happy pair threw token handfuls of silver to the gathering, leaving most of the contents however to be handed out in more judicious and dignified fashion as they progressed through the narrow streets. A horse-litter was waiting for her, but Matilda dismissed it, despite the weather, saying that they had walked together from the first wedding that they had attended, almost seven years ago, and they would walk again – even though Northampton's cobbled causeways were scarcely so well-cleaned for the occasion as had been royal Winchester's. Henry and Maud, who had come round to join them, drew the line at this; but the children were there, eager, excited, and David asserted his husbandly authority for the first time by insisting that they should accompany them. So, with young Simon, Earl of North-ampton, proudly leading the way, small Matilda clutching her mother's left hand – difficult, in that the Countess had to use it also to hitch up her long silver skirts above the cobbles' filth – and Waltheof holding David's right, they moved on towards the castle, through the packed streets and alleys, the steward and his men clearing the way as well as distributing the largesse. Popular proceeding as this was naturally, there could be no doubt as to the Countess being well-loved, in herself, by the townsfolk. That this was not lost on Matilda was revealed when David asked if she was not cold, and she asked in return who could be cold when wrapped, not only in his love and in her children's but in that of her people?

There was no privacy for them at the castle, where the royal party and most of the guests had arrived before them, and there was nothing for it but to submit to the prolonged wedding-feast and the still more prolonged entertainment and dancing there-after.

But as the short winter's day drew to an early dusk, David decided that enough was sufficient. He went to Henry and told him that they had eight miles to ride to Earl's Barton, east-wards, and it was almost dark already, and beginning to rain. He begged leave for his wife and himself to retire, and if possible discreetly.

The King, after the usual comments and innuendoes, with his wife's helpful touch and nod, gave the required permission. Thankfully David returned to Matilda, who said that she must say farewell to the children, now in a private chamber of the castle, with the woman Editha. So they slipped out of the hall, and David accompanied her to the children's room, where there was a touching scene of parting. The boys were not greatly upset, but the little girl was much distressed and clung to her mother, sobbing. They were going back to Normandy with their Aunt Alicia, Countess of Leicester, for a month or two, then on to Matilda's own uncle, the Count Stephen d'Aumale, her mother Judith's brother and nephew of the Conqueror. This promised adventure for the boys, but their sister saw it otherwise. The farewell left the adults feeling guilty, the mother at the desertion, David at being the cause of it.

Without returning to the hall and company, the pair reached

the courtyard by a side-door, collected their horses from the stables, and wrapping themselves in heavy travelling-cloaks, took the road eastwards, in the rain, alone together at last.

It took some time for the feeling of guilt to wear off.

*　　*　　*

Earl's Barton was the principal manor of the Honour of Huntingdon – as was Earl's Thorpe for Northampton – although not the *caput* or seat of the earldom, which was at Huntingdon Castle itself, in the small town of the name, sited on the River Ouse. Earl's Barton was placed just over the shire's border, on the Nene near Wellingborough, a fine place apparently – as it certainly should be if it was the choicest of no fewer than one hundred and ninety manors in the Honour of Huntingdon, scattered over eleven counties, although mainly in Hunting-donshire itself, all since last night David's personal property. He could by no means take it all in, as Matilda told him the scope of it as they rode into the wet fenland wind. He had realised that the earldom was rich; but one-hundred-and-ninety manors was almost incomprehensible as a conception. The vast majority of them, to be sure, were in the hands of the earldom's vassals, who paid for them to their lord in money, grain, wool, hides and knight's service, the last so important to the entire feudal system which the Normans had perfected. The Honour, she revealed, could total no fewer than two-hundred-and-twenty-five knight's fees. These were not knights in the sense that he had just been made a knight, of course, but only in that each so-called knight's fee required the vassal to provide a knightly leader, trained in war, mounted and fully armoured, along with two sergeants and a troop of armed men or archers, varying from ten to fifty, ready for war, for up to forty days' service in any given year. Some great manors were worth a dozen knights' fees, others only half of one, depending on size, richness of the land and of population, although most fees ran to eight hundred acres or one plough-gate. This general system was well known to David, naturally – it was the extent of the Honour of Huntingdon which so surprised him. In theory, therefore, his personal armed strength could reach seven or eight thousand men, Northampton's slightly more. Of these, since all was held of the Crown, Henry could call upon him at any time to field two-thirds for war at home, and up to one-third for foreign war. Hence the significance of fealty and the control of earldoms.

As for Earl's Barton itself, although David had never been there, he was assured that it was a fair and pleasant place amongst the Nene meadows, with its own Barton Chase and the two-miles-long lake of Ashby Water nearby, this one of the finest wildfowl haunts in the county, with other hunting and hawking facilities not far off. Huntingdonshire was notably rich in forest, hurst and brake as well as fen, indeed one of the sheriffdoms entirely subject to the Norman forest laws. Matilda had always preferred this manor to that of Earl's Thorpe, but her husband had favoured the latter.

That evening, reaching the place in the windy dark, it might have been anywhere to David. But blazing log fires and warm rooms held their own welcome, and discreet servants were attentive without being intrusive. The couple had eaten more than sufficient at the castle banquet, and although an excellent repast awaited them here, they contented themselves with sipping mulled wine before the hall fire.

They eyed each other questioningly, almost warily, as a silence grew, save for the crackle of the fire and the whine of the wind outside. Matilda suddenly reached out a hand to him. "David – we said that we would always be honest with each other, did we not? Let us be honest now. We have both longed for this day, this night, for years. Longed for each other, our bodies as well as our hearts and souls. Are we children, to dissemble now?"

"God bless you!" he exclaimed, and throwing an arm about her, moved for the stairway.

In the large bedchamber above, in the warmly genial light of another aromatic birch-log fire, they held each other close. Then urgently David began to undress her, less than expertly perhaps, so that, laughing, she had to assist him. He was no untutored innocent as far as women were concerned, but his engagements hitherto had been apt to be of the earthy sort, with uncomplicated country girls and co-operative females of only intermittent virtue, not with high-born ladies, richly clad, who might well have different priorities and preferences as well as much more difficult garb. So Matilda's frank co-operation now was a comfort and a relief – and he swiftly recognised that there was no lack of basic enthusiasm here either, no coy pretences. Indeed, naked presently, when she drew away a little from eager hands, it was not in any shrinking fashion but to stand there before him, turning a little this way and that in the firelight, most clearly offering display of herself – yet peering at his face, it seemed almost anxiously.

She was in fact, superb, her person as proudly rich and fulfilling as her facial features were beautiful, mature yes but firm, generously rounded, essentially, challengingly woman, lissom still, long-legged, deep-breasted, dark of aureola and groin, gleaming white elsewhere, belly swelling to match her hips.

He swallowed, all but groaned, and shook his head.

"Say it!" she got out "Tell me – tell me, I say! Am I . . . still desirable? I am no longer young. With three children borne. No man has seen me thus, for many years. Indeed never, just so. For, for . . ." She faltered. "I have sought to keep myself as, as once I was. For this day. But . . ." Her voice tailed away.

"My dear, my dear," he cried. "You do not know what you say! You are lovely, utterly desirable, an incomparable delight beyond all telling. You, you wring the heart of me with your beauty. And more than the heart, by God . . .!"

"In truth, David? You do not kindly cozen? This *firelight* is kindly . . ."

"Lord, woman – look at me! Do I seem to cozen? Does my body not speak full truth, even if my tongue were to lie! A plague – aid me off with these wretched clothes . . ."

Nothing loth she came to help him – yet by her nearness delayed the business by distracting his hands to her delectable self. So they wrestled and laughed and panted, until at length he was rid of his clinging, restraining garments – and the proof of his assertions was amply evident to still any last doubts she might have entertained.

Picking her up bodily, he ran with her to the great canopied bed, time for talk undoubtedly over.

There were over twelve hours until day would dawn.

Part Two

13

AFTER TWO WEEKS of unalloyed bliss, days spent in splendid
idleness, or hawking or visiting parts and personages in the
great Honour of Huntingdon, with long nights of delight, the
Earl and Countess set out for the North. David, although now to
be styled Earl of Huntingdon, was still governor of Cumbria,
and in a more vague and unofficial way ruler of Strathclyde
also. So he had no lack of responsibilities, and was a little
anxious as to what might have transpired in his absence –
although winter was the time when incidents were least likely,
with all campaigning and sea-raiding difficult. Matilda had
made it clear that she expected to accompany him, although he
assured her that travelling conditions would be less trying later;
but she insisted that she had married him to be with him, not to
be some stay-at-home guardian of his new southern posses-
sions. She would not have sent her children to Normandy
otherwise. Besides, she had been constrained and trammelled
hereabouts for too long as it was. She was commencing a new
life and was eager to make a start.

David had no reason to complain of any delay or hampering
on their journey – not because of the women anyway, for she
took a tirewoman and a maid-servant with her, and ensured
that they were good horsewomen. Nevertheless it took eight
days to reach Caer-luel, through a rain-soaked and high-
rivered countryside.

There he found all reasonably well, although the Viscount
Richard had broken a leg hunting and Hugo de Morville, not
wishing to trouble David in the circumstances, had taken temporary command – and appeared to have done very well. David
was thankful that it was not Hervey de Warenne who had taken
this initiative, and whose methods might well have displayed
more vigour than tact. Fergus of Galloway, of course, was a
tower of strength, to the north – even though his own methods
likewise caused David some little anxiety.

Matilda settled in well amongst the mainly Norman establishment at Caer-luel, all young men and appreciative of
feminine company, especially when good-looking. From the
first, David found her a positive help in his administration,

indeed, not only in that he could discuss problems and policies with her, knowing that she understood and approved his general attitudes, but that, in backing them up before the others she enhanced his authority. He had ample powers, to be sure, to *enforce* his authority, but preferred to carry his colleagues with him. And Matilda emanated a quiet but unmistakable air of authority of her own.

To remind all that he was back, and in the saddle, David made a tour round the Scottish territories under his supervision, when April made travel through the Lowland hills practicable. He took Matilda – indeed part of the object was to introduce her to Scotland in general and, if possible, to Alexander its king in particular.

Of course Shiel Kirk was early on the list of calls. Matilda was enchanted with the place and much interested in all that went on. Clearly she made a great impression on Prior Ralph. In fact, her enthusiasm was such that her husband began to judge her almost as much a danger to his treasury as was the Prior, approving of this extension and that and suggesting further improvements and refinements of her own. And she was in a position to all but choke off his guarded doubts and protests by asking him why he thought that she had handed over to him in its entirety one of the richest earldoms in England, if it was not that the might no longer have to worry over matters such as this? What more worthy use was there for Huntingdon's wealth then glorifying God adequately in this lovely place?

The work was, in fact, proceeding apace, although winter conditions had apparently held things up somewhat. Least progress showed on the church itself, inevitably, for on this all must be perfection, the masonry hewn to an exacting standard, the carving meticulous – and skilled masons did not grow on every tree of the Forest of Ettrick. As well as the building work, ground was being cleared for crop-growing, orchards and gardens, essential drainage put in hand, and the beginnings of the sheep and cattle stock accumulated. More money was urgently required.

From Shiel Kirk they made their way down Tweed to Ersildoune in Lauderdale, where Cospatrick welcomed them warmly. He took them to see the small Benedictine monastery of Melross, founded by his father for his own purposes, and now rather run-down and neglected, with only three or four monks remaining. The site was dramatic, on a high spine of land where Leader met Tweed, the place all but islanded. The buildings however were utilitarian, modest. David found himself inclined to boast moderately how much finer the Abbey of Shiel Kirk was going to be – until he caught Matilda's amused glance.

Whilst at Ersildoune they made an excursion further down Tweed a dozen miles, to where Teviotdale branched off westwards. Two items took David there. In the Forest of Jedworth, near the mouth of Teviotdale, his eldest brother Edward, Prince of Strathclyde, had died in 1093, wounded at Alnmouth where his father had been slain, the spot now marked and being called Edward's Aisle. Also, the Northumbrian border came close here, and there had been a number of raids by Northumbrians recently into Cospatrick's territories, which called for redress. So David made a pilgrimage to Edward's Aisle, and arranged to have a stone carved, in the Celtic fashion, and set up there. He had been only nine years at Edward's death but remembered him as quite the finest, noblest of his brothers as well as the eldest, a most grievous loss to Scotland. Surveying part of the march with Northumbria, David was struck by the remarkably strong natural position and strategic significance of a site there named Rook's Burgh, where Teviot joined Tweed, the two great rivers forming a long whaleback ridge at their confluence, this with a notably narrow neck which, if ditched and moated, would make the position all but impregnable. Indeed there were the remains of fortifications crumbling thereon, presumably Pictish. A strong castle sited there would be of enormous value in protecting a vulnerable section of the borderline from Northumbrian invasion. David promised to speak to Alexander about this. Cospatrick pointed out, incidentally, that the Forest of Jedworth, part of the greater Ettrick, was quite the finest piece of hunting territory in Southern Scotland.

Leaving Cospatrick after a couple of days, they moved on northwards up Lauderdale, Matilda delighted with this fair land of tall green hills, foaming rivers, heather moors and forests of gnarled and ancient pines, such as they never saw in the South. From the head of Lauderdale they climbed over a lofty pass of the Lammermuir hills, and from its summit looked out over the lovely land of Lothian, wide, rich and fertile, to the gleaming cordon of the Scottish Sea, blue and silver, with Fife beyond, and away to the north-west the jagged purple outliers of the Highland mountains. In the middle distance rose the isolated peak of Arthur's Chair and its neighbouring fort-crowned rock of Dunedin, where David had watched at his mother's death-bed twenty-one years before and at Edgar's unhappy couch more recently. The sight aroused mixed feelings in that man, but his wife, used to the more level landscapes of East Anglia and the Fens, exclaimed that she had never seen so magnificent a vista.

They came to Edinburgh, tired, in the long light of an early May evening, with the afterglow behind the hills beyond the Scotwater. Less than eager for the gloomy atmosphere of the fortress-palace up on the rock, David sought the hospitality of the Celtic Church cashel of St. Nicholas, under Arthur's Chair, where they were kindly, if simply, entertained, despite the suspicions with which that Church viewed the Rome-inclined present royal house. They got on very well with the Columban monks, in fact.

In the morning they climbed up to Dunedin, mainly to visit the tiny, plain Queen's Chapel which Margaret had built for her own private worship, so astonishingly different from the splendid minster she had erected at Dunfermline. In this quiet and humble shrine, so much more like a Celtic cell indeed than one of her own Romish churches, they said a prayer for her soul's peace – which was not in doubt – and another for their own, which might well be. Then they set off on the thirty-five mile journey through the west of Lothian and Calatria, for Stirling, with the Scottish Sea narrowing to the Firth of Forth on their right.

But once again Stirling, Alexander's capital, where the Forth narrowed itself sufficiently to be bridged, and another rock like Dunedin, fort-crowned, dominated the crossing, failed to produce the King. A restless man, he was always off somewhere, they were told, this time apparently up into Drumalban, North Atholl where, on an island in Loch Tay of all places, he was building a nunnery in his mother's memory – why there, was obscure. But Sir Eustace de Morville, Hugo's uncle, first Edgar's and now Alexander's Great Constable, was there, and received them warmly, declaring that it was not worth their while to go further, for the King was due back within two days for a council meeting. On enquiry, they learned that Queen Sybilla was not with her husband, indeed it appeared that she seldom was, maintaining her own establishment on her dowry lands of Clunie, on the Ore, in Fife, and going her own way.

So the visitors waited at Stirling. The following day David took Matilda for an excursion into the Highland hills readily accessible, where her joy in fine scenery was further stimulated by the sight of Lochs Menteith, Ard and Chon and their surrounding bens of rock and heather.

They got back to Stirling to find Alexander returned, and glad to see them, especially Matilda. He had a roving eye for women, and quickly came to a due appreciation of his new sister-in-law's qualities. He had seen her before, at his wedding, but only briefly. Now he did not hide his admiration – and it was clear that he was used to having his way with women.

To temper the process David enquired after the Queen – and was unprepared for the answer.

Alexander snorted. "Henry dealt me an ill bargain there!" he declared, without the least constraint. "Sybilla serves me little, as wife or queen!"

"I am sorry. And . . . still no children?"

"She is barren." The King grinned. "I have proved sufficiently otherwhere that the fault is not mine! Indeed, she glories in it, lies with whom she will, in despite of me! It was an ill match you came making that day, Davie! You have done a deal better for yourself!" He turned to Matilda.

"Think you he did it of a purpose?"

She looked surprised. "How that, Sire?"

"Did he not tell you? He brought me Henry's offer of Sybilla. Advising acceptance. To bind our two kingdoms closer. Like a fool I agreed. I wonder if he *knew* that she would never bear me a son? So Davie himself is now my heir! Is it not simple?"

"Never heed him, Matilda," David said. "He but cozens you."

"Is it cozening to say that you are heir to my throne? And brought me Henry Beauclerc's proposal?"

"I have never thought of myself as heir," David declared. "You are young yet – not two years older than am I. You could yet have lawful sons . . ."

"But not on Sybilla – and there's the rub! And, since she is Henry's daughter, I can by no means put her away. I am held fast. So you, my dear new sister, God willing, will one day be Queen of Scots!"

She shook her lovely head. "I am older than you, if David is not."

"Ah, but you do not have men seeking your blood – whatever else they may seek of you, woman!" he said, deep-voiced. "As they will seek *yours*, if so be you become King one day!" he added, pointing a finger at his brother. "Mind it. Three times I have been assailed, with intent to slay. Our father slew Mac-Beth and Lulach. Their kin will slay me if they can – and you after me. Never forget that. The northern line seek the throne and will have it if they can."

There was an uncomfortable silence.

"You had a close escape at Invergowrie last year, Alex, I heard," David said.

"It was MacBeth's grandsons, with a host from Moray and Ross. That was sufficiently ill. But I esteem it worse that the Mormaors of Mar and the Mearns sent me no word. They must have known that this force marched through their lands. Only Gillibride of Angus sent me warning, just in time. I shall not forget that."

"You believe that Mar and the Mearns deliberately withheld warning to you? That they do not support the Crown? Two of your lesser kings?"

"Yes."

"Why? Have you done aught to offend them?"

"No more than any firm hand can offend, at times. And this Scotland needs a firm hand, God knows! Edgar, whose hand was palsied, proved that. Our Father's hand was sufficiently firm, although he was not loved. But since then . . ."

"If some of your mormaors do not support you, Alex – whom *do* they support? You are crowned High King, on the Stone of Destiny. To whom they have given their oaths of fealty. What is the alternative?"

"There are over-many alternatives, man – with aspirations to the throne. A plague of them! There are these MacBeth's grandsons, Murdoch and Airbertach. There are Lulach's grandsons, the sons of Malsnechtan. And now, I hear, there are some who declare that Eth's son, Malcolm, should be Prince of Strathclyde. Eth himself is debarred, as a churchman – and besides, he has no desire for the throne. But he is our elder brother, and his son is not debarred from the succession. Moreover, he represents both the north and south lines of our house. Eth's wife was Malsnechtan's sister, Lulach's daughter. There is no question but that Lulach's line, through MacBeth's Queen Gruoch, was the senior branch of our royal house. MacBeth himself recognised it, by naming Lulach, his stepson, as heir, not his own sons. And, since I have produced no heir, and you are considered to be an Englishman, there is this talk."

"I have never thought of myself as in line for the throne, I tell you. If this other, Malcolm, our nephew, would help to unite the realm, then make him Prince of Strathclyde indeed."

"No, no. That would raise as many problems as it would solve! MacBeth's grandsons of Moray and Ross would have none of it. They see Malcolm MacEth as representing the northern line only through the female side, whereas they are sons of sons. Forby, there could still be another objector to either of these. Our cousin Madach of Atholl. His father, Melmore, was lawful brother to *our* father, who was illegitimate. Moreover he has married Hakon of Orkney's daughter, who is great-grand-daughter of Thorfinn Raven Feeder, himself grandson of Malcolm the Second. Madach says that he has no ambitions for the throne, himself. But if I am without heir, and you are one of Henry's earls, then he believes that his child Angus has more right to be King than any of these others. Saints help us – what a coil! You see what friendship with Henry has cost our house? You, one of his earls, myself his sonless good-son!"

David stared from brother to wife, unhappily. "I had no notion of all this. I suppose that I should have known it, all this of descents, but . . ."

"Edgar believed that there was a curse on our house – and perhaps he was right. But . . . I am King and shall remain so, despite all these dogs yapping round my throne. But the heir, the heir to Scotland, must be made clear to all. I have thought on this. That heir must be you, Davie. None other could I trust. Besides, you have the wits for it. But – how do you stand with Henry? As Earl of Huntingdon – *his* earl. As King of Scots, you would be subservient to Henry? So it is being claimed."

"Not so. I expressly paid my fealty to him *only* for Huntingdon. I stated before all that my prior fealty and loyalty was to you, the King of Scots."

"He did – and most roundly," Matilda confirmed. "I rejoiced – even if Henry did not!"

"Thank God for that, at least!" Alexander said. "I shall see that all hear of it. And that you, meantime, are my heir. Yet, Davie – I cannot make you Prince of Strathclyde. Even though, as recognised heir to my throne, I wish you to rule all south of Forth and Clyde. You understand, man? I am not old, as you said – not yet thirty-one. Sybilla could die. I could then marry again and have a son. If I made you Prince of Strathclyde, my son would be deprived of his birthright. I cannot do that . . ."

"I understand very well, Alex. And agree. I have no wish to be Prince of Strathclyde. I shall be heir-presumptive, if it is your wish, not heir-apparent, as the phrase goes. Although not desiring to be heir at all . . ."

"Good, Davie – good! And you will govern the South for me? As well as Henry's Cumbria? You do so now, in some measure. But I would have it made full rule – to be viceroy. For I cannot spare the time, the men or the siller for it, placed as I am. My treasury is all but empty – Edgar saw to that! And you – you are rich, all say! Thanks to this lady."

David looked at his wife – and forbore to remind his brother that Edgar had also wanted to make him ruler of the southern half of Scotland, but that he, Alexander, had refused it, saying that the kingdom could not be divided.

Matilda nodded. "David is rich, yes. And able. I think that he will rule your southlands for you very well, Sire. The gold and the silver will be the least of it."

"I rejoice to hear you say so, Sister."

"How free are to be my hands in this, Alex? In ruling for you? In Cumbria, I rule for Henry, but he holds the purse-strings. Here, it seems, that is not to be – since the purse is to be mine own! But how far may I govern, without reference to you, the King?"

"So long as you support my throne and interests, always, your hands are free, Davie. Indeed, I will thank you not to trouble me overmuch with decisions. Save in matters which affect the whole realm. I have more than sufficient to consider here. You will be viceroy, making the King' decisions for him, in general. Keeping me informed. What more do you want?"

"It is not more that I want, but clarity, assurance, knowledge of what are to be my powers and limitations. See you, the Merse and Teviotdale are being much raided by Northumbrians. Cospatrick of Dunbar receives no aid from you. A fort, a castle in the Norman style, built at a place called Rook's Burgh, where Teviot joins Tweed, and garrisoned always, would greatly assist in controlling the march there. *Your* march. A royal castle . . ."

"Then build it, Davie – build it. But do not ask me to pay for it! Take what measures you see fit. You are my brother, our mother's son, as well as my heir. If I cannot trust you, whom can I trust?"

"Very well. Put it in a paper, signed and sealed . . ."

David sat in at the council-meeting next day, to underline his new authority in the realm and, amongst much else, to have his position as heir-presumptive and Viceroy of the South confirmed and ratified – even though the councillors involved appeared to him less than representative. But it was sufficiently lawful, with the King presiding, the Chancellor, the High Judex or Justiciar and the Great Constable present, although only two of the *ri*, Madach of Atholl and Constantine of Fife, as well as the new Bishop Cormac of Dunkeld and sundry lesser lords and Celtic Church abbots. All, even Madach, seemed

186

relieved over David's adherence. Presumably the situation was not all merely fortuitous, and something of it would have been conveyed to him at Caer-luel, by messenger, had he not chosen to make this journey. Not for the first time, David wondered what quality of monarch Alexander made? Compared with Henry Beauclerc's careful planning and organisation, government here seemed very rough-and-ready – not how he himself would conduct a kingdom's affairs. Which seemed now to be a subject to which it might be wise to devote a little thought.

Two days later they left for the South, both of them more thoughtful than when they had arrived.

14

IN THE MONTHS that followed, David found himself to be filling the role of buildings-supervisor and master-of-works more often than that of viceroy. He seemed to be involved, personally and perpetually, in stone-and-lime, not only with the abbey at Shiel Kirk but with the new castle at Rook's Burgh which, since he must now have a suitable base on his Scottish territories, was being erected not just as a stronghold but as a reasonably comfortable residence and hunting-lodge as well. Moreover, with Matilda expressing no intentions of returning to Earl's Barton or Northampton meantime, it became incumbent upon him to provide more comfortable quarters at Caer-luel than the gaunt castle there could offer, and more permanent than their lodgings in the monastery. This requirement was much enhanced when, one morning in July, Matilda announced that she was fairly sure that she was pregnant.

David was overjoyed. "My dear, my dear – can it be true? Are you sure? The saints in heaven be praised! A son, a son! It is wonderful, a, a miracle!" He picked her up bodily – and then set her down again as quickly, indeed almost with a jolt. "Oh, I am sorry, my love – sorry! Forgive me. I have not hurt you . . . ?"

"Foolish! I am well, well! Is it so strange? Was it not to be

187

expected? We have not .., stinted our efforts, have we, my love? No miracle! But I cannot promise you a son . . ."

"It will be a son – I know it. I suppose that we will have to name him Henry. He said that – Henry. He said that our first son should be called Henry after himself, and he will be god-father. But – you will be able? Sufficiently well? We must be careful, very careful . . ."

"I am none so old as all that, David! Perfectly able. I have done it before, after all – three times. With little to-do. But – you are happy? That is what matters . . ."

So the building-work at Caer-luel was hastened on and improved, a pleasant house at the riverside, near but not part of the castle complex. This was still not finished when another and rather similar residence was commenced almost alongside, for Hugo de Morville. Hugo had been sent south to Hunting-don twice or thrice to see to David's and Matilda's interests there – for the de Morvilles were prominent vassals of that earldom – and had come back the last time with a wife, Beatrix de Beauchamp, daughter of one of the Honour's Bedfordshire vassals, a cheeful, generously-made creature, all warmth and smiles, who quickly became a favourite of all and Matilda's companion and aide. So another house was called for.

All this building was not allowed to come between David and his essential duties, of course. The Viscount Richard was re-covered, and South Cumbria could be left largely in his care. But David had to spend considerable time in Strathclyde pro-per, long neglected. Fergus was well able to look after Gallo-way, Dunegal's Nithsdale, and his own original lordship of Carrick, to the north. But that left huge areas without due supervision. Annandale in especial was a problem, unsettled after Hakon Claw's devastations, and subject to depredations by broken men from the adjoining Forest of Ettrick, yet carry-ing the principal route from Caer-luel to both Shiel Kirk and Rook's Burgh. David sent Robert de Brus there, one of the most effective of his young Normans, as resident, based on Annan. Liddesdale was another haunt of thieves and cattle-stealers, probing deep into the Cheviot hill-mass, and so a convenient highway for Northumbrian raiders. There he sent Ranulf de Soulis, a tough character. The other great dales, if less signifi-cantly important, nearly all called for resident lieutenants. They had their native lords and chiefs, to be sure, but these seldom sought to keep the King's peace, indeed more often than not led the disharmony. So Walter de Avenal was despatched to Eskdale, Ranulf de Limesay to Wauchopedale, the Lovel brothers to Upper Teviotdale and Bernard de Baliol to Lower, and so on. Cospatrick of Dunbar and March was given general over-sight of most of these, which flanked his own lands; and even his brother the Earl Dolfin was prised out of comfortable sloth in Allerdale and sent to establish a presence on the western skirts of the Forest area – where, to be sure, he could still hunt to his heart's content. Still further afield, Walter and Simon fitz Alan were given charge of Ayrdale, Cunningham and Renfrew, with Lower Clydesdale, and Simon Loccard with Upper. They all were given precise instructions as to how they were to behave, the King of Scots' representatives at two removes.

So Caer-luel became a very different place for those remaining, taking on a rather more dramatic character, and with most of its fire-eating young Normans seen only intermittently. The local inhabitants were on the whole relieved – especially those with daughters.

Thus passed the months. In February, exactly a year after her wedding, Matilda was brought to bed. David was right, as well as elated and enormously relieved; she produced a fine son. They duly called him Henry mac David. The birth was not a difficult one, and joy was unconfined. Alexander, although envious no doubt, should have been pleased, that there was now an heir to the heir to the throne – always a stabilising influence.

Matilda's new offspring brought to a head her motherly desire to have back her other children, whom she had been missing more and more. She felt that they had been quite long enough in Normandy. Now that she was inevitably going to be restricted in her movements by this new arrival, it seemed only right to have them back with her. David was nothing loth. He loved children and had felt some guilt at being the cause of his wife's separation from them. So Hugo was sent off on the long journey to Aumale on the Seine, where the youngsters were now with their great-uncle Count Stephen, to fetch them home. They would spend the summer here in the North, and go to Earl's Barton for the winter.

All these preoccupations and developments were interrupted for a space in the late spring of that year 1115, with the start of the campaigning season bringing word that the Norsemen were boarding their longships once more – and it behoved wise men to be on the alert. Alexander sent the news – the first they had heard from him – that Madach's good-father, Hakon of Orkney, reported that Sigurd Half Deacon the King had sent a large army and fleet under the Jarl Ivar of Fiodir, which had been living off his islands and devouring his substance all winter. But now they were off westwards, Ivar said to win great treasure, so that Sigurd could afford to go on Crusade – this being the object of the expedition. He had said that he was going to Ireland for this treasure – but Hakon had heard some of the Vikings boasting in their cups that it was really Scotland they aimed for, Strathclyde and Galloway, which were thought to be richer than Ireland. So beware.

David wasted no time in sending warning to Fergus – for Galloway and Strathclyde were indeed favoured stamping-grounds for the Norsemen – and in summoning all his wide-scattered lieutenants to drop whatever they were at, assemble their fighting men and march to given centres down the coast-line fronting the Western Sea. His own Cumbrian army was organised for swift muster, and such shipping as was available he concentrated at the deep-water ports of Silloth and Whithorn and Ayr. David sent word to Henry.

So they waited. No attack developed on Scottish soil, nor English. As the weeks passed, the information reached them that Ulster indeed was the target and that bloody ruin was spreading through that Ua-Neill kingdom and its neighbours. Others everywhere breathed a sigh of relief – for a large-scale Norse hosting was the most terrible scourge known to Christendom – but knew no call to go to the rescue of the victims. But still men stood to arms, watching, ready. Because Viking hordes had glutted themselves in Ireland, it did not necessarily mean that thereafter they would return quietly to Norway, satisfied. They had notable appetites – and crusading was notoriously expensive.

Then a new preoccupation developed, for David at least – and again it emanated from Alexander at Stirling. Turgot, their mother's friend and confessor, had died, in his self-imposed exile at Monk's Wearmouth, leaving the vital bishopric of St. Andrews vacant. And Thurstan, Arch'bishop of York, had taken the opportunity, in his campaign for spiritual hegemony over Scotland, to declare that he intended to appoint the successor. Alexander declared that that would be over his dead body – but the alternatives open to him were not readily evident. He could, to be sure, appoint whomsoever he chose; but getting him consecrated thereafter was the difficulty. His nominee for the new bishopric of Dunkeld, Cormac, was still awaiting consecration, and there was nobody in Scotland competent to do it – so his appointment was all but useless. He,

Alexander, had written to the Pope on the subject of Cormac, but had merely been referred to the Archbishops of Canterbury or York. In the Romish polity only an archbishop, or in special circumstances another bishop, could consecrate and lay hands on a bishop. Since Turgot had absented himself from Scotland, a year before, Alexander had approached Ralph of Canterbury to agree to consecrate, since he was well-known to be in perpetual conflict with York. But without positive result. Could David help? Use his renowned wits to help solve this problem? Otherwise all their mother's devoted efforts to establish the Roman Church in Scotland looked like going for nothing, and the native Columban Church winning by default. Would Henry help? It seemed unlikely, in the circumstances.

David cudgelled his brains. Alexander's position was, in a way, ironical. He was little of a religious man, and might have been just as well content with a resurgence of the old Columban Church, which at least would have spared him this sort of trouble. But he had a very great attachment to his mother's memory, and seemed to feel himself bound to continue her work of establishing the Romish Church supreme in Scotland. Moreover this course was politically advisable. The Pope could be a most useful ally, a helpful lever in dealings with other realms. The Vatican could provide pressure as no other authority could do. Even though in this instance the Pontiff had failed him, he would not always do so, for England was often at odds with the Holy See. Moreover, Popes changed not infrequently. Ireland excepted, and disunited under its warring kinglets, no other kingdom in Northern Christendom remained outside the Roman acceptance. To revert to the Celtic Church now would be too costly a step. This York hegemony threat had to be solved otherwise. Flambard was unlikely to be able to help in this, even if he was prepared to be bribed again; he could scarcely consecrate another bishop contrary to his own archbishop's express policy. Henry would probably back Canterbury; but with Ralph refusing to become involved, he could hardly be expected to bring pressure to bear in a matter, on the face of it, to England's disadvantage. Rome had to support its archbishops.

Neither Matilda nor his chaplain, John, whom he consulted, could think of any way out of the impasse.

It was in their bed that August night the David suddenly sat up, awaking Matilda. "I think I have it!" he exclaimed. "Or . . . possibly I have. A chance, at least." He turned. "Oh, I am sorry, my heart. For waking you. Forgive me. I have been lying thinking of this coil, this of bishops."

"That is Alexander's coil, my dear – not your's," she told him, yawning. "You should be sleeping, not fighting his battles for him. But – what have you hatched in that mind of yours?"

"See you – I rule Cumbria and Strathclyde. Cumbria for England, Strathclyde for Scotland. Yet they used to be one – Cumbria was part of the kingdom of Strathclyde. My rule has the support of both monarchs. So far as Holy Church is concerned, both provinces are backward, wholly neglected. In an area larger than Wales, there is no single bishop, no Church establishment greater than two or three monasteries. This is grievous, wrong – and militates against all good government."

"So? That is true. But what . . ."

"Cumbria *should* be the responsibility of Thurstan of York. But successive archbishops, and Bishops of Durham, have done nothing. So far as they are concerned, it could be a foreign land. I spoke to Flambard of Durham about it, at the time of my father's disinterring – but nothing has been done. So – am I not entitled to go to Ralph of Canterbury, the senior archbishop, to ask *him* to do something?"

"Perhaps, yes. But how would this serve Alexander?"

"It would serve both of us. I much need the spiritual help of Holy Church in my rule here. Hard and lawless chiefs fear the anathemas of the Church often more than the threats of governors! It is not just a device. John is ever stressing the need for the Church's presence. Well, then! I send John to Canterbury with a message for Ralph, requesting that he consecrate him, John himself, a bishop here! With responsibility for Cumbria and Strathclyde both – since I can get no help from York. Then, consecrated, I appoint him Bishop of Strathclyde – or some such title. He becomes a bishop in Scotland. He then could consecrate another – the Bishops of St. Andrews or Dunkeld!"

"Save us, David – what a head you have on you! But yes, it could be so, if the Archbishop of Canterbury would do it."

"Why not? I am entitled to ask it, as viceroy. None can deny the need. Nor the neglect. And John would make an excellent bishop, able, of good blood and better-learned than many. I could ask Henry to aid in this. For the benefit of his province of Cumbria. I say that Ralph could scarce refuse."

"And afterwards? When you make him a bishop of Scotland?"

"Then it would be too late to object! He would be consecrated – and could consecrate in turn. Lay on hands. Once

made, a bishop cannot be unmade – save by Papal excommunication, I think. And John would do good work for Holy Church
here. There would be no complaints on that score, I swear."

"You may be right. Indeed, it all sounds well-founded. Now
– forget it all, my love. Come back to sleep . . ."

The next day, David thrashed the thing out with Brother
John the Benedictine, his former tutor – who, after initial alarm
at finding himself chosen for the role of bishop, and of a diocese
one-fifth the size of England, grew intrigued by the challenge
and by the mechanics of the case, and certainly did not question
the need. Two points arose from their discussion; it must be
stipulated from the first that any such Canterbury ordination
did not imply spiritual hegemony over any part of Scotland, as
was York's claim; secondly, that the bishopric to which John
should be appointed must be left vague as to title and territorial
designation, or it would be difficult to change later. Bishop *in*
Cumbria and Strathclyde would serve meantime. The entire
area was too vast for any one diocese – all must recognise that.
Yet Cumbria alone, or any other *English* designation, would not
do.

David went to write his letters to Henry and Ralph, and John
to prepare for his unexpected journey to London.

Whilst they awaited the outcome of this move, and still no
Viking invasion materialised, allowing some proportion of the
men standing to arms to go off and ingather the harvest, a more
personal problem struck David's household. Hugo de Morville
arrived back from Normandy bringing with him only Waltheof
and young Matilda. Simon, the elder boy had not wanted to
come, and Count Stephen d'Aumale had actually encouraged
him in his refusal, saying that he, a young Norman with a great
future, was much better in Normandy, learning to be a good
knight, than up amongst the barbarians of the English-Scottish
border. He refused to let him be brought away. Hugo had a
notion that there was more to this than met the eye. As future
Earl of Northampton and to be very rich, young Simon might
one day be a useful prize, almost a hostage for an ambitious
man.

Matilda, delighted to have her two younger children back,
was much upset by this of her first-born, both his lack of desire
to return to her, and the suggestion that he might be used in
some game of her uncle. She and David wrote another letter to
Henry, requesting him to intervene, as kin of Stephen
d'Aumale, and possibly pressing his brother Robert, Duke of
Normandy, to bring the Count to order.

In mid-September Fergus transmitted the news that his cousin Somerled of Coll declared that the Norsemen menace was overpast. The Jarl Ivar's fleet had sailed through the Hebridean sea eastwards, laden down with booty, on its way back to Norway. Honest men could now go about their proper business again, of harvesting, peat-cutting and pleasuring their wives.

After an absence of a month, John returned to Caer-luel a fully fledged and mitred bishop. There had been no least difficulty. King Henry had made his endorsement of the need for spiritual advancement in Cumbria and his lack of confidence in the York archdiocese. Ralph had agreed that something had to be done – and obviously was not displeased to be in a position to emphasise his displeasure towards Thurstan. The question of title, which might have proved a serious stumbling-block, provided no difficulty in fact, the Archbishop acceding that Cumbria and Strathclyde was far too large an area to be designated one diocese, and content that John should have something in the nature of a roving episcopal commission, title unspecified. So all was well, and he was Bishop in Cumbria and Strathclyde.

David was perhaps more elated than was suitable on purely spiritual grounds – although happy on that score also. He had thought considerably on the matter meantime, and had come to the conclusion that the title of the new bishopric ought to be Glasgow. The only traditional diocesan names in the entire area from Lune to Clyde were Whithorn, or Candida Casa, and Glasgow; and almost certainly archiepiscopal eyebrows would be less likely to rise, in the circumstances, over a traditional see name than one newly forged. For their purposes, it had to be in Scotland proper, and Glasgow was more unassailably so than Whithorn in Galloway, which had once been a small kingdom on its own. Also, its resounding connections with the Blessed Kentigern, patron saint of all Cumbria, was notable and worth emphasising at this juncture – even though there had not been a Bishop of Glasgow for long. Moreover, there had been pressure from York, during MacBeth's reign, to revive the diocese of Whithorn – under York of course – so that dog would best be left asleep. Early Bishops of Glasgow had claimed that their diocese reached as far south as even Stainmore in Yorkshire – so such title would be hard to refute by the traditionalists. Glasgow let it be, then. Not that David suggested that John should take up his abode, save nominally, so far north as the Clyde; Caer-luel would serve as episcopal centre very well, meantime.

David sent a message to Alexander thereafter, informing that he now possessed a Scottish bishop, duly consecrated, who could consecrate in turn. That problem was solved. The next moves were up to the King of Scots.

15

As IT TURNED out, one of the Bishop John's first significant episcopal acts was to consecrate Prior Ralph as the Abbot of the new Abbey of Saints Mary and John of Shiel Kirk, the first Roman Church abbey in Scotland, in the spring of 1116. The establishment at the confluence of Ettrick and Yarrow had been functioning as a monastery in some measure for many months of course, and all the subsidiary buildings were finished – or at least in use – by the previous autumn, and Ralph was ready for the grand opening to take place then. But David had been called urgently away to Huntingdon, where the earldom's affairs were suffering some inevitable neglect in the circumstances and where, besides, he had to take Matilda and the children for their winter stay, as arranged. But by the Feast of St. John the Evangelist, in early May, the family were back in the North – Matilda vowing that she was not going to endure another months-long separation of that sort – and they could all attend the auspicious occasion, her husband and Ralph both agreeing that it was unthinkable that the celebration should be held lacking the Countess's presence, whose treasure and support had made it all possible.

So a great company assembled in that fair valley, from far and near, to signalise the achievement, with the abbey precincts temporarily looking more like a tented armed camp. Taking a leaf out of Henry's book, David saw this event as an opportunity of indicating to all and sundry that the achievements of peace and patience, artistry and industry, with sheer faith and goodness, could be every bit as exciting, colourful and rewarding as deeds of arms and martial valour – a lesson admittedly difficult to drive home to the Normans in especial. So all was stage-managed to the best of his ability, every opportunity for display and flourish utilised, no expense spared. All the local lords and chieftains were present, most of his Norman lieutenants, and large numbers of the people, considering the under-populated nature of the terrain.

The church was by no means finished yet, to be sure; that would take years of devoted work. But roofless as it was, the walls were sufficiently complete to have the impressive consecration service held within, with the May weather fortunately kind. The bare stone was decorated with evergreen boughs and spring flowers and blossom, and the Caer-luel party had brought fine hangings and tapestries. The Tironensian Order tended to eschew all pomp and display; but Prior Ralph accepted that this day was an exception.

David was deliberately playing the viceroy and heir to the Scots throne, dressed in his finest, with Matilda looking magnificent, and attended, for the occasion, by a train of ladies led by Beatrix de Beauchamp.

Bishop John, in mitre and splendid vestments, conducted the service, assisted by David's new chaplain, Alwin, a Saxon Augustinian canon found for him by Queen Maud from the Priory of Merton, south of London, in which she was interested. Not only so, but adding lustre and recognition to the scene was another Saxon prelate, a colleague and friend of Alwin, the quite renowned young Abbot Ailred of Rosedale, in Yorkshire, who was risking almost certain censure from his archbishop by attending and taking part in this establishing of a new abbey outwith his authority.

The ceremony commenced out-of-doors, with the Bishop drawing a chalice of water from the holy well of St. Mungo – David's suggestion this, to link up with the ancient Celtic missionaries who had first established Christian worship here – blessing it before them all and then going in procession, accompanied by choristers and instrumentalists, to sprinkle drops of the holy water in the corners and lintels of all the monastic buildings, intoning a blessing at each construction, bakehouse, dairy, tannery, mill, dormitories, refectory and so on. Finally they came to the uncompleted church, taking longer over this, the various points of the masonry where the water was to be sprinkled being marked, for crosses to be carved thereon in due course. Thus, the edifice itself consecrated, all who could get inside moved in, to see the high altar dedicated in its turn.

Then after the altar, the officiating clergy turned to wait, while Prior Ralph and his original dozen colleagues from Pennant-Bachwy, plus some new adherents, paced in through

196

the throng, to fine singing. Advancing to the altar-steps Ralph knelt, and Bishop John laid hands on him, to bless and declare him Abbot of this new Abbey of Saints Mary and John the Evangelist, and to pray God's divine aid and guidance in the furtherance of this His work in this place. He raised him to his feet.

Abbot Ailred stepped forward and presented the new prelate with his crozier or abbatial staff, whilst singers and players burst forth in praise and thanksgiving.

So, ceremonial over, all filed out, to do justice to the ample cold provision and ale set out on trestles by the riverside, again to the sound of music.

It was upon this pleasant scene of peace and easement that disharmony erupted in the shape of two weary messengers from Ersildoune, sent by Cospatrick's steward there, that earl being here amongst the guests. They announced that a major raid of Northumbrians was in progress, more than any mere raid in fact, for they had been reported as crossing the march at three points simultaneously – more, perhaps, but that was all that they had heard of at Ersildoune – so that it looked more like a planned invasion. The object was not evident as yet, nor were the full numbers involved. But clearly it was a serious matter.

David wasted no time. Calling for all his colleagues and lieutenants to attend on him in the refectory, he there had the messengers repeat their story, more slowly and coherently. They revealed that the Northumbrian forces had crossed into Scotland, on the west by the ancient Roman road of Dere Street, from Redesdale, to Jed Water and to cross Teviot at Nisbet, a few miles upstream of Rook's Burgh. Centrally, they had come, also from Redesdale, down Kale Water to Morebattle, to ford Tweed at Sprouston. And their third probe had come up the age-old invasion route through the Till valley, six or seven miles further east, to cross Tweed at Coldstream and Wark.

"Who leads?" David demanded.

"We do not know, lord. There are many banners."

"What can be their aim? This is no cattle-reiving venture – not in such strength and style. Men of note are behind this. Have we such unfriends in Northumbria? Another of Henry's earldoms?"

None answered that, but de Soulis, who was responsible for Liddesdale and the eastern Cheviot passes involved, exclaimed that it must have been carefull planned indeed, to coincide with this celebration – for they would never have got past him otherwise. All the North knew that the Earl David's assistants and officers would be congregated here today, would not be in their own places, ready with their men. It had been well thought out. There was no hiding the criticism implied there, with a viceroy who placed more importance on abbey-building and the like than on military virtues.

David did not argue. He turned to Cospatrick. "You know this part of the march better than any, my lord. What think you could be the reason?"

"God knows!" the Earl said. "Small men's raiding is easily understood – cattle, gear, women! But this is different. Who is it against? Myself and my earldom? Or you, my lord? If we knew who led, we might be wiser."

"Three different forces means many men. None could move such large numbers northwards without the knowledge and permission of Ivo de Vesci, who presently acts Earl of Northumbria. Why should de Vesci countenance this? Against me? Or against you, either?"

"Perhaps . . . perhaps it is against us both, David. For *I* claim Northumbria, of which my father was once earl. And does not your lady-wife also claim it, in right of *her* father Waltheof son of Siward, whom the Conqueror used to displace my father? De Vesci now rules Northumbria, in Henry's name. He may think to warn us off, both . . ."

"King Henry it is who decides who will be Earl of Northumbria – not de Vesci, nor you, nor me!"

"Will Henry fight for your claim, or mine? I think not. This is Scotland, a long way from London or Winchester. What happens here will concern him little. It is not only the Norman barons on the Welsh marches who may draw sword to carve their own sway."

"We shall see. But – enough of talk. We must move, and fast. Unfortunately our armed strength is far from us here, dispersed. I cannot bring up any part of my Cumbrian force into the Tweed valley in less than four days. The same applies to my Lord Fergus and most others. Only de Soulis and de Brus can put men in that field fairly quickly – and you, my lord of Dunbar. But to wait even for these to be mustered and brought, is unthinkable. By then these invaders could have overrun Tweeddale and the Merse, Lauderdale and Teviotdale. Or wherever they aim. So we must move my friends – ourselves! Down Tweed. Here we are but some score of miles from Rook's Burgh. Well mounted, we can be there before evening. We are not many – but we are strong in trained knights. We will be

198

poor creatures if we cannot give these Northumbrians pause, one way or another, until our own forces come up."

There were growls of agreement from almost all.

"So, de Soulis and de Brus – off with you. Bring your men, so many as you can quickly muster, by the swiftest route to Lower Tweedale. That will be down Teviot and Jed. I shall seek to keep you informed, by courier. The rest, my friends, to horse. Clad as we are! Time only to say a brief farewell to our women. Every able man to ride – the women to bide here at the abbey meantime. We shall plan it as we ride . . ."

In haste and disorder, then, the great celebration broke up. In fact, some three hundred men prepared to ride off, for the lords and chieftains and Norman knights had all brought small mounted escorts with them; also some of the local herders and foresters were possessed of garrons, and well able to bear arms. Nevertheless they made up a rather extraordinary company with almost as many officers as men and anything but a unified force, their finery of apparel and lack of armour and chain-mail notable.

David's parting with Matilda gave him cause to think. Although she did not seek to dissuade nor delay him, she did venture a warning note.

"My dear – have you considered well? That there may be more to this than appears? Henry. If this de Vesci it is who leads, or at least permits, he may be acting not *against* Henry's wishes and interests but at Henry's instigation. Have you thought of this?"

"Henry would never desire this armed invasion. What could it serve him?"

"Do not be so sure. Henry has a devious mind. It could be his way of warning you off any claim to the Northumbrian earldom, through myself. Warning off Cospatrick likewise. At no cost to himself, not seeming to be involved, using de Vesci as tool. I am sure that Henry does not intend that my claim to Northumbria should be granted. Not that I care for it – but it could benefit you. He may reckon that you have ambitions there. Especially as the Kings of Scots have long considered it as truly part of their realm – and now you are heir to Scotland. He may see it as a danger. So would have you to perceive that it would be . . . difficult. Encourages de Vesci."

"I do not believe that. If he thinks that way, could he not tell me so?"

"That would not be Henry's way. This may well be."

So David rode off thoughtfully. They went, in fact, not down

199

Tweedside, north-eastwards as he had intended, but up into the hills due eastwards of Shiel Kirk, on the advice of locals, who pointed out that they could cut a great corner by so doing, even though the terrain was more difficult. By climbing over the high common lands by Midlem to the Ale Water, they could reach Teviot at Ancrum and so save four or five miles. Thereafter it was only some six more miles to the joining of Teviot and Tweed at Rook's Burgh.

He had intended to plan as he rode, but it was difficult to do so without any real knowledge of the strengths, positions and objectives of the invaders. Only generalities could be envisaged. Clearly they must rely upon their wits rather than on armed strength. Surprise must be exploited to the utmost, for their presence could hardly be expected so soon. Authority too ought to be brought into play, if at all possible. Men were conditioned, to some extent, to respect authority – and he, David, was the viceroy of both kings. Even if Henry was in any degree behind this adventure, he could not be present and so in no position to over-rule his representative's voice.

They followed the Ale Water down into Teviotdale, to reach Ancrum in late afternoon. Here was the rath of one of Cospatrick's vassals, Colbain mac Comgall, who was able to inform them that the raiders – or some of them – had crossed Teviot from the south that morning about three miles downstream and then turned eastwards, not coming in this direction. He had men out shadowing them, but no further word so far. So whatever the enemy's objective, it did not appear to be Teviotdale and its subsidiary valleys.

They moved on, taking Colbain of Ancrum with them, plus about a score of his men, all additions welcome. They approached Nisbet ford warily, in case the Northumbrians should have left the crossing guarded, the more so as they saw smoke rising from the area of the nearby mill. But scouts reported no enemy presence, no presence at all save for a maddened, raped woman and sundry dead bodies, the mill and its cothouses burned down.

The woman, only part-clothed, fled screaming into scrub woodland at sight of them; and there was nothing to be done for Nisbet Mill. David steeled himself, and they rode on leaving behind this all-too-normal detritus of war.

As they moved on eastwards they passed other similar evidences that they were following the tracks of the raiders, and David had to take himself very much in hand, reminding himself that he was here for the larger purpose of ridding the

200

land of the invaders, not for comforting and assisting the victims. They were heading up into an ever-narrowing tongue of land between Teviot and Tweed, which would come to a point at the confluence, where his new castle of Rook's Burgh was being built. Such advance could be dangerous, David did not have to be told, for they could be trapped between the rivers. They maintained scouts ahead and to the flanks, of course. The question as to where the enemy were heading became ever more vital, and where their other two forces might be. Near the confluence, Tweed took on a somewhat different character as it entered the Merse, the lowland plain which stretched for nearly twenty-five miles due eastwards to the river's mouth at Berwick, through an ever-widening and open vale – where, according to the reports, the invaders had crossed at two points. In the other direction, the great river coiled its way through closer country, presently to turn almost due northwards, to pass the mouth of Lauderdale and circle the tall peaks of the Eildon Hills. Cospatrick was growing ever more anxious about his castle and town of Ersildoune, where were his wife and family.

David decided, although it would weaken his little force, that they should part company meantime. By striking due northwards from their present position on Nisbet Moor, Cospatrick could utilise one of the very few crossings possible on this stretch of Tweed, at Rutherford, and so be able to reach Ersildoune, some seven miles north, cross-country by Bemersyde, in about an hour. More than fifty men, including Colbain's people, could not be spared; but at least Cospatrick would be able to send back news as to any enemy presence on that side of Tweed. Also, he could raise as much as possible of his armed strength in Lauderdale, and if he found all well at Ersildoune, come back to aid in the situation here.

So they split up. David's company had not gone more than a mile further, eastwards, when his scouts brought back one of Colbain's people who had been sent earlier to shadow the invaders, and whom they had picked up returning. This man reported that the Northumbrians who had crossed at Nisbet had halted some three miles ahead, a bare mile this side of the joining of Teviot with Tweed, where the neck of land had narrowed to less than half-a-mile. There they had taken up a defensive position across the peninsula, backs to the township of Rook's Burgh, facing this way, making use of burn-channels, outcropping rock and the like to form a protective line.

"Halted? Facing *this* way? Defensive?" David exclaimed. "Why? To what end? They must have learned that we come.

201

But – how could they? If they had left scouts behind to watch their rear, *our* scouts would surely have seen them . . ."

"I know not, lord," the Ancrum man said. "But there they wait."

"How many?"

"Many. More than you, lord. Who can tell? Six hundred, perhaps, Seven. I could not see them all."

"And the town? Of Rook's Burgh. Are they occupying that? Have they sacked it?"

"I know not. But they must hold it, yes."

"I do not understand this. Somehow they must have learned of our approach. But – if they so outnumber us, why wait in a defensive position? Why not turn and attack us?"

"Does it matter why, David?" Fergus of Galloway asked. "The fact is, they wait for *us* to attack. So they must fear us. So be it – let us do so! If they are stretched across a half-mile neck, they must make a fairly thin front. Even a thousand men would not look very many over half-a-mile. With our charging cavalry we can break through such line, and then turn and roll them up."

There were cries of agreement, especially from the Normans, for whom such tactics were basic.

"Perhaps, Sweenie – but first we must *see* the situation. There are other invading forces than this one, remember." David turned to the Ancrum man again. "Are there any of the enemy nearer? This side of their line?"

"I think not. I saw none. Two more of my lord Colbain's men are forward there, watching."

"Then we shall go look. Fergus, Hugo, Hervey – come with me. Richard – bring you the company on, more slowly. Watchful. Be ready for action. You, friend," he said to the local man. "Is there a ford across Teviot between here and Rook's Burgh? We must watch our flank."

"Yes, lord – below Heiton. Heiton Mill ford. Yonder, a mile." He pointed south-eastwards.

"Richard d'Avranches – send a small patrol to inspect that ford. To cross and discover if there is any enemy presence on that side of Teviot. We have to know."

With the Ancrum man as guide, David's little group rode forward, at speed.

The land soon began to fall gently but steadily before them, the moorland giving way to scattered open wood and rough pasture, the trees providing ample cover – although this could cut both ways. Smoke rose high and murky ahead in a number of places in the middle and farther distance, no doubt burning, harried farmeries and hamlets. The township of Rook's Burgh itself was not actually visible, because of the trees, it being on still lower ground near the confluence; but no great smokes billowed there, so presumably it had so far escaped devastation.

Two miles or so they rode, taking advantage of the shelter of the woodland and saw only cattle and sheep, with now the rivers' troughs on either side becoming ever more evident, the feeling of enclosure manifest. Presently they came to the edge of the cover, only the open spaces of Rook's Burgh common ahead. And there they found the two other Ancrum men waiting, watching, hidden behind scrub and bush.

One of these watchers pointed, unspeaking.

Some six hundred yards out there the line of the enemy was clear to be seen, although scarcely as a recognisable line or front, more as groups and parties of men stretching away on either hand, with gaps between, occasioned by undulations in the ground, outcrops of rocks, clumps of whin-bushes and the like. Men came and went, without any attempt at hiding. Numbers were very difficult to calculate, but what was not difficult to recognise was the confidence, the assurance that all was well, with camp-fires sending up their slender blue columns into the evening air, so very different from the dense brown clouds from burning thatch. Also it was clear that however unconcerned these Northumbrians were, they were most certainly facing this direction, westwards, as positioned.

Significant as all this was, David's glance lifted nevertheless beyond, to where, on the rocky spine which formed the very tip of the peninsula, the new castle was being built. Standing considerably higher than the township, it was quite visible from his stance, under one mile away. And although it was too far to distinguish much in the way of detail, it was entirely evident what was going on there. Large numbers of men were at work on the great building – but work of destruction. The masonry was being smashed and cast down, containing walls levelled, ramparts undermined, scaffolding-poles felled and burned, dressed stones hurled down into the rivers. David's new bastion of the East March was in process of demolition.

He stared, lips tight, fists clenched, but said no word.

Hugo coughed. "Ill work" he said. "Much toil, much thought, brought to naught. There is spleen there! Who would do that, David? And why?"

"Someone who mislikes you!" Fergus jerked. "But – what of

it? That is only stone and lime. These here, before us, are flesh and blood! Time that we showed them whose land this is!"

"Stone and lime . . . !" David echoed. "There is hatred behind this, I think. So be it." He turned his eyes back to the foreground. "This . . . this is passing strange. These men. They face us, backs to that destruction. Yet they look as though they feared nothing, no attack, knew nothing of our near presence. It scarcely makes sense . . ."

Fergus's mind dwelt on other aspects of the situation. He jabbed a pointing finger eastwards. "If we drove through there, and there – yonder between those whins. There would be no stopping us. And there, the rocky slope up to that scarp. They could by no means hold that line against cavalry."

"They would reform behind us," Hervey said.

"Even so, we could wheel and break them up. Three places, four, along this line, and we would have them. Their defence would serve against foot, never against trained cavalry."

"Which it seems, they do not look for. Let us ride further along, northwards," David said. "Look for other points to breach. So that our people may charge straight for their objectives, with no milling here. That the enemy gain no warning . . ."

Still in the cover of the trees, they turned back a little way and then trotted some distance northwards, towards Tweed. Their guide told them that the land there eventually dropped sheer into the greater river in quite high cliffs. Either side driven in that direction would be trapped.

Satisfied that they knew the terrain sufficiently, they cantered back towards the Viscount's main party.

D'Avranches had two fresh items of news for David. Messengers had arrived back from the Earl Cospatrick. He sent word that no enemy appeared to have proceeded up Tweed as far as the area opposite Rutherford – local folk had seen no sign of invaders. So, the urgency off him as far as Ersildoune was concerned, he had turned eastwards, down river, for some way, scouts out. They had found a force of Northumbrians, encamped, settled for the night evidently, and facing westwards, some two miles down, in a defensive position near the Trows, where the Tweed narrowed and ran through a rocky gorge. Numbers were uncertain but there were some hundreds. The other tidings were from the patrol sent down to the Teviot ford at Heiton. These had found the ford unmanned, but at the village above, on the far side, they had learned that a large number of the invaders were massed about a mile further east, at a place where a tributary burn entered Teviot amidst bog, difficult of passage. They had been there for some hours.

David smashed down his fist on his saddle-bow. "You see it?" he exclaimed. "You hear? It can only be . . . All these enemy forces at the same ploy. All in position, settled, facing westwards, waiting. No doubt there are others, at the other side of Rook's Burgh, facing eastwards. Or north. They are placed for one purpose – to protect the men who are pulling down my new castle! That is the objective. Whoever leads them, or sent them, wants no castle at Rook's Burgh. It is all to wreck that."

Considering it, none could disagree.

"Who would do this . . . ?" Hugo was demanding, when Fergus interrupted.

"There is one way to find out! Attack! At once, before they learn of our presence. This line, in front. We have seen their positions and weakness. We can cut through them like a dirk – like four dirks! Then round on them."

"Yes," David nodded. "It must be that, now. We have here some two hundred and seventy men. Four horsed wedges of fifty each. The others as reserve. The Norman knights, trained in this, to be the spearheads of each wedge. There is good cover until less than half-a-mile. There, at a blast of my horn, we charge, together. Each wedge perhaps two hundred yards apart. Once through, each to split into two, and turning, ride down on the enemy from behind. Is it understood?"

There were no questions.

"The reserve will go to the aid where most needed. But, first – Cospatrick's couriers. Go you back to the Earl, and tell him what we do. Tell him to ride forward with his party, openly, to just before the enemy on that side. At this place you spoke of – aye, the Trows. Make a show of marshalling and the like, in front of them. No need to fight. Only to keep them occupied, so that they do not come to the aid of the men at the castle. You have it? Then off with you . . ."

Without further delay the five parties formed up, with only minor dispute as to who should lead which. Then, in file as yet, they trotted forward behind David, to take best advantage of the available cover, until at length they came to the last of the trees. There, they spread out, the four wedges in line abreast, David placing them. Despite the urge to lead one of the groups himself, he remained with the reserve, in the centre. There appeared to be no change in the situation ahead.

He blew his horn.

The four teams burst from the shelter of the woodland almost simultaneously and spurred swiftly into a full gallop, to thunder across the rough pasture in tight arrowhead formations, the foremost and outer riders swinging drawn swords and maces, the inner men ready to replace them. Seldom can any cavalry wedge have hurled themselves upon an enemy dressed in such unarmoured finery.

It was almost too easy, with the Northumbrians totally unprepared, indeed with most of them clustered around camp-fires eating their evening meal of stolen beef. Six hundred yards are quickly covered by galloping horses, so that they had not time to be given orders or to form up effectively in any defensive posture. Many rushed for their due positions, but as many did not, the sight of sword-wielding horsemen hurtling down upon them sufficiently dissuasive.

All four wedges crashed through that only token line almost without pause or major hindrance, the whin-bushes and rocks, which were to have aided them, tending to offer the greater obstruction. David perceived no need to go to the help of any. The swinging round and dividing process, thereafter, was rather less effectively executed, with some going further than others, and the breaking-up apt to degenerate into a free-for-all. But since the enemy themselves were in chaos, and milling about without any recognisable line anywhere, it could have been that the individual horsemen, slashing and beating, wheeling and caracoling where they would, actually proved to be the best offensive tactic.

David and the reserve rode in on a shambles – but a shambles in which the blood spilled and the disaster was almost all on one side. One or two of the horses were hamstrung or had their bellies dirked open, and a few riders fell or were slashed. But compared with the Northumbrian casualties theirs were negligible.

Those of the invaders who could, began to stream away eastwards, for the township of Rook's Burgh.

David blew his horn again, waving all his people in on himself, to halt the carnage and form up again into troops, for a descent upon the village before there could be any sort of defensive stand made there.

Leaving the ravaged battleground, most of the force – not all, for many of the northern wedge had gone chasing after Northumbrians fleeing towards the Tweedside cliffs – went off at a canter, in some sort of order behind their leaders, over-running many of the refugees on their way to Rook's Burgh.

The township was not very large, although it had doubled in size with the advent of David's castle-builders, an old village, successor to that of the Pictish fort, still mainly contained within the crumbling earthen walls of its one-time stockade. But there was no attempt to man those green ramparts in the face of the pounding horsemen. Only panic prevailed, the fleeing men from the broken line, those camping there already and the frightened local folk, all in cowering turmoil.

Clearly nothing demanded their immediate attention here, David pointed upwards to the castle-site towering above.

To reach it, on its spine of rock, there was only the one route – which was a great part of its strength, of course. They had to go round to the west end of the spine, where it was less steep, and a corkscrewing track led up to the summit. But even here, the natural defences did not cease, for the spine was gapped and cut across by a quite deep cleft, which had to be crossed. David planned to dam this at each end and fill it with water, the moat thus formed to have a drawbridge as the only access. Meantime a fixed timber bridge crossed it, however.

The site could have been defended against them, had the bridge been cast down. But nothing of the sort was attempted. The people up here were not there to fight, only demolish – and the bridge would be the last item to be demolished. They all must have seen much of what transpired on the lower ground, but no plan of action had eventuated. Men watched, stared and waited. Some moved as far away from the advancing horsemen as they could get. Some even continued with their work of destruction as though nothing of what went on had anything to do with them. Some, however, sought to flee by trying to scramble down the steep rocky sides of the spine.

David and his people swept into the castle area – and none there were left in any doubt as to the newcomers' feelings about the demolitions.

While his riders drove the folk out, David and some of his lieutenants climbed to the highest part of what was left of the castle, to peer eastwards. The light was now fading and the more distant prospects towards the Merse were hidden in the gathering dusk. But entirely clear to be seen, something over a mile away down Tweedside, were the gleam of camp-fires amongst woodland.

"More work to do!" David declared. "Come, before they are warned."

So, leaving the castle, they rode down to the Calchou ford, a little way to the north but east of the cliffs, and splashed across.

They headed quietly thereafter down the haughland towards those gleaming flickering fires.

This time they did not trouble to form wedges, but in line abreast, in three waves, they charged down upon the camp area – where most evidently they were not expected, there seeming to be little communication between the various groupings of the invading force. Again it was something of a massacre, with no defence possible or attempted. Bewildered men, eating, lounging or sleeping, were struck down right and left, or herded like sheep to be slaughtered or driven down into the river to drown; until, sickened, David blew his horn to order a halt it all, and to cease from chasing the many fugitives who fled into the shadowy woodland.

A prisoner was brought to him, wounded, a heavy, bulky man of the better sort, wearing a somewhat stained surcoat decorated with a gold cross on blue, the first seeming leader captured alive so far. David looked down at him thoughtfully.

"That device you wear, sir, I have seen before. Who are you? What do you here? And in whose service?" he demanded.

"I am Oslac of Felkington, my lord. Steward at Norham for my lord Bishop of Durham. Have mercy, lord . . ."

"Ha – Durham! Flambard! Dear Lord – Flambard! I had not thought of Flambard of Durham. You are here on the Bishop's orders?"

"Yes. I but obey . . ."

"And the others? These other companies? Who sent them?"

"These are from Hexham, lord. And Warkworth. And Redesmouth. And Corbridge. And the Islands. My lord Bishop's lands and manors. Most, that is. Some are from otherwhere . . ."

"So-o-o! This is Flambard's work. Why, man – why"

"Who knows, lord? The great ones do not tell such as myself. We were but told to go and pull down this great new castle a-building here . . ."

"*My* castle. In Scotland. What has your bishop to do with my Rook's Burgh? That his servants should cross into Scotland, to harry and kill?"

"I know not, my good lord. We but obey . . ."

"Fool – if you think that *I* am fool enough to believe that you know so little! You and your friends have tongues in your heads, have you not? Even if Bishop Flambard told you little, you must have talked of this. If you look for any mercy from me, Master Steward, you will tell me . . ."

"*I* can make this clerk's get find his tongue, never fear!" Fergus declared. "Give him to me!"

"No, lord – no!" the man cried. "We talked, yes – but know nothing for certain. Some say that the lord Bishop sees this new castle as threat against his manors at Norham and Cornhill. It is built just across from his lands. Some say that he is wrath that moneys have not been paid to him from lands in the Merse, lands which are his. In Coldingham, is it? Some say that since the Scots are in rebellion against Holy Church, they must be shown their error. *I* do not say that, lord . . ."

"Coldingham, eh?" David glanced over at Hugo and Hervey. "That old story! I wonder . . . ?"

They rode back to Rook's Burgh, their prisoners herded along behind. It was now almost as dark as a May night ever is in Scotland, and there was no point in any pursuit for further activities. Anyway, all were tired and hungry. So they settled for the night at Rook's Burgh, where at least there was plenty of stolen beef and meal. David was careful to set out sentries. Also to send a party of about one hundred under Fergus, to see how Cospatrick was faring at the Trows area; but these returned in only a short time, with that earl himself, who announced that the enemy there had melted away. Presumably they had received word of the débâcle at Rook's Burgh – some of the fugitives may have reached them. Anyway, they had gone, slipped away into the dusk. Cospatrick had sent a few men after them, to keep track of their whereabouts, before himself coming on here, without having struck a blow.

There was some discussion, over meat, as to what should be done now. A few enthusiasts were for setting out in pursuit of the fleeing invaders, darkness notwithstanding. More advised waiting for the morning light. Some even suggested a retaliatory raid into Northumbria – Norham for instance. But David saw all such as profitless. The Northumbrians would not rally now, and were therefore no further threat. What would it serve to kill and wound a few more? Let them trickle, defeated, back to Flambard, their lesson learned. And it was certainly not for King Henry's Viceroy of Cumbria to go raiding into King Henry's earldom of Northumbria. Even if Ivo de Vesci must have known about this venture and had not stopped it, there were better ways of dealing with the matter than by unlawful counter-invasion. Cospatrick's assertion that such limitations did not apply to him, an earl of Scotland whose lands had been invaded, met with no encouragement.

David sent off two of Colbain's men, who knew the land well, even by night, to try to intercept and turn back the Liddesdale and Annandale forces under de Soulis and de Brus, which presumably should be on the move north-eastwards.

Then he might sleep.

In the morning he inspected the castle. A grievous amount of damage had been done, the labours of months nullified. However, there was nothing that could not be restored and made good. More men must be employed, that was all, the work speeded up; even one or two improvements to the original design incorporated.

They sent the Northumbrian prisoners home, on their own, with their wounded but minus their arms and equipment – and of course, booty; they took leave of Cospatrick, who was at last making for Ersildoune; and leaving the quarrymen and masons, the wood-cutters and carpenters, the scaffolders and carvers and the crushers of shells for mortar, all working harder than they had ever worked before, the armed cavalcade turned horses' heads westwards to cross the Forest to Shiel Kirk, finery now somewhat jaded, but feeling on the whole satisfied.

As he rode, David had ample time to think about Flambard. And Ivo de Vesci. And Archbishop Thurstan. And Henry Beauclerc indeed. And, for that matter, his brother Alexander. And to wonder.

16

THE DISADVANTAGE OF being viceroy to two monarchs at the same time was demonstrated the following spring, when David received almost simultaneous summons to attend on both kings, for purposes unspecified. These came at an inconvenient moment, too, for Matilda was expecting their second child within a week or so – she saying that since her child-bearing period was unlikely to last for many more years, they should not delay but have what they could while they could.

David did not really require to debate at any length on his decision as to priorities. He would go to see Alexander first and be back in only four or five days, hopefully, before the birth; and go south when that was safely over. So he sent off the English royal courier to tell Henry at London that he would come on in a few days time, after his wife's delivery — since, with no reason stated, it was to be assumed that there was no great urgency in the summons. He did not add that his first duty must be to his own High King and brother.

With Matilda weary but well, and assuring him that all was in order and that she was not in the least concerned over the birth of her fifth child, he left on his journey northwards, by Annandale and Upper Clydesdale, over the North Lanark moors to Strathkelvin, and so across the Kilsyth Hills to the Upper Forth and Stirling, with only Hugo and Hervey as companions, completing the one hundred and fifty mile ride in two very hard days.

He was irritated, almost resentful, there to learn that Alexander was at Invergowrie again, on the Angus border. This time he could not afford to wait, so they set off again at dawn next morning to ride the further fifty miles across Fothrif and Fife and to ferry over wide Tay at Balmerino. They reached the rath of Invergowrie, at the eastern end of its carse, in the early afternoon – only to find that the King was off on a salmon-spearing expedition to the River Isla, some dozen miles away. Changing horses once more, and in no very kindly frame of mind, they went on northwards.

They found Alexander, at length, stripped to the waist despite a chill easterly wind, splashing about in only comparative shallows of a stretch of the Isla in the Meigle area. He was wielding a three-pronged leister or salmon-spear, while the fish were driven up to him by a party of wading men who spanned the river below and beat the water, shouting and hallooing, for all the world like any boar or game drive in forest. Two personable young females watched and skirled laughter.

When the King perceived his visitors, he waved his spear, but went on with his energetic sport. David and his friends had never before seen this practised. It looked easy enough, although clearly it was not, for Alexander achieved only two spearings in the fifteen or so minutes that they had to watch, despite the large number of tries and plentiful supply of targets. No doubt the refraction effects of the water, as well as the lightning-swift movement of the salmon accounted for the high proportion of failures; also, of course, the unsteady stance of the would-be spearer on the slippery stones of the stream-bed under two or three feet of rushing river – proved when the King suddenly sat down with a great swash, at one miss, to the vast

211

amusement of the ladies and the monarch's uninhibited cursing. Even when a hit was achieved, success was far from certain, for a powerful fish weighing many pounds could take a lot of holding, could pull a man over if his feet were not well-planted, or could wriggle itself free even though the spear-point were barbed. All these aspects of the business were amply demonstrated before, the beaters drawing close and the supply of salmon tailing off meantime, Alexander tossed his leister ashore beside some half-a-dozen fine if scarred fish, and clambered out, dripping and grinning, his lean, hard body all rippling muscle.

"Good sport, Davie – but difficult, taxing," he cried. "Are you for trying it? We can find you a fresh beat further upstream."

"Thank you – no. Another time perhaps. I have come far in answer to your summons. Far and fast. At some cost. I did not come to catch fish, Alex!"

"Ha! Do I hear some lack of goodwill in your voice, Brother? Some impatience? Towards your liege lord!"

"It may be that you do, Sire! We looked for you at Stirling. I left Matilda awaiting childbirth, at Caer-luel. And would return to her, at the soonest."

"So that is it. I congratulate you! Instead of being sour, man, you should be rejoiced. I would that *my* wife was presenting me with a child – so long as it *was* mine! These would be glad to do so, I think – but that is scarce the same!" And he gestured towards the young women. "Donna and Echilda. Or, it may be, Echilda and Donna!" The King was struggling wet torso into shirt and doublet.

David bowed stiffly towards the giggling females, clearly no ladies. "I rejoice, yes. But would prefer to be at my wife's side, in this. Had you been at Stirling, as your courier said, we could have been returning to Caer-luel by this."

"Lord, Davie – you fuss like some callow youth! Or as though *you* it was who was to produce the bairn! Your lady will do very well lacking you – better, I swear! Or have you turned midwife, as well as old woman!"

In front of the others, David had to restrain his tongue. "You commanded my presence here for better talk than this, I think, my lord King?" he said.

"To be sure. But – do you wish to discuss the business of the realm here amongst queans and salmons?"

"The sooner I know your royal wishes, the sooner I may return to my wife's side, Sire."

"Oh, do not be so devilish prickly, man! How should I know of this childbirth? You take all to such damnably serious intent!"

"It is no doubt thanks to my serious intent that you have asked me to come, Alex? You want something that I can do for you, I think? Else I never hear from you!"

"M'mm." His brother frowned. "You are heir to this realm, man – and so must bear your share of the burdens. Be thankful that I do not call on you more often. But, yes – I have a task for you, Davie. I desire you to go to Ralph of Canterbury, for me. I cannot leave Scotland, to go myself. You will mind that I asked that he find me a new Bishop of St. Andrews. He has never done so, but has put off . . ."

"I did not know of this. I know that you sought a new bishop to replace Turgot. And I worked to get John consecrated Bishop of Glasgow, so that he in turn might consecrate a bishop for you. If you have never appointed a new man for him to consecrate, then the fault is yours, surely? You were sufficiently concerned, at the time. I went to much trouble . . ."

"No, no. You did well. For Dunkeld, this of Bishop John was excellent. But St. Andrews is different. Whoever sits there has to be King's Bishop. *Ard Episcop.* First of bishops. To outdo the Abbot of Iona, of the Columbans. This is necessary if we are to have the Roman Church supreme, as our mother desired. I have taken the Primacy away from Ethelred. The new Bishop of St. Andrews must be Primate, and speak with the voice of full spiritual authority. You must see this? It will not serve that he should be consecrated by a bishop junior to himself. Your John would seem to all to have the greater authority. The realm needs a Primate appointed by myself but sent and consecrated by the highest authority in Holy Church. I sent to Pope Paschal, but he has done nothing. So, since it must not be York, it has to be Canterbury."

"And the Archbishop does not agree?"

"He neither agrees nor disagrees, only puts off. I have a notion that Henry may be behind it."

"Henry? Why Henry?"

"Henry has not named himself Lord Paramount of Scotland, as did his father and brother. But he would wish to be so, I swear! He has sought to *influence* Scotland, without drawing sword, as no other English king has done, wedding our sister, marrying his daughter to me, making much of you and giving you his niece and Huntingdon. And this of Cumbria. I say that if he could see Scotland as under the *spiritual* rule of England, he would be much pleased."

213

They were walking to the horses, the women being left to trail along behind, ignored.

"If this is so, why should he hold back Canterbury from finding your Primate?"

"Because it is not Canterbury which does, or could, claim any hegemony over Scotland, but York, Davie. If Canterbury will not give me what I want, I may be forced to turn to York. Since there is no other. Do you not see it? Henry is a fox! He prefers to work through others, by hidden ways."

David did not deny that, at least. "What could *I* do, in this?" he asked.

"Go there, and use your famed wits, what else? You are a friend to Henry – much more so than am I, his good-son. Convince him that I will never accept a bishop from York. Tell him that if Canterbury will not aid, me, I must needs go to the Pope. He will not know that the Holy See has already failed me. Say that you will go seek the help of this Bernard of Tiron, or Clairvaux. We raised up this abbey to his Order, so he should be grateful. Play on this – for Bernard is much admired by Pope Paschal, they say. It may serve. But look also for a suitable monk for me to have as Primate. Strong – but not too strong, see you! One who will lead, but not seek to lead *me*! Not as Turgot. There is one I have heard of, at Canterbury. A Saxon, named Eadmer. It had better not be a Norman. This Eadmer was friend and chaplain to the late Anselm. Might have been archbishop himself thereafter, it is said, but the Normans preferred one of their own kind, this Ralph. Eadmer writes a book on the life of Anselm, I am told. A scholar. Seek him out, Davie. Having been passed over for Ralph, he may well be discontented. Might well wish to be a bishop and Primate. And Ralph glad to be rid of him."

"A lot to build on such small foundation!" David said.

"You will go?"

"If you wish it, command it, I must. Is it not so?"

"I would sooner that you went in goodwill, man. This is important to the realm . . ."

As they rode back to Invergowrie, Hugo and Hervey squiring the young women, David felt entitled to raise a related subject, likewise to the weal of the realm of Scotland. "Did you stop payment of the Coldingham Priory rents to Flambard of Durham?" he asked his brother.

"That man is a scoundrel! Behind Thurstan's claims and obduracy."

"No doubt. But we made a bargain with him. I did, in your

name. And you have broken it. To *my* cost. I lost many months' work on my castle of Rook's Burgh. I have had much trouble . . ."

"I heard of that. But what reason have you to believe that was behind the raid?"

"One of the prisoners said as much. One of Flambard's stewards. What did *you* think the reason for it?"

"The good God knows. But if Henry did not order it, I swear that he knew of it! That castle of yours, Davie, is too near to Northumbria for English liking."

"Henry never told me not to build it. Nor to stop building it."

"Would he? That is not Henry's way. I would guard it well hereafter!"

"Never fear. Cospatrick aids me in keeping a strong guard there always. It is necessary, to protect our march. It will soon be finished, already strong enough to withstand ordinary attack, lacking siege-machines."

"When you go see Henry, put it to him!"

"I shall go, Alex – if you will promise to allow the Coldingham payments again. I love Flambard no better than you do, but a bargain is a bargain. It was the price of our father's body being able to lie beside our mother's. Should they not sleep in peace?"

Alexander shrugged. "Very well. But I do not believe that it will save your castle from assault . . ."

At first light in the morning, without benefit of royal farewells, they left for the South.

*　　*　　*

Matilda had had her baby before they got back to Caer-luel. It was a girl, whom she was already calling Claricia. All apparently had gone well, and although she admitted that giving birth was never an easy or enjoyable experience, the mother made light of it all. They would have more children yet.

Listening to David's bedside account of his meeting with Alexander, Matilda declared that it all fell out very conveniently. He had to go to London anyway, whatever Henry wanted him for, and could now go also as his brother's spokesman, always a help where there might be dealing and chaffering involved. This of a Primate for Scotland deserved support. And if Henry and the Archbishop proved obdurate let him indeed cross over to France, to Tiron. Or was it not now Clairvaux, where Bernard ruled? He had always wished to

215

meet the great Bernard had he not? And the Abbot Ralph was ever talking of the need for monks from Tiron, trained men to add to his dozen, now that Shiel Kirk was a full abbey, not just a priory. Indeed, she thought that David should go over to France anyway, whatever the result of his meetings in London. It was an opportunity such as did not often occur. For herself, she would be much taken up with baby care for a month or two, of little use to him.

All of which seemed to make good sense.

The journey to London, over three hundred miles, was accomplished in unseasonably poor weather conditions, with the inevitable consequence of delay from floods, impassable fords and the like, as well as discomfort, so that it took nine days to reach Thames. Only Hervey de Warenne accompanied David, with a small escort, Hugo's wife Beatrix requiring his attendance.

At the great Tower of London, started by the Conqueror, enlarged by Rufus and not yet completed, which Henry was now using as his base, they found the bird had flown once more, the King having gone to his country palace of Woodstock near Oxford. However, the Queen, it seemed, was still in London, at her lodgings in the Abbey of Westminster. Thither they repaired.

David was much upset at sight of his sister. Maud was only in her mid-thirties, younger indeed than Matilda; but she looked almost an old woman, pale, haggard, stooping. Clearly she was ill, but she was dispirited too, although glad to see her brother, pathetically so.

"What is wrong, lass?" he demanded. She felt brittle in his embrace. "You are not well? Have you been sick? You are thin . . ."

"Sick a little, yes, Davie. Sick a little in body – but more at heart, I think. But – you? You thrive? And Matilda? And the boy . . .?"

"Yes, yes – thanks be to God. And now there is a girl, also. But . . . you said sick at heart? What do you mean? Sick at heart?"

"I should not have said that, Davie. I am selfish. Ungrateful. I have had so much. That perhaps is what is wrong. I mourn for what was, when I should thank God for it."

"We all do that, Sister. But what is it that you have lost? You mean your health?"

"Not that, no – although that is a trial. No – it is Henry's love that I have lost. He did love me – you know that he did."

216

"To be sure he much loved you, my dear – and still does, I vow. Why should he not? You, the best of wives . . . ?"

"No, Davie, he does not. That is past, gone. Why, think you, I am here? Living in this abbey. As good as a nun!"

"You mean . . . you mean that Henry no longer lives with you? You, the Queen?"

"No. Not for months. A year and more. He wants none of me, now – and I live here to escape the clamour of his infidelities."

"Dear Lord – I knew none of this. See you, men . . . men are often that way. Too often. But still love their wives. Alex – I have recently seen Alex. He has many women. But they mean nothing to him . . ."

"Alex never loved Sybilla."

"No. But others I know . . ."

"Henry has changed, Davie. Not only in this, I fear. I have watched it happening for some time. He is not the man that he was. He has grown cold, cruel, deceitful, harsh. Not only with me. Others will tell you. I have watched it and grieved. As he ages, he grows more like his father. And Rufus. He who was so different."

"I am sorry, lass, sorry, Perhaps it will pass . . . ?"

She shook her head. "Worst of all, he keeps our son William from me. He holds him, ever. William is but fourteen years. Matilda our daughter he does not care for. Her I may see, now and again. Surely he could let me see William? After all, Henry has thirteen illegitimate children they tell me . . ."

It was David's turn to shake his head. "What is the other?" he asked, to change the subject. "Your sickness of the body?"

The Queen did not seem much interested in that. "Some mere woman's ailment. Of which the physicians can make naught. But this I can bear. It is Henry . . ." She sighed. "Oh, forgive me, Davie – I am wickedly selfish. To weary you so. I am become a sorry creature, bewailing my lot. Our mother would not have behaved so! I am weak. It is being alone so much – I am not used to being alone. But – speak no more of my troubles. You – you will have come to see Henry?"

"Yes. He summoned me. For what I know not."

"He is gone to Woodstock. With his latest woman, the Norman Adelicia. And William. I fear that you will gain little joy there. I am told that he blames you, in certain matters. In especial over Huntingdon."

"Huntingdon? How that? What of Huntingdon?"

"I do not know for sure. But I think that it is neglect of the earldom."

217

"Save us – how can it be that? And how can I do otherwise than live there little? How can the Viceroy of Cumbria and Strathclyde also be present at Huntingdon? We have stewards there, a-many."

"I know it, Davie – I know. It is unreasonable. But it may be only a stick to beat you. And through you, myself."

"Why should he wish to beat me? Or you either? I have served him well."

She spread her hands.

Next day they rode the sixty miles up Thames and Cherwell to Woodstock. Here, at least, they had no difficulty in locating the King. Henry had established a great menagerie, where he kept large numbers, hundreds, of birds and animals, which he gathered from lands near and far, from the Muscovy snows to the burning sands of Nubia, a costly pastime which the Crusaders had much facilitated. David found him with William the Atheling and the Lady Adelicia of Louvain, superintending the erection of a long line of new cages built of willow saplings, to supplement the hundreds already there, and filled.

Any stiffness in their greetings tended to be on David's part, with Henry affable, even jocular. Prince William was a good-looking, slender youth, fair-haired and long-limbed, seeming more Saxon than Norman or Celt, with the watchful eye of one who saw life as uncertain. The Lady Adelicia, although only a couple of years older, had the assured confidence which came from possessing a richly burgeoning body, early ripened, such as men desired, and a precocious recognition of her own subsequent power. She was the daughter of Godfrey, Count of Louvain and a distant cousin of Henry's.

"So, my good brother-in-law – you have not slain many horses in hastening to my call!" the King charged, although genially. "I looked to see you days past."

"My wife was giving birth to a daughter, Sire. Would you have had me to leave her side, when your messenger gave no reason for your summons?"

"Ha – a daughter! Daughters can be both joy and problem, you will discover. Matilda survived, I take it? And how is my godson and namesake?"

"Well, Sire – all are well. Which is more than I can say of the Queen, my sister. To my sorrow."

"Ah – so you have seen Maud? Then you will be full of woes and sorrows, yes. She has a talent for sorrows!"

"She has reason, I think!"

"Have we not all?" Henry glanced over at his son. "But,

come – I will show you my new camelopard. But recently come from the King of Ethiop. It is scarcely to be believed! William will entertain Adelicia . . ."

As they strolled amongst the cages and enclosures, Henry's affability ebbed. "I sent for you, David, for your own good," he said. "Building abbeys and castles is all excellent. But there are duties as well as such delights. I fear that you may be forgetting some of yours."

"Which are those, Sire? Of the many."

"*Too* many, is it? Have I laid too much upon you? Shall I relieve you?"

"That is for your decision. In what have I been remiss?"

"As one of my earls, one of the greatest, you have certain responsibilities. To me, as also to the earldom."

"And in this I have failed?"

"In some way, yes. In Huntingdon and Northampton. These, amongst the richest in my realm. You skim the cream – but leave the milking and the churning to others! There is discontent there, trouble – and *my* interests suffer. My revenues and my entitlement in armed men. When fiefs are neglected, those go down."

"I know of no neglect, Sire. My stewards render their accounts regularly. And have reported nothing untoward."

"Would they, if they were themselves at fault? An earldom requires more than stewards – it requires an earl!"

"I cannot be in Cumbria and Strathclyde, and at the same time in Huntingdon and Northampton."

"Perhaps Strathclyde, then, is too much for you?"

"You *wished* me to accept Strathclyde from Alexander."

"Not to the hurt of Huntingdon and Northampton. The revenues of which you use to build abbeys in Scotland. Not to mention castles!"

So that was it – Rook's Burgh.

"Even when the castle, Sire, is built to keep the peace on *both* sides of march?"

"Castles do not always keep the peace, David. And this one sits on Scottish soil, threatening Northumbria. Built of English gold!"

"My, lord Henry – the peace of your realm, and of my brother's, is endangered by Northumbrian raiding. This I *know*, sufficiently well – all in Cumbria know. These raiders remain unchecked by de Vesci, who acts as your Earl of Northumbria. Or by any of your officers. Or yet by Ranulf Flambard, Bishop of Durham. The Earl Cospatrick of Dunbar makes strong and frequent complaint. So, as my brother's deputy, I build the castle of Rook's Burgh at the most expedient point on the march. If Flambard, or other, feels himself to be threatened, he should complain to de Vesci, who should approach me . . ."

"God's blood, man – are you telling me, Henry, what should or should not be done in my realm!"

"I am but telling you why I build Rook's Burgh, Sire. And why *you* should not be concerned."

"I am concerned if my Northumbrian folk are concerned."

"Your Northumbrian folk – or Ranulf Flambard? Whom you used very much to distrust.!"

"Flambard has learned his lesson. He is a rogue – but a shrewd rogue. Firmly handled he can be a useful subject and servant."

"The day was when Your Grace would not have employed such servant!"

"Perhaps. But kings cannot always be so nice as to whom they would have to serve them. One day, *you* may learn that! But – this of Huntingdon and Northampton. If you cannot yourself spend more time in these earldoms, then I say that you must appoint a deputy who can. A viscount or sheriff. I cannot have two such important fiefs mismanaged."

David, staring at a black Muscovy bear in a cage little longer than itself, sought to hold his voice steady. "I shall go to Earl's Thorpe and Earl's Barton before I return to the North, Highness. And seek to discover what may be wrong – which I have not heard of. And consider such appointment."

"You will do better than that, my friend! I have the man for you, the very man. Sir Gilbert of Leicester, my Sheriff of Cambridge. He is a most able man, and honest. A scholar. A benefactor of Holy Church, for he is well-born, with his own riches. Since he already administers my royal earldom of Cambridge for me, which flanks Huntingdon, it will be entirely convenient."

"But – I do not know the man!"

"But I do, David – I do! Is *my* recommendation insufficient for you?"

"If you say it must be so, Sire . . ."

"Exactly. Come – you have looked at that bear sufficiently long! The camelopard is yonder. You can see its neck from here . . ."

It took the younger man some little time to control his temper, marshal his wits and seek to rescue something from this sorry interview.

"If I agree to the appointment of this man, Sire, as deputy and sheriff – will you do something in my interest? Or in Scotland's? Some small matter to aid the good harmony between the two realms, to mutual benefit."

"If . . . ?" Henry was immediately wary.

"It is the matter of providing a new Bishop of St. Andrews. Alexander asked the Archbishop of Canterbury's aid two years past, but he has done nothing."

"If he had asked Thurstan of York, would he not have fared better?"

"You know that he will not do that, Sire. So long as York seeks hegemony over Scotland."

"It is not for me to interfere in the affairs of Holy Church."

"You said not so with Archbishop Anselm!"

"Anselm interfered in matters of *state*, David."

"Nevertheless, your good-son the King of Scots, requests your aid."

"What can I do?"

"The Archbishop Ralph was of your appointing. He will much heed you."

"In such matters, I fear not."

"May I put it to the test, Sire? Can I go to Ralph and give him Alexander's message? Say that I have seen Your Grace and that you make no objection?"

"Why should I make objection?"

"Ah – I rejoice that you do not!"

"Not so fast, man – not so fast! I asked a question, did not give answer."

"*I* answer – no reason why you should find objection."

"And I see no reason why I should intervene in no affair of mine."

"Perhaps then, Sire, that would be sufficient! May I tell the Archbishop that? That you see no reason to intervene in the matter?"

Henry turned to look at him, narrow-eyed. "You, my friend, grow importunate, I think!"

"How can you say that, Sire – if this matter is no concern of yours?"

"David – I will not be hedged and baited like this! Do not trade on my patience, man! Go to Ralph, if you must. But do not take him any message from me. You understand?"

"I do, Sire – oh, yes, I do!"

They stared at the extraordinary creature, the giraffe, but neither was really seeing it, despite its physical oddities.

221

David played his last card. "If the Archbishop will do nothing, I am authorised to go further, Sire. To the Abbot Bernard, at Clairvaux. To ask him use his influence with Pope Paschal to appoint the necessary bishop."

"Ha! So you would go that far! Alexander must be concerned, indeed? Is his position so precarious? But – at least I may save you a profitless journey, David. The good Abbot Bernard is dead."

"Dead? Bernard of Tiron . . . ?"

"The same. I had word that he died some months ago. A sad loss, no . . . ?"

David recognised that he was beaten. He could do no more here. Henry was equally percipient. He became affable again, particularly anent the giraffe.

As his visitors left next morning for Canterbury in Kent, they traded one last exchange.

"You will find Sheriff Gilbert a notable help, David," the King said. "Seek him at Cambridge. And, see you – build bridges, like your sister, rather than castles and abbeys! Maud has built a great bridge at London. This I can recommend. Bridges bring folk together – castles keep them apart."

"Maud would, I think, have *you* to build a bridge, Henry – back to her side. She is unhappy – she who was your chief delight."

"And still is, to be sure – but a sad delight! She pines, man – she pines overmuch."

"She pines for her husband's company. She pines for William, her son."

"Then why shut herself up in that abbey? She should be here, at Woodstock. None to stop the Queen coming here!"

"Ask her, Henry – ask her to come. Send William to ask her."

"My salutations to the Archbishop," the King said abruptly. "And, mind it – that is the only message I send him!"

* * *

At the great cathedral and abbey of Canterbury in the Kentish plain of the Stour, David found the Archbishop Ralph to be an amiable man but weak, carefully chosen by Henry so that the frictions of Anselm's regime would not be repeated – and his choice no doubt acquiesced in by the Pope for similar reasons. Strong and opinionated archbishops were not always appreciated.

Ralph was defensive about his failure to do as the King of

Scots had requested, to send up a consecrated bishop for St. Andrews, making sundry excuses, and even claiming that there was no one suitable available. But when David insisted, and hinted at going direct to the Pope, also declaring that he had come from King Henry who left the matter entirely to the Archbishop, Ralph capitulated. Indeed, when David suggested the monk Eadmer, the Primate actually seemed to be slightly relieved. When that man was sent for, and proved to be a tall, thin, scholarly Saxon, short of sight and of a somewhat gloomy countenance, but strong-featured – stronger than his superior, David guessed – no real obstruction was put forward. Admittedly Eadmer showed no enthusiasm for the appointment, but he could scarcely refuse, and the Archbishop did not so advise. David clinched the matter by telling the monk that he could continue with writing his book on the life and miracles of the Blessed Anselm as readily in Scotland as here at Canterbury.

Thus, fairly easily, the visit was concluded, and David rode off after declaring that his royal brother, King Henry's son-in-law, would be well content – a sentiment which both prelate and monk rather noticeably failed to applaud.

They went northwards by Cambridge, as commanded, but visited Northampton and Huntingdon first. There, although David questioned his chief stewards for both earldoms closely, he could uncover no hint of any serious troubles or problems. In fact, the men were clearly mystified over his probings – and he would swear that they were honest, and long employed by the Countess Matilda. Unable to fault them, he asked, casually, what they knew of the Sheriff Gilbert of Cambridge?

They answered readily enough, both of them. Only good, they said. The Sheriff, although a King's officer, was a fine man, honest, fair, just. He had even founded a monastery, at a place called Merton.

Knowing something of the cost of founding monasteries, David wondered; but his informants assured him that Sir Gilbert's riches were not obtained by any oppressions, nor harsh appropriations of the tenantry, in the manner of so many. He appeared to have private wealth, and was clearly well-reared, even though his ancestry was something of a mystery. It was even suggested that he was one of the numerous natural sons of King William the Conqueror, and so a half-brother of King Henry.

So David journeyed eastwards from Huntingdon sixteen miles to Cambridge, where at Grantbridge Castle he found the Sheriff Gilbert, a busy man of affairs, working amongst papers and records and ledgers, with an office of clerks and secretaries – for it seemed that this strange man administered not only the royal earldom of Cambridge but those of other King's lands also, as well as certain wealth-creating matters for various monasteries, including the Cluniac St. Andrews of Northampton – which David had not realised. Although prepared to find this individual, who had been foisted upon him, more or less objectionable, in fact during the day he spent with him, David could not but like as well as admire the man. He judged him to be as effective as he was unassuming and tactful. It was evident that he had already been informed by Henry of the new duties he was to take up, even though he obviously assumed that it was all with the Earl's agreement, if not at his behest. David did not disillusion him. They discussed the business and concerns of the two earldoms at some length – and here too David learned of no serious difficulties or irregularities. He came to the conclusion that these were no more than an invention of the King to provide excuse for the imposition of this Sir Gilbert's care and oversight. This, in turn, might have inclined him to be the more resentful – only that, talking to the Sheriff, he could not fail to realise that it might well be much to his advantage to have such an able, scrupulous and experienced deputy on the spot. In fact, even whilst they talked, Gilbert, a man old enough to be David's father, tentatively suggested half-a-dozen alterations and improvements in the administration of various aspects of the vast estates, which patently could be beneficial and profitable to all concerned. David, indeed, in their short time together, really recognised for the first time something of the great potential of the lands, manors, fishings, villages, even towns, which he had acquired by his marriage, something Matilda herself had scarcely been competent to explain.

As a consequence, he rode northwards thereafter thoughtful, his feelings mixed, after signing sundry documents which gave the Sheriff authority to act in his name. He realised that he *had* been neglecting his responsibilities here in some measure, however inevitably and unknowingly – and to that extent Henry had excuse for his interference. The earldoms should be better managed now than they had ever been under Simon de St. Liz. On the other hand, Henry had now put himself in a position practically to control them – and that man did not usually act without due thought and forward planning. It could mean that from now on the King had an additionally firm grip over his Viceroy of Cumbria. David might spend most of his time three hundred and more miles away from Henry's Court, and seem to be almost an independent princeling; but his royal brother-in-law's displeasure could now be demonstrated, and at longer range than that, in no uncertain terms.

Life, he perceived, was to be a battle of wits with Henry Beauclerc.

17

Rook's Burgh Castle was completed at last. Far from being put off by Henry's clear disapproval, David had pressed ahead more urgently with the building programme. It was not mere stubbornness – although an element of that may have entered into it. There were sufficiently good reasons to risk Henry's frowns, he felt. For one thing, it was necessary to show that he was not cowed by the King's intimidations and devious methods – or he would never again be his own man. Again, to halt the construction of a Scots castle on Scottish soil at the behest of an English monarch, would be to admit a quite unwarrantable influence and pressure, and cause offence to Alexander; as heir-presumptive to the Scots throne he could by no means countenance that. But more immediately vital was the sheer need for the place, locally. There had been no more large-scale incursions, admittedly; but small-scale raiding remained rife, almost as much on the Scots side as the Northumbrian, and David was concerned that this must stop, for lawlessness was infectious and small things often led to great. As it was, the vast Forest of Ettrick and its subsidiary hereabouts, the Forest of Jedworth, offered notable refuge for broken men, outlaws and refugees from authority on both sides of the march, and consequently a haven for raiders. A large part of the necessity for Rook's Burgh was to help to control at least these eastern parts of the Forest area; and David had plans for other, if less ambitious castles elsewhere. Until both the march or border country, along the Tweed, and the Forest no-man's-land, were under control, neither kings' writs would run hereabouts; and David had no doubts as to his duties in the matter. He had solved the Cumbria-Galloway problem, in the west; he would solve this one on the east, God willing. If Henry, misled by Flambard, did not understand, then he must take that risk. And if Henry thought to withhold the revenues from Huntingdon, which he was using for his work of pacification and rule up here, then it would be wise to get as much done as possible whilst the money lasted. Thus he argued, and Matilda agreed.

So, to mark the completion of the work, and to emphasise the start of a new phase in the maintenance of law and peace on the border, David held a major celebration the following midsummer, to which he brought his wife and children and much of his entourage at Caer-luel, as well as inviting a large representation of local people. He had learned that Teviotdale held a peculiar festival each year at this time, a traditional affair evidently compounded partly of Pictish and partly of Norse or Viking origins, for it involved elements of sun and fire worship connected with the summer solstice, and also homage to Thor and Odin, the Norse gods, with fertility rites relating to land, beast and man. David, whilst nowise countenancing these pagan practices, saw the advantage of making use of local enthusiasms and established custom. So, with Matilda's and Cospatrick's help, he concocted an amended programme for the festival, much as the Celtic Christian missionaries from Ireland had done towards the Druidical ceremonies five centuries before, seeking to retain the colour and vigour of the revelry whilst expunging most of the obvious heathen references, to substitute Christian themes as far as possible. Some of these might sit only oddly on the age-old rituals and observances, but the thing should still be vivid and unusual, not to say dramatic. This was all to be staged at Rook's Burgh, to coincide with the opening of the castle, so that it might be seen as no symbol of oppression and dread – as were so many Norman-style castles – but as a friendly place put there for the people's welfare and protection. In fact, David intended to reside there for considerable periods, for it was a highly attractive vicinity, more so than Caer-luel, and matters in Cumbria were now so well organised and established that they could be left to his lieutenants for periods at a time.

So, on Midsummer's Eve, 21st June, the celebration began, with an outdoor banquet held partly in the forecourt of the new castle, just east of the gatehouse and drawbridge and partly down below the cliff, there being insufficient space for all above. This did not commence until late in the evening, for it was to go on all night. As a great treat Matilda's children, Waltheof, Matilda and Henry, now three years, were allowed to stay up,

226

although Henry slept peacefully in a blanket most of the time. Great fires were lit, scores of them, and the carcases of oxen, deer and sheep roasted whole, whilst dances took place round them, David drawing the line, however, at young men running into and leaping through the flames, as was part of the old Norse fire ritual. It was never truly dark, of course, and there were still traces of sunset in the north at midnight. So there were only some four hours to wait until sunrise and the time went swiftly enough in revelry and singing, as well as dancing – and, it must be admitted, in fairly extensive horseplay, for there was unlimited ale provided, and David, despite his religious inclinations, was no spoil-sport.

Amongst the songs, repeated time and again, was a traditional one which the locals called 'Teribus y Teri Odin', which obviously glorified Thor and Odin, to a rousing and suitably martial tune which, chanted by the light of the fires and punctuated by the stamping of feet and the wailing of bulls' horns, raised the hairs on even Norman necks. David, presently, found himself shouting its challenging refrain with the best, so strangely effective was its rhythm and theme – although he was careful to counter this by ordering the singing of some of the best-known hymns of the more forceful kind, in between, including the general favourite of Saint Serf's pet lamb which baa-ed in its eater's stomach.

The hours passed without any sense of weary waiting, to culminate, one hour before dawn, with a torchlight procession in which all took part, chanting, leading down from the castle to the haughland, along the river-bank, through the little town and back up to the castle again. Even young Henry was wakened up to toddle in this, amidst much excitement. Just to emphasise who and what they were worshipping, David had Abbot Ralph lead the way, bearing aloft a tall golden cross which gleamed in the flaming light, with other simple wooden crosses held up at intervals down the line.

Up on the rock again, the flaming torches were used to make new fires on the topmost towers of the castle, within the parapets and along the wall-walks, so that the whole great building was illuminated, its turrets and bartisans picked out in light and shade. All had been timed carefully, so that there was little further waiting. The sky was lightening. Suddenly the singing of 'Teribus y Teri Odin' was stilled by the high bugling notes of a single trumpet from the loftiest pinnacle of the castle, seeming to shiver the air and cause throats to constrict. Every eye turned north-eastwards as the flourish died. There, across the com-

227

paratively level plain of the Merse, the first fiery red rim of the sun arose, seen just those moments earlier by the higher-placed trumpeter. A great shout lifted and continued.

Then a bell began to toll, with the hollow deep note of a Celtic saint's bell, St. Boisel's own, brought by Cospatrick from the monastery of Melross. David climbed up on to the parapet-walk of the northern curtain-wall of the precinct, to address the company.

"My friends," he called, strong-voiced. "I, David mac Malcolm, greet you well, this new day of the Blessed John the Baptist. It is a new day, a new season, and I hope and believe, a new time of peace and prosperity and the rule of law and justice, in this ancient marchland. On this rock, the Picts or Cruithne, our ancestors, called in their tongue the March Mount, above the town of Rook's Burgh, watched, as we now watch, the new-born sun in its splendour dim and extinguish the feebler fires and flames of the night of darkness. The Picts, knowing no better, but recognising that there *was* a better, worshipped here the sun itself and what it foretold and heralded, the new and better life. But *we* know what the midsummer sun foretold – new life, yes, the birth of the Lord Christ and His promise of life and love and peace to men of goodwill."

He paused, and a murmur rose from the shadowy, listening crowds, as cocks crowed in the village below.

"So Midsummer's Day is now John the Baptist's Day throughout Christendom. For the Blessed John prophesied that, as at this solstice, *he* would grow less as the new sun, the Son of God and Man, grew greater, eleven centuries ago, John of the shortening days. So watching this sun rise today, we worship not it but the Son of God Himself, of whom the Baptist foretold. We glorify Him, humbly, and pledge ourselves to work for His peace, the peace He was to die for, not war and bloodshed and rapine, but love and caring, man for man, honest labour, the fair rule of law, and above all, peace. This castle of mine, of *yours*, is a stronghold yes – but a stronghold for peace, not war. To uphold your liberties and safety, not to oppress. To restrain evil men and all who would disturb that peace. See it as the March Mount indeed, to maintain the peace of the marches. I pledge you that so long as I live it shall so do! I commend it to you all, my friends – the March Mount of Rook's Burgh, now completed!"

Hesitant at first, for folk were a little uncertain as to what all this might mean and signify, applause grew and presently swelled to great cheering and acclaim. Even so not one in a dozen probably recognised what really was intended, the vision behind it all. But some did, and led the acclamation.

David then called upon Abbot Ralph to pronounce the Benediction – adding that thereafter all would breakfast on the traditional curds and cream.

At Matilda's side again, she gripped David's arm.

"That was splendid, splendid!" she exclaimed. "I am proud of you, indeed. What matter if few here understood? David – I feel that we should celebrate this great occasion. So that none should forget . . ."

"This *is* a celebration, my love!" he pointed out, smiling. "Have you forgot? It is to celebrate the completion of the castle and the start of a new regime along the march."

"Yes, yes – that I know. I mean something different, something to commemorate this night. What you have just said, Promised . . ."

The breakfasting on curds and cream and ale followed. This was as traditional as the rest, representing the fertility of the land contributing to the fertility of the people. Great bowls of cold curds were produced, with jugs and pitchers of thick cream, all washed down with barrels of ale and mead, eaten and drunk with much hilarity. On this unconventional morning's diet, all were expected to perform prodigies and feats of strength, skill and endurance – for despite the fact that no one had had any sleep, the day was given over to sporting contests and trials of agility, races, wrestling, swimming, archery, stone-putting, caber-tossing and the like. Surprisingly there seemed to be no lack of energy and enthusiasm, and mighty feats were achieved. Even the Norman knights, with their slightly superior attitude, were spurred into demonstrations of their especial prowess in horsemanship, jousting and lance-work. David himself put up a reasonable performance, especially at running, at which he had always been proficient – although he by no means sought to emulate his brother Alex, who prided himself on his pre-eminence at sports.

By mid-day, however, physical vigour was beginning to flag and the standard of achievements sinking somewhat. So now the real feasting commenced, out there in the open, with food and drink for all and to spare. At David's own trestle-board, in the shade of ash-trees above the swift-running Teviot, Matilda returned to her theme expressed at sunrise.

"I say that this day's doings, and what you said up there on the castle-wall, should be commemorated," she declared. "All, ourselves with others, should be reminded of what was done and said, what attempted and what must be maintained and brought to pass. For it will be a great and lengthy task, and all must be frequently reminded, ourselves not least."

"The castle itself will do that, lass."

"I think not. That is not in the nature of castles, David. While you are here yourself it might serve. But you cannot be here for many months in the year. And when you are not, what will it be? A fortress, with a garrison of armed men. Is that what we would have as commemoration of this day? Oh, I know that you intend the castle to be a strong place for good and order and peace. But will not the people of these parts see it rather as the Earl David's Norman castle, full of soldiers, who may or may not be as gentle as you would wish! How many will then remember your splendid words?"

That produced silence at the table.

"So we must do other," she went on. "If we would prove and establish our good purpose. I have been thinking about this, whilst you men ran and jumped and frolicked like colts! I say that we should found another abbey! Here!"

They stared at her – they all stared, even Abbot Ralph.

"But . . . but . . . !' David began.

"Why not?" she asked. "Shiel Kirk has been notably successful. But – is it to be the only true abbey in Scotland? It has brought already much of good to the west side of this Forest – as well as glorifying God. Would not another, in the east, be as valuable? It is costly, I know well – but meantime we have sufficient moneys to make a start. And, once started, by God's good grace it will be completed. Somehow."

"I think that is right, what should be done," Beatrix de Beauchamp supported loyally. "The moneys will come."

"When King Henry hears of it, will they?" David wondered. "He is displeased with me for building this castle with what he names English gold. How would he look on another Scots abbey?"

"Must it be *English* gold?" Cospatrick demanded. "Can sufficient not be found in Scotland? *I* would find some. For a great monastery here would much aid Teviotdale. As Shiel Kirk has aided Ettrick and Yarrow and Upper Tweed. Bringing trade and all manner of good."

"Yes, best if indeed it could be built with Scots moneys," Matilda agreed. "I believe, once it was started, support would come. But it would require you to start it, David. And you could, surely? Since this Sheriff Gilbert has been acting for you in Huntingdon and Northampton, the revenues have increased. He is an excellent man. Let us use the more moneys, while we may. If Henry stops them, as you fear, then we must find other moneys."

David still looked very doubtful.

"This is still the Forest, is it not?" she went on. "Ettrick Forest – royal demesne. Would not Alexander give you more land of it?"

"The Forest, and the royal lands, end here. Where Teviot joins Tweed. Eastwards is Cospatrick's earldom of the March."

"I would give land," Cospatrick said. "But, see you – I would rather that you placed your abbey further up Teviot. Where it would serve more purpose. Here, at Rook's Burgh, there is a church, small as it is and Columban. And now there is this castle. But up the dale, for long miles, there is nothing. The old abandoned cashel at Jedworth, that is all. A new abbey up there would do great things for Teviotdale."

"Ah, yes – Jedworth," David took him up. "The old Columban monastery there – that is a thought. To revive a house of God which has sunk away . . . ? Better that than a new one. Better in all respects – even for Henry's ears! Not any new abbey, but a renewal. And reformed to the Roman obedience . . ."

"Yes, yes – that would be it!" Matilda agreed eagerly. "Jedworth Abbey! That is good . . ."

It was at this juncture that a weary messenger arrived. He came from King Alexander, at Stirling, but via Caer-luel. His errand was of the saddest. Alex sent word that both their brother Ethelred, Earl of Moray, and their sister Mary, Countess of Boulogne, were dead. Mary, it seemed, had died some time earlier, in France, but the news had been slow in reaching Scotland. She left four children. Eth had actually been on a visit to London to see Maud when he suddenly sickened and died within a day or two. Alex was anxious that his body should be brought back to Scotland for burial at Dunfermline beside their parents and brothers. Would David see to this?

David was much upset. He had not been as close to Eth as he had been to his sisters, who had shared his long exile in Romsey Abbey; but he had liked what he had seen of him. Also he had a strong sense of family. In a way, he felt almost responsible, for he had sent word of Maud's poor state to Alex and had urged him to go to see their sister if he could, and if that was not possible, at least to send Eth, for Maud was ill, lonely and felt deserted. And now – this! As for Mary, he had not seen her for

231

years, but had thought of her a lot and hoped that she was faring better than was Maud.

It was, of course, a major inconvenience for him to leave all, at short notice, and travel down to London; but he felt that it was the least that he could do in his brother's memory – beside it being something in the nature of a royal command. There was no desperate hurry, to be sure, for presumably Maud would have the body embalmed for the journey back. But he could scarcely look forward to the occasion. He had not enjoyed his previous and much shorter pilgrimage with his father's corpse. He had hoped that it was not to become a habit. At least, it would provide an opportunity to call at Huntingdon and see the Sheriff over certain issues – and deprive Henry of another chance to say that he was neglecting his earldoms.

Matilda announced that she would come with him, and would not be dissuaded. She quite enjoyed travel with her husband, finding it a break from the responsibilities of châtelaine and mother – and she did not often achieve this. Besides, she wanted to see Maud again, of whom she was fond. She had never met Ethelred, so it would be a strange encounter.

There was no more talk about a new abbey that Midsummer's Day.

18

IT SEEMED THAT death stalked the royal houses of Scotland and England. David and Matilda were only weeks back from their London journey, with its melancholy return with Eth's body, when the tidings reached them that Maud had died. Admittedly she had been in a sorry state when they had left her, still at the Abbey of Westminster, with no reconciliation with Henry; but she had seemed little worse than on David's previous visit. There was no great surprise in this tragedy, of course; it had seemed to be only a question of time, with the Queen having little will to live. But it was sad news, for Maud had been quite the favourite of all David's family. That the English people were apparently everywhere mourning the Good Queen Maud, was only moderate consolation.

Then, not long afterwards, there were further drastic tidings to reach Caer-luel. William the Atheling, Henry's only lawful son and heir, was dead aged barely seventeen and just married. Henry had been over in Normandy, where he spent a lot of his time these days – he had imprisoned his brother Robert the Duke in Bristol Castle for life – and he and his family were returning to England from Barfleur. At the last moment, Henry sent his family in a different ship from his own. This vessel had run into a reef and began to sink. The prince had got away in one of the small boats, when he learned that his illegitimate half-sister, Marie, Countess de Perche, was still aboard, left behind in the confusion. He insisted on turning back to save her. But on reaching the sinking ship's side so many other desperate folk jumped down into the small boat that it over-turned and sank, all being drowned.

Henry was reported to be desolated, for William was the apple of his eye as well as his only male heir born lawfully, a youth of great promise. For England too it was a disaster, for William was the representative, through his mother, of the ancient Saxon line.

So perhaps Maud was re-united with her son in the next world, although denied his company in this.

Only the following year there was still another demise in the family, when Alexander's Queen Sybilla died suddenly. Details of her passing were scanty, unlike those of her half-brother and sister. All that was told was that she had died at Loch Tay in Highland Druim-Alban, whether likewise from drowning or other accident, or from sickness, was not stated. What she was doing up at Loch Tay was not reported either, she who lived her own life; but apparently the King was not present. All that was added was that Alexander, significantly, did not want her to be buried with the rest of the royal family at Dunfermline, and had had her interred merely on an islet in the loch there. Even by Alexander's standards this seemed distinctly drastic for a Queen of Scotland; but it was said that the King intended to found a nunnery on the island, in Sybilla's memory – a nice touch for the Queen, who had been no nun.

If this last fatality affected David a great deal less, emotion-ally, than did the others, it nevertheless affected him more keenly otherwise. For it meant, of couse, that Alexander was now a widower and free to marry again and possibly produce a son to heir the throne; so that David's position as heir-presumptive might now be short-lived. This did not greatly worry him, for he had never set his heart on becoming King of

Scots; but it obviously could much affect his future life. And it might conceivably affect Alex's attitude towards him. With Henry no longer his close friend, and Alexander possibly requiring him less, his secure position relative to both kingdoms could change notably. He might be glad to be merely and modestly Earl of Huntingdon one of these days.

Meantime there were developments and problems nearer home. Surprisingly, Abbot Ralph was summoned back to Tiron to try to fill the shoes of the late Bernard, a great compliment to him but a sad loss. His coadjutor, the monk William, reigned as Abbot of Shiel Kirk in his stead. Unfortunately the hiatus coincided with a raid on Shiel Kirk by a large band of caterans from the Forest. The Abbey itself was not greatly damaged but most of the now substantial cattle and sheep stocks were driven off and much gear and plenishing stolen. There had been minor raids previously but nothing on this scale. David personally led a quite strong punitive expedition to try to comb out that north-westerly quarter of the huge Ettrick Forest – an expedition which was less successful than its size and illustrious composition warranted. They managed to catch, try and hang a few outlaws; but the terrain was so wild and difficult that they lost many more than they could apprehend. The Normans suggested that they should burn the entire area systematically – which was how the Conqueror and Rufus had dealt with such situations – but David would not countenance such indiscriminate devastation. Better a few rogues escaped, than that.

The Rook's Burgh Castle experiment was a success, at any rate, with an undeniably settling influence on the eastern marches area. David sought to reside there for ever longer periods. Matilda greatly liked the place, as did the children. Moreover, the new monastery at Jedworth, only eight miles up-river, was growing apace and requiring superintendence. They had decided that it should be only a priory, meantime, not an abbey, as less ambitious – for David was spending money elsewhere in the prodigal style, whilst it lasted, egged on by Matilda. As some kind of memorial to his sister Maud – as also to his brother Edward, who had died nearby – he had sent to the monastery of Canons Regular which she had founded in London, for a group of monks to form a nucleus. A Saxon named Osbert came, with half-a-dozen others. Although not another Ralph, Osbert was an able man with considerable initiative; but never having been a prior or master of an establishment, he lacked the experience to plan and set up a new

234

community in all its ramifications, so that he required much assistance and guidance.

As well as this project, the other destination for the Huntingdon revenues was a series of smaller castles all over the Forest area, and elsewhere, which David saw as an answer to the lawlessness problem which bedevilled that great green wilderness, and to some extent all the borderland. These would not be powerful strongholds like Rook's Burgh, set up to deal with English invasion and major border raiding, but more modest strengths, with small garrisons, designed to keep a curb on bands of brigands and broken men, and to which local folk could turn for protection and help. It was a new conception of David's own, to meet a pressing need – and although not so costly as abbey-building, still demanded a great deal of money, for he envisaged fully a score of such keeps and towers, some of them, as at Peebles and Hawick and Lochmaben, large enough to act also as hunting-lodges. He likewise encouraged his lieutenants, de Brus, de Soulis, de Lindsay and the rest, to erect similar strengths in their own bailiwicks.

All this finding of sites for castles, and superintending the work, entailed much quartering of the country, constant travel, not only of the central Forest area but of the East and West Marches likewise, with Galloway also – for David was concerned that his pacification and settlement policy should apply to all the territory over which, meantime, he had control – so that he came to know the land probably better than any other one man before him. None other had had his farflung oversight and responsibility; certainly none had taken it so seriously. He did not pursue his building campaign in Cumbria, however, lacking Henry's authority. He wrote to that king suggesting it but did not receive any reply. Henry was back in Normandy, which dukedom he was now ruling with a heavy hand, and where he now married the youthful Adelicia, daughter of Godfrey, Count of Louvain, whom David had encountered at Woodstock. If there was a new heir to the English throne, he would not have any of the ancient Saxon blood.

These Normandy preoccupations of Henry's perhaps had the effect of lessening his concern for details in England; for the monk Eadmer was permitted to come to Scotland as Bishop of St. Andrews, at last. Satisfaction with this long-delayed development was short-lived, however. Even before the new Primate was installed formally, he fell out with Alexander. The King claimed that he must ceremonially invest the Bishop as Primate and *Ard Episcop* of Scotland. But Eadmer refused any-

thing such, saying that in all matters religious Ralph of Canterbury was his superior, not any earthly monarch; and Ralph had
already invested him as Primate of Scotland as well as consecrating him bishop. Furiously, Alexander pointed out that
Archbishop Ralph had no least authority to invest anyone as
anything in Scotland. Why did he think that he, Alexander,
had refused Thurstan of York's nominations if it was to have
Canterbury claiming hegemony in his place? There had been
complete impasse for some time until both agreed to a reluctant
compromise. Eadmer would accept the episcopal ring of investiture from off the altar, at Alexander's hands, in ceremony,
whilst he himself took up the pastoral staff, as from the hand of
God Himself. With this uneasy device, the new Bishop was
declared *Ard Episcop*, King's Bishop and Primate.

However, one of Eadmer's first authoritative acts thereafter
much upset David, as well as the King. He denounced the
episcopate of John, Bishop of Glasgow, and claimed Papal
instructions that it was invalid – clearly something engineered
long before he came to Scotland. Pope Paschal had died and
there was a new Pontiff, Calixtus the Second. He was a friend of
Henry's, it appeared, and that monarch had already managed
to detach the Papacy from the French interest to the side of
Normandy; now this – so perhaps Henry Beauclerc was not so
unmindful of English–Scots affairs after all, in far-away Normandy. At any rate Eadmer announced that, through Archbishop Ralph, Calixtus had ordered him to declare John's
episcopate of Glasgow as invalid, on the grounds that he had
been consecrated a bishop of England, not of Scotland. He
must cease all functions in Scotland immediately.

This enraged Alexander as much as it worried David – for of
course it made doubtful the position of Cormac, Bishop of
Dunkeld, whom John had consecrated. The King demanded
retraction from Eadmer, and an announcement that Cormac's
ordination was valid. When neither were forthcoming, a complete rift developed between monarch and prelate. Alexander
refused to see or speak with Eadmer, and that Saxon
announced that he would return to Canterbury for solace and
instruction – to which the King, and most other Scots, declared
Amen, so be it, or words less dignified. So, having been in
Scotland less than one year, Eadmer departed.

Something of a relief as this might be, at first sight, it left
behind serious gaps and problems. Eadmer was still Bishop of
St. Andrews, so Scotland had no head of its Romish Church,
and no *Ard Episcop*. And of its two other bishops, one was under

Papal interdict and the second, in consequence, might be also. The supporters of the old Celtic Church – to which the main mass of the people belonged, of course – might have been forgiven if they chuckled and said I-told-you-so.

Less stern Romanists and reformers than the Margaretsons might well, at this stage, have given up their long and frustrating campaign to turn Scotland to Rome, and returned to the ancient spiritual allegiance of Columba, however tired it was in Romish eyes, decadent and in error. Scotland was never nearer reverting to Iona. But that was not how the Blessed Margaret had brought up her family. Alexander and David reacted differently. Typically defiant, the King founded and endowed a new see of Moray, and ordered Cormac to consecrate as its bishop Gregory, a monk of Scone. David, typically also perhaps, sent Bishop John off on a pilgrimage to Rome, via Tiron, where he was to see Abbot Ralph, now head of the Tironensian Order, to solicit his influential aid with Calixtus. At the Holy See John was to explain the true position in Scotland to the Pope, and the dire danger to the Romish faith from the present unhappy situation.

In the midst of all this, Matilda was brought to bed with her sixth child. She had no easy time of it. She was now forty-two years, and had never had a really troublesome birth with any of the other five. David decided that this girl must be the last. They called her Hodierna, a traditional name in the Waltheof family, shortened almost immediately to Erna. Young Henry was now nearly six and Claricia three. Waltheof, now fourteen, and a grave child religiously-inclined, was ever asking to be allowed to go to Shiel Kirk to be enrolled as a novice; they let him go to the new Jedworth Priory on a part-time basis, to see how he got on. Of his elder brother Simon, in far Aumale, they heard nothing, to Matilda's distress, although she wrote to him frequently. David had sought Henry Beauclerc's aid to have the lad returned, but to no effect. Undoubtedly the future Earl of Northampton was more or less a hostage, even if originally a willing one.

David's own thirty-sixth birthday reminded him of something which he seldom remembered – that he was no longer a young man, however slender and almost boyish his appearance.

19

DAVID AND MATILDA were attending the wedding celebrations of Robert de Brus – who very sensibly was marrying the daughter of the Celtic Lord of Annadale, over whose lands he had oversight, and so settling comfortably into the local landscape – this at the town of Annan, in August, the ceremony over and suitable feasting commencing, when a special courier arrived from the North. Weary and dishevelled, for he had travelled long and at speed, via both Rook's Burgh and Caer-luel, he louted low to David – lower than usual. Yet he was his own nephew, Malcolm, the late Eth's third son.

"My lord," he panted. "My lord David. My lord Prince – who knows, it may be my lord King!"

"Eh . . . ? Malcolm – what is this? What do you mean, man?"

"The King, my lord. It is the King. Alexander. He is amissing. We, we fear that he is drowned. The Earl Madach of Atholl sent me to you . . ."

"Alexander? Drowned!" David stared from the young man to the wine-cup in his own hand. He raised it to his lips, then bethought him that the other probably had greater need, and thrust the cup at his nephew. "Drink, man. Then sit. You are wearied. Tell us these tidings. However evil."

"Yes, evil, Uncle." Malcolm emptied the beaker at a draught. "It was three days back – four, now. The King was out fishing in the Firth of Forth. Out from Culross Abbey. You know how he is fond of fishing. In a boat with three others. A great storm of wind arose. And rain. The boat was lost to sight. It did not come back to Culross that night. Next day the body of one of the boatmen was washed up on the shore. There is no word of the King."

"Merciful Lord!" David breathed. "Alex!"

"Oh, my love!" Matilda took his arm. "It may not be . . . it *need* not be . . ."

"No. It may not. Pray God! Malcolm – there has been a search? No sign of the boat? No wreckage?"

"The sea was still very rough. Strong west winds . . ."

"From Culross, you say? That is quite far up Forth, from the Queen's Ferries. It should not have been so rough there."

"I know not, my lord. I was not there. I was at Stirling. But it was wild, wild. Of a sudden . . ."

There was silence amongst the wedding-guests.

"The Earl Madach of Atholl was at Stirling," Malcolm mac Eth went on, out of a full mouth. "He waited for two days. Then, then he sent me to tell you. If Alexander is indeed drowned, you are now the King, my lord. He asks that you come. At once. Before, before all learn . . ."

"Yes. Yes, to be sure. I must go. Without delay. But – I will not accept that Alexander is dead! I will not . . . !

It was a sorry interruption of a wedding-feast. Making hasty apologies to their host and to the bride and groom, and leaving Matilda to represent him, David took Hugo and Hervey with only one or two others, and in their finery as they were, took horse for the Forth and Stirling.

Although they rode well into that May night, it was evening of the next day before they looked down from the Gargunnock Hills on to the fort-crowned rock of Stirling rising starkly from the flood-plain of the Forth. At the castle, Hugo's uncle Eustace, the Great Constable, now an ageing man, greeted him uncertainly, not knowing whether to go down on one knee to him as monarch – but being left in no doubt that he should not. There was still no word of Alexander. The Earl Madach was away in Fothrif superintending the search.

It was too late to do anything worthwhile that night. Tired and dispirited, David sought a couch.

They were on their way to Culross, along the north shore of the Forth, when they met a party from Madach spurring in the other direction. These announced that the King had been found. He was alive, although weak and in a poor state. They had no details save that Alexander was lying at Culross Abbey. They were sent to inform the Constable and Chancellor at Stirling.

Thankfully David rode on.

Culross Abbey of St. Serf lay on the Fothrif coast of the Firth midway between Stirling and Dunfermline. It was an ancient establishment, very different from any Romish monastery, lacking any edifice of stone-and-lime and consisting of many clay and timber buildings, with thatched roofs, within a large stockaded enclosure. But it was a pleasant place amongst gardens and orchards, with its own boat-haven, quite famous in the Columban Church as where the renowned St. Serf had reared the still more renowned St. Mungo or Kentigern.

Madach greeted his cousin thankfully, a worried man still.

239

The King was very ill, he reported, coughing blood. Abbot Murdoch, skilled in such matters, said that he had crushed ribs and one or more had punctured the lung. He was sleeping just now, after tossing and coughing all night. One of his companions was in little better state, but the third had come out of the ordeal fairly well and had been able to give an account of what had happened.

It seemed that the King's fishing-boat, caught in the sudden squall of a week before, had been overturned, tossing its four occupants into the water. One of the boatmen had been swept away at once – he whose body had been recovered on the shore nearby. But the boat had not actually sunk, floating on keel-up, and the three survivors had managed to get back to it and to cling thereto. Then had commenced a grim and prolonged ordeal as, at the mercy of strong winds, high waves and an ebbing tide, they had drifted seawards. There was nothing that they could do to guide or affect the course. Hour after hour they had clung on desperately, chilled and losing hope. In time they had passed right out between the headlands where Queen Margaret's Ferry crossed, and on into the widening Scottish Sea. By then it was growing dark, and all three had said their last prayers and committed their souls to God and His saints, not believing that it was possible than they could survive even another hour. Anyway, what hope was there for them in the broad Scotwater, in these high seas and darkness?

None knew when it was that, still clinging although barely conscious, they had become aware of change, the sea suddenly seeming to grow even rougher and the noise greater. Then they were smashing and grinding amongst rocks and spray. Helpless, they were smashed and battered and tossed clear of the splintering boat. The man reporting had lost consciousness at this stage, presumably stunned against a rock.

When he had come to, he and his two companions were lying in a small hut made of drift-wood and turf, being tended by a wild-looking hairy man in rags and skins, who proved to be an anchorite of the Columban Church, a holy man living alone on the small island of Inch Colm, on which they had been cast up, with a single cow for sustenance. Although the man looked a mere skeleton, he had dragged all three of them up from the rocky shore to his cabin, treated their hurts as best he could and was cherishing them on milk and cheese and shell-fish and edible weeds – although the King, who was sorest hurt, was unable to eat anything. The hermit had no boat, and they were in his care, storm-bound, for five days before the seas abated

240

and their saviour's three fires, lit as signals, could be seen from the mainland, and a boat had duly come out from Aberdour to their rescue. The search for them, of course, had not extended nearly as far east as this, fifteen miles and more from Culross.

His listeners could only wonder and give thanks to God, St. Columba and the hermit.

It was some hours before the King awakened and David saw his brother. Alexander, who so prided himself on his physical fitness, hardly seemed the same man. He was gaunt and drawn and grey, hollow-eyed and still coughing blood despite Abbot Murdoch's remedies. Nevertheless he was clearly glad to see David, more so than the latter could recollect, since their childhood, in a strange state of mind, gripping David's arm and talking fast, almost incoherently, between his coughings and blood-splutterings. Evidently his dire experiences had affected him almost as greatly emotionally as physically.

"I have looked on death, cast within the very jaws of doom, Davie!" he exclaimed. "Fore God, I as good as died! For I lost all consciousness on those rocks, and would have slipped away into the shades without further knowing. Had not this blessed eremite Malbride rescued me. He delivered me, took me out of the power of the enemy! God put him on that island to save me, I tell you! It was a miracle! God must have work for me to do, yet, Davie. It must be so . . ."

"Of course He has, Alex. You are but forty years old. You have much good work ahead of you. But – I thank God indeed that you are safe. That our prayers were answered."

"I shall build an abbey on that island, Davie. As I lay there in that hut, I vowed a vow that I would, if God permitted my rescue." A great bout of coughing brought up much scarlet froth into a basin which the Abbot held out, shaking his grey head, and for a while the King could not speak. Indeed the Abbot signed to David that he should withdraw, murmuring that His Grace was better not to talk. But Alexander found his voice again, however brokenly.

"An abbey, I say . . . instead of that hut! A true abbey, of stone, with a noble church. I shall dedicate it to St. Columba himself, since it is his isle. But it will not be a Columban abbey but a Roman, see you. This I swear! And that eremite shall have my protection all his days. This I swear also. I, I . . ." The rest was lost in a red flood.

David slipped away.

They remained three days at Culross, with David acting for his brother on certain matters brought by the Chancellor and

241

other officers of state. Alexander improved only slowly, the coughing lessening in intensity but still producing blood. It was clear that he would be in no fit state to be moved for some time yet. David could not linger indefinitely, with many issues requiring his attention in the South and left suddenly.

At their parting, on the fourth morning, Alexander indicated that he wished to speak with his brother alone. "Davie," he said, "if this should yet go ill with me, watch you for Angus, Ethelred's elder son now that Duff is dead. Now Earl of Moray. Young Angus MacEth, he calls himself, Malcolm's brother. I am told that he has ambitions to be king. Claims that as son of our elder brother, he has the right. Also his mother was Lulach's daughter. So he represents the old line. Watch him, I say. Malcolm is well enough, I think – but watch Angus!"

"The lad may dream dreams, Alex. But you are crowned on the Stone of Destiny. You are undoubted High King. That is all that signifies."

"While I live, yes – while I live, perhaps . . ."

They left it at that.

*   *   *

It was as well that David returned to Caer-luel when he did, for it was to find major developments in train. First of all, sadly, his viscount, Richard d'Avranches, had broken his neck in a buck-hunting incident, leaving a major gap to be filled in the Cumbrian leadership as well as a personal loss. Then Bishop John had at last arrived back from his prolonged exile-pilgrimage. He came back in modest triumph, his cause vindicated. Pope Calixtus was dead and Honorius the Second reigned in his stead, a very different man who was no friend to Henry Beauclerc. Now the Vatican had confirmed that Glasgow was the pontifical see of Cumbria and that John was lawfully bishop both in Scotland and England. At first it had seemed as though there would be no success, for on John's arrival at Rome he could by no means again an audience with Calixtus – who admittedly was ill but who also was unsympathetic towards his cause. He was told to wait, and wait again. So, partly to fill in the time of waiting and partly to register protest, he had gone off on an onward pilgrimage to Jerusalem, as great a joy and privilege as it was a device. And when he returned to Rome, Calixtus was dead and Honorius was Pontiff – and was engaged in undoing much of his predecessor's work. He made no difficulties over John's plea, ordered him to return

242

to his see; and at the same time declared against Eadmer's retiral from Scotland as neglect of duty, pronouncing that if Eadmer refused to resume his episcopal duties in Scotland and the primatial see, he was unworthy to be Bishop of St. Andrews, and another must be appointed. So all was well, and the Scottish episcopate was endorsed. Incidentally Eadmer's own domestic position was no longer secure, for as John had learned only a few days previously, Ralph of Canterbury himself had died. When a new Archbishop came to be appointed, King Henry would find it more difficult to get his nominee endorsed by Honorius. So the situation was improved on all counts.

Most of this much pleased David, needless to say. But Bishop John's other news was less satisfactory. King Henry was back in England, indeed in the *North* of England. He was apparently engaged in something which he had never previously thought to do – visiting York and Northumbria and the word was that he intended to come to Cumbria also, thereafter.

John had another item of information regarding Henry. Possibly as a counter-stroke to his reduction of influence at the Vatican, he had just married his sole remaining legitimate child, Matilda, to the Holy Roman Emperor, Henry the Fifth.

David was, of course, much exercised over the news of Henry's northern tour, especially the prospect of his coming to Cumbria. This was something quite new and presumably significant, meaning – what? Henry had for long seemed to be more interested in Normandy and France than in England. Also in the past when he had wanted to see his subjects, he summoned them to his presence, did not go visiting them. So far as David knew, he had not been further north than Woodstock for years. York, Northumbria, Cumbria – what did it mean?

Confirmation reached Caer-luel presently. The King was at Durham with a large train, and was expected to cross the spine of England, by Weardale and Gilderdale, into Cumbria. Durham – Flambard!

To show that he was not lacking in courtesy any more than in due alertness, David despatched a welcoming party to meet the monarch at the Cumbrian border – although Henry had sent *him* no intimation of approach. He made what preparations he could for Henry's reception, doing so not without some sense of foreboding.

When the King's cavalcade eventually arrived at Caer-luel, David was surprised at its size and splendour – even though he had been warned that it was large. It was indeed a royal progress, a Court on the move, with earls and barons and bishops as well as officers of state, together with two members of his own family, illegitimate as they were, Robert and Elizabeth; although notably his new young wife, still disappointingly childless, was not of the party. Henry had allegedly taken a vow that he would never smile again, on hearing of the drowning of William the Atheling; nevertheless he was now showing a sudden and marked interest in his hitherto neglected bastard Robert, aged sixteen, for whom he had found an heiress wife, and created Earl of Gloucester. Of the girl, Elizabeth, aged a year or so younger, David had not heard.

The King's greeting to his former brother-in-law was carefully civil but not warm. He was looking his age of fifty-five and inclining to fat – although nothing like the dimensions of Bishop Flambard, who bulked massively behind him.

"Ah, David – it is good to see you, good to catch you!" he exclaimed. "I feared that we might not, that you might be . . . elsewhere. So busy a man! Ever on the move, I am told."

"I have large territories to govern, Sire. I hope that I see you well? Not fatigued with *your* much travelling?"

"Why should I be, man? I am none so old, yet!" That was quick. "I am very well. Sufficiently well to look to my kingdom. To look closely!"

"I rejoice, my lord King. And hope that you approve what you see?"

"Not altogether, David – not altogether!" Henry turned. "Ha – here is the fair Matilda – so blooming, so altogether a delight! How excellent a wife I found for you, David!"

"That I have never questioned, Sire. Although I thought that I had found her for myself!" David managed a smile at that.

"More fool you, then! I planned it before you thought aught of it, man!"

"Then Your Grace had the gift of prophesy!" Matilda put in, calmly. "Moreover, you traduced one of your own earls! For the Earl Simon was still much alive when David first expressed his devotion to me. And I to him. We did nothing, nothing to injure Simon's rights as husband. But we *knew* our own hearts. Did Your Grace plan that also?"

David looked at his wife with a surge of affection and admiration, that she should speak out thus in front of all.

Henry frowned, but recovered himself quickly. "So we were of a like mind! Our judgment concurring. But . . . did we judge aright, woman? Did we judge this man aright? Was he worth it?" With that thrust Henry moved on into the castle.

Just when the King had intended to announce the reasons for

his visit was not to be known. But undoubtedly it was precipitated by an encounter of the two bishops, Flambard and John, which took place whilst first refreshment was being dispensed and before the larger banquet. These two had long known and disliked each other, from Winchester days. Flambard was not long in referring John's presence there to the King.

"Here is one whom we looked not to see on Your Grace's soil of England!" he said. "The clerk John, still calling himself bishop! I had thought him . . . gone. And deservedly. At the Holy Father's command."

Henry stared where he pointed. "The tutor, yes. As such, responsible for much, perhaps!" He turned to David. "How is it that this man is still here? Was he not to be dismissed?"

"Dismissed, Sire? By whom? Not by me. Nor yet by you, surely? We scarcely can dismiss from the episcopate!"

"By the Pope in Rome, man."

"But he is new back from Rome. Confirmed in his bishopric of Glasgow, as pontifical see of Cumbria. By Pope Honorius."

"What . . . !"

"Confirmed, yes. Is it not most satisfactory? For all. No further disruption nor doubts. Your Archbiship Ralph was mistaken – may he rest in peace, nevertheless, for we hear that he has died."

Henry looked at Flambard. It seemed evident whence the initiative for John's demotion had come.

"The new Pope has been . . . misled," that man said, with difficulty. "He must be informed, Sire. Better advised."

John spoke up. "His Holiness questioned me, and others more illustrious, closely, my lord King," he said. "He was well and truthfully informed. And advised by his College of Cardinals. He had no doubts as to his decision. About my humble self. Or about Bishop Eadmer . . ."

"Eadmer?" Henry barked. "What of Eadmer, man?"

"He is to return to his see of St. Andrews, forthwith. Or yield it to another. A papal command to that effect was being sent to Canterbury."

The King glared around him. "This is . . . insufferable! Why have I heard nothing of it?"

None cared to answer that. But Flambard did his best.

"Your Grace will recognise that there are advantages also," he said, smoothly now. "For since the good Ralph is gone, until a new appointment is made to Canterbury, the excellent Archbishop Thurstan is Primate. And so will be the new Pope's chiefest adviser in England!"

"Ah, yes – true," Henry nodded. "So we may yet look for better things and an end to these follies. In matters of religion." He turned back, to look straight at David. "But there are other matters to be put to rights. Not involving churchmen, thank God! Matters where I alone must make decision. I find that all is not well, on my return from Normandy. I find neglect and failure – and where I should not think to look for it. Not least in my province of Cumbria, David!"

The other had been more or less waiting for this. "I regret to hear it, Sire," he said carefully. "And shall be interested to hear wherein I have failed you in Cumbria?"

"Are you blind, man? I think not. You have failed me in that you ever seek to be more King Alexander's viceroy than mine! You spend more time in Scotland than in my Cumbria. You build castles amany, as well as abbeys, in Scotland, with gold from *my* earldoms. You fortify the Scots march against England. You make a Scots bishop to have sway over my English province – as you have just shamelessly announced. None of this can you deny."

"With all respect, Sire, I do so deny." David strove to keep his voice even, reasonable. "In none of these matters has your province of Cumbria suffered hurt. The reverse indeed. All has led to the pacification of these parts. Instead of the lawlessness from which Cumbria used much to suffer. This no more – save for raids from Northumbria, which still go unchecked by those whose duty it is to halt them." And his glance switched to Flambard and the Earl Ivo de Vesci.

"That is no denial, man, but an admission. You are your brother's representative now, rather than mine."

"Can I not be both, Sire? To the advantage of all the march and border country? Which, I am assured, has never known peace and security such as it has today. Is that to your hurt?"

"It is to my hurt that you are now seldom at this Caer-luel. And still less often further south in Cumbria. The issues concerning my Cumbrian lords have to go to Scotland for decision – which is intolerable. While at the snap of Alexander's fingers, you are off to his side! He who humiliated my daughter Sybilla! Abandoned her. Then buried her on some remote island in that barbarous country, like any serving-wench!"

"Of that I know little, Sire. Save that Queen Sybilla had chosen to go her own way, for long. And now a nunnery is to rise in her memory."

"Do not fence with me, man! You, whom I cherished and made much of, from youth up. Whom I knighted and elevated

to earl. Appointed my viceroy here. I say that you have failed
me. At Huntingdon and Northampton, I had to take steps to
see that my interests – aye, and your own – did not suffer
further. Here, I see that I must do the same. As king it is my
simple duty. I do not dismiss you from my service, as I might
do. But the realm's interests must be safeguarded." Henry
paused, and turned. "Randolph de Meschin, there, from this
day is Governor of Cumbria. Governor, not viceroy. He will
govern it as I require. Athelulf, Prior of St. Oswalds, has been
consecrated bishop, by Thurston of York. He will be Bishop of
Caer-luel, with sway over Cumbria. And the Lady Elizabeth,
my daughter, will wed the Lord Fergus of Galloway – who, as
my son-in-law, will not fail to protect Cumbria's northern
borders. These, for the realm's weal, by my royal command!"

There was silence in that great chamber for long moments, as
men sought to take it all in. Matilda moved closer, to hold
David's arm tightly.

That man drew a deep breath. "I am in Your Grace's
hands," he said, into the hush. "I see that you came prepared.
Without hearing what I had to say. You recognise, I have no
doubt, what this will do to these border lands? It will divide,
where I have sought to bring together. Cause strife and enmity
instead of the peace I have worked for . . ."

"Not so. No need for strife – unless *you* foment it, from the
Scots side!"

"That I shall not do. But others may . . ."

"I think not. We shall *see* that they do not. We shall guard our
marches, never fear. You are not the only one who can build
castles, David. We shall build many. The good Bishop Flambard has already plans to erect a great new strength. On his
lands of Norham-on-Tweed. Conveniently close to your Rook's
Burgh! We shall preserve my peace, I tell you."

David bowed. "You are the King," he said.

Despite all Matilda's fine provision, the repast which followed was not a success. Reserve, suspicion, hostility were
evident on every hand. David's people acted but poor hosts to
the visitors. At the dais-table, Henry, between David and
Matilda, made little attempt at the civilities, and not unnaturally received only distant courtesies in return. An outright
quarrel developed between Hervey de Warenne and the new
Governor, de Meschin, a dark, saturnine man of middle years,
and their hands dropped to their dirks. David had to rise and
strongly rebuke both men, and their eager adherents, for daring
to raise their voices in the King's royal presence.

As host, David decided to countermand the appearance of the entertainers, since these would give opportunity for further drinking, with possible unfortunate results. The banquet in consequence broke up notably early, with Henry agreeing that he and his people were tired after their long riding, and with another lengthy journey in the morning, for he planned to be at Rufus's great castle on the Tyne next evening.

In their own bedchamber that night, David and Matilda discussed the situation. She was indignant, as well as sore-at-heart for him; but he was less distressed than he might have been, for he had seen something of the sort coming for long. He was surprised, admittedly, at the extent and detail of Henry's actions, and the forward planning involved. Also he was uncertain as to his own position now. But what did hurt him was Fergus MacSween's deceit, guile and almost betrayal, in agreeing to a marriage with this young daughter of Henry's, without any word to himself, his superior and friend. It must have been under arrangement for long. Fergus was not present; so far as they knew he was at one of his houses in Galloway. How he had been got at, David did not know; there must have been comings and goings for some time, for Henry had said that the wedding would be so soon as the Eve of St. Luke, at Westminster. Fergus, of course, had been a hostage in the South, with David, and would have many Norman links still.

In the morning, the royal entourage took longer to move off than Henry had indicated. When at length it was departure and farewells were being said, however stiffly, David put his question.

"Your Grace has appointed a new Governor of Cumbria, in your wisdom. Where does that leave me? I require to know my position now, Sire."

"Have I changed your position, David? I said that I did not dismiss you from my service – as I might have done."

"But . . . you have put this de Meschin in my place."

"Not so. He is governor. You viceroy."

"You mean . . . that I am still your viceroy? Yet de Meschin governs. How can that be?"

"You represent myself, the Crown, in these parts. Better than you have done hitherto, I hope! De Meschin *rules* Cumbria. To my requirements. It is a sufficiently large territory. Between you, pray God, you will do it justice! Or I must needs make other arrangements still. Now – we must ride. Matilda my dear – you used to have a good head on your shoulders. Guide this one well – for he needs it! God keep you all . . ."

No wiser, they watched the King go, leaving the taciturn de Meschin and the new Bishop Athelulf behind. If he left mystification also, it was very much mixed with warning. Henry Beauclerc might be devious, but his actions were seldom unplanned.

For his part, uncertain as to his position as he still was, David did not take long to decide on his own immediate actions. When he learned that de Meschin intended to take over at least part of Caer-luel Castle for his own headquarters, and recognised that resentment between his own supporters and lieutenants and the newcomers was going to boil over into trouble, and quickly, he called together his people. He told them that he saw this new position as impossible. There could not be two masters at Caer-luel. So he was going to pack up and go to Rook's Burgh, to reside. Since they were all subjects of King Henry, however, he advised, reluctantly, that they came to terms with the new Governor, who would no doubt be glad to have the advantage of their knowledge and experience here and would probably maintain them in the most of their positions. If, however, any of them were strongly against this course, they could come with him to Rook's Burgh – but he reminded them that this was in the realm of Scotland, and any removal thereto on a permanent basis could put them much at Henry's displeasure. He was distinctly surprised and much moved when every one of his Cumbrian team, Norman and Saxon alike, vehemently opted to move with him into Scotland. Nothing would change their minds; they would not stay to serve under this interloper, de Meschin, and his upjumped crew. Let him seek to govern Cumbria as best he could. King Henry and he would soon be sending for the Earl David and themselves to come back and clear up the mess. There was room for all in Strathclyde, they were all aware.

Matilda glowed with pride in her husband's capacity to generate loyalty – even though not in Fergus Mac Sween apparently – and gave orders for all their domestic establishment at Caer-luel to be dismantled ready for transport northwards. They would move in a matter of days.

So ended the experiment of mutual and unified government of the borderlands. Despite its success, it was probably fated from the start, given the prejudices and failings of human nature.

The move to Rook's Burgh was like a tribal migration, for many of David's people had found wives amongst the local folk and produced children. No regrets were expressed on either side – but undoubtedly lists of names would be compiled by de Meschin and sent to Henry.

As Viceroy and Governor of Strathclyde, David sent for Fergus, Lord of Galloway to attend him at Rook's Burgh – only to be informed that he had already departed to the South for his wedding.

They settled in comfortably and indeed somewhat relievedly, where Teviot joined Tweed, David sending out his lieutenants to overseeing duties all over Strathclyde. He had some difficulty in restraining those who remained, together with de Soulis in Liddesdale and de Brus in Annandale, from marching the fifteen miles or so to Norham-on-Tweed, there to demolish the preliminary work on Flambard's new and rival castle. Bishop John, not grievously upset by being spared spiritual responsibility for English Cumbria, went to take up his abode at Glasgow on the Clyde, towards which David would have to turn his attention more frequently.

So that winter passed, with precious little coming and going between Caer-luel and Rook's Burgh, David expecting any day to receive word of Henry's further displeasure and an end to his now merely nominal viceroyalty. But the word which reached him first came from Stirling, not London, and put a final end to this limbo period. It came in late April 1124, and not by any courier but by an illustrious deputation, led by his cousin Madach of Atholl, Constantine, Earl of Fife, Robert the Chancellor, young Malcolm mac Eth and others. Madach dropped to his knees before him – they all did.

"My lord David – greetings!" he said. "The lord Alexander died at Stirling three days back. In the presence of myself and others, after long ailing. God rest his soul. He named you heir. You are by God's grace, undoubted King of Scots. I claim proudly to be first to render fealty to my liege lord." And he held out his two hands, to enclose David's, in age-old gesture of homage.

Part Three

20

THE MINSTER OF the Holy Trinity at Dunfermline was full to overflowing for the first ceremony of the new reign – or was it the last of the old? The great church was now to be turned into an abbey, in accordance with one of the last of Alexander's commands, with impressive rights and privileges and endowments of lands, as befitted his own last resting-place. David, with Matilda on his arm paced out from the sacristy which opened off the south transept, and on to the crossing, beneath the tall central tower. He turned towards the high altar and bowed deeply, Matilda curtsying. Then they turned right about, to face the crowded congregation massed in the still unroofed nave, and bowed and curtsyed again, although a shade less deeply. There was a stir throughout the church at this unexpected gesture from monarch to people at first encounter. Facing front again, the royal pair waited at the chancel-steps, alone. No word was spoken. Only the great bell tolled slowly, steadily, as it had done since sunrise that St. Mark's Day, the air in the minster seeming to quiver to the resonant clanging.

After a few moments the great west doors were thrown wide, and the funeral procession entered. First came a group of eight cymbalists, treading slowly and clashing their cymbals in time and tune with the mighty tolling bell overhead, a strangely, almost savagely impressive sound and progress which made more than the air to shiver. Then came a large choir of men and boys, but silent, heads bowed. There followed the Prior of Dunfermline, black stole over his gorgeous vestments – which had been sewn by the hands of Queen Margaret herself. He bore aloft the famous Black Rood, containing its revered portion of the true Cross of Calvary, brought for the occasion from Margaret's private chapel at the fort of Dunedin in Edinburgh. Behind this walked the Chancellor, Robert, Abbot of Scone. Alexander had appointed him *Ard Episcop* and Bishop-Elect of St. Andrews, in place of the dead Eadmer; but he was not yet consecrated to the episcopate. Bishop John of Glasgow had offered to do this, but it had been rejected for the same reason as heretofore – the Primate could not receive ordination at the hands of a lesser prelate without compromising his authority. So Robert must either journey to Rome, await the coming of some papal legate, or hope that the newly appointed William, Archbishop of Canterbury, would prove sympathetic and undemanding. So now only an acolyte carried the magnificent crozier of St. Andrews, as symbol.

Finally came the dead King, borne in an open coffin upon the shoulders of his *ri*, the lesser kings of the Scots realm, young and old. There should have been eleven of these mormaors or earls, but three were missing and one was too ill to be present. However, Cospatrick of Dunbar, although not one of the *ri*, was an earl of Scotland and took station on the left at the foot, so that there were eight to carry the High King, *Ard Righ*, on his last earthly journey.

Breaths were caught and prayers muttered as this illustrious group, so seldom seen all together, sombrely made its burdened way up towards the chancel, to the heavy clangour of bell and cymbals.

At the steps, the instrumentalists and choir moved left and right, to allow the clergy, with crucifix and crozier, to lead the coffin-bearers onwards. David and Matilda fell in behind them.

Before the high altar a great greenish Iona marble slab had been raised from the floor and moved aside, to reveal a gaping hole. On the lip of this the procession paused, the clergy to move round to the east of the cavity, the earls and their burden to remain on the west. David led Matilda to a throne-like chair on the right of the chancel, and then returned to take his place now at the head of the coffin, under which he placed a shoulder.

The cymbals ceased their clanging and two strokes later the minster bell at last fell silent.

The Chancellor Robert intoned the first part of the burial service, his voice sorrowful but rich, the Latin phrases sonorous enough to sound almost as though they had taken over from the bell. But he did not prolong it, merciful towards those who had to stand holding up the massive coffin.

At a sign, a single cymbalist came forward, and at the same deliberate tempo as before, began to lead the clergy and bier-bearers down the stone steps into the underground crypt, which Alexander himself had had excavated. Slowly, heedfully negotiating those steps, the burial party dropped out of sight of all others in the church, while the clashing beat grew fainter, more hollow, sepulchral indeed, to most remarkable effect.

Below, in the dim light of candles, under the lowering vaulted roof, David watched, much moved, as the coffin was at last lowered, with much care, into the great leaden casket prepared for it at the head of the sad row of others – his family, mother, father, Edward, Ethelred, Edgar, with their half-brother Duncan the Second a little apart, now four kings and a queen and two princes. Apart from the unhappy Edmund, who was none-knew-where and might well be dead also, David was the last of that large family which had wrought such changes in Scotland, his sisters lying in foreign graves. Here, then, it all ended. Or, perhaps, here it all more truly began? In a row of leaden caskets under a stone vault. If and when he might tend to grow above himself, to see himself, as monarch, more illustrious than other men, let him remember this row of boxes, and pray for humility.

The Chancellor finished the burial rite, and the pall-bearers performed their last service to their chief, picking up the enormously weighty leaden lid from the floor and placing it over the embalmed corpse – where, despite all their care, it fell with a most final thud that seemed to shake the very crypt.

The cymbalist led the living up and out. At their appearance the choir began to chant an anthem, sweet but sorrowful, before the Prior pronounced benediction.

As the royal couple led the earls down through the congregation in the roofless nave to the west door and out, many sank on knee at their passing. But David gestured them upright. For he was not king yet, and it was important that this should be realised. He could only be Hing King by the election and decision of his lesser kings – which was still to come. He and Matilda had only arrived at Dunfermline from Rook's Burgh the previous night.

Out in the early May sunshine, they walked the short distance to Malcolm Canmore's small palace, David's old home, through crowds uncertain whether or not to cheer – for this was after all the return from a funeral. Most smiled – but not all, for kings were in general far from being objects of popular affection. Alexander, although more so than the withdrawn Edgar, had scarcely been beloved by his people – his by-name had been the Fierce, after all, and he had a reputation for being terrible towards those who opposed him. And Malcolm, their father, had been hated – but feared. Which he had said was as it should be. So David scarcely looked for adulation.

In a private chamber of the palace the all-important meeting was held. For tradition's sake David would have preferred to have held it in Iona. But that was now impossible, with all the Hebrides in Norse hands, thanks to Edgar's weakness. None of the Margaretsons had gone there. But Dunfermline would serve – and the outcome was certain enough. Only numbers were in doubt.

It did not take long. They sat round a table with beakers of wine, nine of them only, although the Chancellor stood by the door. Constantine, Earl of Fife, not David, sat at the head. On his right were the Earls of Atholl, Angus, Mar and the Mearns. On his left, Strathearn, Buchan and Dunbar. David sat at the foot.

"I see the *ri* of Alba," Fife said the time-honoured phrase. And added, "And I see the Earl of Dunbar. I do not see Moray or Ross or Sutherland."

The Chancellor spoke from behind them. "All were sent message, my lords. There has been due time. My lord of Sutherland is not of age."

"So be it," Fife said. "We are eight – sufficient. Six would be sufficient. Who names a name?"

"I do," Madách said. "I name David mac Malcolm, brother of the late *Ard Righ*."

"I say likewise," Malise of Strathearn seconded.

"Does any say other?"

No voice was raised.

"Then I, Constantine of Fife, declare that David mac Malcolm is *Ard Righ* of Alba, High King of Scots, by consent of all here. Who pledge to support him to the death, with their voices, their swords, their mortuaths and their all. So say I."

"So say I!" each of the others repeated in turn round that table, until they came to Cospatrick, who added, "I have no vote. But I proclaim the same support."

David rose and went to each man, not for any kneeling of fealty hand-holding but to clasp every man, forearm to forearm in the symbolic, firm Pictish grip. To each he said,

"I, *Ard Righ*, will uphold you as you uphold me."

That was all. It was as simple as it was brief. Yet only one other ceremony was more important in all the Scottish scene.

Yet there was the shadow. Although summoned, two of their number had failed to come. Admittedly they were the farthest off, the mortuaths of Moray and Ross, with Sutherland, embracing all the very North of Scotland. But both the Earls of Moray and Ross were young men, and could have reached Dunfermline in time had they so desired. That they had not come for this most essential meeting, if not the funeral, was ominous. Especially when both were nephews of David – Angus, eldest son and heir of Ethelred, Earl of Moray; and

Malcolm, a bastard son of Alexander's own, whom he had made Earl of Ross in room of a descendant of King MacBeth, deceased. So both could conceivably make claim to the throne. Alexander's last words to his brother had been to warn him against Angus – but he had not mentioned his own illegitimate son Malcolm.

Normally there was no great hurry about the coronation ceremonial, which always took place at Scone, the traditional heart of Alba. But David felt strongly that he would not be truly and undeniably king until he had sat as such on Scotland's talisman, the *Lia Faill*, the Stone of Destiny. Also many of these mormaors, earls and lords would require to be present, and it would be convenient to have it while they were still assembled. So the ceremony was fixed for only two days hence.

It was Matilda's first visit to Alba or Scotland proper, as distinct from Strathclyde, Lothian and the border lands, and she was greatly taken with what she saw of the country its colour, its scenery and its people, all so strangely different from England. To come to it, for the first time, as its queen, made its impact the greater. Hills everywhere affected her with a great feeling of excitement, an urge to be amongst them, to master them, to see what lay beyond, unlikely as this might seem for a woman reared in the level fenlands around Huntingdon. On every hand were hills, great and small, green and heather-clad or rocky, forested or bare. Especially the unending jagged barrier of the Highland massif, which rimmed all distant prospects to north and west, drew her eyes. Scone was not in the Highlands, but it was on the edge of them, only a few miles from where great Tay came surging out through the famous woodland jaws of the Pass of Birnam, from the vast mountain womb which gave it birth. This was the mightiest river in all Scotland, greater than Tweed or Spey or Dee – and Matilda had thought Tweed unsurpassable.

Scone, in fact, was placed exactly where it was *because* of the splendid river. For this was the point, over thirty miles inland from the sea, where the tidal ebb and flow ended and the life-giving fresh water conquered the death-dealing salt, a vital matter for the ancient Pictish folk who, although pagan, had been so concerned with the worship of the very elements of God's creation, fire and water, sun and air and the seasons. So they venerated not Tay itself but what Tay represented, the power of water, running water, which could not only defeat fire but could make the land fertile to support man and beast, provide fish for food – the salmon was a sacred symbol – drive mills to grind, and defend their forts with moats and marshes, and provide lochs for crannogs. So at Scone their priests and druids had set up an important temple of standing-stones; and later Columba and his missionaries from Iona had taken it over for a Christian monastery of the Celtic Church. And this Alexander had turned into an Augustinian abbey of the Roman Church. So although Romish ritual had been established only for a few years, worship had been offered here for millenia. It made an entirely suitable resting-place for the strange, mystic Stone which represented rule and timeless authority in this northern land.

Robert, the Chancellor, was still Abbot of Scone as well as Bishop-Elect and so in charge of the ceremonial. Nevertheless this was his first coronation, so he required the guidance and assistance of the Celtic Church, which was steeped in it. Fortunately this was readily forthcoming for, thanks to Margaret's skilful handling and little-by-little methods, the Columban clergy were in the main co-operative with their Roman superseders, naively so according to some, accepting the changes as perhaps necessary reforms.

The coronation service, as far as the ecclesiastical part was concerned, was still mainly Celtic therefore; and like most such, simple and brief, with only a few Romish additions. It was when, after the ritual washing, dedication, laying-on of hands, communion and benediction, the principals emerged from the abbey-church on to the Moot-hill outside, that the unique and dramatic aspect of it all took over. For like so much of the Celtic ceremonial, coronations in Scotland were held in God's open air and not in men's buildings – perhaps a strange conception for a land with such a doubtful climate.

The Moot-hill, or *Tom a Mhoid*, the Hill of Vows, was a low, grassy, flat-topped mound, not impressive until it was understood that it was made literally by bootfuls of soil from all over Scotland. Here was where, from time immemorial, the land-holders of Scotland had come, from far and near, to swear allegiance and fealty to their High King. But on their own soil, not his – which was why David's title would be King of Scots not King of Scotland. For the land was not his, only the people on the land, and held in trust by him for the said people, a conception seldom understood by visitors from other kingdoms, and especially difficult for Normans to comprehend, with their elaborate feudal system based on the King's ultimate ownership of all. So, when the land-holders, mormaors, earls, thanes, lords and chiefs, came to coronation, each brought with him a bag of earth from his own property. At the right moment he took off his boots and put a layer of the soil in each before re-inserting his feet, so that when he took his oath of allegiance he did so as a free man should, standing on his own soil. Thereafter the earth from boots and bags was emptied out, so that the Moot-hill grew that little bit at each coronation – for there were hundreds upon hundreds of samples to add each time.

When David and Matilda issued from the church it was to find vast crowds thronging the Moot-hill and spreading down the slopes towards the riverside haughlands – but not a soul on the hill itself. There, on the summit, stood only two stones; at first sight only one, for the second was small and flat. On a plinth of slabs stood the Stone of Destiny, black, gleaming dully in the early May sunlight, solid, enduring. It was oddly-shaped seat-height, round at base but squared off above to the oblong, with curved volutes at each end and a hollow in the centre of the top. Highly carved with typical Celtic interlacing and strange animals, it looked heavy, heavy, most probably formed from a meteorite. To this Stone David was led by his seven *ri* and the Abbot. Some said that it was Jacob's pillow, on which he had dreamed of angels ascending and descending at Bethel, which Pharoah's daughter Scota had brought to Ireland on her marriage to a Celtic prince. Those less credulous, opined that it had been a Roman altar. Others said that it was Columba's own portable font-cum-altar – the hollow for holding the holy water – or that of some other early saint. Whatever its origins it had been brought from Ireland in the sixth century by the Dalriadic Scots when they came to found their Argyll kingdom of Dalar, and installed at Dunadd their capital and transferred later to Scone in 844 when Kenneth MacAlpin united by marriage the Scots and Pictish monarchies.

Before this Stone, the High Sennachie came, colourfully garbed. He filled a role similar to that of chief herald and king's skald or saga-man. He now declared to all present that David mac Malcolm had been selected and chosen, most rightfully, by the mormaors of Scotland as *Ard Righ* and High King in the room of their late and mighty lord Alexander. That the rightness of their choice should be known and understood by all, he thereupon recited the royal genealogy. If this might represent a comparatively modest exercise for some of the monarchs of Christendom, it was far from it for the King of Scots. For a thousand years was as nothing in the Celtic race-memory, and where authentic ancestors failed mythical ones were never in short supply, right back to Biblical times. Moreover both Scots and Pictish lines had to be rehearsed, one rivalling the other as to magnitude, complexity and colour. So what started out sanely enough as David mac Malcolm mac Duncan mac Bethoc nic Malcolm mac Kenneth mac Malcolm and so on, ended up some seemingly immeasurable time later in unpronounceable fantasy. Yet none would have dreamed of interrupting or cutting short this quite unbelievable catalogue for the most ancestor-conscious race this side of Cathay.

When at last it was over, Abbot Robert led David to the two-stepped plinth of the Stone. There he administered the oath, on a magnificent illuminated vellum of the Scriptures, David repeating after him that he would maintain the true worship of God, protect the realm, uphold the laws and do justice without favour. Then bowing, he left David alone to mount the steps and turn, to stand facing all. So in silence he waited.

He stared around him, a lump in his throat. As well that he had no speech to make. This was the moment, the greatest moment there could be in any Scot's life. Once seated there could be no going back. This Stone would make him into a different man.

There was absolute silence on every hand, save for the sleepy quacking of mallards down in the water-meadows.

David took a deep breath and looked over at Matilda as Abbot Robert came behind him and placing a hand on each shoulder, pressed him gently down. He sat.

Like a flood released, the pent-up emotion of the crowds erupted into shouting. "God save the King! God save the King! God save the King!" On and on it went until the very hills surrounding seemed to shake. There was much more to be done, but this was what the thousands had come to see. David sat silent, watching, waiting, his mind as much in a turmoil as on his wedding-day at Northampton.

Then at last a trumpeter blew for quiet. Constantine of Fife came forward with his son Gillimichael, who bore the crown of Scotland on a cushion. The Earl picked this up and bowing, placed it around David's brows. Madach of Atholl came with the sword of state, to lay across David's thighs. Ruari of Mar brought the sceptre, Malise of Statherarn the Book of Laws, other *ri* the remaining symbols of rule and governance. Finally Matilda was led to stand behind the Stone, with Henry mac David, undoubted heir to the throne.

David had no hand to spare to clasp his Queen's, but she

gripped his shoulder proudly, in support. He needed support then.

He rose, burdened, and one by one, save for the crown which he kept on his head, he handed the other symbols to the Abbot and Sennachie to be laid on the Stone. Then he moved over to the other lesser stone. This was merely a simple granite boulder half-imbedded in the ground. But on it was carved the imprint of a man's right foot, cut to perhaps an inch of depth. This also had been brought from Dunadd. Here each of the *ri*, but they only, drew from pocket or pouch a small bag. From these each poured a little earth into the carved footprint. Then kicking off his right sandal, David placed his bare foot on top, pressing down the symbolic soil under his sole, in token of *his* authority.

There remained only the fealty-giving. But since this involved many hundreds of land-holders, in their due order of precedence, names read out by a team of sennachies, not to mention the formal soil-emptying thereafter, it took as long as all the rest together. Throughout David had to sit on the Stone again, crowned, and take each man's hands within his own and repeat his name and style after the High Sennachie. Before that was finished he was weary and stiff indeed and Matilda beside him pale with her long standing.

But the thing was done at last, and need not be done again, God willing, until it was young Henry's turn. Now, only refreshment, feasting, for all, there on the riverside grassland. They had still to play host, the gracious king and queen, to greet and smile and listen. But that would not tax them too greatly. And tomorrow, whatever anyone wanted him to do, whatever else was planned, David would say them nay and take Matilda off into those Highland mountains which beckoned her, to be just themselves. That was a promise.

Even monarch and consort were entitled to that, surely?

21

ROOK'S BURGH WAS perhaps not the most convenient position for a royal palace – as David's ministers and officers were apt to tell him. Situated on the very southern edge of the kingdom, it was highly difficult of access from most of the rest, and a long way for official folk to travel from central parts. Moreover, the King's normal residence, as well as being reasonably central, ought surely to be in Scotland proper, ancient Alba, the heartland, not down here on the rim of the Merse, territory which was incorporated in the realm only a century or so before. David mildly accepted that, but stubbornly continued to make Rook's Burgh his main home. He pointed out that he was quite prepared to call Stirling his capital, as Alexander had done; or his father's Dunfermline, if that was preferred; or Scone or Dunsinane or Forteviot, even Edinburgh, or any other of the more central places favoured by his predecessors. He would go thereto for all necessary duties, councils, ceremonial and so on. But the March Mount of Rook's Burgh was his own house chosen and built by himself, in country of which he and his wife and family were fond. After all, other monarchs had had their favourite seats, often far from their capitals – Alexander at Invergowrie, MacBeth far away up in Moray, Kenneth at Kincardine in the Mearns. But as well as all this, there was an excellent reason why the royal presence should be made very evident here in the border lands. For this was the most vulnerable part of his kingdom. The fact that it was the latest addition, not part of the old Alba, meant that it could be most easily detached again. And the English nearby were ever ready to detach it – as they had done fairly recently to the Cumbrian part of Strathclyde. Nothing would be more likely to deter any such attempts, he asserted, than the frequent residence of the King of Scots therein.

It was a telling argument – whether or not he really believed it himself.

But Rook's Burgh had another disadvantage even more frequently pointed out, also concerned with accessibility – but on a different level. Built as a strength, a fortress, at the junction of two rivers, it was damnably difficult to get at. Both rivers were wide and the peninsula between steep and rock-bound. Access had to be gained by going half-a-mile up Teviotdale, to the nearest fording-place, and there crossing and approaching the castle from the west, climbing on to its spine, a most round-about route for all visitors save from the west itself. In fact, from the north, it required a ford of Tweed first, at Kelshaugh; from the Merse likewise. This David could by no means deny – although he pointed out that it did give the occupants the advantage of warning of all approachers, which could be helpful. After all, Stirling Castle, and Dunedin likewise, on their lofty rocks, were scarcely easy of access either.

This disadvantage of the site was in fact rather self-evident this June afternoon of 1125, when David had been on his throne for thirteen months – yet he had deliberately chosen this venue for what was certainly the first really important essay in statecraft of the reign. As he saw it, the meeting had to take place somewhere in Bishop John of Glasgow's see, since this was the only one with papal recognition in Scotland, as yet.

Bishop John, his old tutor, rode with him now as he splashed across the Rook's Burgh ford, with others, to climb to the higher ground beyond and rein up, facing eastwards. Some, including the Chancellor, Robert – who was inclined to be stuffy – suggested that even this was unsuitable, that the King should actually go out to meet his guests instead of letting them come to him; all right for lesser men, but . . . To which David had pointed out that this was no ordinary guest – and had gone.

"A large company," he commented to John, peering into the middle distance. "Hugo would not have sufficient horses. He would have to hire more at Berwick. Do princes of the Church usually travel in such state?"

"In Rome, yes, Sire. But for a sea voyage, I would not have looked for it."

"Holy Church proving that there is more to holiness than meek looks!" Hervey de Warenne, Lord of Keith, the new Knight Marischal of Scotland, growled. He had ever been the least religiously inclined of John's pupils.

The approaching cavalcade was almost a mile off still, coming along at a suitably dignified pace after fording Tweed, all banners and glitter, the music of instrumentalists, which David had sent with Hugo, wafted faintly on the easterly air-stream. The watchers, however, perceived that a single rider spurred ahead of the main body, towards them.

This proved to be young Thomas de Mautelent, esquire to Hugo, from the de Morville manor in Huntingdon. "Sire," he cried, "the Lord Hugo sends me. To tell you that all is well. With the Cardinal. But he says to tell you also that the Lord Fergus is here. With his lady. They came in the cardinal's ship, from London. To Berwick . . ."

"Fergus! *Fergus*, you say? Of Galloway?"

"Yes, my lord. With a large train."

"That viper . . . !" Hervey snorted – he who had been Sweenie Mac Sween's closest friend once. "What does *he* want?"

"I know not, lord . . ."

"Forget Fergus for the present," David said. "What is important is the Cardinal. How does he seem, Thomas?"

"A dark-avised man, Sire. But softly-spoken. Smiling little . . ."

When the company of perhaps five-score came up, gorgeously-dressed and decked-about, Hugo silenced the musicians.

"My lord King – it is my honour to present to you the Most Illustrious lord Cardinal John of Crema, papal legate of His Holiness at Rome."

David had dismounted. "I rejoice to hail the illustrious lord Cardinal, and welcome him most warmly to my realm," he declared. "This is a notable day, the Eve of St. Columba – the first visit of a papal legate to Scotland. My lord Cardinal – have you a blessing for me – who need it?" And King though he was, he sank to his knees there on the grass – as so perforce must all the waiting group, however much Hervey muttered.

"The Holy Father sends his warm greetings, my son David," the other said, in a mildly sibilant voice in contrast to his stern, almost cadaverous appearance, a younger man than David had looked for, younger than himself. "And gives his Pontifical Benediction," he added, and raised two fingers to make the sign of the cross.

"I thank His Holiness. And yourself, my lord," David rose. "Here is the Bishop John of Glasgow."

"Ah, yes. I have, to be sure, heard much of this Bishop. Although I did not meet him when he was in Rome. Or in Jerusalem! His Holiness sends him greetings also." The Bishop was given something between a cross and a flick.

John bowed over the Cardinal's ring. "I am much honoured that the Holy Father remembered my unworthy self," he said – although David recognised well that it was only because Pope Honorius had remembered John of Glasgow that this momentous visit had come about.

"Sir Hervey of Keith, Knight Marischal of my realm . . ."

David turned to look at the other and larger party behind the Cardinal-Legate's group. Fergus Mac Sween grinned at him boldly enough. They had not seen each other, these two, for long. Fergus had kept out of the King's way ever since his surprising marriage to Henry's daughter, indeed spending much of his time in the South, with that young woman's brother, Robert the new Earl of Gloucester, and leaving Galloway in the care of his kinsman Dunegal of Nithsdale.

"Here's a happy occasion, my lord David!" he cried. "You

264

King, and myself in wedded bliss! Here is the Lady Elizabeth –
who has heard much of Your Grace."

David was not a man to harbour resentment, but it
demanded some effort to greet Fergus and his wife with civility.
his old school-fellow had not in fact, committed any major
offence against him, nothing that he could be charged with –
only entered into negotiations with King Henry secretly, without informing his superior and friend, to the extent of marrying
the daughter. Was that so ill? Only, Henry always had sufficient reason for all he did; and to give this Elizabeth to anyone
so remotely situated and comparatively unimportant as the Lord
of Galloway, not even a subject of his, he must have gained
something substantial in return. That was what worried David.

"I wondered when I would see you – and this lady," he said,
stiffly for him. "But I welcome you back to my kingdom, Fergus
– for there are matters in Galloway requiring attention. As to
your wife, I wish her well. For her own sake, and as her father's
daughter." That was the best he could do.

The new Lady of Galloway was a thick-built, pale but pert
young woman, who reminded him of the late Sybilla, but with a
less calculating eye. The Conqueror's line did not breed good
looks. She curtsied and smirked. David wondered what Fergus
would get out of this match, as well as Henry.

It seemed that the Cardinal's ship, from Italy had put in at
London on its way north, for the Legate to have some discussion with William, the new Archbishop of Canterbury; and
whilst there, Fergus had heard that the vessel was bound for
Berwick-on-Tweed and had sought passage. As the King's
son-in-law, the Cardinal could scarcely refuse. There appeared
to be no more to it than that.

They remounted and rode down to the ford.

If Fergus's arrival was a surprise, a further surprise awaited
the King, for after refreshment and settling in, with introduction of the others who would take part in the discussions, when
David, who was seldom one for delay, suggested in early evening that they might make a start on preliminary matters, it was
to be told by the Cardinal that it might be better to wait a little
to allow the Archbishop Thurstan time to arrive.

"Thurstan? The Archbishop of York!" David exclaimed.
"Do I hear you aright, sir? Thurstan – coming here?"

"Indeed, yes, my son," the other said calmly. "Did you not
know? Not realise that he must be here? We can scarcely
enquire fully into this matter lacking his point-of-view, can
we?"

"He agreed to come? Himself? To Scotland? Into my house?"

"I required him to do so, in His Holiness's name," the other said simply.

So they had to wait, David now in some disquiet. When he had written to the Pope, as one of the monarchs of Christendom, requesting a papal pronouncement on the ubdoubted independence of the Scottish Church and a decision on the vexed matter of the consecration of Robert to the see of St. Andrews, making use of Bishop John's new-forged links with the Vatican as lever; and had been rewarded by the announcement that a special papal legate would be sent to resolve the matter, he had been elated. But this bringing in of Thurstan might well put a very different complexion on the business, for of course Scotland had no churchman to speak with the authority of an archbishop. Clearly the debate was not going to amount to any mere formal pronunciamento, as David had hoped.

Another aspect which began to disturb David was some evident lack of sympathy between the Cardinal and Bishop John. It was no doubt more on the Italian's part, but it was unfortunate, to say the least, with John the only accepted episcopal dignitary present; for although Cormac of Dunkeld and Gregory of Moray were there, the Legate appeared to be very doubtful as to their authenticity as bishops, neither having been consecrated by an archbishop or primate. There seemed to the Scots to be an arrogance about the Cardinal, partly hierarchal no doubt but possibly also racial, for although he appeared to be quite able to accept Normans as perhaps fit to be shepherds of God's flock, Saxons and Celts were a different matter – and of course both Cormac and Gregory were Celtic Scots, who had started their ministries in the Columban Church. David realised that he would have to keep his temper very much in hand if any success was to come out of this exercise.

Happily, Matilda seemed to make a great impression on the Italian, who surprisingly appeared to be something of a lady's man. Her husband reluctantly urged her to do her best with the Cardinal.

They took him to see the still unfinished Priory of Jedworth in the morning – with which he did not seem much impressed, being more interested in the castle being built nearby, for which he suggested some improvements. One visitor *was* very interested in the new monastery, however, a Saxon Benedictine monk named Gosfrid, whom William of Canterbury had sent north, in the same ship, in answer to an appeal from David for an experienced canon to make abbot of the new abbey at Dunfermline. The Cardinal ignored him completely, as no concern of his. But this Gosfrid appeared to be a useful, pleasant and effective youngish man; and he was exercised over the problems and stages of setting up a monastery here in Scotland, as he himself would be called upon to do.

When they returned to the March Mount, it was to find Thurstan of York arrived, with a large entourage – which included, to David's further displeasure, Flambard, Bishop of Durham.

Thurstan was now an elderly man, getting frail and brittle-seeming. He had thin, intellectual features which, although distinguished, seemed to lack strength, his whole bearing a strange mixture of surface authority and underlying uncertainty. He was frostily correct towards David, but appeared to be much more in awe of the Papal Legate – an awe which was far from reciprocated. He was, of course, another Saxon. Flambard, on the other hand, was easy, affable, assured, clearly the power behind the archiepiscopal throne, very much the former Lord Chief Justice of England, however grossly unwieldy now. The Cardinal paid rather more attention to him.

In the great hall of the castle the council took place. David sat at the centre of a long table facing directly across to the Cardinal. On the King's right was Bishop John, and on his left the Chancellor and Bishop-Elect Robert, while the Legate had the Archbishop and Flambard on his right and a couple of secretaries – both apparently titular bishops – on the left. The other two Scots bishops, with Abbot William of Shiel Kirk and Prior Osbert of Jedworth – and it was noted, the new Abbot-to-be of Dunfermline, Gosfrid – sat on John's right. David was a little uneasy over this apparent line-up of sides, as it were; that had not been his intention. It looked all too like a confrontation, and with the Cardinal on the wrong side. The rest of the hall filled up with spectators and members of the various trains. The Queen sat prominently.

David asked Bishop John to open the proceedings with prayer, and then, as introduction, read out the letter the Pope had sent him in answer to his own, asking him to cause the bishops of Scotland to meet together, in synod, and to receive with reverence his personal legate, the Cardinal John of Crema, to put the issues in dispute before him. This, although seeming to place their fate rather too much in the Italian's hands, at least indicated the Pope's acceptance that there was more than one bishop in Scotland, and so might give Cormac and Gregory authority to speak as such.

Since it was thus a synod and not a royal council, John took the lead thereafter. He declared their satisfaction in having the presence of the personal representative of His Holiness – and less warmly – the company of the Archbishop and his advisers. Without preamble he went on to declare that there were two major matters before them, one bearing on the other. Namely the claims of the archdiocese of York to spiritual hegemony over Scotland; and the refusal of Archbishop Thurstan to consecrate the Bishop of St. Andrews, or other Scots bishops, without recognition of such superiority. Which Holy Church in Scotland, an entirely independent kingdom, could nowise accept. Other problems stemmed from these – but did all agree that these were the vital issues?

Without waiting for any others, the Cardinal nodded curtly and ordered John to proceed.

After a glance at the King, who half-shrugged, half-nodded, the Bishop went on to point out that never, at any time, had the Scottish Church come under the authority of York, or Canterbury either. Indeed, as the Columban branch of the Celtic Church of Ireland, it had not even recognised the hegemony of Rome itself, for long centuries. It was only when the late and sainted Queen Margaret, His Grace's mother, introduced the Roman rite and rule into Scotland less than fifty years before, that papal authority was recognised. How then could the Archbishop of York, or any other claim such authority?

The Legate glanced at Thurstan.

That man coughed. "My lord Cardinal," he said, "There are three good reasons why I do so, must do so. Firstly Scotland is *not* an independent kingdom, since its monarchs owe allegiance to the Kings of England, as Lords Paramount. This as established by King Canute, by King William the First, King William the Second and now King Henry . . ."

"Untrue!" David intervened, although quietly, restrainedly. "I cannot sit silent while such statement is made in my royal presence, in this my realm. I owe allegiance to Almighty God alone, and to King Henry only in respect of my English earldom of Huntingdon. That stands."

"You, you may not admit it, Sire – but that does not alter the fact that the King of England so asserts. And did not your own brother, King Edgar, carry the sword of state, *England's* sword of state, at King William the Second's Crown-wearing? Surely symbol of allegiance and subservience?" The old man's voice shook, but he went on. "I say that, as my own liege lord asserts, the Kingdom of Scotland is subject to his paramountcy in matters temporal, so in matters spiritual it must be subject to the paramountcy of Holy Church in the King of England's dominions. As metropolitan of Holy Church in the northern parts of those dominions, I can do no other than assert such superiority."

Bishop John began to speak but the Cardinal held up his beringed hand. "Brother Thurstan – you said *three* reasons?"

"Yes, Illustrious – three. The second is this. The fact that the mistaken and heretical Columban Church in Scotland did not *recognise* the authority of Holy Mother Church at Rome and of St. Peter's glorious and undoubted successors, does not in any way affect their authority. The Pope's holy sway over Christendom is indisputable and indivisible, whatever blindness or error may prevail from time to time in any part. The fact that the Columbans estranged themselves from Rome does not mean that they were therefore outside the Holy Father's love and care. So this bishop's contention, for that sad period, means nothing. You cannot but accede, Illustrious?"

"We shall see. And your third point?"

"It is that Holy Church has never ceased to have spiritual charge and direction over Scotland from York. The Blessed Ninian who brought Christ to that land established a line of bishops at Candida Casa, which owed allegiance to York and were appointed therefrom. Later the Blessed Cuthbert also. And since then, in Queen Margaret's time, since there were no properly ordained or consecrated clergy in her land, she had to bring them in from York or Canterbury. Her sons likewise, as His Grace still is doing. So how can they claim independence?"

"Bishop – you wished to speak?"

"I do. If my lord Archbishop's last reasoning is accepted, no nation's Church could ever be independent, for at first all have to accept ordinands from otherwhere. There has been no Bishop of Candida Casa or Whithorn since the eighth century, when it and Strathclyde were not then in the realm of Scotland. There is no reason, other than spiritual pride and wordly vainglory, why York should seek to lord it over Scotland – save as an aid to English monarchial ambitions!"

"Insolent . . . !" the Archbishop quavered.

"May I speak, Illustrious?" Flambard intervened smoothly. "Does not the Bishop of Glasgow agree that one of the most potent forces for establishing Christ in Southern Scotland was

St. Cuthbert; who ruled from Holy Island and was consecrated bishop at York in 685? He held sway over all these parts – there is even a town and water with his name in Galloway. And Melross near to here was his monastery. He set up many of your churches . . .''

"May I remind the Bishop of Durham that St. Cuthbert was, in his Scottish period a bishop of the Celtic Church, not the Roman?'' Cormac of Dunkeld, said.

"That is not important, Illustrious – since he saw the error in time! What is important is that this country has traditionally been ruled ecclesiastically from York. And, if you will bear with me, there is another point to consider. Is Holy Church not divided, pontifically by law, into provinces or metropolitan primacies? Each under a metropolitan or archbishop. This Scotland, then, must come under some archbishop. The obvious and nearest is York. It can scarcely be otherwise.''

"The metropolitan need not be an archbishop,'' John contended. "There are provinces of the Church, independent, where the metropolitans are bishops. As in the Kingdom of Man. As should be Scotland's Bishop of St. Andrews, the King's Bishop – when he is consecrated. Which brings us to the second representation, Illustrious . . .''

"Let us be finished with the first first, Bishop!'' the Cardinal directed. "I have heard all these assertions. Has other any point not yet put forward on the first issue?''

"I am no bishop nor cleric,'' David said carefully. "But as well as supporting all that the Bishop of Glasgow has said, I would put a point before your lordships which you may conceivably not have considered. This of metropolitans. I had word one time with Magnus, son to the Earl of Orkney. He assured me that the Archbishop of Hamburg claimed to be metropolitan, not only over his own Germanic lands but over Norway, Denmark and Sweden and therefore over Orkney, Iceland, Man and the Hebrides, which the Norsemen had dominated. More still, over the coastal lands of Scotland and Ireland, where the Norse had settled. I agree that this is out of all reason. But – so much for metropolitans! I urge you to consider Hamburg when you talk of the claims of metropolitans.''

It was a long shot indeed – but it registered the first recognisable hit, on the Cardinal at least. For Hamburg archdiocese, being vitally important to the Emperor Henry, who was being difficult in his relationship with the Vatican, was therefore a delicate matter for Pope Honorius, who certainly would be concerned not to gratuitously offend its archbishop or the Emperor. The Legate's dark eyes flickered and for a moment or two his long fingers drummed on the table-top.

But Thurstan was not interested in Hamburg. "Orkney and Zetland are in *my* archdiocese," he declared strongly. "*I* appoint the bishops there. The rest is nonsense, as all must agree."

"Yet your lordship's Bishop Ralph of Orkney never leaves York!" Gregory of Moray pointed out, mildly. "Whereas the Archbishop of Hamburg's Bishop of Orkney lives and rules in those islands."

"Ralph was driven out by evil men . . ."

"This of Orkney and Hamburg is scarcely relevant," the Cardinal interrupted sternly. "I have heard enough." He all but glared round the table. "This other matter. Of the consecration. It appears to me that until this more important issue of the alleged superiority of York is settled, the consecration of the Bishop-Elect of St. Andrews must remain in abeyance. I spoke with William of Canterbury on this and he – I say rightfully – would not wish to consecrate in what could be Archbishop Thurstan's province. So the matter must wait until the other is resolved."

"We had hoped, Cardinal, that you yourself would consecrate the Abbot Robert as bishop. Here and now. You could well do so," David said.

"That would be . . . inconvenient, my lord King. A disturbance of due order."

"What of the inconvenience to my realm, Illustrious? To my Christian people? The thousands of them. That there should be no Primate, year after year. No sure authority. What of the disturbance of due order in a whole nation?"

"Holy Church, Sire, has its own divine order."

"But you are here, surely, with all the power of Pope Honorious. His Legate to deal with this very problem. Is it not for you to impose order on the discord here? Disorder which none can deny."

"Your impatience, my son, is understandable. But decisions must I fear await God's own good time. His Holiness instructed me to come, hear all the contentions and then to return to Rome for his personal decision. He will, I am sure, pay due heed to my own advice. But the decisions must be the Holy Father's own."

"Then all this has been but a beating of the air? For all that has been said the Pope already knows. Bishop John explained it

271

all when he was in Rome, and was consecrated by Honorius. And *I* wrote it again in letter."

"Letters and special pleadings are not the same as personal inquisition, my lord King. I have not come all this long way to beat the air, I promise you. I have been much informed and shall return well able to advise."

"And . . . that is all?"

"That is all, my son. The matter will be decided in due course."

David rose – as much to keep himself from further hot speech as anything else, although clearly there was nothing more to be gained by continuing talk there. They all rose, and bowed, as the King retired, his displeasure and disappointment a palpable thing – which was unlike him.

Matilda followed him out, to comfort and commiserate and to tell him what she thought of the Lombard Cardinal – and of Pope Honorius too, who presumably was ultimately responsible for this charade.

Nevertheless it was the Queen who, later, after the feasting, came to her husband – who had made a less attentive host than usual – with a word of encouragement. She had been plying the loathsome Legate with both wine and blandishments, she confessed, and he had become sufficiently mellowed to hint that his advice to the Pontiff would be that Thurstan's claims were no more substantial than they were in the best interests of Holy Church.

Which seemed to suggest that diplomacy and statecraft could operate on more than one level.

When the Cardinal started on his return to Rome next day, again apparently via London and Canterbury, David sent Bishop John with him – whether wanted or not – on Matilda's advice.

22

IT WAS TWO whole years before Holy Church's due order and God's good time produced decision. The Pope finally resolved the matter by declaring that Scotland's Church was in no way a dependency of York. And in order to forestall trouble in England, with Henry, he pushed the action on to William of Canterbury, creating him especial papal legate for the occasion, and directed him, as such, to order Thurstan of York to consecrate Robert of Scone as Bishop of St. Andrews and Primate, with the status of minor but undoubted metropolitan. So it turned out a triumph for David, however long delayed.

But by that time events had moved on somewhat drastically on the wider front, with Scotland not unaffected. The Emperor Henry the Fifth died suddenly, and there was trouble about the election of his successor, Lothair, producing a distinct hiatus in Christendom, and leaving Henry's daughter Matilda – now also being called Maud – a young widow. Henry was not one to let the grass grow, even over new graves, and within the year had married the sorrowing Empress off to Geoffrey, son of the Count of Anjou, by-named Plantagenet on account of the sprig of broom he wore in his jousting helmet as identification; no doubt, he deemed him a useful son-in-law in his unending struggle with the King of France. Hardly were the nuptials celebrated than Henry had the bemused bride back to England, from Rouen, minus her husband, for a further display of statecraft. He made formal announcement that Maud, his remaining legitimate offspring, was to be his heir in the dukedom of Normandy and the kingdom of England.

This of course set the cat amongst the pigeons. For a woman to be reigning monarch was unheard-of amongst the Normans, where the so-called Salic Law prevailed and rulers were essentially sword-wielders. Moreover, the Angevins were unpopular in Normandy. There was immediate trouble in that dukedom – where, however, Count Geoffrey was in a good position to help impose order; also murmurings all over Norman England. As a consequence of which Henry issued a peremptory summons to every major land-holder in his kingdom to come to Windsor on the Feast of Epiphany, there to swear to support the Empress – she was still being so called for prestige reasons – under pain of treason.

And, as Earl of Huntingdon, King David was summoned with the rest.

This, of course, put David in a quandary. To obey the bald summons could look as though he was indeed a subsidiary, a vassal King. Yet to refuse would be considered a hostile act, treason as far as Huntingdon was concerned; and Matilda's great lands there liable to forfeiture. Moreover Maud was his own niece, his sister's daughter, and he had no reason not to

273

support her. Scotland not being a subscriber to any Salic Law, David decided that he had no option but to go, although he must make most clear his position to all concerned. Although it was mid-winter and an interruption of the Yuletide festivities, the worst time of the year for travel, he took Matilda with him, along with a large and impressive train, as befitted a visiting monarch – including Chancellor Robert, for Thurstan to consecrate, however reluctantly.

At Windsor on the Thames, where the enormous castle of the Conqueror was being added to, Henry had all planned and stage-managed. All England that mattered was there, including many lords and counts from Normandy summoned on account of their English holdings – partly to keep them from making trouble in their own dukedom. Included amongst these was Stephen of Blois, Count of Boulogne, Henry's nephew and married to David's sister Mary's daughter, a handsome if petulant-seeming young man whom he had never previously seen.

David and Henry had not met since the former's accession, indeed not since the unhappy interlude at Caer-luel four years before. But now Henry was in affable mood, one monarch to another, apparently prepared to forget past differences.

David took the first available opportunity to emphasise that his answer to Henry's summons must be made entirely manifest to all as that of the Earl of Huntingdon, not the King of Scots.

"I well understand your position, David," the other said. "And I intend that it shall be emphasised by having you to be first of all to swear support for Maud. Before all my family and my earls and lords."

"That could be seen in another light, Henry – as though the King of Scots was but the first of your vassals. I would ask that it be announced, before I take this oath, that I do so with all my heart but only as Earl of Huntingdon, not as King."

"This oath is not one of fealty, man! Be not so thin-skinned. It is only to support my daughter in her legitimate and rightful claim to the throne of England, should I die. An oath which any monarch could swear without hurt to his position."

"Nevertheless, it could be seen otherwise. All others will be swearing as vassals, owing fealty."

"As so do you, for Huntingdon."

"*Only* for Huntingdon. Which is what must be made abundantly evident to all. Otherwise, Henry, I cannot swear."

The two kings eyed each other directly for a moment, Henry frowning. Then he shrugged.

"Very well. I shall see to it. Although it is unnecessary."

But on the morrow, when all was ready for the great cere-mony in the chapel of the castle, and all the lords and prelates of England, and much of Normandy, were massed, crowding the place uncomfortably, there was a hitch – whether spontaneous or contrived David did not know. But there, before all, when the line-up of the various categories of magnates was being marshalled by the heralds, young Stephen of Blois made vehe-ment and dramatic protest when he discovered that David was to take precedence in the swearing ceremony.

"It will not do!" he cried. "I am undoubted heir-male to the throne of England, as son of Adela, William the First's daugh-ter, and nephew of King Henry. If my cousin Maud, a woman, is to heir that throne, then at least it should be myself who first offers support."

There was some cheering for this, especially from the Nor-mandy Normans.

Since David could scarcely enter into an unseemly wrangle in front of all, there was an uncomfortable pause. Henry, from his chair-of-state up near the altar, sat unmoving. Roger, Bishop of Salisbury, the Justiciar, who was acting master-of-ceremonies, wrung his hands and looked unhappily at David – who gave a single brief but decided shake of the head.

Robert, Bishop-Elect and Chancellor of Scotland, although not involved in the proceedings, stepped forward from amongst the distinguished visitors, and spoke up.

"My lords – it is unconceivable that any should take prece-dence of a crowned king! My lord of Boulogne cannot fail to see that, surely?"

"King of *Scotland*, only!" Stephen sneered.

"Your lady's uncle, my lord!"

David had to speak. "My lord Bishop," he said to Salisbury. "May we proceed? I take the oath first – or not at all. And as Earl of Huntingdon."

"Yes. Yes, my lord King. My lord of Boulogne – you will swear second."

"Not so!" Another voice rang out through the crowded chapel. "*I* will swear second. I am the King's son, and an earl of England. I will not take place behind any count of France!" That was Robert, Earl of Gloucester, Henry's favourite illegitimate son.

"Curse you, Bastard!" Stephen shouted. "Are whores' gets now to rank before honest men?"

"My lords, my lords . . . !" Bishop Roger wailed.

David turned around and stalked up the chancel-steps to Henry's chair – the only man there who might have done so.

"This is intolerable!" he said low-voiced, tense. "And an offence in God's house. Stop it, Henry – or I leave this church."

"Tush, man – puppies must bark!" the other said. But he raised a hand, nevertheless, and raised voice also. "My lord Bishop – proceed. With the form as set forth."

David nodded curtly and returned to his place below the chancel-steps.

Roger pointed, wordless, for Stephen to stand behind David, and his cousin Robert behind him. Then Reginald de Dunster-ville, new Earl of Cornwall, another of Henry's bastards, Henry de Beaumont, Earl of Warwick, Hugh d'Avranches, Earl of Chester and the other earls according to seniority. The heralds had already marshalled the lesser lords of all degrees; and the archbishops and many bishops, who were not to swear but only to affirm their devotion to Maud's cause, were waiting in a side-chapel. The two young men at the front muttered and scowled, but they could not disobey the King's voiced command.

Bishop Roger bowed low to the King, and then to the Empress Maud, who sat in another chair at the opposite side of the chancel. Then he moved up to the altar, where he genuflected, took an illuminated gospel therefrom, and with this in hand, intoned a prayer. Then he turned back to mid-chancel.

"In the name of God the Father, God the Son and God the Holy Spirit, Amen," he said. "Before the throne of the Most High God, before which all earthly thrones must bow, we are gathered, at the command of the King's Highness, solemnly to pledge our support, one and all, to the cause of the excellent princess, the Empress Maud, daughter of our liege lord, to defend her rights hereafter against any and all so ever. In token of which I now call upon the King's Grace of Scotland, the Lord David, to swear first of all his adherence and most full support of the said princess; that when, in the fullness of God's providence the throne of this realm of England shall become vacant through the passage of our liege lord Henry to still greater glory, the said Lady Maud shall succeed to the said throne of England, as undoubted monarch. Although this, we pray Almighty God, may be long delayed. The said lord David to swear as an earl of England, Earl of Huntingdon in this realm, rather than as King of the Scots."

David stepped forward, and putting one hand on the gospel held out and the other raised, said,

"I, David, Earl of Huntingdon, swear my support as an earl of this realm for the right of the Princess Maud, my sister's daughter, to the throne of England when it shall be vacant by God's action, in the name of God the Father, Son and Holy Ghost, Amen."

As David bowed to the altar and turned to walk over to where Matilda sat in the south transept, Stephen of Blois waited for distinct moments after the Bishop's signal, before he came forward, muttered his declaration and turned to grin at Robert of Gloucester before strolling off.

Robert made a ringing affirmation, as son of the King and brother of the Princess, adding his own condemnation of all would-be usurpers, self-seekers and vainglorious pretenders.

After that the lengthy process went smoothly and without hitch.

Both monarchs had to be satisfied.

The next day, the chapel was the stage for a very different scene, with only a very few to witness it. Under the supervision of Archbishop William of Canterbury, a blandly genial prelate, stronger than he looked, Thurstan of York consecrated Robert of Scone Bishop of St. Andrews and Primate of the Scottish Church. William was acting as special papal legate, for, because of the peculiar situation in the English Church with its two metropolitans, whilst Canterbury was senior to York, it was not in a position to command York's obedience. The new Biship of Caer-luel, and Thurstan's vicar-general, the purely titular Bishop of Orkney, acted suffragans for the occasion, and all was done as briefly as could be, old Thurstan putting a stiff face on it. David and Matilda, with their chaplain Alwin and Bishop John of Glasgow watched. It was noticeable that Bishop Flambard of Durham absented himself, although he too was at Windsor.

Brief as it was, the actual ceremony and laying-on-of-hands had to be an amended and compromise version, as well as shortened, to suit both sides. The usual professions of obedience to the archbishop's authority had to be dispensed with, and Thurstan felt bound to declare that what he did was done to the orders of the Papal Legate and saving all rights of the archdiocese of York. For all that, the thing was done, and Scotland had a Primate again, duly, however reluctantly, ordained.

Thereafter David did not long delay at Windsor, professing the urgent affairs and demands of his kingdom. Henry did not seek to hold him back.

They returned north by way of Huntingdon where, as well as seeing the useful and reliable Sheriff Gilbert, David had an important function to perform. Matilda had advised that he ought to seek to lessen criticism, Henry's and others', that he spent most of the great Huntingdon revenues on building monasteries and castles in Scotland, by establishing a new monastery here at Huntingdon. So a suitable site had been selected at Great Paxton, on the Ouse six miles to the south, and the Sheriff had been instructed to gather a large and representative company to see the foundation of what was to be a new Augustinian priory.

Despite a thin rain off the fenland to the east, this proved to be a successful occasion. Archbishop William had found them one more suitable canon of Canterbury, as prior, another Saxon named Osbert. They brought him with them, endowing the establishment, in his presence, with rich lands, revenues, multures and the like, dedicating it to the Blessed Virgin Mary, as were all Augustinian foundations, that prayers might be offered daily for the souls of the Countess Matilda, her children and her husband the Earl David.

Then it was the long road back to Scotland.

23

If councils were to be judged by their length and the amount of business transacted, this one held in September in the fortress of Dunedin at Edinburgh, was surely notable. The first major royal assembly of the reign, with representatives from all over the kingdom, it had started on the Feast of St. Hyacinthus, the 11th, in the great bare dining-hall of the castle, in good style and even some initial enthusiasm, for there was much novel and potentially exciting for all the realm in what was to be discussed and decided, the impact of a fresh and vigorous mind on the affairs of the nation. But it was now the 14th and enthusiasm was flagging noticeably, especially amongst the young Normans, barons, knights and officers, on whom David was attempting to remodel and revitalise the distinctly jaded, haphazard, not to say crumbling patriarchal realm he had inherited, into a modern, twelfth century feudal-system state, organised, law-abiding, productive and effective. The King recognised that it would all take time, a lot of time and patience and learning by experience. But a start had to be made – and this was that start, at Edinburgh, however tedious for those unaccustomed to such indoor and non-martial exercises, debate, exposition, patient listening and decision-drafting.

It was not helped, to be sure, by the fact that few of the Normans could read or write, this applying also to many of the Scots lords; so that inevitably much of the detailed work of the council had to be in the hands of churchmen, always apt to be long-winded by fighting-men's standards. Added to the fact that the new Chancellor, who acted chairman under the King's presidency, was inexperienced – for now that Robert was Bishop and Primate, he had had to be replaced by Herbert the new Abbot of Shiel Kirk – and expedition could scarcely be expected.

It had taken until this fourth morning to get to the matter of the proposed parish system, an issue close to David's heart, whereby the entire land would in time be divided up into parishes with dioceses, for civil as well as religious administration, this not only greatly increasing efficiency, it was hoped, but bringing much closer church and state in a way which should benefit both.

It was when Chancellor Herbert had announced this as the fourth day's main programme, pointing out that it was bound to be a very large issue and must be very carefully considered, that there developed a revolt. Hugo de Morville, now Deputy Great Constable, came to David presently to inform him that his fellow-Normans had had enough and to spare. They could take no more of this endless talk. They beseeched the King to show mercy and call a halt. Let them have respite. One day, at least.

"Are they so quickly wearied in well-doing?" David demanded. "Like bairns! They think to be leaders of a kingdom, yet tire after three days debate?"

"They are little used to this, Sire," Hugo pointed out. "They would fight for you for three weeks, I swear – three months, three years! But this of clerks' talk and sitting still, ruling with their bottoms as Hervey calls it . . ."

"Aye, Hervey would! What do they want, these infants I

have brought to Scotland? A day's respite to do what? Whilst prolonging this council for all others?"

"Hervey . . . they all say that this Edinburgh is a notable place for hunting, Sire. In the forest and glades and marshes around yonder King Arthur's Chair mountain. There is much deer. Boars also and other beasts. A day's hunting, they say – and they will be the better councillors tomorrow!"

David grimaced. "You make a persuasive envoy, Hugo! Clearly you are of the same mind. Very well – but not a whole day. This afternoon we shall go hunting – if this forenoon my bairns work at this of the parishes. Tell them so, tell Hervey . . ."

But there was other kind of protest than one to come between a monarch and his reforms. It was his Saxon chaplain Alwin who came to him thereafter, reproachfully.

"Sire – they tell me that you are going hunting this afternoon. Have you forgot the day, my lord King? I reminded you last night. It is the Day of the Holy Rood, the Feast of the Exaltation of the Holy Cross."

"Save us – I had forgotten! In all this work of council and parishes. It is God's work too, Alwin, mind you. But . . . it is not one of the major feasts, see you. Not any grievous sin to miss it. This once."

"*You* say that, Sire – you, whose blessed mother brought the Black Rood to this land. Part of the Holy Rood itself, which now stands in this very castle! Surely of all days, and Your Grace of all men . . . ?"

"M'mm. Yes. Ah, well – we can do both, Alwin. Have a celebration, a mass for the Holy Rood. Then go hunting afterwards."

"But that is scarce suitable, Sire . . ."

"I have given my word, man. They shall have their hunt – but shall attend your mass first. See you to it."

"Where, my lord? The Queen's chapel here, wherein is the Rood, is too small to hold more than a dozen . . ."

"It is a fair autumn day, man – hold your service in God's open air. As the Columbans would do. Bring the Black Rood with you. My friends will approve it, and you, the more!"

So, soon after mid-day the large and lively company assembled down in the valley, below the dramatically abrupt and lofty hill which soared from mighty brown-stone crags about a mile to the east of Dunedin's fortress-rock. Here, in a green glade with the autumn colours just beginning to stain the trees, Alwin held his mass amidst the calling of birds and the stamping and snorting of horses – and, most agreed, none the worse for that. He had brought the famous Black Rood, the late Queen Margaret's most prized possession, from her chapel, a silver-gilt reliquary in the shape of a cross, having on the outside a figure of the crucified Christ in ebony – hence the adjective black – and containing within a small portion of the true Cross of Calvary, brought with her from Hungary. This Alwin set up on an improvised altar in the midst.

After the service, the huntsmen, impatient to be off, divided into a number of small groups – for stag-hunting could not be done successfully in the mass. Fortunately the terrain was sufficiently widespread to accommodate all, and allegedly full of game, with a number of local foresters to act as guides and beaters. The area around the mountain spread, in forest and scrub, far and wide, especially to east and south, and some way up the steep slopes. Close below the hill itself the ground tended to be boggy, where the water drained from the high ground and accumulated. Here three lochs formed, haunts of wildfowl. The bogs also attracted the deer and boar, where they could wallow in mud and keep the flies at bay.

David was fond of hunting, but today he had a different ploy in mind. One of the hillfoot lochs had been a favourite place for his mother to take her children, when they stayed in Dunedin, to watch the fowl and play at the water's edge; and many a happy hour David had spent at what was now being called Queen Margaret's Loch. He had not been there for thirty-five years, and he decided to make the little pilgrimage. He let all the hunting parties get away, not to become involved in their activities, and leaving Alwin to pack up his temporary altar and silverware, and telling him where he was going, set off, riding eastwards along the woodland path, which twisted and turned erratically to avoid the burns, bogs and swampy hollows. Deliberately he went alone, the last of the large family which had laughed and sung here so long ago.

He had less than a mile to go, and was, he felt sure, nearing the loch, thoughts far away, when he was jerked back to the present abruptly. Above the distant shouts and hound-bayings of the hunters, he heard a crashing noise from along the narrow track ahead of him, a sound rapidly approaching. The wood-land was thick here, the path little more than a grassy causeway through swampy ground which drained into the loch. Into sight in front, round a bend only some three-score yards away, came charging, not a galloping horse, nor even a boar as he feared, but a tall and heavy woodland stag.

Even if no tusker, this made a sufficiently fearsome sight, great antlers held high, shaggy mane tossing, snorting breath from wide nostrils. It was an old beast obviously, almost white, its coat patched with the mud of its wallowing. No doubt it had been disturbed by the hunters. At the sight of the mounted man it did not falter, lessen speed or seek to turn aside. Instead, it lowered his great head and charged on, if anything with increased impetus, white-tipped antlers forward.

David had little time for thought. He, no more than the stag, could pull off the track without plunging deep into mire and reeds and decaying elder trunks. He was unarmed, save for his small dirk. He could only flee.

Savagely he reined round his rearing, frightened horse on the narrow way, and as he did so his glance caught sight of the feathered shaft of an arrow projecting from the rump of the racing stag. The brute was a victim of the hunt, wounded and maddened with pain.

The alarmed horse did a poor job of turning completely round, staggering partly into the flanking slime and losing precious moments. Spurring it fiercely, David dragged it round, with the stag now only a few yards off. But starting from the stationary again, his mount could not work up to any great speed inside a considerable distance; and anyway it would never rival the pace of a deer.

In only a few seconds the inevitable happened. David was aware of a jarring pain in his left thigh, which then went numb. His horse screamed in sudden agony and terror, then reared up on its hind legs, pawing the air. Unable to grip with his numbed thigh, the man lurched sideways, was flung over by his staggering mount, and fell to the ground. The animal plunged off, a great bloody gash in its haunch opened by a neighbouring antler-tine to the one which had pierced its rider's leg.

The stag's headlong rush itself halted by the impact, the brute reeled and all but fell over. But it recovered itself, and seeing the fallen man lying directly in its path, launched itself upon him, head lowered again.

As well for David that the creature's head was such a fine one, with such wide-branching antlers. If it had been a switch-horn or any narrower headed beast, he would have been skewered there and then. But the huge spread of horn did in fact dig into the soil on either side of the man's head, bringing the stag up with a jolt. David found himself dizzily staring into the great pain-crazed eyes, the sharp white-tipped brow-trays thrusting only an inch or two from his face, and the hot snorted breath from red nostrils puffing over him, himself helpless to move.

In those desperate moments his mind went back to that other stag and fallen king, in the New Forest, twenty-eight years ago, and the strange fate which should give him a death similar to Rufus's, alone in the greenwood. He tried to pray, but got no further than whispering Lord, Lord, at the stag's protruding eyes.

He may have swooned away for a moment or two, for he had fallen on the back of his head and was dazed anyway with the searing pain. But suddenly he was aware of a new dimension, changed circumstances. God had indeed come for him. A gleaming cross was before his unsteady eyes. There was no doubt about it, a cross shining between him and the stag. A vision, a joy. A great peace came upon him then.

Just when he realised that, although it might indeed be a miracle, it was not yet his reception at the heavenly portals, he never thereafter could make up his mind. But two facts did register – that the cross was no vision but a solid one of silver-gilt; and the the stag above him was still snorting and puffing but backing off, tossing its now raised head and stepping foot by foot away from the crucifix.

He recognised now that an arm was attached to the cross, a man's arm holding it out in front of the animal's face, which it seemed to push back and back, until abruptly the creature wheeled round and went off at a scrabbling run eastwards whence it had come.

"My lord, my lord David! God and Christ Jesu and His Holy Rood be praised!" Alwin cried, sobbed. "My good lord – thanks be to God! You are hurt – but you are alive! The evil beast is gone, praises be!"

David was beyond speech, but he nodded his aching, reeling head.

Alwin, after those first almost hysterical minutes, tended his fallen monarch as best he could, telling the swooning King, babbling rather, how he had come on after him, on foot, refusing to leave the precious Black Rood in servants' hands, along with the other furnishings for the open-air mass, and so, by God's blessed providence, was carrying it when he saw the King's horse bolting past and then the fallen man and the straining, savaging white hart. He had been afraid, desperately afraid, but with the Holy Rood in his hands he could do no other than go forward and thrust the sacred relic in front of the brute's eyes. And God had blessed his sinful servants and the evil had fled away. All glory in the highest!

After a while David forced himself to try to walk, leaning on the chaplain – and made but a poor business of it. A nasty gash had laid open his thigh, causing continous pain, and the leg had stiffened up. They were hobbling along slowly thus when one of the hunting parties, with the brothers Sir John and Sir Gregan d'Alleyne of Crawford, came trotting back. Appalled to discover their liege lord in such state, they improvised a litter from saddle-cloths slung between two horses, and hoisting the King carefully thereon, took him at a most heedful walking pace back to the town and up the long ascent to the fortress on the rock, there to place him in his wife's alarmed but efficient care.

That long night, in a strange state between waking and sleeping, David asked himself again and again whether it was all a judgment on him for failing properly to keep the Feast of the Holy Cross? If so, was it not strange that it had been the Holy Cross itself which had saved him? Was it a sign? It was a miracle, certainly. Could it have been his blessed mother who had stepped in, to save him, with her Black Rood? Saved him for greater efforts in God's cause?

Whatever it was, one thing he vowed – that he would build and endow a great abbey there, where he had fallen and risen, in gratitude, an abbey beneath King Arthur's Chair, dedicated to the Holy Rood . . .

Tomorrow he would give the necessary orders.

24

THE THREE-HUNDRED-AND-FIFTY-MILE journey back to Scotland had never seemed so long, so irritating, so frustrating – but then, David was in an irritated and frustrated state of mind that early summer of 1130. He was irritated that he should have to be back in England at all, so soon after the support-swearing business; and at the methods Henry Beauclerc had used to get him there. And frustrated that Matilda, who should have accompanied him, had fallen unwell just when they were about to set out from Rook's Burgh, and had persuaded him to go on without her. The whole thing had been a farce, merely a device on Henry's part to emphasise his superior position and claims. He, Henry, had had one of David's Huntingdon vassals arrested on a charge of treason, in that he had failed to send his due number of knights and armed men to the latest Normandy adventure – as had many another English lord and baron – and then insisted that the offender in this instance must be tried by his own earl, David, but in his, Henry's presence, the most transparent means of forcing the Scots king to come hastening south by a given date. Yet to have refused to go would once again have made Matilda's inheritance liable to forfeiture – and never were its vast revenues more urgently needed for the great and ambitious programme of governmental and church reform David had initiated, as well as for work on the new abbeys and border castles. The trial had in fact been little more than a formality, and the penalty the same substantial fine that Henry was imposing on others of his barons guilty of the same offence. There was no good reason why David should have had to preside over this charade, when Sheriff Gilbert could have done the thing equally well as his deputy. But Henry's fondness for showing his power grew with age. David told himself that this Huntingdon weakness must somehow be remedied.

The only redeeming feature of the entire episode was the word received while he was at Woodstock that Bishop Flambard of Durham had taken a heart attack and died – so Scotland had one less inveterate enemy.

But then had also come the other news – revolt in Scotland. So now he was bursting the hearts of a succession of horses, to cover those three hundred and fifty miles in the minimum possible time, a worried man indeed.

Details of the revolt had necessarily been in outline only. It was his nephew Angus MacEth, Earl of Moray, Lulach's daughter's son, he of whom Alexander had warned. He had risen in arms, and with a great force of Moraymen, estimated at ten thousand at least, was marching south by the east coast route; whilst his brother Malcolm, evidently finding his loyalty to his uncle less binding than to his brother, had gathered a smaller force from his patrimony of the Stormounth, and was marching to join Angus. Edward the Constable – son of old Sir Eustace now dead, and cousin of Hugo – with Hervey the Knight Marishcal, were mustering all loyal forces. But the King's presence was desperately required.

David, with Hugo and only four others, had left most of his train behind in this headlong dash for home, in the interests of speed, in no state to wait for laggards. He aimed to reach the border in four days, if it was humanly and equinely possible.

It proved to be not quite possible; but they crossed Tweed at Berwick bridge before noon on the fifth day, exhausted men on dying horses. At Berwick there was fresh news. The Constable had marched north to meet the rebels with about eight thousand men, as many as he could raise at short notice, less than Angus's numbers but including much Norman armoured cavalry – which the northerners totally lacked. When last heard of the Moray host had crossed Dee and were advancing into the Mearns by the Cairn o' Mounth pass. There was no further word of Malcolm MacEth, but it was now reported that another Malcolm, Alexander's bastard son, the Earl of Ross, had joined Angus with a contingent. All his lieutenants urged King David's appearance at the earliest possible moment.

David was only twenty-five miles from Rook's Burgh, and Matilda with his family. He had intended to call there, if only briefly, concerned for his wife's health. But the urgency of the news and appeals persuaded him. He sent Hugo westwards along the Tweed's valley with news of his return to Scotland, the situation and his loving greetings, and himself pressed on, up through the Merse by Dunbar for North Berwick, where the Earl of Fife's ferry would take him across the Scottish Sea to Fife, sparing him the enormous detour round the Scotwater and the Forth estuary, by Stirling.

He was halfway across Fife thereafter, heading for the Tay estuary and another ferry opposite Dundee, with only two companions now, Walter de Lindsay and Simon de Frizell, when they encountered more couriers. These were not in fact looking for the King but for the Countess of Fife at Kennoway, for whom they had heavy tidings. Her husband Earl Constantine, was dead. He amongst many. There had been a great battle, at Stracathro in the Mearns. The rebels were defeated, with great slaughter – but at grim cost to the royal forces. The Earl Cospatrick of Dunbar was also slain, with many Norman knights.

David, almost dropping with fatigue, demanded details, with lips which would scarcely form words.

The battle had been the day before, it seemed, near the ford of Inchbare, and had continued almost all day, so hardly fought was it. Undoubtedly it was the Norman cavalry which the Constable had to thank for final victory. When the rebels had eventually fled the field, they had left over four thousand dead behind, including their leader, Angus, Earl of Moray. His brother Malcolm MacEth, and Malcolm Earl of Ross, had escaped apparently. On the loyalist side the deaths were greatly less, perhaps one thousand – but included many illustrious besides the Earls of Fife and Dunbar.

Leaving the couriers to carry their sad story to the widowed Countess, David proceeded on his way northwards, although in less haste now, heavy at heart at the loss of so many of his subjects, even those in rebellion, and including his own brother's son. Particularly, of course, his good friend Cospatrick, a sore blow. The relief of victory was too dearly bought. He ought at least to have been there when his friends were dying for him, in hazard himself . . .

Two days later David held a council at Brechin, only a few miles from the battlefield, to thank all concerned in the victory and to deal with the results. At this, he learned for the first time that Fergus of Galloway had been involved, and fighting on the wrong side – a shock indeed. He was amongst those who had made good their escape. There were loud demands for his apprehension and punishment, even his execution as a traitor, along with the other surviving leaders of the revolt, including Malcolm MacEth and the Earl of Ross. But David countered this attitude. He pointed out that he had a kingdom to rule and the realm's wounds to heal, not to exacerbate. Mercy and forgiveness, as well as being incumbent upon a Christian monarch, were likely to achieve more for all concerned than revenge and harshness. He would certainly forfeit the earldom and mortuath of Moray, meantime, from Ethelred's descendants – although as one of the ancient lesser kingdoms of Scotland, he could not suppress it altogether. But Angus had been very much the ambitious one, the trouble-maker, and his defeat was so shattering that there would be little danger of another Moray rising for long. Young Malcolm MacEth had been a good subject until this lapse. Let him be warned, but go free – so long as he kept away from Moray. As for the Earl of Ross, he was a weakling and something of a fool. Let him roost in his far northern fastnesses; anyway, they had no means of extracting him therefrom. He too was unlikely to risk troubling them again. And Fergus of Galloway was Henry of England's son-in-law, and had just had his illegitimate daughter married to King Olaf Morsel of Man. He was a grave disappointment and something of a danger, no doubt – but he might well be more of a danger if drastically punished. He must be dealt with, shown the error of his ways; but not so direly as to upset his royal in-laws.

Not all present fully appreciated this attitude.

They were discussing the reported death of King Sigurd Half Deacon of Norway, and how this might affect the West Highland coastal regions, with the Hebrides presently under Norse rule – for Sigurd had proved a reasonably good neighbour, so much better than the late and unlamented Eystein, and his son Magnus was an unknown quantity – when there was an interruption. Hugo de Morville came hurrying into the hall or the rath where the council was being held, weary and travel-worn. He made straight for David's chair.

"Sire," he said tensely, "the Queen! She is sorely ill. Her strength failing. She asks for you. If it is possible for you to come . . ."

The King was on his feet before that was finished, his chair knocked over with a clatter. "God's mercy!" he exclaimed. "Matilda!" He grasped Hugo's arm fiercely. "How ill, man? What is wrong with her? She was sick, yes – but it was only some woman's ailment, she said."

"It is a wasting sickness, Sire. And a grievous pain . . ."

He had to all but run after his friend, who was striding for the door calling for horses as he went, the entire council on its feet, staring.

As they pounded southwards thereafter, lashing their mounts into even greater efforts than on the northern journey. David cursed himself, cursed Henry Beauclerc, cursed Angus MacEth, cursed cruel fate and his own decisions, which had kept him from Matilda's side in her sore need. He prayed as well as cursing – but somehow it was the cursing which tended to prevail; for despite his friends' assertions, almost accusations, he was but a sorry saint, and a poor son of his sainted mother, more of his father in him than he liked to contemplate. Even using the ferries again, they had about one hundred and twenty miles to ride to Rook's Burgh, so there was no lack of either form of mental activity for comparison.

That night, at Kincraig Point on the Fife shore, impatiently awaiting the arrival of the ferry-boat crew, David did not so much as close his eyes, although his friends managed to snatch an hour or so of sleep. Hugo, needless to say, had been all but asleep in his saddle, for long.

They reached the March Mount in late afternoon. Stiff as he was, David flung himself up the stairs to their bedchamber, glaring at the long faces of the servants, even brushing aside young Henry and Erna who tried to cling to him. But in the room itself he was pulled up sharp, his panted breath catching in his throat.

He scarcely recognised his wife, so pale and gaunt and shrunken was she, only her fine eyes the same, if not larger, and dark-rimmed. He had been gone only three weeks, but she had changed almost unbelievably from a slender but well-built, shapely woman to a mere frail shadow of herself, wan, brittle-seeming. But her great eyes were at least open for him, even lightened at sight of him.

"David! Thank God, thank God!" she whispered, and managed to raise a thin white hand, although it dropped back on the bedclothes in the same motion.

"My heart, my love, my most dear!" he exclaimed, and came to the bedside, to sink on his knees and gather her into his arms. Their children stood at the door, in wide-eyed distress and uncertainty.

He could scarcely keep himself from crying out at the scanty, fragile feel of her, so frighteningly different from what he knew so well and loved so dearly. He tried to speak, but his voice broke.

"Dear David . . . I knew . . . that you would come . . . in time! I waited . . . waited . . ."

"No!" he choked. "No!"

"Yes. I could not go . . . without you . . . to hold me, David. I was . . . afraid. But . . . not now. Not . . . in your arms." Clearly she had great difficulty in speaking.

"Hush, lass – hush!" he said, stroking her hair, kissing her damp brow. "Do not talk now. Later. Just let me hold you . . ."

"I must. There is . . . so little time . . . left. Here. Time in . . . plenty . . . where I go! I waited . . . for you here. I shall . . . wait for you again . . . there."

"Oh, my dear heart . . . !"

"So much to say. Yet . . . cannot. You . . . understand, David?"

"Surely, surely, lass. Do not fret. Are you in pain?"

"Not much, now. That . . . is past. If it comes again . . . I can bear it . . . with you holding me. I needed you . . . you see."

"And I failed you, God forgive me! I did not come."

"No. You are . . . the King. You had to . . . do your duty. And you came . . . in time. David – hear me. Huntingdon. It is become . . . a millstone. It served us well. We did much with it. But now . . . it costs you dear. Let it go, David."

"But . . . it is our children's heritage."

"Then give it to . . . Simon. It has become a trap. For you . . . for Scotland. Do not hold it . . . for my sake."

He shook his head.

She was silent for a long time thereafter, her eyes closed, her breathing quick, shallow. He thought that perhaps she slept. Then she was gripping his arm again, if feebly.

"David – you are still there? God . . . be praised! I thought . . . I thought . . . It will be . . . soon now. Soon. David . . . never change. Be true. To yourself. Ever. Kings so often . . . change. Henry. Do not let power . . . change you. Dear David."

"No. No. But hush, lass. Care nothing for that now. Rest you . . ."

"Time enough . . . to rest . . . hereafter. The children . . ." She stopped suddenly, stiffened in his arms, her breathing catching in a choking groan of pain. It did not seem to resume. Frantically he clutched her, afraid that she was gone, until he realised that her heart still beat, and he all but wept in relief.

But if not gone. Matilda seemed far away now and there was no more of the difficult talking. Presently he gently disengaged, smoothed her damp hair and arranged the bedclothes. He moved quietly over to the young people. He talked to them, low-voiced, incoherently sought to comfort them, he who had no comfort in him. But he did not leave that room. He would not leave it again while still she had need of him.

When darkness fell, he sent their children to their beds, and went to lie beside his wife in the lamplight, arms around her. He did not mean to sleep, but he was desperately tired. Matilda had not spoken again, eyes closed.

He must have dropped off almost immediately.

He wakened to her strange jerking, in the small hours of the morning. She was mumbling incoherently, and gasping through it as though being strangled, a horrible sound. Then suddenly she spoke out lucidly, perfectly clearly.

"Now, David – now! It is time. Hold me close. I go now. Hold, hold! I will be waiting, looking for you. I am not frightened, not frightened, not . . ."

She shuddered and shuddered and died, held tight in his arms, as she had wanted. And he was left alone.

25

Work, labour, toil, action, stern almost unending application, as to a treadmill – like many another before him, David mac Malcolm drove himself, to fill his days and much of his nights, with occupation and busyness, in order to drug himself with fatigue, so that when he came to throw himself down on his bed at length, he might be the less aware of what was no longer there, his irreparable, searing loss. For months on end he laboured as though possessed, while his children, his friends and his officers, eyed him askance, fearing almost for his sanity.

And yet, he was never more effective, more capable, more decisive. No problem was too much for him, no obstacle too great, every challenge to be not so much accepted as grimly welcomed. In the year after the Queen's death, Scotland was hurled into a new age by one man's feverish energy and dogged determination.

And there was no lack of work to his hand, with all his plans for his realm – *their* plans, for always Matilda's influence was close, often she seemed to be at his very shoulder, for so many of the plans they had concocted together. Yet, strangely, he deliberately did not carry out one of those last urgings of hers. He did not give up the earldom of Huntingdon, either to young Earl Simon in Normandy or to King Henry. He thought much on this, and decided against it. Its revenues were just too valuable for what he was doing. And why should he hand Henry Beauclerc or Simon's uncle of Aumale what they both were undoubtedly scheming for? His beloved Matilda in this misjudged, he believed. She was right in that Huntingdon had become something of a millstone and trap for him, as King of Scots. But the answer was not to throw it away, surely, with all that it could do for Scotland; but to counter the danger and use it to best purpose. He would indeed resign the earldom, so that he could no longer be summoned ignominiously to Henry's side like a vassal – but he would bestow it on his son and heir, Henry's namesake. The boy was now nearly sixteen, and mature for his years. Henry Beauclerc's own children were married at his age. Time that he was taking his part. Admittedly this would not affect the necessary fealty for the English earldom; but so long as young Henry was below the full age of twenty-one years when, and not before, he could enter into outright possession of the earldom, he would have to be represented in it by a deputy or viscount – and David was sure that King Henry would get little satisfaction from summoning such deputy before him at intervals, since it was undoubtedly the King of Scots he aimed to humble and embarrass. Sheriff Gilbert could very well serve as viscount.

So an investiture was held at Stirling, and young Henry was formally created Prince of Strathclyde, as heir-apparent to the throne, and Earl of Huntingdon in the room of his father. And while they were at it, the youth was officially stated to be claimant to the earldom of Northumbria – as sign to Henry Beauclerc not to refuse to endorse the Huntingdon position, or he might stir up a hornet's nest. Northampton no longer was to be involved in such manoeuvres, for Simon de St. Liz had come of age two years before, and David had thereupon resigned his titular holding – although Henry had refused to ratify the earldom to Simon whilst that young man remained in Normandy.

But this, although an important development, took up but little of the King's time and energies. The great labour was the setting up, at least in outline, of the parish and diocesan system whereby the whole of Scotland's administration, either of justice, local government or taxation, was to be revolutionised – indeed, there had been precious little coherent administration hitherto, save what individual lords imposed of their own whims. This process would take years, of course, generations probably; but a start had to be made, and the detailed planning done, if all was not to be haphazard and chaotic.

In this, strangely enough, David found it considerably more simple to found and set up dioceses than parishes. He had a Primate and Bishop of St. Andrews, now, competent to consecrate and instal new bishops, and a supply of fairly suitable clergy from his fine new monasteries; also funds, and the power to allocate royal lands and revenues to the said sees – even though some of them would remain little more than names and titles for some time to come. So, in addition to the dioceses of St. Andrews, Glasgow, Dunkeld and Moray, already in existence, new ones were established at Galloway, Brechin, Aberdeen and Caithness, for a start. Others would follow later. These locations were selected each for good reason – Galloway, so that David would have legitimate excuse to take action, if necessary in Fergus's lordship, and also to counter any claims of the new

English Bishop of Caer-luel towards Candida Casa or Whithorn; Brechin in the Mearns mortuath, because, after the Stracathro battle, it had become most evident that this area much needed some such influence, for here the Celtic Church was notably strong and reactionary and had been inclined to support the rebel Angus; Aberdeen for much the same reasons, for though the Earl of Mar had not joined the revolt, many of his people had; and Caithness, to have a good influence on the Earl of Ross and the far North.

But the dividing up of these dioceses into parishes was much more difficult, at least as meaningful entities; hundreds of parishes, and almost all, at first, without churches or clergy, their borders sketchily defined, their responsibilities and privileges vague. But the idea, which was largely David's own, thrashed out in many a long discussion with Matilda and Bishop John, and owing only a little to the English system introduced by the Normans, was never in doubt. One day it would be a manageable, working scheme, to the enormous benefit of the entire kingdom and its people, not just its rulers. It was not the religious aspect of this great project which was concerning David meantime; that was for the churchmen to implement, and would have to await the availability of trained clergy – although the Columban clergy were pressed into service meantime, of course; it was the dividing up of Scotland into recognisable and official sections and small territorial units, irrespective of the great domains and lordships of the barons and chiefs, where the royal writ, not the lord's, would run and the ordinary people's needs and well-being be catered for. Indeed this was one of the main objects of the exercise, the limiting of the powers of the great nobles, as against that of the Crown – David having had ample demonstration, in England, of the overweening might and tyranny of the Norman barons and the dangers to the throne.

Needless to say, in all this, he had less than enthusiastic support from most of his nobility.

As example, he set up a parish structure at Ednam, or Edenham, on the edge of the Merse not far from Rook's Burgh, where an able small landowner named Thor was already working an excellent manor system and had built a small church. David imposed a tithe or tiend arrangement here, from the produce of the lands, for the support of a parish priest from Jedworth – and to show the way, dedicated a tenth of his own personal revenues to the Church. So, in effect, this became the first parish in the land.

Parallel with the parish plan he envisaged a system of burghs, for urban settlements. There were already burghs in the land, mainly havens and ports like Berwick and Inverkeithing, or the castletons of raths and duns, like Dunbar or Edinburgh. But these were only burghs in name. Now seats of population would be regulated and encouraged, for the increase of trade and crafts, given duties and privileges, but also required to pay customs for the royal revenue. They would have councils to govern themselves, in many respects, with even some judicial functions in minor offences, to relieve the realm's justiciars, set up by King MacBeth. Indeed, MacBeth's reforms were a great help in David's plans; although after that enlightened monarch's death, his successors, David's own father and brothers, had allowed much to lapse.

As well as these many ordinary burghs, great and small, he moved to establish more important centres, with special powers delegated directly from the Crown – again to counter the dominant tendencies of great lords – and these would be called king's or royal burghs. Usually they would be castletons of royal palaces and forts – such as Rook's Burgh and Dunfermline – but not only such.

In the midst of this enormous work and planning, there developed a more local problem. Ever since Abbot Ralph's translation to Tiron, his succesors had been complaining that Shiel Kirk was not really a viable site for a major abbey. It was too remote, deep in the forest; it still suffered from sporadic raids of broken and robbers; and its surrounding lands, although beautiful, were insufficiently fertile and productive to support the establishment. If this seemed an extraordinary state of affairs, there was another and less openly-voiced reason behind the discontent – simple jealousy. This had been provoked by the growing power and royal favour towards the Priory of Jedworth, so comparatively near to the King's seat of Rook's Burgh. This was an Augustinian establishment, of course, and the Tironensians considered themselves to be a step above this, or other, rival Order – and theirs was an abbey where Jedworth was only a priory. Bishop John, in whose diocese were both monasteries, and who personally maintained close links with Tiron, came to the King and urged that something should be done. This ill-feeling was unsuitable and must be put an end to. But he pointed out also that Tiron was more important on the wide scene than were the Augustinians, in its influence with the Vatican, Pope Honorius being a strong supporter thereof. It would be a pity to offend, in any way, the Pontiff who had maintained Scotland's case against York.

With so much else on his mind, David asked his old tutor what he proposed?

'The real reason behind this matter is but simple human failing, Sire," he asserted. "This of jealousy. Shiel Kirk was the first monastery you founded. It was therefore your favourite. Its monks considered themselves *your* especial friars. Then you came to dwell at Rook's Burgh, and in due course set up this new foundation of Jedworth, a mere eight or nine miles away. Now Jedworth's monks see more of you than do Shiel Kirk's, minister to your household, gain more privileges, have better land. The religious have their weaknesses, like other men – all too many, I fear."

"What then is to be done, John?"

"I see only the one answer, my lord David. Move Shiel Kirk."

"*Move* Shiel Kirk? Lord, man – what do you mean? Move an abbey?"

"Just that, Sire. It may seem folly – but it would, I think, be a greater folly to allow this ill-feeling to grow, to the hurt of all Holy Church in Scotland, at so delicate a stage. It could do untold harm to your plans and hopes for this land, if there is trouble between these two, if feuding develops between Tironensians and Augustinians. Better far to effect a move."

"But how, John? How move a great abbey?"

"None so difficult, Sire. Not so difficult as to start a new one – as you are proposing to do at Melrose and Brechin and Urquhart, I am told. As you *are* doing at Edinburgh and Dunfermline. Give the Tironensians land near here, nearer Rook's Burgh than Jedworth! Fertile land. It must only help your town and royal burgh of Rook's Burgh. Then tell them to move their abbey. It will be much work – but they will do it gladly, I vow. They will have to take down every stone and slate and timber that they have put up with such labour, and have all carried down Tweed the twenty-five miles or so, perhaps on rafts or barges, and rebuilt here. Make them sweat, Sire, for their jealousy! But they could do it. All the materials are there. They will need little that is new – only hard toil and much time. It may teach them a valuable lesson . . ."

"But it is not only buildings. What of the farms, the orchards and gardens and fields. The mills and fisheries?"

"Let these remain as a grange, my lord, a small, working

daughter-house at Shiel Kirk. Many abbeys have such. Tiron itself has many."

"All this – to give in to petty jealousy!"

"Little cost to you, Sire. The toil and sweat will be theirs. But – you could gain from it. Burden the new abbey with some task, some duty to perform. In token . . ."

They were standing on a flanking-tower of the March Mount castle, with David gazing down on what had been Matilda's favourite prospect, the joining of the two great rivers to eastwards and the fair meadowlands on the far side of Tweed, where cattle grazed in lush pasture and where had been the abandoned cashel of Kelshaugh, the haugh of the Keledei, its associated salmon-fishers' hamlet still there. Suddenly he pointed.

"There! The ford, to be sure. Kelshaugh! Let them have Kelshaugh. Let them work and drain that rich land, and build there. And maintain for me a free ferry, for goods and foot-folk, above the ford! Across to this Rook's Burgh. This we have needed, since ever we came. That is it! A useful service for our jealous friars! For all time. Tell them that, John. Let them build their barges, to ship all the stones and carving and gear down Tweed. Then use the barges as a ferry across Tweed to Rook's Burgh. We shall see who crows the loudest and longest in the end!"

* * *

The King's detailed planning labours suffered another and much greater interruption that autumn – and again it was Bishop John who presented it. David was at Stirling, putting theories into practice, when the Bishop came in haste from the South. He had had serious tidings from Rome. The Bishop William of Man had been there, and on his way home had halted at Kirk Cuthbert's Town on the Galloway coast on hearing that there was trouble in Man, Olaf Morsel having had to flee to Dublin meantime, three of his illegitimate sons running riot in the island kingdom. The prudent William had decided to delay his return until matters simmered down, and Bishop John had offered him shelter – and learned of the Rome situation. Pope Honorius was dead, and the College of Cardinals had split in two over electing a successor. Equal numbers had voted on each side, and only the casting vote of the presiding cardinal had declared Innocent the Second, a Roman noble, to be Pontiff. This was not accepted by the other half, who

296

declared the Spaniard, Peter of Leon, Pope, under the title of Anacletus the Second. So there were now two Holy Fathers, and confusion reigned, with bloody fighting in the streets of Rome.

David was shocked, but asserted that sanity and God's order would prevail – until he heard that the rival Pontiffs were each seeking the support of the monarchs of Christendom. Innocent was known to be friendly with King Henry and also with the Emperor Lothair; but Anacletus had Lombardy, Venice and Spain behind him, and occupied the Vatican buildings, St. Peter's and most of Rome. The Bishop of Winchester, Henry's nephew and brother of Stephen of Boulogne, had been present in Rome at the time, and had boasted to the Bishop of Man that Innocent would triumph and would quickly overturn the decision of the late Honorius regarding York and Scotland and bring the wretched Scots to heel.

John did not have to enlarge on the dangers and problems this situation could and probably would produce.

David took little time to make his initial decisions. He would send immediate word to Rome of his support for Anacletus as Pope, with a message for that prelate himself. Nothing could undo Thurstan's consecration of Robert as Bishop of St. Andrews; but there might well be declarations that he was no longer Primate and that Scotland had no other metropolitan than Thurstan. So all arrangements for the new bishoprics must be speeded up and finalised, before any Vatican pronouncements and prohibitions could reach Scotland, in the event of Innocent becoming established. There was, of course, one particularly vulnerable area – the new diocese of Galloway. This almost certainly would be Thurstan's first target, the thin end of the English wedge, as it had been before. Thurstan would declare that its establishment was an infringement of the old York bishopric of Candida Casa or Whithorn, and either appoint a completely new bishop thereof, in opposition, with papal support, or put Galloway under the rule of his Bishop of Caer-luel. So the Scots would have to act fast. David had already chosen his nominee, one Gillialdan, a former Celtic monk and a kinsman of Fergus. But he had delayed actual implementation because of the admittedly rather difficult situation regarding Fergus, Galloway being different from other Scottish provinces, a semi-independent principality. Indeed, since his marital alliances with the royal houses of England and Man, Fergus had taken to styling himself Prince, not Lord of Galloway. The appointment of a Bishop of

Galloway, therefore, could hardly go ahead without his know-ledge and concurrence, at least.

So now David went in some haste down to Galloway, included in his train the Bishops John and Robert, and the episcopal candidate Gillialdan. With trouble in Man and Olaf fled, Fergus, who had been roosting there since Stracathro, would almost certainly have come home.

When the royal cavalcade reached Kirk Cuthbert's Town eventually – clerics tending to be less than urgent horsemen – it was to learn that Fergus was indeed back in Galloway. But not here. He was at his remote stronghold of Cruggleton, possibly hiding himself away discreetly – although discretion was scarcely one of his normal attributes. Cruggleton lay some forty miles further west, on the shore of the great Wigtown Bay. Prelatical groans greeted this information.

Their reception at Cruggleton, an eagle's nest of a place on top of a cliff high above the tide, was as though Fergus's cup of joy was now full to overflowing, his delight untrammelled by doubts of any sort – although his renowned grin had a distinctly determined aspect. He looked at his clerical kinsman, Gillial-dan somewhat askance, however. No doubt his spies had been able to give him a few hours' warning of the royal approach, enabling him to decide on his attitude – which was evidently not to be that of any penitent rebel.

Cruggleton was no great establishment, however impressive the site, and with the visitors and Fergus's own quite large entourage, was uncomfortably crowded. Certainly there was little opportunity for private converse – which perhaps suited both sides. David decided that something in the nature of a conference was probably the best way of attaining his objec-tives – although Hervey and even Hugo, suggested that the best course was just to arrest and depose the man there and then, and appoint a successor who would do what he was told. But that was not the King's way, and would be to reckon without Henry and the Vatican.

So they sat at the long table in the draughty bare hall, David at one end, Fergus at the other, rough Galloway chieftains glowering across at the prelates and Norman knights.

David led off, picking his words carefully. "We are here to deal with a matter of considerable importance to my realm and to the Lordship of Galloway. All know, none better than the Lord Fergus, that the Archbishop of York, with insufferable arrogance, has long claimed spiritual dominance over Scot-land. And especially over the one-time see of Candida Casa or

Whithorn here. This the Pope has controverted. But Popes come and go, and it behoves us to take steps to ensure our position." He looked down at Fergus, who made no comment – so that it seemed as though, fortunately, he had not yet heard of Honorius's death.

"It is my fear," he went on, "that the new Bishop Athelulf of Caer-luel will, at Archbishop Thurstan's bidding, lay claim to Whithorn, and so to Galloway. Indeed this has already been done, in name, but so far no moves have been made to enforce that claim. It is my belief that this may soon be attempted."

"Why?" Fergus asked.

"Information received," the King answered briefly. "It seems necessary, therefore that our own Bishop of Candida Casa – or better, of Galloway – be appointed forthwith, before any such move can be made. It is long since there was such a bishop – many centuries. Before Galloway was within the kingdom of Scotland. So there is no precedent. The appointment would seem to be a joint matter."

"Any appointment of a Bishop of Galloway must be the responsibility of the Lord of Galloway, Sire," Fergus said. "The former Bishops of Candida Casa, whoever they paid allegiance to as priests, would assuredly be appointed by the Kings or Princes of Galloway. *I* am Prince of Galloway."

"You are *Lord* of Galloway, within my realm of Scotland, my friend. Made so, at my recommendation, by my brother King Alexander. Even if you have not always remembered it!"

There was a growl from down the right side of the table, responded to by a similar growl from opposite.

"I suggest a *joint* appointment," David went on, conversationally. "This would seem fair and suitable. I further suggest your own kinsman, here, Gillialdan, a worthy priest and man of Galloway. Bishop Robert of St. Andrews is prepared to consecrate him, and Bishop John of Glasgow to yield him spiritual rule over Galloway, which hitherto has been his. Without such acceptance and yielding no incumbent could be installed." That last was pointed.

Fergus looked round the table and stroked his small beard. "I prefer to choose and appoint my own bishop – if such there is to be, my lord King," he said, smiling strongly. "King Alexander may have named me Lord of Galloway, in his kingdom. But long before that I and my ancestors were King or Prince of Galloway."

There was a quivering silence in the hall.

When David spoke his voice had lost only a little of its ease

299

and conversational tone. "Ah, yes. And was it, therefore, as King or Prince of Galloway that you married, without informing me, the King of England's daughter? And fought with my rebels against me at Stracathro, this year? Do you no longer accept me as liege lord, my friend? Or do you prefer your father-in-law of England?"

Again there was silence. Both sides had now thrown down their gauntlets.

Fergus took his time to answer – as well he might. Wording it as the other had, he was placed in something of a cleft stick. To agree with these suggestions, to assert that he could act as an independent prince, was as good as a declaration of war: whereas not to do so, to agree that David was indeed his liege lord, made his two breaches of conduct and good faith, admitted sedition if not treason.

He took refuge in subterfuge. "Not so, Sire. King Henry is not my liege lord. Only my good friend. As yours. I have had to act as is best for Galloway. But . . ."

David's voice hardened perceptibly now. "Am I your liege lord or am I not? Answer, Fergus."

The other moistened his lips. "Yes, my lord King. But . . ."

David held up his hand. "Very well. No buts on my kingship, friend!" He sat back and allowed his tones to relax again. "Now we know where we stand, in this realm. You, Fergus, Lord of Galloway, and I your overlord. But, that there be no further such confusion, I propose to make our relationship fully clear, Fergus. I propose to create and appoint you an earl of Scotland. Fergus, Earl of Galloway. How say you, my friend?"

There were gasps not only from Fergus but from all around the hall. David's own friends stared at him, scarcely believing their ears. To shrug off treachery and rebellion was bad enough; but to reward it with an earldom, the highest honour in the land, was beyond all credibility.

Fergus for once looked bewildered, at a complete loss. "I . . . I do not understand, Sire."

"Yet it is entirely simple. We come to an agreement, you and I, Fergus Mac Sween – a final agreement. Galloway becomes an earldom and you an earl of Scotland with all an earl's privileges. And together we appoint Gillialdan as Bishop of Galloway. Together we seal our leal compact by founding a monastery here in Galloway, for the glory of God and the good of our souls, in token and enduring symbol of our accord and good faith, in the eyes of God and man. Is it not the best outcome of our meeting and conference?"

Fergus swallowed, as just an inkling of what all this implied dawned on him, and on others around that table. An earl of Scotland had distinct, well-defined and unquestionable duties to the monarch, as well as privileges, to fail in which was outright and accepted treason. No longer would it be possible to talk about a vaguely defined independent principality. He might be enhanced in status, but he was now tied down to the King of Scots. And a bishopric and a monastery or abbey were to witness to the fact, for all time to come – as well as to help forward David's diocesan and parish system.

Yet to refuse was all but impossible in the circumstances.

Later, Fergus, however doubtfully, was duly invested as Earl of Galloway, with a golden earl's belt David had brought for the purpose. And the following day they all moved the five miles down the coast to Whithorn, at the tip of the peninsula, where, at the old ruined chapel of St. Ninian on the rocky seashore, the two bishops duly consecrated and installed Gillialdan as Bishop of Galloway.

Before the royal party left for the North again, they decided on a site for the new abbey, at Trahil, where there was a jutting tidal island of fertile land at the head of Saint Cuthbert's Bay, near Kirk Cuthbert's Town. Fergus would provide the land and the workmen, while David would find the monks and most of the money.

26

SITTING IN HIS chair-of-state in Edinburgh Castle, flanked by his two Chief Justiciars, of North and South of Forth, the new Earl of Fife and Walter de Lindsay, David nodded to the Great Constable for the prisoner to be brought in. He was much troubled – partly on account of the business on hand, but more by the fact that his son Henry was reported to be unwell at Rook's Burgh. He must be truly ill, not merely somewhat sick, for he was to have taken part in the forenoon's ceremony of the opening of the newly-completed abbey beneath King Arthur's Chair, and the handing over to its abbot's keeping, for all time, of the sacred Black Rood, from Queen Margaret's Chapel here in the castle – the establishment thereafter to be known as the Abbey of the Holy Rood. Henry himself had been going to hand over his grandmother's precious relic, and keenly conscientious young man as he had grown to be, would have been loth indeed to miss this great occasion, which also celebrated his father's almost miraculous escape from death. So David was worried, and would have been well on his way to Rook's Burgh by now had it not been for this wretched matter of the trial, which he could by no means either miss or dismiss.

The Constable's men led in the prisoner, clanking, shackled with iron and a rope around his neck and trailing behind, as custom required – although this young man might well assert that he could nowise be hanged. For he could not only claim that he was rightfully an earl of Scotland, one of the *ri*, but might choose to lay claim to the throne itself. He was Malcolm MacEth, David's nephew, and since his brother's death at Stracathro, representative of the northern and senior royal line, grandson of Lulach. Having been on the run for almost four years, he had been captured in Moray.

He bowed stiffly to his uncle, but thereafter kept his head high. He looked as though he had received rough handling.

Edward de Morville spoke up. "My lord King – I, Constable, bring before you for your royal judgment the man Malcolm by-named MacEth, styling himself Earl of Moray, although that earldom has been forfeited for rebellion. Apprehended in the said province of Moray, from which Your Grace has debarred him. Four years ago he took arms against Your Grace. That he cannot deny. I saw him with my own eyes, on the field of Stracathro. Such act is highest treason. I ask for due judgment – death by hanging."

David nodded towards the prisoner. "Malcolm – do you deny the accusation?"

"I do not." That was almost curt. A murmur ran through the hall.

"Answer with proper respect, fellow!" the Constable barked.

The other said nothing.

David looked at his nephew thoughtfully. It was the first time that he had seen him for six years. "Why did you rise against me, Malcolm?" he asked. "You, who acted my loyal friend before, who brought me news of King Alexander's supposed drowning, hailing me as probable King. Then swearing allegiance to me a year later. Why change? Had I done aught to injure you?"

"No, my lord."

"Why, then?"

Silence.

"Answer the King's Grace, man!" the Constable cried.

"I have nothing to say, Norman!"

"You must have had reason, nephew," David persisted. "If I am to judge honestly, I should know it. You changed. Why? Did your brother Angus convince you?"

"Angus should have been King. Son of your elder brother and grandson of King Lulach, last of the true line. As therefore now should I. Not you, Uncle."

"This you knew or believed before you took your oath. Before ever I sat on the Stone. Why wait, and then break the oath?"

"Because you filled the land with these!" Malcolm had to raise both hands shackled together to point at the Constable and other Normans. "Frenchmen! You flood Scotland with English monks, to bring down our ancient Church. You change all. Our customs, our faith. You are not the King this realm requires . . ."

There was uproar in the hall, threats and outrage.

David raised his hand for silence. "I asked my nephew for his reasons. Do we abuse him for giving them? We know his reasons, even if we conceive them to be mistaken."

"Sire – the prisoner is condemned out of his own mouth," the Constable said. "I press for sentence – since there is no doubt of guilt."

"My lords – how say you?" David turned to the Justiciars on either side.

"Guilty, my lord King. Worthy of death," MacDuff of Fife said.

"Agreed," Lindsay confirmed.

"I claim death by hanging," the Constable repeated, and picked up the trailing end of the rope round the young man's neck.

"I will *not* be hanged!" Malcolm said tensely. "As my brother's only heir, I am an earl of Scotland, as well as your rightful King. You cannot hang me."

"Have you considered what is the alternative, man?" the Earl of Fife demanded grimly.

"I have."

"Blinding and emasculation!" the Justiciar added, in case there was any misunderstanding.

The other inclined his head.

"That I will not have!" David exclaimed vehemently. "There will be no mutilation in my realm."

"It is the accepted penalty for treason, Sire, for those too high of rank to hang."

"Perhaps. But not acceptable to me."

"What then, my lord King?" the Constable asked. "Since punished he must be, his treason admitted, flaunted. If example is not made, the throne will never be secure."

"I know it, my Lord Constable. Judgment there has to be – but not hanging nor mutilation. I pronounce it – perpetual imprisonment. How say you, my Lords Justiciar?"

Doubtfully both his companions nodded.

"So be it. Malcolm – I adjudge you guilty of treason, on your own admission. I sentence you to perpetual imprisonment until the day you die. But because you are my own brother's son, I myself shall be your gaoler. You will remain in my house all the days of your life, and act as clerk in my projects. This for judgment. This trial is over." He rose.

A groan arose. None there appeared to be satisfied – not even Malcolm.

When the King rode for Rook's Burgh an hour or so later, Malcolm MacEth rode with him, however hostile the rest of the company.

David found his son Henry in a dire state. He was lying on a bed, shivering and shaking violently, his complexion of a peculiarly bluish hue. Although his eyes were open, staring, he did not recognise his father. The monkish physicians from Jedworth and Kelshaugh were utterly at a loss. They had tried every remedy they could think of, including prolonged prayer, but to no effect. None could even suggest what the illness was. Henry had been smitten suddenly, about eight days before, whilst riding with hawks. Since when no nourishment had passed his lips. Never very robust, he had been a fit enough young man, now of nineteen years; but clearly his strength was failing fast.

David was appalled, desperately worried. After Matilda's death, this menace to his only son was almost more than he could contemplate. He asked himself if indeed there could be a curse on him? Or on this Rook's Burgh? Or was it rather on all his family, the Margaretsons? Six sons of Margaret and Malcolm, and now but two male heirs, one a convicted traitor, the other direly sick.

He sat up at his son's bedside all night, in an agony of near despair.

304

There was no improvement, no change, in the morning. But the new day brought a new preoccupation for the weary and dispirited father. Bishop John arrived from Berwick, bringing with him that notable character widely known as St. Malachy O'Moore. Not truly a saint, in that he had not been canonised, he was nevertheless popularly endowed with more than usual piety and fame. The title of saint had almost certainly stuck to him because he had been a colourfully renowned Celtic Church abbot in Ireland, where saints were in rich supply; he had transferred to the Roman rite and become a vigorous and successful reformer in the Cistercian-Tironensian tradition – so much so that even distant Rome itself had taken note, and he had been summoned thither. He was now on his way home to Ireland, not only consecrated Bishop of Armagh but official papal legate to that land, with full authority to build up the Romish Church and to appoint new bishops.

It was not this enhancement which exercised Bishop John however; it was the news he brought from the Vatican. Innocent had more or less won his battle with Anacletus apparently, who had retired to Lombardy leaving his rival Pope in possession of Rome. Innocent was bearing down predictably on all his opponent's supporters – which included Scotland. He had declared that the Bishop of St. Andrews was not truly a metropolitan, and that Scotland was indeed, and always had been, subservient to York. He would require all Scottish bishops, beginning with John of Glasgow, whom he conceived to the main source of disaffection, to make their humble submission to Archbishop Thurstan, on pain of papal dismissal from their sees. Hence this Papal Legate's return to Ireland via Berwick and Rook's Burgh, to convey this ultimatum.

John was much perturbed, naturally; but David, in his present state of anxiety, was scarcely in a condition to devote as much attention to the matter as it deserved. He declared that he would still support Anacletus, and ignore Innocent's fiats, until such time as there was no doubt as to the Pope's identity and authority.

St. Malachy – whose real name was Maelmadoc Ua Morgair – did not seem in the least put out by the reaction at Rook's Burgh to his message from Innocent. He was an oddity, both in appearance and behaviour, a little birdlike man, but a cheerfully sardonic bird, a crow perhaps, and markedly unlike the normal notion of any bishop, much less a metropolitan or legate. He chuckled a lot, cracked his finger-joints, and appeared to consider the entire human scene with a sort of

305

cynical amusement – an unlikely reformer. The clerics around David did not know whether to be impressed, upset or to look down their noses at this near-mountebank.

It was Alwin, however, David's chaplain, who recollected that St. Malachy had, amongst his other semi-fabulous endowments, a reputation for healing, back in Ireland – no doubt much exaggerated. When the King heard this, clutching at any straw, and besought the little man's aid for Henry, it was to be pooh-poohed and assured that such talk was only foolish tattle, not to be taken seriously; besides, he had not done any healing for a long time. But when David insisted that he should at least come and look at the sufferer, he allowed himself to be led up the twisting turnpike stairway.

In the bedchamber he eyed the shaking, staring young man, rubbed his blue and jutting chin, and quite quickly broke into one of his chuckles.

"Oho, oho!" he said. "It's the Devil that's in him! The Old One, Himself! Yes, oh yes – old Satanicus in person! We know each other well, Satanicus and I, so we do – the old rascal!" And he laughed aloud.

"You mean . . . ? You mean that he is possessed? Devil-possessed? Henry . . . ?"

"I would not just be saying possessed, David my son – no, no. Borrowed, maybe – taken loan of, just. The Old One likes innocents, especially young ones. He is old, you see. So do I, mind you – so do I. I am getting old, too . . . ."

"But – what is to be done? You cannot just stand there and laugh, man! Is there nothing that you can do?"

"Och, well – maybe, maybe. Och, yes – we'll get Him out of there, to be sure. Water! He does not like water, does old Satanicus – cold water. He likes the heat, you see, the old rascal. Water . . . ?"

He looked around. There was a bowl of water on a table, which David had used for bathing his son's fevered brow, although to no effect. St. Malachy took this, slopping it, and laughing as it spilled. He dipped a finger in, as though to test its temperature, nodded, and then raised another finger to make two, to mutter the briefest of blessings and sketch the sign of the cross. Then moving to the bedside he proceeded to flick and splash the water over the twitching figure in both generous and haphazard fashion, spilling more than he used but soaking everything around, including himself and the King.

"Out! Out! Out!" he chanted, through chuckles. "Out, I say

306

– I, Maelmadoc Ua Morgair say it! Enough, Satanicus you old devil!"

The water supply finished, he handed the empty bowl to David, and without another word started for the door.

"But . . . Bishop! What now?" the distraught father cried. "What now?"

"Och, let him be, let him be," he was told.

"But . . . is that all? All you can do?"

The Legate did not pause, but looked over his hunched shoulder. "Have some confidence, my son – confidence. That's it – confidence. This time he will not die – this time, mind." And he went off through the door cheerfully.

David looked at his soaking son. The eyes were closed at last, and the twitching had stopped.

Next morning the fever had gone and Henry, though pale, had lost the blue colouration. Weak but lucid he shook no more.

Although all at Rook's Burgh were loud in praise and thanksgiving, St. Malachy appeared to think nothing of it. He brushed away wonder, questions and thanks alike. He must be on his way, he said, with God's work to do in old Ireland. David, heaping him with gifts, sent him, with an escort, by Annan and Kirk Cuthbert's Town, with a message for Fergus to provide a ship to take him across the Irish Sea.

David and all his friends rejoiced as Henry progressed steadily and grew strong again. The months that followed were the happiest since Matilda had died, with Yule celebrated again as it should be – in Scotland, at least. For that winter and the following spring there was dire famine in England with the failure of the harvest and pestilence amongst cattle – men said as a judgment on King Henry, whose savagery was increasing strangely, his rapacity for taxation almost crazy. In the belief that the coinage was being debased, he had all the moneyers of the kingdom, who minted the silver for him, to the number of over fifty, and chopped off the right hands of all but four. At one village in Leicestershire, Huncot, he hanged forty-four persons at once, charged with robbery. And so on. There was dire civil war in Norway too, that year of 1135, with Sigurd's death, his two sons competing for the throne, with Harold Gillichrist winning, blinding his brother Magnus and sending him to a monastery. But in Scotland there was peace.

In the summer they heard that the Empress Maud had had a son to Geoffrey Plantagenet, whom she was calling Henry after her father, a male heir to the throne of England. And only months later came the word that the proud grandfather had died, suddenly, totally unexpectedly, at Gisors in Normandy, after eating too much of his favourite dish, lamprey pie. Henry Beauclerc had gone on, in his sixty-eighth year, David's friend and enemy for so long. Nothing would be quite the same again.

27

NOTHING WAS THE same indeed, thereafter, in England – and it did not take long for that to become evident to all. Stephen of Boulogne might be weak and headstrong, but he was not dilatory. No sooner had he heard of his uncle's death than he took ship to England, called on all the many dissident nobles of Norman extraction to join him, and had himself proclaimed King, despite his reluctant oath of support for his cousin Maud. The Empress, in the early stages of motherhood, was a deal less prompt. She issued a proclamation that she was true and legitimate monarch, and called upon all leal men to rally to her standard, naming Robert of Gloucester, her half-brother, as her general, to lead her cause. She also called upon all who had sworn support to redeem their oaths – including the Earl of Huntingdon. But she herself remained in Aquitaine meantime.

David, of course, was put in a quandary. His oath was sacred to him, and he had every intention of turning his promised support into fact. But unfortunately Maud's delay in making any move enabled Stephen to stage a fairly convincing corona-tion. He even managed to get William of Canterbury to do the crowning, through the expedient of arranging for the Steward of the royal household, Hugh Bigod, to swear that on his death-bed Henry had turned against his daughter the Empress and declared that he left the throne to Stephen. Whether Wil-liam believed this or not, he allowed himself to be convinced by the other bishops, led by Stephen's brother of Winchester, and Roger of Salisbury, and the thing was done – no doubt, as he claimed afterwards, to avoid civil war in England. So, however much of a usurper, Stephen could claim to be lawful and anointed King of England – which meant that any positive action against him by the King of Scots could be construed as an act of war against England. This had to be very carefully considered. He might have wriggled out of his dilemma by asserting that his oath was sworn only as Earl of Huntingdon and that he was no longer that, having been succeeded by his son Henry – and Henry had taken no such oath. But David was no wriggler, and rejected this device, however strongly advised.

Weighing it all up, he decided that his honour left him without option but to answer his niece's appeal. He did not particularly like her, did not even feel that she would make a satisfactory monarch. But an oath was an oath . . .

There was, of course, another aspect of the situation, and one which appealed to his lords and lieutenants where the oath-and-honour conception did not. This was the Northumbrian dimension. His father had always claimed that his realm should extend right down to the Tees – and had spent much of his time and energies trying to enforce this belief – Northumbria being the southern portion of the ancient Kingdom of Bernicia, of which Lothian, the Merse and Tweeddale were the northern sector. The late Cospatrick's father, had been Earl of Northumbria, under Scots overlordship, until William the Conqueror took it from him by force and gave it to Siward the Strong; whose son, Waltheof, Matilda's father, in due course inherited it, and was himself later dispossessed by the Conqueror and executed. So both as overlord and father of Matilda's son, David could make claim to that great province – and had reminded all of the fact when he had declared Henry as claimant at the same time as naming him Earl of Huntingdon. He had done nothing more about it. But now there was a new situation. With Stephen usurping the throne of England, Northumbria, possibly even Cumbria also, could well come back to Scotland. David was not a man for territorial aggression; but he recognised that there were distinct advantages to be gained here. It gave him an excellent excuse to marshal an army and march over the border, without actually having to declare war; also, the recovering of Northumbria was much more the sort of thing to rally his people to action than any mere declaration of redeeming a royal promise regarding a woman.

So, despite the unsuitable winter conditions, David mustered a force of some five thousand, deliberately not a major army but with a great display of lords, chiefs and knights, under a forest of banners and his own Boar Standard of Scotland, and marched from Rook's Burgh into Northumberland, his first deliberately warlike gesture as King.

Almost at once they come to the late Flambard's castle of

Norham – which surrendered after the merest token resistance. David had decided upon his policy in this respect, and ordered the place's demolition. Then he moved on southwards up the Till valley.

He was, as ever, concerned with good discipline, leaving his people in no doubt as to his royal wrath at any unprovoked attacks on the local population, as was almost normal procedure once a border was crossed. This was, of course, unpopular; but fortunately the Northumbrian folk all but welcomed the Scots, esteeming David, son of a Saxon queen with no Norman blood in his veins, as something like a deliverer from the excesses of the Norman barons who had taken over the province since the Conqueror's time, their hatred of de Vesci and the late Flambard notable – this despite the large numbers of Norman knights in the Scots train.

Castles were a different matter, however, Norman stone keeps which had arisen and were still building, all over Northumbria, centres of oppression in the main. These the local people all but pleaded with the Scots to take and destroy. David was nothing loth, recognising that these would be thorns-in-the-flesh in any eventual administration of the province by himself. Although they were strongholds, minor fortresses, they were built to withstand small raids and petty warfare, not armies of thousands, and they all either yielded after a token defence, like Norham, or else were prudently abandoned in the face of the advancing Scots. All except Bamburgh itself, that is, the principal seat of the former Earls of Northumbria, and now de Vesci's headquarters, a massive and powerful strength set on top of a sea-girt rocky cliff, which defied them and which would have required siege-engines and much time to reduce or starve out. This they left behind unassailed.

If the capture of most of these castles did not take so very long, the destruction and demolition of them afterwards did, ten-foot-thick walling being difficult to cast down. Squads had to be left behind to work at each, a delaying process, again less than popular with the troops. However, as far as David was concerned, there was no hurry, at this stage. The expedition was a gesture in support of Maud. He had sent word of it, before starting, to Robert of Gloucester at Arundel, and anticipating suitable reaction, some co-ordinated move by the Empress's forces, he hoped that Stephen would be caught between two or more armies and be forced to retreat or negotiate. So until he heard from the south, David could afford to dawdle – and to strengthen his hold on Northumbria.

In due course they reached the Tyne, still without any word from the Earl Robert. Here Rufus's great castle, which guarded the first suitable and sheltered ferrying-place above the estuary, again yielded after an exchange of pleasantries. If many of the Scots could scarcely credit their good fortune, and the ease with which they won these strengths, David reminded them that it was an expression of the unpopularity of the usurping Stephen, here in the North at least, indicating that most in the land, Normans as well as Saxons, were in fact faithful to the Empress. It was not all some vaunted prowess of the Scots, however much they might like to think so.

But the said Empress seemed notably slow to move in her own cause – or to see that her supporters in England did so, if she was still in Aquitaine. David began to get seriously concerned at the lack of any sign of positive action against the usurper, other than his own. So much for Henry Beauclerc's oath-swearing at Windsor.

They moved on towards Durham. Northumbria stopped at the Tees, where York commenced. They would go no farther meantime.

But before they reached Durham, information at last reached them – although it was not the news they looked for. Stephen himself was on the way north to meet them, and allegedly with the largest army ever to have been seen in England. He was no farther off than York.

Decison had to be swift. The Scots gesture looked like changing character drastically. It was no part of David's strategy at this stage to fight any major battle, especially not against what sounded like a vastly superior force, and with no least indication that there was any support in the offing. He plumped for discretion meantime. He would forego any idea of taking Durham as warning to Thurstan, and move back to the Tyne, to put himself behind that easily defendable water-barrier. And he would send out scouts to try to ascertain the true strength of Stephen's array, and his intentions as far as was possible.

So retiral was made to the Tyne, and David took up his quarters in Rufus's castle. There was now a feeling of tension in the Scots force.

In due course the scouts returned with what they had gleaned. Stephen's army was indeed large, if not perhaps quite so large as suggested. They reckoned it as perhaps between twenty and thirty thousand, mainly foreign mercenaries from Brittany and Flanders, with no large proportion of chivalry. It seemed that, like Henry before him, Stephen's first act had been to seize the royal treasure chests, in which he had found no less than three hundred thousand marks in silver and gold, it was alleged. He was spending this like water, to consolidate his hold on the throne; granting bribes and subventions left and right and large pensions of as much as three and five thousand marks to powerful men who should have supported Maud; buying the clergy with gifts and grants of land to the Church; above all hiring fighting men by the score of thousands from overseas, to make up for the lack of enthusiasm in England. He and his vast host were now approaching Durham.

Digesting this news David, whilst agreeing with his lieutenants that it was serious indeed, did not accede that it warranted immediate retiral on Scotland, as some urged. He saw more than a gleam of hope in it all. A would-be monarch who was reduced to importing many thousands of mercenaries to support his cause, must be markedly unsure of his position in the country. Stephen therefore was treading on thin ice, and would know it all too well. He would be aware of marching through a land ready to rise behind him, always an unnerving experience for any commander – and Stephen was young, inexperienced, save in jousting and the like, at which he was an expert performer. And he was of an unstable character. David guessed that he would be in a very uncertain state – which must be exploited, if possible. Five thousand Scots, solidly ranked behind the Tyne, with a Northumbria hostile to the usurper all round, and a sullen Middle England behind, would be apt to give any commander pause. Stephen, at the end of a long forced march from the South, might well be prepared to temporise meantime.

Reasoning thus, David sent a deputation forward, under Hugo de Morville, Deputy Constable, to propose a meeting, midway between their armies, say at Chester-le-Street, where they might discuss their differences.

In due course Hugo came back with an indeterminate response. Stephen would consider the matter.

There was much debate as to what this meant. Hugo said that the size of the opposing army certainly had not been exaggerated; but it was also true that it was very obviously composed mainly of mercenaries, and of the roughest type. He had seen very few Norman English lords. Stephen had seemed uneasy, irritable as well as arrogant. His brother Henry, the Bishop, was with him, and Hugo had the impression that he was influential and counselling caution.

It looked then as though Stephen preferred to wait. For

what? Reinforcements? Surely that should be unnecessary. He would certainly have scouts out who would have told him that he had four or five times the numbers of the Scots in front. Then, either he did not trust his own troops, dreaded putting all to the test of war; or else was afraid of what might be going on in his rear, of England perhaps rising behind him. David judged this to be the most likely reason for the uncertainty and delay. In which case waiting was unlikely greatly to benefit him – whilst it might help the Scots, strongly-placed behind the unfordable Tyne. If they could rouse the Northumbrian folk to rise, all over, not actually to fight but to display their sympathy with the Scots and their hostility towards the usurper, especially to disorganise, if not cut off, the necessary food supplies for his large host, which had to live off the country, then the waiting period might well prove to their advantage.

So David sent out emissaries all over the province, urging local musters and marchings, and especially rough handling of Stephen's foraging bands – in all of which the Northumbrians were well content to co-operate. He considered sending for reinforcements from Scotland, but decided against it. Larger numbers of Scots might in the end be counter-productive.

They waited for two whole weeks, the two armies facing each other at a distance of about fifteen miles, inactive – although the folk of Northumbria were busy enough with demonstrations and the like. Many of David's people grew very impatient, especially the Normans, declaring that this was no way to conduct a campaign, arguing that if the enemy was sufficiently scared not to move, it was up to themselves to take advantage, to strike first and keep on striking. Timorousness would avail them nothing. Hervey de Warenne was of this persuasion, needless to say. But David was not to be moved.

Then, at last, Henry, Bishop of Winchester himself arrived from Durham. He declared that King Stephen was now prepared to speak with King David. He would meet him at Chester-le-Street, as suggested, two days hence, one hundred men only to accompany each monarch.

*　　*　　*

It was quite a performance to ensure that both sides arrived at the venue, the site of the former Roman fort, at precisely the same moment, so that neither king could seem to have to wait for the other. All concerned were clad as though for war – although David could not rival Stephen's splendour, in crown-encircled helmet, gold-scaled armour and colourful horse-furniture.

"Mummery!" Hervey scoffed. "Play-acting! Is this what we have come for?"

"It may well be," David told him. "But we may not act quite the same play! In my mummery the costume is less important than the words!"

The two sides drew up in long lines facing each other about a score of yards apart, the principals under their banners in the centre. Stephen was quick to get in the first word.

"I would greet you more warmly, King David, were you not deep in my realm in armed force."

"I am deep in Northumbria, Stephen fitz Stephen – which is scarcely the same. Northumbria has always been part of my realm of Scotland. But . . . I greet you fairly."

"You have brought thousands of men to Northumbria. Why, if it is yours?"

"Five thousand only – but a fifth of yours. I could scarcely have come with less. And might have brought so many more! Is it not so? *You* have!"

Stephen tried another tack. "When last I saw you you were not claiming Northumbria as yours."

"When last I saw *you*, you were swearing support for the Empress should her father die!"

"Conditions change. Kingdoms cannot be ruled by the testaments of dead men! You know that as well as any. The English asked me, the heir-male, to be their King, in place of a woman. It was best. For all."

"The people of England? I think that you . . . exaggerate!"

"All who matter did."

"You say so? Does not the Earl of Gloucester matter? Nor the Earl of Cornwall? Nor the Earl of Surrey? Nor even such as my son the Earl of Huntingdon?"

"I have just heard that my cousin Robert of Gloucester has accepted a pension of five thousand marks for his support of me! I bought Henry's other bastard, Cornwall, for considerably less, some time ago!"

David had difficulty in masking his expression, achieving only a sort of wooden immobility. So that was why there had been no word from Gloucester at Arundel, no move to match his own invasion. It would be, also, why Stephen had waited – for confirmation. So there was to be no uprising. Only *his* own oath apparently had meant anything at all. And he had brought his Scots force into the jaws of disaster for nothing . . .

Or not disaster, yet. The immediate situation had not changed, whatever the longer-term outlook. Hoping that his voice sounded calm, unperturbed, he spoke.

"Bastards may so behave. But I would not rely on bought men to keep their bargains, Stephen – any kind of bought men, high or low! You should watch your back, I think! There is still a lot of England who care nothing for Henry's bastards. Too many to find pensions for, with even Henry's treasure!"

"We shall see. As for you – what do *you* want?"

Again David had to disguise his surprise. "Want?" He swallowed. "*I* am not in the market-place! I want nothing that is not my own. What I have come to take. There is no buying me. I am come only for my provinces of Northumbria and Cumbria. Naught else." He hoped that his voice sounded steady.

There was a long silence, while Stephen chewed at his lip. He turned to exchange a few words, low-voiced, with his brother. At last he spoke.

"If I accede to this, in some measure, will you return to Scotland?"

The Scots could scarcely believe their ears. David inclined his head. "If the arrangement is satisfactory, yes."

"You swear it?"

"I do not require to swear to keep my word, sir! And I would not have believed that *you* put much faith in oaths! But, in the circumstances – yes. I am willing to swear that my main armed strength will return to Scotland forthwith if you agree to cede Northumbria and Cumbria to my realm."

"No – not that, man. Not to your realm. To *you*. Not to Scotland – to yourself. Two earldoms – for which you would do homage to me."

"Ah! That is a different matter altogether. No, my friend – I, King of Scots, will do homage to no man. Your uncle sought that, and did not gain it. I will nowise yield it to you, for Northumbria or Cumbria or any other."

There was another lengthy pause, while Stephen conferred.

"Then I fear we must do battle!" he said at length. "I have been more than reasonable. I cannot do more. And you cannot win such battle, David. My host is many times greater than yours."

"Greater in numbers than the Scots I have brought – who did not come to fight you. But not greater than the Northumbrians! All Northumbria will rise against you, at my behest. Already they are mustering. And you have got to win across Tyne. Think you that will be easy? With an entire province against you, under Scots leadership? You will never do it."

In the further period for thought, young Henry whispered to his father that *he* could do fealty to Stephen for Northumbria and Cumbria, as for Huntingdon, without compromising the Scots crown. David nodded. He had thought of that, but he said to wait.

It was as though the other had heard them. "A pity to shed blood when reason could and should prevail," he called. "Your son, there, is one of my earls – Huntingdon. If he can make homage for Huntingdon, why not Northumbria and Cumbria? I will not part these from England – but could yield them as fiefs to a Scots earl."

"They are Scots soil, I say. But . . . it might be considered."

"Do so consider, then. Unless you desire war."

"I am not afraid of war. But not over Northumbria and Cumbria. But for my oath of support for Maud."

"Your oath was made to Henry, not Maud – and Henry is dead. Would you make war for a dead man? Consider well," Stephen waved a gauntleted hand. "I also go to consider this matter." He turned round, and rode a little way back from his line.

David, for his part, did not move, as a matter of policy. Also there was really nothing to consider. They were gaining infinitely more than they could have hoped for – Cumbria in addition to Northumbria. And without having to fight. Admittedly, not to be part of Scotland – but this in name only. Time could well change that. Young Henry's fealty would not tie the King of Scots. Even David's fire-eating Normans did not require this to be pointed out to them – although their attitudes tended to be that since Stephen, with his great army, was so reluctant to put matters to the test, they ought to fight and win the more.

When presently Stephen returned with his advisers, David was quick to speak first.

"What have you decided, my friend? Do we battle or do we not?"

"It is you who must decide, not me," the other answered. And then, as though that might sound weak, he went on, "I have gone as far as I can with you, man. If you promise to withdraw your array back to Scotland, and no more threaten my realm. And if the Prince your son will do fealty to me for Northumbria and Cumbria, I will convey into his hands the royal castles of Tyne and Caer-luel. Better than that I cannot do. For the friendship of our two realms."

"Rufus's new castle on Tyne is already in my hands," David returned, but not forcefully.

"Do you agree, sir?" That was almost agitated.

"I do." David spoke firmly now. "The castle of Caer-luel. My son does fealty to you for the two provinces, to Tees and Ribble. And I retire to Scotland."

"And you will no more threaten my kingdom?"

"Not unless you give me new cause, Stephen."

"Very well. We are all here witness to your promise. I shall have the documents scribed, signed and sealed. The Prince Henry, Earl of Huntingdon, to accompany me back to York, there to swear fealty with due ceremony. Then to receive the documents. Come if you will, also."

"I thank you – no. I will return to Scotland. One last matter – you will recall Ivo de Vesci, from Bamburgh? And Randolph de Meschin from Caer-luel? With all their people? I do not wish to meet either."

"Very well. They are no friends of mine." Stephen hesitated, then. "David – you have not once addressed me as King. Have you forgot?"

"No, sir. I have not forgotten my oath, to Maud."

"But I *am* King of England, whatever your oath, man! Duly crowned and anointed. By the Archbishop of Canterbury. And all ratified by a Bull of Pope Innocent."

"I do not greatly esteem either of your archbishops – who both also pronounced support for the Empress! And I do not recognise Innocent as Pope, but Anacletus – so his Bulls scarcely concern me!"

They left it at that.

A party of young knights were selected to accompany Henry on his visit to York. David had some advice for his son, but had sufficient confidence in his good sense to be sure that he would know how to cope with most that Stephen might produce.

David turned his face northwards, still scarcely believing that he had achieved, in one short hour and by mere words, gestures, what his father had spent a lifetime trying to achieve with fire and sword.

28

DAVID'S FEAR THAT it had all been just too easy was justified. At first all seemed to go well enough. Young Henry sent back word to his father that Stephen was being notably gracious. The fealty-swearing had gone off without incident and the charters of Northumbria and Cumbria duly handed over – Henry's messenger bringing these back to Scotland with him. Henry himself, at Stephen's pressing invitation, had gone south with the English army, to London, for a visit. He thought it wise to accede to this, so that he might learn more of the true situation there and the mood prevailing in England.

David was well pleased with his son.

Then stories began to come from the South presaging trouble. Stephen, feeling more secure on the throne, was beginning to act the tyrant. Instead of handing out largesse he was raking in fierce taxation again, oppressing the people, riding rough-shod over the sensibilities of rich and poor, Norman and Saxon alike. He was certainly not fulfilling his promise to his subjects. Would he be any more likely to fulfil them towards David his enemy? To gain early support he had said that he would abolish most of the hated forest laws, and the worst excesses of serfdom on the indigenous population. He now did the reverse, and this served to offend both people and nobles – for though the royal forests, covering so vast an area, were to be reduced, the land involved had been promised to the nobles and clergy. Chaos was therefore developing in much of England, with little or no attempts made at good government or any firm control. As far as David and Scotland were concerned, neither de Vesci nor de Meschin was withdrawn from Bamburgh or Caer-luel, both continuing to behave as though nothing was changed. David was prepared to be patient, but he began to fear that steps would require to be taken.

There was, however, no hint of any organised rising in England in favour of the Empress.

Then, after Eastertide, Henry came home. In the end, he had had to leave Stephen's Court in a hurry. There had been some hostility against him from the start, amongst Stephen's motley collection of supporters and hangers-on, although the King

318

himself had seemed to want his guest to stay, just why was not clear. Then, at a feast in the Tower of London on Easter Day, after a special thanksgiving service at Westminster, Stephen had seated Henry in the place of honour at his right hand, above the Archbishop of Canterbury, likewise above his own cousin, the Earl of Chester, the principal noble supporting him. As well as embarrassing Henry, this had infuriated many, and a violent scene had erupted. Henry had been personally assaulted and his Scots party insulted. Stephen had cowered before it all, and then left the hall. The Prince and his friends had departed for home the next day.

David was annoyed, of course – but really more concerned with the news on the wider front which Henry brought back. Geoffrey Plantagenet, the Empress's husband, had agreed to a two-year truce over the contested succession, for a pension of five thousand marks – presumably with Maud's assent. This appeared to make nonsense of her claims and hopes of the throne. Louis of France had accepted Stephen as King of England and was proposing to betroth his daughter to Eustace, Stephen's child son. Most of the Normandy nobles had come over to Stephen's side, and he had put his elder brother, Theobald Count of Blois, at their head meantime, also with a pension, with instructions to put that dukedom in a fit state to receive him, for he would be coming there just as soon as he could safely leave England, to instal the boy Eustace as Duke of Normandy. Robert of Gloucester, like most other of Maud's former supporters, had made the best bargain he could for himself, on condition that his rights and privileges were maintained.

So Maud's cause appeared to be in the dust, possibly deservedly so; although it was a sorry business that the winner should be so poor a character. Sorry also that money, lands, pensions, seemed to be what mattered in England and France these days, not right, honour and good faith.

There was the other side to it all, however. The earls and barons had exacted a great price for their change of allegiance. The late Henry Beauclerc's reforms were largely lost, and every Norman baron was now almost his own master, many going so far as to coin their own silver. Lawlessness and rapine grew daily in England, unchecked.

David foresaw a reckoning, but perceived little that he could do meantime. He wrote to Stephen requesting swift fulfillment of his commitment to withdraw de Vesci and de Meschin and their forces from Northumbria and Cumbria.

In Scotland, by comparison, there was peace and order. The

new system of administration had scarcely begun to work, but the effects of firm government, justice and concern for the people's welfare were notable. There were failures, mistakes, misdeeds and refusals, of course. Malcontents and wrongdoers did not turn into saints, greed and reaction often countered the King's policies. But by and large his reforms went ahead, and his rule was never seriously challenged. David founded a new Cistercian abbey at Melross, a couple of miles up Tweed from the Old Melross one-time Celtic monastery. He endowed and started to build a cathedral church at Glasgow for Bishop John, to be dedicated to St. Kentigern or Mungo, the original founder of the diocese. And, enheartened by the progress now being made in Galloway in conjunction with Fergus, at the Priory of Kirk Cuthbert's Town, now being called St. Mary's Isle, he encouraged his lords and friends to go and do likewise, where they could, offering royal aid and co-operation. This was not only in the interests of piety, of course, but for the furtherance of his governmental system. One of the first to take him up on this was his old friend Hugo, now Lord of Lauderdale, with great lands on the fringes of the earldom of Dunbar and March, as well as elsewhere. Hugo endowed an abbey at Dryburgh on the Tweed, between Melross and Kelshaugh, although much of the initial funds and impetus came from the King. Hervey de Warenne, Knight Marischal, now married to a Celtic heiress, was not yet persuaded to turn abbey-builder; but he did endow a little church at Keith Marischal on the edge of Lammermuir, where he and his heirs might conveniently be buried; and there he set up a parish system. As did others.

All this heartening development was possible, of course, partly because of the moneys still flowing north from the well-managed Honour of Huntingdon, under Sheriff Gilbert; but even more so because for once there were no external threats to Scotland. England was in no state to threaten; there was still civil strife in Norway; and the turbulent Viking earls and kinglets of Iceland, Orkney, the Hebrides and Ireland were involved in internecine struggles of their own, whilst their Norse overlords fought each other. Some of David's advisers, the Celtic ones in especial, urged him to seize the opportunity to wrest back the Hebrides from the slackened Norse grip. But he refused, saying that the Northumbrian and Cumbrian provinces were of far more value to Scotland than the western isles, and, although they were his in name now, they might well have to fight for them yet.

Henry mac David, Prince of Strathclyde, Earl of Huntingdon and titular Earl of Northumbria and Cumbria, came of age the following year, 1137, and great were the celebrations at Rook's Burgh. As an extension of this, David decided upon another of his gestures. He had done little or nothing about actually taking over the two English provinces, waiting for their governors de Vesci and de Meschin to be withdrawn. Neither had been, over a year later. He was reluctant to move in, in armed force again. It might well come to that, but first he would try more peaceful penetration. They would make a progress into Cumbria – or at least Henry would, as Earl thereof, and he would accompany his son – and they would establish a new abbey there as symbol of the new situation and notification to all concerned. One of the few links David had retained with Cumbria was with his own nephew William, Lord of Allerdale. This was a quiet young man known as William fitz Duncan or William the Nobleman, son of David's half-brother Duncan the Second, who had been assassinated after reigning for only six months. His mother had been Ethelreda, Cospatrick the elder's daughter, and Cospatrick's Allerdale lands in upland Cumbria had been given to him. By marriage he had acquired the manor of Holm Cultram on the Solway coast west of Caer-luel; and this he was prepared to exchange with his uncle for lands on the lower Tweed. There they would build their abbey, looking across Solway towards Scotland.

So, with a great train of nobles and clerics, including Bishop John and Abbot Alwin of Holyrood, with mounted musicians and singers and only a comparatively small armed escort, father and son set out for Cumbria.

There was, of course, much interest to see what happened when they came to Caer-luel. But Randolph de Meschin chose discretion – he had had ample time for warning of their approach – and absented himself, leaving only underlings who remained passive, if wary. But Bishop Athelwulf was there. David and Henry, with Bishop John and the Lord William, called upon him. He was sufficiently wary too, naturally, but concerned not to offend if he could help it.

David for his part was placatory. "We seek your help, my lord Bishop," he said. "As you will know, my son is now Earl of Cumbria, this great province his, by agreement of Stephen of Boulogne. He seeks to celebrate this advancement with thanks to God and some act of piety and advantage to all Cumbria. The lands of Holm Cultram are now his, and he proposes, with my aid, to found an abbey there, to the glory of God and the furtherance of Christ's cause in these parts."

321

The Bishop looked the more alarmed at these good tidings, rather than delighted. He swallowed but ventured no comment.

"It will be a large and noble establishment," David went on pleasantly. "I have now built many abbeys, and learned much. We shall, to be sure, need your help. It is in your diocese and will come under your good guidance. It would be suitable, therefore, if you would duly consecrate its foundation."

Athelwulf, a decent Saxon, looked flustered. "But, but . . ." he began. "This is a matter . . . for much thought, Sire. I do not know . . . I would have to consider. Many things . . ."

"So you do not wish to see an abbey established in your diocese, my lord Bishop? There is none in all North Cumbria, I think."

"Oh, yes – yes, to be sure. But . . . does Archbishop Thurstan know of this? Has he agreed?"

"Whether he knows or not is of no matter. This is a matter for the Diocesan. Is it not, Bishop John?"

"Entirely, yes, my lord King. And I have never yet heard of any bishop refusing the splendid gift of an abbey in his see. Have you, Brother Athelwulf?"

"Er . . . no. But in this I would value the Archbishop's . . . guidance."

Henry spoke up. "My lord Bishop – I am Earl of Cumbria. By King Stephen's royal warrant. Do you wish to see the warrant? I have it with me. No? Then do you question my right to erect such abbey? Do you refuse to accept my own abbey in my own earldom? You, a servant of the Lord Christ?"

"No, no, my lord – no." The other wrung his hands.

"Good! And would you have other than yourself consecrate this abbey in *your* diocese?"

"No. But . . ."

"Bishop John of Glasgow, here, will do it if you wish," David intervened.

"But I would think that even Thurstan would prefer it to be you. As Diocesan."

"Would this abbey be indeed under the Archbishop's rule and authority? Owing duty to York, not to Scotland?"

"If *you* consecrate it, in your diocese, yes. If not, it will be different matter. It will reopen the controversy over Strathclyde and hegemony."

"No, no – not that!" For once, a subject interrupted a king. "Not that, Sire. Of a mercy . . . !"

"Then – you *will* consecrate? The foundation-stone?"

Unhappily the prelate nodded his tonsured head.

322

"We proceed there tomorrow. We will endow the new abbey richly. It will greatly benefit your see, my lord Bishop . . ."

So, de Meschin and his people keeping out of sight, the Scots cavalcade, with the reluctant Athelwulf and the Lord William, made a musical and pleasing procession the few miles westwards to Holm Cultram on the Solway shore, where the estuary began to widen. There, after an inspection of the manor, they paced out the bounds of the abbey-precincts, chose the site of its church, and Henry laid the foundation-stone, dedicating the place to the Blessed Virgin, and announcing the lands and revenues for its endowment and support. Thereafter Athelwulf did his consecrating, with holy water and intonations, and however loth, did it well, all agreed. Arrangements were set in hand for the employment of local overseers, masons and craftsmen, and a return made to Caer-luel – where again de Meschin did not materialise.

Then it was home to Scotland.

They arrived at Rook's Burgh to find serious news awaiting them. Peter of Leon, otherwise Anacletus, was seriously ill, thought to be dying. In this state he had finally and formally abandoned his papal pretensions and conceded Innocent's authority, seeking reconcilation before approaching a higher throne, apparently. Whether Innocent made respondent gesture was not reported; but what was made clear was that he had promptly declared all decrees of Anacletus null, and reinforced all his own orders and vetoes concerning those who had supported his rival – making a start by excommunicating King Roger of Sicily. Amongst the many fiats issued were commands for Bishop Robert of St. Andrews to give up all claims to metropolitan status and to admit immediate subservience to York; and for Bishop John of Glasgow also to put himself under Thurstan's authority. Or both to demit their sees. The sanction of excommunication was threatened for all who chose spiritual disobedience.

David was gravely perturbed and hurt, not to say disheartened. There was no denying the power of the papacy for any man of the Roman faith – indeed for any man in Christendom whatsoever. The threat of excommunication could bring even emperors literally to their knees in dust and ashes before the Pontiff, seeking remission. It represented eternal damnation to the individual soul; and to a nation the break-down of all religious authority – in Scotland's case particularly dire, with all the new administrative system based on dioceses and parishes. David felt embittered indeed. After all that he had done to turn his country from the Celtic to the Roman Church, all the abbeys and monasteries and churches he had founded, all the gifts of revenues and lands – as well as all his mother's strivings – this was the reaction from Rome . . .

That man was not often bitter, angry , offended – he did not allow himself to be, as a conscious effort. But was all three now. Those around him eyed him somewhat askance. He ordered Bishop Robert to remain in his place and act as before. He was *Ard Episcop*, King's Bishop of Scotland, whatever the Pope might say – these were offices of the old Celtic Church. They must be used again to serve Scotland now. There would be no truckling to York, with its inevitable corollary of subservience to the English Crown.

Bishop John's position was different. He had no background of the Columban faith. He declared that he had no intention of making submission to Thurstan – but on the other hand, he had no intention of bringing down the wrath of the Holy See upon his liege lord and adopted country, by any act of his. He would vacate his see meantime, as commanded – vacate, not resign. He would do what he had indeed long desired to do, in his inmost heart – go to Tiron and become a simple monk there. As a man of God, surely that was his right?

In his present state of mind, David did not forbid him. Probably it was the best course, for the time being. He said goodbye to his one-time tutor and chaplain sorrowfully, but promised to continue with the building of his cathedral in Glasgow. It would be waiting for him to come back. There would be no new appointment to the see, he promised him. Popes on the whole had short reigns.

29

IN NOVEMBER, WITH winter beginning to cap the Highland mountains with white, David, not yet fully recovered from his mood of resentment, was spurred to further wrath. There had been no least reply from Stephen regarding de Vesci and de Meschin; and news reached him that work had been halted on the new abbey at Holm Cultram, allegedly on orders from Archbishop Thurstan, although it was de Meschin who drove the workmen from the site. It was too much. If he was not to look a complete fool and weakling, the King of Scots must act.

He issued orders for a major mustering of armed men, not five thousand this time but three times that number.

His people were nothing loth, in the main. Peace, order and good government were all very well, but apt to be dull for spirited folk used to more stirring activities. There was no difficulty in raising the required numbers; certainly no suggestion anywhere that the King was being impatient.

There was, however, an unanticipated reaction three weeks later, just as the assembling host was preparing to move off into Cumbria. Old Thurstan himself made his second visit to Rook's Burgh, unannounced, frail as he now was, borne in a horse-litter. It seemed that the news of the Scots muster had not taken long to reach York, and further afield still.

He came on the lord Stephen's behalf, the Archbishop declared. The King had had to go to Normandy on affairs of that dukedom. But he would be back soon after Christmas. He urged that King David did nothing rash. There was no need for armed display. As monarchs, they could compose any differences between them readily enough face to face, without bloodshed. Why resort to the sword? Wait until after Yuletide, and Stephen would come north in person to put matters to rights.

David was surprised and only moderately impressed. Why had the governors not been withdrawn from the two provinces long since, he demanded? And what of Holm Cultram, where his son's works had been insolently stopped? And on his, Thurstan's, instructions it was said.

That was all a mistake, a misunderstanding, the Archbishop asserted. Underlings exceeding their instructions. Work could recommence. Just an unfortunate misapprehension by dolts.

David was placed in something of a quandary. It was evident that his muster of strength had achieved results without a sword being drawn. But how genuine, how worthwhile, was this reaction? Stephen was utterly untrustworthy – and he estimated that the Archbishop was almost equally so. Yet was there any point in marching in force into Cumbria when the object of the enterprise was already gained? Would this not come to look foolish? If there was nobody to fight, nothing to be done but make a progress? He did not want to let loose a large army on a defenceless province, his own province in theory, with no especial aim and target. It would result in sheer slaughter, massacre, pillage and rapine – such invasions always did. On the other hand, if he accepted Thurstan's assurances and dispersed his host, relieving the pressure on the English, had he any certainty that all would not be as before, promises forgotten?

One factor weighed heavily, the coming Yuletide season. He had deliberately chosen a winter-time strike simply because such was practically never attempted on account of adverse conditions, and so offered great opportunities for surprise. But it was one thing to lead an army on a winter campaign and altogether another to keep it standing idle, at home, over Yule, the greatest and longest holiday season in Scotland. It would be as good as condemning the Tweed valley to chaos and spoliation. Indeed, keeping any army, made up of individual lords' levies and innumerable district contingents, in inactive waiting for any length of time, was apt to be a disastrous business.

David decided that he had little choice, in the circumstances. He would accept the Archbishop's assurances meantime, and wait for Stephen, sending all but a nucleus of his force home for Yuletide; but they must be prepared to remuster at short notice, if necessary. As usual, many of his nobles and supporters were grievously disappointed and saw this as weakness.

So Thurstan departed southwards and most of the Scots northwards, and Rook's Burgh prepared itself for a more or less normal Yule.

In mid-January, with no word of or from Stephen, David went north himself for a council-meeting at Stirling, in hard frost but calm weather. That council decided, amongst other things, without actually saying so, that the King had misjudged, acted weakly in not taking Northumbria and Cumbria by main force when he had his army assembled. Clearly strategy by gesture, artifice and wits was much less popular than that of honest cold steel.

It was on his way back to Rook's Burgh from this meeting that an urgent messenger from Ranulph de Soulis met the King. Stephen had landed an army unexpectedly at Berwick-on-Tweed, from a great fleet of ships, and was invading the Merse and Lothian, himself leading.

After the first sickening jolt of near-despair at men's deceit and dishonesty, David acted swiftly. He sent back Hervey the Marischal to Stirling with orders for an immediate full-scale muster of the nation's greatest strength; but while this was assembling, he was to send on all available forces immediately.

He sent warning to Lothian and Clydesdale and Galloway. And he raced on for Rook's Burgh with all speed.

There he learned the details. The English had been cunning. Coming in the usual way, by land, the Scots would have had some warning of a large force approaching; by sea, none. After landing at the mouth of Tweed, Stephen had struck inland, up-river, into the Merse. But of course having no horses, his advance was comparatively slow – the disadvantage of any sea-borne invasion. This had given time for de Soulis, left in charge at Rook's Burgh, to fling forward such troops as remained there from the original muster, with what was quickly obtainable locally, to the number of about fifteen hundred, and these were now fighting a delaying action along Tweedside and the South Merse. Young Earl Cospatrick had scraped together about eight hundred of his people, and with these was harrying the enemy flank on the north. Others like Burnet of Fairnington and de Mautelant, Hugo's vassal at Lauder, were out harassing likewise. But it was reckoned that Stephen had landed at least eight thousand, and these would not hold him up for long. Last reports had put him at Lennel, the other side of Coldstream, only a dozen miles away – although part of his force was said to be heading northwards up the coast towards Dunbar.

David had three courses open to him. He could hurry back northwards to meet the forces which Hervey should be sending on – but that might take days, before any effective counter-stroke could be mentioned. And there was always the possibility that Stephen might be expecting reinforcements by land or sea. He might shut himself up here in the March Mount Castle and wait to be besieged – undignified and probably unprofitable, and preventing him from placing himself at the head of his forces when they did arrive. Or he could attempt some small sally, however limited, here and now.

The trouble was that his total available manpower mean-time, including the party which had accompanied him from Stirling, less the many sent off as couriers, amounted to no more than two hundred. Not a great deal could be done with two hundred against thousands, however gallant. But there was one point in his favour – being the King's companions and escort they were all superbly mounted, lordlings, knights and chivalry. He could move fast, therefore and make rings around dismounted men.

Hugo, supported by William of Allerdale and others, said that they should go add themselves to the delaying, harassing forces, forming two or three powerful cavalry wedges to bore into and disorganise Stephen's leadership group especially. Who could tell what such determined attacks against a dismounted host might achieve? But David shook his head. Later, perhaps. But first he had another notion. Two hundred men on fast horses should be sufficient . . .

Late February afternoon as it was, with the early dusk settling over the Cheviot foothills, he led this company out and across the Teviot ford, to turn eastwards along the south side of Tweed. Despite the poor light, he maintained a fierce pace, which soon had the two hundred considerably strung out. In only about six miles they were over the unmarked march into Northumbria, at Haddenstank. Fortunately all knew the road well, although it was on the wrong side of the Tweed, a Cheviot drovers' road – otherwise there might have been unfortunate spills. Presently the glow of the hundreds of English camp-fires ahead was lighting up the night sky – but on the other side of the great river. As David had anticipated, they saw no troops on this English side, only the occasional salmon-fishers' hamlet and milling township.

Twenty-five miles, most of it in real darkness, on a frosty night of stars but no moon, will take even expert horsemen almost four hours, so that it was well into the evening before they heard the hollow booming of the Norse Sea breakers before them on the Tweedmouth beach. Slowly now, circumspectly, they rode down to the fishing haven and village. They were directly opposite the defensive town of Berwick-on-Tweed across the half-mile-wide estuary basin. Some lights twinkled from windows there.

Local fishermen, with cold steel held before their eyes, confirmed what David had expected. The English invasion fleet lay out in the sheltered waters of the estuary, at the Berwick side. They were packed tight over there, some seventy vessels all told – although some of the smaller craft used for ferrying men and supplies were lying in at the Hospice haven nearby.

Well enough content, they enquired how many fishing-boats, the typical high-prowed cobles of the Tweed area, were available here, at the boat strand; and were informed just under a score were there, drawn up on the sand and shingle. That would serve their purpose – say ten men to a boat. Sufficient fishermen were routed out, to row the boats. Leaving the horses under guard, the Scots helped the Tweedmouth men, doubtful as they were, to push the cobles down into the shallows, then piled aboard.

The flotilla pushed off, the creaking of the long sweeps drowned in the steady thunder of the surf on the sand-bar at the estuary mouth. Only one or two faint lights glimmered from what must be the fleet of sea-going ships lying to anchor. Candles and lamp-oil were apt to be too expensive for sailor-men to burn of a night; besides, most of the crews would be ashore in the town's alehouses, the fishermen assured. David and his men anticipated little difficulty.

As the dark hulks of the vessels loomed up, it seemed as though they constituted a solid barier, so closely were the craft packed, most indeed warped side-by-side. Swiftly the raiders swarmed up from the cobles to the decks of the larger ships, the more agile going first and aiding their companions. David's orders were simple and clear. Every ship was to be set on fire. There was to be no unnecessary bloodshed. Only if crewmen resisted actively were they to be maltreated – he had no real quarrel with the shipmen. Whenever each ship was sufficiently alight, one or two men were to be left to see that it continued to blaze, was not extinguished, the rest to move on to the next vessel. With nearly twenty teams of ten the thing should not be too difficult. Tarred timbers should burn well.

The seizing of the dark, silent fleet was indeed not difficult; but tarry timbers and gear or none, the setting of it all alight was less easy. They found few men aboard, none at all on some craft; and of such as were, most were already in their bunks, asleep or drunken. Only one or two actually showed fight, and these were quickly disposed of. The later ships to be attacked, of course, received some warning, and some of their people may have made their escape either in small boats or merely by jumping overboard. Anyway, resistance was practically non-existent.

But getting major fires started, and then ensuring that these went on to destroy the vessels, was much harder than antici-pated, assiduously as all applied flint and tinder. Fires admit-tedly fairly quickly glowed and flickered all over the fleet; but these seemed notably slow to run together, coalesce and turn into blazing ships. Being a calm, and frosty night, there was little wind to fan the flames. Ships timbers seemed grievously slow to catch. Moreover, presently some proportion of the incendiaries had to break off their efforts to repel boarders in the shape of crewmen from ashore at Berwick, who had seen the fires and come rowing out to their vessels. These did not represent any major challenge to the King's company, for they were mere peaceful seafarers not trained fighting-men – and largely drink-taken at that. But they further delayed the arson.

However, the Scots did learn, by trial and error, and by using bedding, clothing, broken bunk timber and the like, aided by lamp-oil and pitch where it could be found. And once these smaller fires, shrewdly positioned, did set alight to the tarry timbers, the latter burned strongly and did not die out until wholly consumed.

At length, reasonably satisfied, David gave orders to return to Tweedmouth beach. Not every ship would be destroyed, but most of those that were not would be unusable for a considerable time. Stephen would not sail back to England in this fleet, that was certain.

The town of Berwick was most evidently awake now and in an uproar, as they rowed back; but that was all to the good and represented no threat. The more panic the better; the more alarming would be the reports hurried along Tweedside to the invading army – which was part of the objective.

Promising the fishermen some silver for their part in the night's activities, David ordered to horse, and led the way back whence they had come, along the south side of the river.

Their night was not yet finished however. At the little-used ford below Twizel, where the Till came in and deposited much silt to shallow the water, some nine miles west, they crossed the river. It was really too deep and swift for use at this time of year, but by holding each other's stirrup-leathers, keeping close to support each other, and gentling their beasts heedfully, they got over without loss.

They were now, of course, behind Stephen's lines, and must be prepared to come across groups of the enemy, camped or otherwise. But they knew that the main force was camped another four miles ahead, in the Coldstream area, facing their own delaying force; so any troops they might run into hereabouts would be apt to be supply people, stragglers, second-rate fighters, and as such little trouble to themselves. Indeed, it might be advantageous to encounter some of these, in order to spread rumour and possible panic forward.

In the event they saw nobody, and rode northwards into the dark plain of the Merse. About a mile in, they turned west again, parallel with Tweed. It was now well after midnight. They avoided villages and farmsteads, which might be enemy-occupied.

With the glow of camp-fires ahead, somewhat reduced now – although that was perhaps partly the effect of the much brighter glare coming from behind, to the east, where the shipping burned in the estuary – they halted for a brief hour or so of rest. David explained his new strategy. They would split into groups, or wedges, as Hugo and William had suggested – say four, of fifty men each. But they would not descend upon battle-ready troops but on sleeping men. This might not be accepted warfare, nor yet chivalrous; but it should be effective and ought to produce more alarm. It was the spirit of the enemy he was concerned to assail, rather than their bodies. Four wedges of horsemen crashing down out of the night ought to create a deal of apprehension and despondency.

Groups of fifty under David, de Soulis, Hugo and the Lord William were marshalled into approximate arrowhead formations, and riding thus they spread over a fairly wide area north of the camps. Four or five thousand men sleeping in the open take up a lot of space. There were no tents nor pavilions in this encampment; presumably Stephen and his chief leaders slept in Coldstream cottages. But the fighting-men lay on the frosted ground. Hence the large numbers of fires, hundreds of them, each with its tight circle of sleepers as close around as they dared, the sentinels seeking to keep the embers refuelled. Observing this from as near as they dared advance, quietly, David decided that it was all to the good. The fires could be made to assist them, and the sentinels, being preoccupied with wood-gathering, would be the less effective opponents.

The four groups spaced themselves well apart, perhaps four hundred yards. The King, furthest to the west, had a whin-bush set alight as signal, to blaze furiously. Then all the wedges broke into a trot, a canter and a gallop, to thunder down upon the sleeping encampment area.

There could be no coherent description of what followed, utter chaos and wild surprise and panic on the one hand, disciplined and inexorable manoeuvre and quartering on the other. In formation, looser than had they been in actual battle and daylight, the groups bored headlong into and through the circles of recumbent men around the fires, swords flailing, hooves pounding and trampling, causing bloody ruin, scattering the blazing wood and embers, creating utter confusion, then wheeling on to the next circle and the next. Weaving in roughly figure-of-eight patterns, the attackers turned that sleeping army into a fleeing, yelling, leaderless mob in only minutes, ungovernable, every man for himself. Some groupings amongst those not attacked first did seek to rally and put up some defence; but bemused with sleep, in no formation, surrounded by screaming

331

horror and with no central direction, they were no match for the armoured, mounted knightly wedges.

It was bloody nightmare and disaster.

In the midst of it, David himself was trying to think as a general and not as a captain of cavalry, difficult as this was in the fierce action and heady excitement. As it became evident that the English could not rally and form any coherent opposing force for some time, he wondered whether to break off and make a dash for Coldstream township, where he anticipated that Stephen and the enemy leadership were ensconced, to exploit this unconventional victory to the full. But he could not be sure that they were at Coldstream, however probable. They would be warned by now, surely. Again, he did not know what sort of numbers might be with Stephen and his lords – possibly many times more than two hundred, and his best knights probably. So such an attempt might well be a failure and tend to undo much that had been achieved. His own men were tired and in no state to face fresh and rested knights who had had time to marshal themselves, even though they might be dismounted – and no doubt Stephen would have stolen some horses since his landing. It was not practicable.

When there seemed little more that the wedges could usefully do, he had his horn blown to reassemble his scattered company. Three proved to be missing and eight wounded in some degree – extraordinarily light casualties considering the havoc wrought. Leaving the stricken area, they trotted off westwards. Behind them the entire eastern sky was now red with the false dawn of the burning fleet.

In less than two miles they ran into the aroused vanguard of their own defensive force, in the Birgham area, advancing slowly, in mystification as to what was going on ahead. This force was commanded by the young Earl Cospatrick and Simon Loccard, another of Hugo's vassals, an experienced fighter. These David ordered to marshal their entire force, which had been sleeping after an exhausting day, and at once to advance on the disorganised enemy before these could recover and reform, to keep up the pressure. Then he led his weary ten-score back to the village of Eccles nearby, for desperately needed sleep and rest and feed for the horses.

In the morning they learned that the English were in full and disorderly flight, retiring on Berwick. What they would do then was questionable. But finding their fleet destroyed and probably with a much exaggerated idea as to the numbers arrayed against them, the chances were that they would retreat into

Northumbria, and probably keep on retreating. Much would depend on whether reinforcements were on their way; but on the other hand they would realise that, in a hostile invaded country, reinforcements would be apt to reach the defenders more powerfully and effectively.

By mid-afternoon David's scouts sent information that Stephen was indeed in full retreat southwards, by land, leaving his shattered fleet to extricate itself, and the northern detachment which had marched towards Dunbar, as best it could. The invasion was over.

David would have followed up his enemy, but just had not the manpower available, as yet. Besides enough was probably enough, meantime.

30

THEREAFTER, OF COURSE, the King was faced with the same problem as heretofore, only more so. A large army descended upon Tweeddale from all quarters, probably one of the largest Scotland had ever assembled – when the urgent need for it had passed. The actuality of invasion had stirred the land as nothing else would, and contingents had come from as far away as the Highlands and Mar. Fergus even brought six thousand from Galloway. David found himself with a host of over fifty thousand – and all Tweedside quickly groaned under their presence, yet had to feed them.

But this time the King was in a different mood. If anything was clear, it was that Stephen and the English required to be taught a lesson. For once he was disinclined to damp down his warlike supporters and talk peace and patience and the benefits of diplomacy over battle. On every count his policies of restraint, bargain and detente had failed or been cynically made a mock of. Now he had no option but to try main force – with mighty main force to hand. Indeed, he could do no other. Had he sought to disperse this vast army a second time, it was highly doubtful whether he could ever have assembled another. Anyway, his lords would probably have revolted.

So, in late March, it was full-scale invasion. They would punish Stephen, take over Northumbria and Cumbria by force and occupation, establish the Scottish border from Tees to Ribble once and for all, and if advisable march on further south. And, to be sure, they would do so against a usurper, claiming Maud as rightful occupant of the English throne.

Fifty thousand was far too numerous a host to handle conveniently as one unit; besides, since territorial annexation was a large part of the objective, division was called for; although the various forces were to keep in touch as far as possible. Division was advisable for other reasons also. Already there had been fighting between various contingents, the Galloway men being particularly aggressive and unruly, tough warriors but difficult to manage and at odds with all. To some extent the same applied with others, the true Scots from beyond Forth despising the Lothian and Mersemen whom they looked on as little better than Englishmen, the Highlanders decrying the Lowlanders, almost all suspicious of the Normans, and the native Scots earls resentful against the new men and claiming all superior commands.

So David divided his fifty thousand into four, and carefully put native lords nominally at the head of each. The Lord William of Allerdale, being a prince of the royal house, he put in command of the extreme western force, which was to march through Cumbria to the Lancashire border; the Earl Cospatrick, with his Lothian, Merse and Teviotdale host, was to take the eastern coastal route; and in the lofty central area, two divisions were to advance, one under his son Henry and Malise, Earl of Strathearn on the left, keeping in touch with Cospatrick; the other under the Earl Fergus linking with William. David himself, with his remaining earls and a tight bodyguard of some two hundred Norman knights, would march with Fergus – since he reckoned that he alone might be able to keep that man and his Galloway kerns in any sort of order.

The great venture commenced – and Tweedside heaved sighs of relief to see the end of them all. The Lord William set off up Teviotdale, for Esk and the Solway to Caer-luel; whilst Cospatrick went down Tweed to the Northumbrian coast. Henry and Strathearn marched up Rule Water and over Carter Fell for Redesdale, while David and Fergus turned up the Till valley to round the north-eastern end of the Cheviots into the moor country beyond. This, of course, would be no fast-moving invasion, for the vast majority were necessarily on foot. Anyway, there was no rush. They had months, if necessary, before the hay-harvest would demand the return of many, to maintain the land's economy. But some, on the extremities, had further to march than others, inevitably, and it was important to keep an approximate line, ninety miles long as it would be, to avoid any outflanking attempts. The two central arrays would have to proceed more slowly, therefore. There were few castles to reduce this time, most having been dealt with on the previous occasion, with little rebuilding.

David, then, was prepared to stop at Wark Castle, right at the beginning. It had been able to defy him before, being notably strongly-sited, and it would give the over-eager Galloway men something to sober them a little, perhaps. Again they did not manage to take the place, however, and had not the time to starve it out; whether this served to tone down the Galwegians was extremely doubtful.

Leaving Wark, the march southwards went on. They had to face no opposition. Stephen had apparently hurried back to London and left no occupying forces behind. Word from the various component units indicated that the Northumbrians and Cumbrians almost everywhere welcomed the Scots once more. But the difficulty was to keep the invading troops from treating them as conquered enemy, despite all David's exhortations and commands. On the former invasion he had had five thousand men under his own personal command; now he had ten times that number, many of them as far as forty and fifty miles off. News of sackings, burnings and savageries began to loom large in the reports which he insisted should come constantly to him at the centre.

The King grew more and more concerned, as he entered the great and populous inland vale of the Tyne. He did not have to rely on hearsay either, for Fergus's men were the worst offenders of all, and their lord seemed little disposed to stop them. At six thousand, they made up half the force the monarch himself marched with. There were constant recriminations and appeals, but little betterment. When, nearing Hexham, David heard of the burning of two churches, he recognised that drastic measures must be taken. He sent orders that the entire army was to halt for three days, and all senior commanders to report to him in person at Hexham.

Grumbling, they all came, from coast to coast. And at Hexham Priory, which itself had suffered some small damage, he held a council, in which he declared his anger and abhorrence at what was happening, tongue-lashing his lords and leaders in a fashion none of them had ever before experienced, the King markedly unlike the quiet, unassuming and friendly man they knew. The Earl Fergus in especial was lambasted before them all, and told that if he could not control his hordes, he could turn round there and then and march them back to Galloway. Then the said earl was ordered to assemble all his men, and there, before them all and before the Prior of Hexham and the gathered townsfolk, he was made to hang a group of his Galwegians who had been caught red-handed at their looting and ravaging. David had had his clerks write out a large number of brief royal warrants, which he now signed before the company, and handed these out to his lieutenants, for future distribution to churchmen who believed their premises endangered or their lands threatened, promising punishment of offenders and compensation – which compensation, he assured, would be recovered by the royal treasury from the lords and barons of the troops concerned. With this warning he sent all back to their commands, the advance to be resumed in two days.

There was still no news of Stephen or any English reaction. De Vesci and de Meschin were either lying very low somewhere, or had departed south with their monarch. No real fighting took place anywhere along the ninety-mile line – which in itself was something of a test of morale for a spirited and mighty armed host, however satisfactory to the King. But behaviour did improve.

For the mounted men progress seemed desperately slow, this proving another morale problem. Horsed forces did probe far ahead, of course, but with little real opposition, this could very quickly have broken up the army, and the conception of a steadily-advancing line. As it was, the west end of the line, under William, was tending to get ever too far ahead, there being less population and practically no castles in Cumbria to hold them up. David's objective was not any swift advance to the Tees-Ribble line, one hundred and twenty miles deep into England, but an orderly occupation of the country. The mounted chivalry often did not move at all for three or four days at a time, a sure recipe for slackness and indiscipline.

It was May before they neared Durham, and the first major resistance. Flambard had been succeeded as bishop by Raoul, another Norman, and a known fighter, who certainly would not meekly submit. His castle and cathedral together occupied a very strong, defensive position on a high and narrow spine of land within a loop of the River Wear, the only approach a steep climbing road barred by a succession of deep ditches defended by drawbridges and portcullis – not unlike the March Mount

336

Castle itself. Recognising only too clearly the hopelessness of direct assault on such a place, David made no such attempt, but settled down to a starving-out siege, at the same time using Durham town, below, as his semi-permanent headquarters from which the vast area he had over-run might be consolidated and administered. He was waiting, of course, for news, for the inevitable reaction from Stephen and the English generally. He, and all his responsible leadership, were all too well aware of their extraordinary situation, sitting there one hundred miles deep into England, with no sign of any counterstroke – only this bishop's castle glowering down at them.

At Durham, at last, news arrived – two items. Bearer of the first was David's old acquaintance the Saxon Ailred, Abbot of Rievaulx, friend of Abbot Alwin, still with the King as confessor. He came from his Yorkshire abbey on the Rye, on a self-imposed mission of peace. He came, he said, to beseech the King of Scots, whom he greatly admired, not to advance further, or at least, not beyond Tees, which would bring bloody war; but to be content with what he had already gained. There were great stirrings in England. Who could tell, perhaps David would gain all and more than he looked for by holding his hand now rather than pressing ahead?

David himself was prepared to listen to this sort of talk, but it was of course anathema to his lords and supporters, who hooted the Abbot down. Nevertheless, in private conversation later, Ailred was able to make a convincing case.

He explained that Stephen's reverse and hurried retiral from Scotland had had its impact in England. The Normans perceived him to be no effective military leader; and the Saxons saw possible opportunity, at last, for uprising against their Norman conquerors. A strong Norman party was now forming against Stephen; and Robert of Gloucester had gone over to Aquitaine to advise his half-sister to act now. The Saxons were preparing to rise, on all hands, and urging the Welsh to rise again also; but their enmity was against all Normans, not just Stephen. There was even talk of asking David himself, as a great-grandson of Edmund Ironside, to take over the English throne. This might be mere wild talk; but what was certain was that any actual armed invasion of England proper, at this stage, would be counter-productive, would have the effect of uniting the Normans again and alarming the Saxons, who were already frightened of the reputedly wild Scots hordes. Ailred urged a definite and proclaimed halt to the Scots advance whilst the situation in England developed and clarified.

He also informed that Stephen himself was in London and seemed inclined to stay there, where he had made himself popular with the mob by giving them largesse, spectacles and the like. He had ordered Archbishop Thurstan to defend the North, and had detailed the veteran warrior Walter d'Espec to aid him. Whether the Normans would rally to the old churchman's banner remained to be seen. Ailred also revealed that Raoul, Bishop of Durham, was not in fact in his besieged castle here, but at York with Thurstan.

On top of Ailred's tidings came the second item of news. The Lord William in the west, not bothering to keep line, had pressed on to the Ribble already; and there, at Clitheroe, had been confronted by a major Norman force which he had defeated roundly.

The effect of all this information on the Scots main force was marked but contradictory, divisive. The more thoughtful were for taking Ailred's advice and holding their fire meantime; but in any assembly of men the thoughtful are seldom in the majority, especially in an army; and the reaction of most was that if William and Strathclyde men could defeat a Norman host in the west, *they* could at least as much in the east and centre. Forward, advance, no craven holding back, was the cry.

David, needless to say, was of the first persuasion. But he had many things to consider other than long-range strategy, including the dangers of idleness, the morale of his heterogeneous force, and the matter of the inexorable passage of time – for come harvest, nothing would hold a large part of his army from returning home, since neglecting harvest meant probably starvation in the winter for homes and families. So reluctantly the King compromised. They would leave Durham under siege by only a small force, and move on slowly towards the Tees, the age-old boundary of Northumbria.

This pleased no one greatly, but it had to serve.

*   *   *

It was no place, nor time, for reflection, as David sat his horse there on Cowton Moor, the common grazing-land just north of Northallerton, six miles beyond Tees and halfway between Durham and York, and looked across the rough pasture to the assembled enemy half-a-mile away. Yet reflect he did, and unhappily. No doubt he was not the first commander so to do, to realise that though he did not wish to do battle here and now, to recognise that it was against his best interests to do so, yet he would *have* to do so. The circumstances left him no choice. A great armed host is not like some convenient device which can be turned off or on at will. Thousands upon thousands of men, especially an army composed of the contingents of innumerable lords and chiefs, with little in common, indeed deep internal divisions, cannot be a precise instrument on which an overall commander can play at will or change tune suddenly. He had brought this spirited, unruly, violent mass of men one hundred and twenty miles into England, and now at last was face-to-face with a powerful enemy force. By no means, however much he might wish it, or recognise it as wise and desirable, could he now refuse to fight, come to terms, or fall back. Battle now there had to be. It could have dire results – but the result of orders not to fight would be infinitely more dire, now and hereafter. His throne would be the first casualty.

Yet he did not see how he could have done differently. When he had reached the Tees at last, between Stockton and Darlington, and had been informed that there was talk of a great muster of Norman barons being called by Archbishop Thurstan and Walter d'Espec, not at York but at the Bishop of Durham's southern castle of Northallerton, only six miles away, he had had to make a swift decision; either to wait there behind Tees, for the English to assemble and marshal themselves and grow stronger, or to move first, with his larger host, and disperse any such muster before it grew dangerous. He almost inevitably had had to take the second course. Now, he found that the muster had been a deal more advanced than reported, and a major army was already facing him, holding a small, isolated hill rising out of the moor. There were obviously many thousands there, even though less numerous than his own; but more important than numbers, an armoured host, the sun gleaming everywhere on massed steel – Norman steel.

None knew better than David and his own Norman friends what that meant. Few if any of the Scots had had any experience of fighting against steel-clad knights and troops encased in armour. Not one in ten of their number had even the leather jerkins with scales of metal sewn on, which served as mail with the Scots, as with the Saxons and Norse. Only the Normans had developed chain-mail, steel plating and helmets – which might be hampering in movement but of incalculable advantage in defensive warfare especially.

So David reflected, while around him his non-Norman supporters laughed and cheered at the prospect of action at last, promising each other great things, victory the least of it.

The King was aroused from his preoccupation by angry voices, wrath, anger suddenly replacing laughter behind him. It was the Earl Fergus asserting that he led the van. Always, he declared, it had been Galloway's privilege to form the van of the Scottish host in war. They would lead, or not fight at all.

David considered his former friend thoughtfully. Fergus, like himself brought up amongst Normans, knew their prowess and the superiority of armoured men over unarmoured.

"I am surprised that you are so eager, Fergus," he said. "*You* know what the cost will be against all that steel!"

The other, in chain-mail himself, shrugged. "What must be, must."

"*Must*, man! You say must to me?"

"Just that, Sire. My people just will not fight unless they lead. I know them. It is that – or you are six thousand men fewer this day!"

Snarls and growls from around them caused David to raise his hand.

"Do you tell me, my lord, that you cannot control your forces? That they will not obey you if you order them otherwise?"

"God help me – yes! These are some of the fiercest fighters on this earth, man. But the most damnably proud. The true Pictish nation, untainted by your Scottish blood! It is their age-old right to fight the van. If I say otherwise, they would spurn me, throw me aside . . ."

"Damn you, Mac Sween!" Malise of Strathearn cried. "You are not even one of the *ri*! A new-made earl and a rabble of uncouth kerns will not lead Strathearn . . . !"

"Nor Fife!" the young Earl Duncan broke in. "I am premier earl. *I* lead!"

"My lords, my lords!" David exclaimed. "Silence! Will you raise your voices in my royal presence? *I* say who leads my array and who does not. Why think you I have a Knight Marischal? And a Great Constable? Sir Hervey of Keith will marshal the host according to my commands . . ."

"Sire – look!" Hugo called. "A deputation. From the enemy. Under a flag of truce. Yonder!" He pointed.

All eyes turned southwards. Three horsemen were riding towards them from the dismounted and mail-clad mass around and on the hill, one bearing aloft a large white banner.

"Ha! They are none so sure of themselves. They would treat!" Fergus said.

There was a variety of reaction from the waiting Scots leadership, to possibly only David's, with some of his Normans', relief. Then a different note was voiced by someone keen-sighted.

"Lord – see who they are! It is de Brus, I swear! Aye, and de Baliol! Save us – traitors!"

Loud was the astonished and angry comment, amongst Scots and Normans both, as the identity of the newcomers was established. Robert de Brus, Lord of Annandale, and Bernard de Baliol, Lord of Cavers, had both in time succeeded to their fathers' baronies in England – as indeed had others of David's Normans. These two had elected to spend part of their time on their Yorkshire domains, and had been in the South when this campaign started. Now here they were.

In their rich armour, heads bare, they rode up, a man-at-arms behind bearing the white flag. De Brus, a handsome man, a year or two older than David, raised his hand.

"Sire! My lord King – greetings!" he cried.

"Ah, yes. But what sort of greetings, Robert?" David asked evenly. "I never thought to see de Brus – or de Baliol either – riding under *that* flag, and from my enemy's camp!"

A rumble of hostility, of menace, arose from behind the King.

"But they are *not* Your Grace's enemies," de Brus said, urgently. "They are our own kind, good Norman lords, who could be your friends. As are we, as we have long *proved* ourselves. These have no desire to fight you. That is why we are come – to tell you so."

"Then let them disperse and go, de Brus!" Fergus shouted. "There need be no fighting, then." This time he did not lack for support.

David raised hand for quiet. "If they seek terms, I am ready to discuss them," he said.

"No – it is not terms they seek, Sire. Only goodwill, reason, friendship. You cannot draw sword against your friends."

"I have no desire to, my Lord of Annandale. We have come thus far without fighting. If there is sword-drawing now it is because this host bars my way. My way to York. Where I would speak with the Archbishop."

"That is the Archbishop's host, my lord King."

"Ha! And does he come to speak with me? He who now represents Stephen the Usurper?"

"Er . . . no, Sire. But the Bishop of Durham is there."

"The King of Scots does not treat with underlings, my Lord. If that is the Archbishop's host, what is the Archbishop's word to me?"

341

"He bids you go in peace, Sire. He asks that you retire behind your own borders. Then any differences shall be settled later, by fair agreement."

"Fair agreement! We have had a sufficiency of fair agreement, Robert. And always the agreement broken. By Stephen and the Archbishop, both. This time we choose other methods. Go tell your new masters so!"

Again the growling behind the King.

De Baliol tried, on a different note. "Your Grace – do not bring this to a test of steel, I beseech you. For you cannot prevail. You must know it. There stand fifteen thousand of mailed men. You may number more, but how few are armoured or trained in battle as are we Normans. Your tribesmen and bare-shanked churls have no least chance of winning this day.'

"There speaks French arrogance!" Fergus cried. "Let us put it to test."

De Brus frowned at his colleague, clearly preferring a less abrasive approach. "Sire – you are a man of peace, all know. You cannot wish bloodshed. Especially in the face of the bodily presence of the Lord Christ!"

"What?" David stared. They all did.

The other turned in his saddle, to point. "There, yonder, is what you pitch yourself against, my lord King – you, a Christian monarch. Not against merely steel and armed might. But against the Most High God Himself! See you that standard raised against you? Look well, Sire. For the great mast lifted high there carries the holy pyx, the consecrated host of the Body and Blood of the Lord Christ. And flanked by the sacred banners of St. Peter of York, St. John of Beverley and St. Wilfred of Ripon. There, see them fly. If you draw sword, Sire, you draw it against Holy Church and Holy Church's Master – you, of all men!"

Even David was rendered speechless for moments in the face of this extraordinary and most terrible conception. Around him men held their breaths, aghast at something the like of which none had ever heard.

Fergus of Galloway was differently made. "By the Powers!" he exclaimed, "Old Thurstan must be scared out of his tonsured pate to think of such device!"

A sigh, an outlet of breath in sheer relief escaped from the listening men, the dire threat at least reduced to manageable proportions. Shouts, reproaches, curses resounded.

David strove to keep his voice steady when he had gained

silence. "This is . . . a great sin, a shame!" he declared. "To use the Blessed Sacraments so. To claim Christ and His holy saints as, as partisans. And for a usurper, an oath-breaker, a liar! I do not congratulate your Archbishop or your new friends, my lords!"

The Scots leadership cheered that to the echo.

"Then, then, my lord King – you reject the hand of friendship?" Baliol asked. "It is to be war . . . ?"

Again de Brus intervened. "Sire, hear me – while there is yet time. Think who you, and these my friends, seek to slay. Honest Normans all. Remember how, from the first, we Normans have aided you. To set up your kingdom. Trust *them*, rather than these Scots tribesmen. Can you, my lord, subject them to your governance without Norman aid? That Fergus! Who reduced him to obedience, but your Norman knights? Will you throw all away? For these?"

In the uproar, one voice overbore all, tense, that of the King's Knight Marischal. "Curse you, de Brus – all Normans are not as you!" Hervey de Warenne shouted. "You are vassal to my own father for your Cleveland manors – the Earl of Surrey. I am son, not vassal! And I support the lord David to my last breath!"

"And I! And I! And I!" David's other Normans cried, snatching out swords to hold high.

De Brus inclined his handsome head. "So be it," he acceded. "If that is your answer, Sire, I shall convey it to those who sent us." He squared his mailed shoulders. "For myself, I must now declare before all that I hereby renounce my oath of fealty to you for my lands in Scotland. Forfeit me Annandale if you will."

"And I for Cavers in Teviotdale," de Baliol added.

David nodded wordless, too hurt to speak. These had been his friends, de Brus one of the closest.

"These are the words of traitors, I say!" That was a new voice for that day, but one all there knew. David turned to find the Lord William of Allerdale, who must have crossed the spine of England to reach them here, from his Cumbrian host. "As well they sit under that white banner!"

There was loud acclaim for the new arrival and his sentiments.

William jabbed a finger towards the Norman army. "We beat them at Clitheroe!" he cried. "Let us beat them again!"

In the wild cheering, the two emissaries bowed, reined round their mounts and rode back whence they had come.

The die, it seemed, was cast. David, far from cheering, sighed deeply. So fate decided – not himself. Was he no more than a cipher, a weakling wearing a crown, to allow it to go thus? He who hated the sword was going to allow the sword to be the arbiter, after all.

*   *   *

Two hours later, in the early afternoon, the thing had come to the moment of truth. The Scots army, of about twenty-five thousand – for many of the original fifty thousand were by now scattered over two provinces in garrisons – was marshalled and ready, eager, indeed scarcely to be restrained any longer. In the end, there had been little further demur over Fergus and his Galwegians forming the vanguard. These were now drawn up in three impatient masses, of some two thousand each, in front of the main array. Behind them were three much larger and rather more disciplined bodies. On the extreme right, the cavalry wing, most of the Norman lords with their mounted levies, plus the Borderers, who were never to be parted from their horses, this under Prince Henry and the Earl of Fife. In the centre, commanded by the victorious Lord William and Earl Malise of Strathearn, was the greatest concentration, footmen from every part of Scotland, with many volunteers from Northumbria and Cumbria. On the left, Cospatrick of Dunbar had his men of Lothian, the Merse and Teviotdale – sharing his command, oddly enough, with Malcolm MacEth, former Earl of Moray, whom David had allowed to come on the campaign from his open imprisonment at Rook's Burgh. In the rear the King himself, supported by Hervey the Knight Marischal and Hugo the Deputy Constable, held the reserve of about four thousand, with his personal bodyguard of some two hundred Norman knights.

At least, there seemed to be no question as to the enemy's tactics. They were evidently going to stand fast on the defensive round their hill, facing north, though with flanking wings stretching a little way east and west – grimly wise strategy for a force of massed armour confident in its invulnerability. Plain to be seen now, dragged to the top of the hill, was a waggon with what could only be a ship's mast rising from it. The three banners of the saints flew plainly at its head, but it was too far to see the pyx, the casket containing the consecrated bread and wine. The Scots tried not to look at that dire standard, to tell themselves that it was false, did not matter – but its presence

344

was like a leaden weight at the back of many minds, nevertheless.

It was two hours past noon. There was nothing more to wait for. The speeches had been made, the assurances given, the boasts boasted and some prayers said. It but remained to do, and to go on doing, until . . .

With a mighty yell which drowned the trumpet-notes, Galloway surged forward at the run, Fergus himself, under the white-lion-on-blue banner, well to the fore. They had some five hundred yards to cover to reach the enemy. All the rest of the ranked army cheered them on.

David waited only until they were about half-way to the hill – their pride must be satisfied with that. Then again he signed to the trumpeter.

Now the entire main array moved into action. But inevitably, not at the same pace. The right wing under Henry, being horsed, broke into a trot, swiftly increased to a canter, a gallop, drawing quickly ahead of all the rest, the very ground shaking to the thunder of their hooves. But this David had reckoned on – his method of supporting the Galwegians, however much they might resent it. Lord William's centre marched forward in fairly ordered ranks, spears at the slope. But Cospatrick's left, starting at a steady pace, quickly broke into a run. So the vast front became an uneven, moving crescent. This also was planned. There were some twenty thousand men on the move.

The scale, the *élan*, the sheer drama of it all, produced a corresponding surge of elation in the watching reserve force, even though, from the King downwards, they all but cringed from the anticipated shock of impact. But, in fact, it was not any such expected clash of collision which shook them, but a very different reaction, the impression, almost unreal as it was unacceptable, of the Galloway host melting, dissolving, before their very eyes. Like standing grain before the sickle the forward ranks went down in swathe after swathe, still one hundred yards and more from the enemy front. It was too distant for the watchers to see the arrows, of course – but their effect was stouningly evident. Higher on the hill, behind the phalanx of armour, the massed archers were shooting over their colleague's heads, with steady, deadly efficiency and accuracy, at short range, into the close-packed unprotected masses.

Men were falling in their hundreds, almost thousands, for the unhurt were tripping and stumbling over their fallen comrades. Three times the lion banner sank and was snatched up to fly again. But though the Galloway front wavered and shrank

in size, it pressed on, still yelling "Albani! Albani!" the ancient
Pictish war-cry, climbing over the fallen.

Efficient as the bowmen were, they just could not fit and
shoot sufficient arrows, in the time, to dispose of more than
perhaps a quarter of the leaping, shouting horde, before these
were able to fling themselves upon the serried ranks of the
kneeling spearmen. The slaughter thereafter looked only a little
less terrible. But again weight of numbers told. Even the
longest, firmest-held spear could not impale more that two or
three men at once – and extracting the weapon thereafter from
flailing bodies took time. Pressed on from behind, the Galloway
ranks might crumple and collapse, but dead, dying and
wounded, they weighed down and neutralised many of the
spears and spearmen both. Over and through this bloody
chaos, the swordsmen, the mace-wielders, the axemen and the
dirk-stabbers poured, even though not much more than half of
the six thousand. The van had not failed.

The right wing, too, struck the enemy's west flanking force
almost simultaneously – and as so often with cavalry charging
standing infantry, broke right through them at the first rush.
Some fell to arrows, mounts and men, some were pierced by
spears, others crashed over fallen comrades and screaming
horseflesh. But the great majority drove on and through,
swords smiting. The centre enemy archers on the hill, when
they could no longer shoot at the Galwegians for fear of hitting
their own men, switched targets to the cavalry.

On the east, Cospatrick's force had not yet reached the
enemy right wing. So this stood idle, its archers waiting for
point-blank range.

David, watching all, sickened by the carnage but with some
hope that sheer impetus and ignoring of losses might carry the
day, became aware of a new situation developing. From his
position he could not see clearly what was happening on the far
right, where his son's advance had carried them considerably
forward and where it had evidently run into trouble of some
sort. Then it became apparent that it was cavalry that Henry
was meeting now. Obviously behind the hill, out of sight, had
been drawn up the Norman mounted chivalry. These were
attacking Henry's and Fife's force, with their impetus partly
spent and their ranks somewhat broken.

David's impulse was to send his two hundred horsed bodyguard to aid his son, there and then. But he forced himself to act
the general, not the father. Biting his lip he waited, agonised.

Cospatrick's people were now dying under the arrow-hail.

But they had the Galloway example before them, and the added advantage that the enemy right wing they were attacking was formed up on the low ground east of the hill, and so its archers did not have the benefit of height, to shoot over the heads of their spearmen. So they were less effective. But unhappily, on the ranked spears, the Lothian and Mersemen died equally disastrously.

The centre, marching with admirable steadiness, had to surmount the great swathes and mounds of Galloway slain and wounded. But Fergus's people had opened a way for them through the spearmen cordon, and though they suffered in turn from the high-placed bowmen, they reached the massed armour of the English centre with considerably less loss than had the other forces. With their arrival, what was left of the van began to withdraw, through their ranks, to reform – a sorry proportion of six thousand.

David perceived that Henry's cavalry were at least holding their own if not pressing back the enemy horse – for which he thanked God. But on the left, Cospatrick's and MacEth's folk were partially held up by the spearmen, their formation in dire danger of being fragmented. The reserve was divided into eight units of five hundred. The King ordered Ranulph de Soulis and Walter fitz Alan, his new Steward, to take two units and hurry to the left's aid.

Some of David's lieutenants were comparatively cheerful as to the situation so far. But the King himself knew that the real test was still to come. Hitherto the fighting had been only around the hill-skirts. The main mass of the English armour, solidly ranked and packed on the hill itself, was not yet engaged.

It was at this dire mount of steel that the Lord William and Malise of Strathearn sought to hurl their strength – and swiftly it became evident how desperate a business it was. Wave after wave of their people were repulsed, flung back like breakers against a cliff. Swords and maces and axes and short stabbing-spears could make but little impression on the massed mail above them. It was appalling to watch the repeated assaults, each falling back in bloody ruin, nothing gained.

Mainly for something to do, to at last seem to be more than idle watchers at this slaughter, David ordered his reserve to move, with him, nearer to the battle. At least there they would see the details more clearly and be able to react more swiftly where necessary.

What they did see from the new position, and all too clearly,

347

was that Henry and Fife had indeed won their cavalry engage-
ment but, having put the enemy to flight, had now gone in
pursuit. Both very young men, in their triumph no doubt they
had forgotten both orders and the ever-present danger of any
cavalry victory on a wing – following up the fleeing foe and
leaving the main battle, leaving that flank exposed. If the
enemy had any reserve behind there, the main Scots front could
be outflanked and possibly rolled up.

David detached another thousand men and most of his Normans to hurry over to hold that flank.

The remnant of the Galwegians had now reformed and
hurled themselves back into the struggle, still under the lion
banner – so presumably Fergus was still leading. But neither
they nor the main centre force appeared to be making any real
impression on the mail-clad steep. The hill was now obviously
slippery with blood, to add to the difficulty.

David began to consider the advisability of ordering a retiral
– if that was possible.

Stalemate appeared to have been reached on the left, the
east, as a result presumably of de Soulis's and the Steward's
reinforcement, something like a mere slogging-match developing. The King sent another five hundred to help, reluctantly.
Now he had a mere fifteen hundred left in reserve. If there was
to be a retiral, as seemed almost inevitable now, all of these
would be needed to cover it. He said as much to Hugo. And he
was worried about Henry and his force.

"We cannot retire." That was Hervey, at his other side. "It
would be to admit defeat. Besides, how could you enforce it?
How many would obey? Break off?"

"I care not about admitting defeat, man. I care about
extracting my people from this attempt in which they cannot
prevail. As for obeying, men are falling there by the hundred.
Every minute. They are gaining nothing. Think you they
do not know it? They must see it is hopeless. They will
retire."

"Will the enemy *allow* us to retire, Sire?" Hugo demanded.
"Would they not sweep down on us, slaughter us as we sought
to withdraw?"

"I think not. They are fighting a defensive battle. To change
to offence would not be easy. They have no horses – Henry has
at least seen to that! Their flanks are in disorder. In that state,
in the state of the field, to come down off that hill and marshal
themselves to attack our retiral would be difficult. Take much
time. And if Henry's cavalry came back, they could be over-

348

whelmed." He paused. "Hervey – go tell de Soulis to return here with his mounted men. Forthwith."

David forced himself not to think of the fearful, continuing slaughter going on just out of bowshot before them; nor of his son and the cavalry wing, what might be happening to them, what *would* happen if they did not get back here before a withdrawal of the main array; instead to concentrate on how best to extricate his battered forces from this bloody coil. To order retiral was one thing – to effect it successfully was quite another, he realised well. It was not easy to visualise, plan and marshal such a complex manoeuvre in his mind, with the wounded to consider also, with all that desperate, yelling, screaming butchery riveting the attention.

When Hervey returned with the mounted bodyguard, David ordered the trumpeter to sound the recall. But, well aware that men engaged in life-and-death, hand-to-hand fighting might not all either hear or heed such summons, he sent forward many messengers to carry the word to the commanders and all whom they could reach. It was to be a fighting retiral, not any hurried flight.

To describe what followed as any sort of orderly exercise would be ridiculous. It was indeed a dire and horrible confusion. But then so was the entire battle which they were breaking off. Battle is seldom anything else but multiple confusion, with purpose, tactics and strategy mere underlying influences, often quite non-apparent to the actual battlers. Disengagement is always more difficult than assault. Men fighting for their lives, or in process of killing someone else, are, to say the least, preoccupied. Some may be glad to desist, others furious, others again unable to do so, and large numbers utterly oblivious of all but the blood-red haze of war. So David's retiral was not effected quickly or coherently nor without grievous mistakes and losses. But it might have been worse, a deal worse. The physical formation of the battlefield helped, in that the central hill was like some rocky stack or islet from which the tide could naturally ebb. Also the disintegration of the enemy left wing meant that there was little danger of any outflanking move on that side. So the Scots cavalry screen, thin as it was, could be used to throw between the disengaging Cospatrick and the English right, with good effect.

But undoubtedly the main feature in their favour was, as David had foreseen, the mental attitude of the main enemy armoured mass on the hill itself. The English strategy had been defensive from the start – and successfully so. They had survived, with little of casualties. To change that now, after some two hours of fierce fighting, into any disciplined offensive posture would have been very difficult and asking almost too much of flesh and blood – especially as almost certainly the Scots still outnumbered their foes. Moreover these mail-clad knights and their men-at-arms were used to fighting on horseback. The very armour which had protected them would be a serious handicap in any chase on foot. So, as the Scots tide ebbed, however raggedly and reluctantly, the English, by and large remained where they were, most of them probably well enough content to claim victory without further effort and danger. Some, to be sure, did seek to continue the fight and pursue – but these quickly paid for their temerity, with David's fifteen hundred rearguard still fresh and playing their first active role – confirming the more sensible majority in their wisdom.

The withdrawal proceeded then, and, as it became clear that there was to be no immediate English surge forward, and that the low-level right wing perceived the fact and prudently did not seek to thrust themselves into the role of martyrs, David was able to call in his two hundred horsemen and use them like sheep-dogs to round up, marshal and divide the exhausted, excited and unruly survivors and send them marching off northwards in some sort of ordered columns. The wounded were the greatest problem, and many advised abandoning them, as standard military practice. But the King would not hear of it, would not consider leaving the field before all who could be moved were aided and borne on their way. At the back of his mind, of course, was the hope that Henry and the cavalry wing would turn up, making him almost reluctant to quit the scene.

And all the time the English ranks watched from their hill. They stood all but silent, neither cheering nor jeering. It could well be that they considered that this might be merely a temporary withdrawal, to regroup and return to the attack, a mere pause in the battle. They too, no doubt, were anxious about the missing cavalry, and what it might do when it returned. At any rate, they stayed grouped tightly around their peculiar standard, waiting, while slowly the Scots drew off.

Back at their former marshalling-point, David reined up and turned to look back. "God forgive me!" he said. "I drew the sword in vain! And leave behind those who had to pay the price. God in Heaven forgive me!"

Unable to say more, he turned to point northwards, for the Tees.

31

WHAT BECAME KNOWN as the Battle of the Standard was surely one of the most unusual engagements in the history of warfare. Not only on account of the peculiar strategies employed and the aura of piety with which the English invested it, a personal intervention of the Almighty, but because of the results. For although a victory and a defeat, in one sense clear-cut enough, there was little of that about it in another. The English were left in possession of the field; but the Scots made an orderly retiral therefrom, and although they left many dead behind, they by no means considered themselves a defeated army. There was no actual retreat, indeed, for they moved back only as far as their original final objective, the River Tees, six miles away, there to reorganise and take up major defensive positions protected by the river-line, summoning their wide-scattered units from all over Northumbria to join them. They may have lost as many as six thousand men, dead and wounded, in those two hours, a large percentage of them Galwegians – whom many of the rest considered to be expendable anyway – but there were still some twenty thousand, with more coming in all the time. Henry and his cavalry did rejoin them there, safe and sound and, oddly, much elated, considering themselves victors. They had utterly routed the enemy horse, driven them far away, dispersing them thoroughly – and then of course had difficulty in reassembling. When they had at last got back to the main battlefield, they had been able to make a further impact on the enemy foot, and so ridden off northwards, triumphant. If Henry and Duncan of Fife expected plaudits, they were sadly disillusioned, and left in no doubts as to what their inexperienced *élan* had cost the main army. But the cavalry's victory undoubtedly had a large effect on the English morale, and left them without any great sense of ultimate gain. So, the Scots stood, one hundred and twenty miles inside England, with nothing of the defeated about them.

In fact, as reports came in, David began to perceive that, far from being in a position of defeat, it was almost as though he had been a victor. His opponents made no move against him, and appeared to accept the Scots occupation of Northumbria and Cumbria. The force at Northallerton actually retired to York, where it had come from. It was, of course, Archbishop Thurstan's force, not Stephen's; and many of its important nobles had very divided loyalties. Stephen's cause was in very low water behind them. News came to the Scots that there was wholesale revolt against the usurper all over the South. Even Hugo Bigod, hitherto his most active supporter, he who had announced the false death-bed change-of-heart of the late King Henry in favour of Stephen, had switched allegiance again and seized the castles of Norwich and Badington, proclaiming for the Empress and calling for all Normans to do likewise. Robert of Gloucester was reputed to be back in England with much Plantagenet gold, to rally support. And the Archbishop of Canterbury was wavering.

David, considering it all, recognised that he might be in a stronger position than he had ever anticipated, not only militarily, despite the sorry business of Northallerton. With the English in such disarray, now was the time to bargain. Why wait for Maud to triumph? Better to deal with Stephen, in his extremity, and in due course present Maud with a *fait accompli*. With the Scots army drawn up and forming a dire threat from the Irish to the Norse Seas, and the Northern English in ever growing doubt as to where their allegiance lay, Stephen was in no position to take any strong line. So David sent off deputations, one to London, offering to treat with Stephen face-to-face, if he would come north, say to Durham – but it would have to be swiftly done; the other to Thurstan at York, in reproachful terms, complaining that he should have sent armed force to deny him access to the archiepiscopal presence, and requesting assurance that he and his forces were in fact loyal and strong in their support of the King of Scots' favoured niece, the Empress Maud, true Queen of England, who was undoubtedly now about to take over her throne. He also added, in conciliatory fashion, that he had decided not to forfeit the Scots properties of de Brus and de Baliol, whom he hoped would now behave in friendly style.

This done, David left his army under the command of Henry, assisted by older and more experienced leaders, gave orders for the administration of the two great provinces he had occupied, and hurried northwards. He re-instituted the siege of that old sore, Wark Castle, and then proceeded back into Scotland, from which he had been absent much too long for his comfort. Not that comfort, physical or mental, was a state with which David mac Malcolm had much acquaintance, these days. Particularly he was unhappy over that Battle of the Standard, it tending to come between him and his sleep of nights. Others might not blame him for that slaughter – Fergus, wounded but far from deflated, was now actually hailing it as a victory for Galloway – but he blamed himself, grievously, whatever the ultimate outcome.

Scotland, left in the care of the Chancellor, the Great Constable, the Bishop of St. Andrews and others, was in a fair enough state, with abbey and church building proceeding, the diocesan, parish and burgh systems being steadily set up, justiciars making their presence felt. David sent new forces southwards, to relieve many of his host who would be itching to return for their harvesting – many indeed had quietly left the occupying army without anybody's leave. Touring some of the country, to show his presence and to reassure any anxieties, he made his way south-westwards to Caer-luel. All the time he was waiting for word from Henry, ready to turn and head for Durham and the Tees again, at short notice.

It was, in fact, a quite unexpected courier who brought the news he had been awaiting, to Caer-luel, no less than another Papal Legate, one Alberic, Bishop of Ostia. Visiting northern monarchs on behalf of Pope Innocent, he had been persuaded by Stephen's Queen Matilda – the daughter of David's younger sister Mary – to act mediator. He announced that King Stephen could not possibly come north to Durham to treat, being heavily involved with the uprising in the west, where the Empress Maud had now landed and was holding Bristol; also there was another rising in East Anglia. But he, the Legate, was empowered to treat on King Stephen's behalf.

This was almost better than David could have hoped for, better than Stephen's own unreliable presence. Terms arranged through and involving the Pope's representative would be much more likely to be fulfilled than otherwise. Moreover he could put terms to the Legate which Stephen might have been unable to accept, face-to-face, but which he might well be persuaded to agree thereafter.

So Bishop Alberic was sent off with David's demands, with instructions to return in due course to Durham, with the answers in the form of signed and sealed documents, charters and confirmations, each paper to be countersigned by the Legate. There was to be no mistake this time.

David went back to Dunfermline to wait. Any waiting at Durham would be done by the Legate. When eventually couriers reached him that Alberic was indeed across Tees again, he set sail from Inverkeithing, Dunfermline's port, in the fine ship he himself had gifted to Dunfermline Abbey, for trading ventures. With the prevailing north-westerly winds, he was at the mouth of Tees in two days.

The Legate brought back practically all that David had stipulated. Stephen had been prepared to agree to almost anything, in the circumstances; and while no doubt he would resile where and when he could, this time he had been forced to put everything under the Great Seal of England, in his need to get rid of the threat in the North. Cumbria and Northumbria were to be part of the Scottish realm, no longer mere English earldoms held by Henry. It was agreed that de Meschin had no remaining authority in Cumbria, and de Vesci none in Northumbria save for the lordship of his own personal fief of Alnwick. The two royal castles of Newcastle-upon-Tyne and Bamburgh were to remain the English Crown's possession but under Scots suzerainty. The English Crown no longer claimed paramountcy over Scotland, with the admission that this had been the merest device. On his part, David promised not to claim any territory south of Tees and Ribble, nor to seek nor accept the crown of England – which Stephen seemed to believe was a possibility.

David was content – with this progress, at least. He did not think that Stephen would occupy his throne for much longer. He had now gained for Scotland what his forefathers had fought in vain for, and which would be difficult for Stephen's successors to take away again – although they would almost certainly try. It would serve.

As they watched the Legate's party ride away from Durham, the Scots were able to turn to happier matters. Whilst David had been back in Scotland, Hervey de Warenne had established contact with his eldest brother, now Earl of Surrey. He was a prominent Maud supporter and had been up in Yorkshire rallying aid for the Empress amongst his vassals in the great de Warenne estates there. Hervey had taken the opportunity, during the lull, to visit him at Richmond, on the Swale. There he had found another two brothers also, Robert, now Earl of Leicester and Hugh, Earl of Bedford, as well as his two sisters – all, he recognised, keeping well away from entanglement in hostilities. Later, since Richmond was only a dozen miles from their main Scots base on the Tees, he had taken Henry and Hugo on a visit. And young Henry had straightway fallen headlong in love with the younger sister, the Lady Ada. Apparently the esteem was mutual, and marriage became more or less taken for granted. The young woman was lively, spirited and talented, if not beautiful. David, when he met her, was much taken with her, acclaiming his son's choice. She would, one day, make a good queen for Scotland, he decided. And she had three English earls for brothers, another Count de Meulan in Normandy, and her mother kin to the King of France. So now it was decided that Ada, with her brothers Hervey and Robert, should join the King of Scots and his party on their return to Scotland, to be wed to Henry at Dunfermline Abbey. It would be the final and excellent outcome of a strange campaign.

*   *   *

Alas for such hopes. The wedding took place amidst much rejoicing – but the final outcome of David's embroilment in England was not yet, even though campaigning was scarcely the word for it. He left that to the Empress, for as long as he might, arguing that she and her party had done nothing to warrant his further active participation in her affairs, with himself indeed practically the only one who had hitherto taken his oath of support seriously. For some eighteen months thereafter Maud and her adherents did their own campaigning without Scots help – with varying success, with England divided roughly down the centre, the west for the Empress, the east for Stephen; not the Saxon English, of course, who had no interest in either, only the Normans, both sides of which savaged the country with equal ferocity in their spleen and in efforts to provide the sinews of war. That Maud gradually gained the upper hand was more on account of Stephen's follies and unpopularity than out of any superior military genius, strategy or ability. Nobles switched sides with bewildering rapidity, offended by one rival or the other. Loyalty became a meaningless term, with families as split as the realm itself. Even Henry, Bishop of Winchester, Stephen's own brother, came over to Maud's side; and the Earl of Surrey, Ada's eldest brother, went over to Stephen. Looking on it all from afar, David minded his own business and was thankful to keep out.

He spent much of his time at Caer-luel, strengthening the castle and turning the town into a fortified walled city, in the recognition that, whoever won the struggle in England, if Scotland was to keep Cumbria, Caer-luel would require to be a strong bastion.

Then, in February 1141, came tidings that not only had Stephen lost a major battle at Lincoln but that he had been captured and was now in chains in Bristol Castle's dungeons. It seemed that at last there was decision. All opposition seemed to have collapsed. Maud moved to Winchester, her father's and grandfather's old capital, and summoned a great assembly of all Normans, nobles and bishops, which duly elected her Queen. And from Winchester she wrote inviting her Uncle David to come to Westminster Abbey to attend her coronation.

He could scarcely refuse, reluctant as he was. The more he heard of this niece of his, the less he liked it. But as fellow-monarch and kinsman, liking scarcely entered into it.

In early November, with only a small company, he rode south, intending to make his visit as brief as possible. Henry remained behind, pointing out that he had taken an oath of fealty to Stephen for Huntingdon, and whilst that man remained a prisoner, he could not decently attend his rival's enthronement. Besides, Ada was expecting a baby.

David arrived at Winchester to find all in renewed turmoil. Earl William of Surrey had been treated with contumely by Maud – as she was treating many, in her arrogance – and had made a gesture of his own, by capturing Maud's own brother, Robert of Gloucester, and offering to exchange him for Stephen. Extraordinary as it seemed, the new Queen had agreed; and now Stephen was free again, admittedly having promised to leave England. But instead of heading for the Channel and France, he had turned northwards, with Surrey, calling for the war to be resumed.

Profoundly wishing that he had not come, David was for returning home. But Maud would have none of it. She was going ahead with her coronation in London, and the least her uncle could do was to attend her there. With dire forebodings, he went along.

That coronation never took place, the London mob being otherwise minded. Stephen, it transpired, was no further away than Oxford, where his Queen Matilda, loyal and capable, with Surrey, had collected an army. Stephen had always made a point of favouring the Londoners, excepting them from his savageries, and now this policy paid off. The city was in an uproar, and Maud and her company were forced into ignominious flight, David with them, a humbling procedure.

They returned to Winchester.

But there conditions had changed. Bishop Henry had reverted to his former allegiance and declared for his brother Stephen, holding the town and royal castle-palace against Maud. She and her supporters decided to besiege it – since it held what was left of the kingdom's treasure – although David advised against any such time-consuming activity, in the circumstances. He also declared that he was going home to Scotland forthwith. Unfortunately, before he could ride, news was brought that Matilda's and Surrey's army had moved south-westwards swiftly and now almost totally surrounded them and Winchester, Normans deserting to it from all quarters.

A kind of panic ensued, Maud's forces disintegrating, every man for himself. David was utterly disgusted; but felt that he could not desert his now desperate niece in her extremity, at least until she was out of danger, however powerless he was to help.

Curiously enough it was David's less than enthusiastic or effective support which did save Queen Maud in this particular situation. For in making a secret dash to win through the enemy lines, in the early December dusk, managing to dodge a large grouping led of all people by the Earl Simon de St. Liz of Northampton, become a Stephen supporter, they ran into a lesser patrol under one of the Earl's vassals, David Olifard by name. This young man was son to Walter Olifard whom David had much befriended when *he* was acting Earl of Northampton. The son had not forgotten – indeed he was named after David. Although he had no use for Maud, he was not going to act captor to the King of Scots – and David prevailed upon him at least to let Maud and a few of her attendants go free. He escorted them to a point where they might safely make their escape.

Here was the parting of the ways, David determined to head north for Scotland, Maud west for Bristol. They made a hurried and unemotional leave-taking – for Maud was not one to inspire affection any more than loyalty. David put it to young Olifard then that he might suffer for this evening's work – which the other did not deny. So the King told him that if he and any of his men cared to escort him to Scotland, he could promise him and them sufficient reward, lands and position. No great persuasion was required. In the fluid state of loyalties and the certainty of continuing strife in England, Scotland may have seemed like a haven of peace and promise indeed. David had acquired a useful new subject as well as an escort.

After that it was merely long and hard riding. David did not exactly take a vow never to set foot in England again, but it was almost that. Unless they attacked him, the English could conduct their affairs without further involvement of the King of Scots. Enough was enough.

357

Part Four

32

How was a man to speak to God when face to face with the death of his only and beloved son? God had faced this situation Himself, of course, eleven hundred years before; but He presumably had the comforting knowledge that the Son would rise again in three days time. David had no such expectation or hope. The priests said to pray – as though he had not been praying for days and nights on end. They also advised him to say, 'Thy will be done'. How could he, how could he, in God's own name, when it was Henry who lay there fitfully breathing his last – and this time no St. Malachy O'Moore to come and drive out Satanicus who was slowly and steadily choking him?

The King, kneeling beside his son's bed, beat his clenched fists on the blankets. Unfair, unjust! He, who had tried so hard, sought ever to do God's work, built a dozen abbeys and cathedrals to His glory, worshipped and praised Him all his days. Other men had sons amany; he, the King, only this one. And now the physicians said that he could not live more than another hour or so. After weeks of racking sickness, inability to keep food in his stomach, Henry's strength was wholly gone. He would not see the dawn, all agreed.

Was it punishment for sins? His own sins, not Henry's – for Henry had been almost unnaturally sinless. But he, *he* had taken the sword, led armed hosts against the very Body and Blood of Christ Himself – however unjust it seemed that Thurstan should have raised such against him. He had been the cause of death of thousands, all those years ago. Was this the price to be paid, in God's chosen time? His own mother had died believing herself condemned for her sins – the blessed Margaret. Edgar also. As for Alexander who could tell what he believed? Was there a curse on their house? If so, why not on himself? Why on Henry . . . ?

Ada came into the bedchamber, still fully clothed although it was well after midnight. Hollow-eyed, quietly, she came to stand beside her kneeling father-in-law, a hand to his bent shoulder.

"Sire – go sleep," she urged, gently. "I shall watch again now. You must rest. There is . . . no change?"

361

"None. Save that the breathing weakens the more, I think. Weakens, lass. I fear that, that . . ."

"Yes," she said. She had given up hope long since, accepting what must be. "Go, my lord. I shall wake you if . . . there is need."

"No – I shall stay. It will not be long, God ordains. I could not sleep. The last hours of, of . . ."

She nodded, wordless.

"The children? They sleep?"

"Yes. Malcolm took long. But the others – they were tired. Why do you still pray, Sire? I cannot. Not any more . . ."

She sat on a chair beside the bed, but the King remained kneeling. He might not be praying but at least he was in the posture of prayer. Save for the puff and rustle of the sinking log-fire there was practically no sound in that tower-room of the March Mount Castle. Certainly the Earl Henry's breathing made little disturbance, however much the watchers' ears were listening for it.

"Malachy O'Moore said 'This time he will not die – *this* time!' " David spoke into the silence, some time later. "I remember that. Always have remembered it, behind my mind. Although I put it from me. That was many years ago. And now, now Malachy is dead . . ."

She did not comment.

"Henry was never strong of body . . ."

David did not sleep, but sank away into a sort of suspended consciousness such as the elderly may achieve for the harbouring of their strength. The Countess Ada's hand on his shoulder again, some unknown time later, roused him.

"It is over, my lord," she said quietly. "He has . . . moved on. My Henry . . . is gone."

"Gone . . . ?" He uttered a strangled sound, between groan and gulp. All the loss in the world was in that single word.

"He but . . . stopped breathing."

David flung himself on his son's poor shrunken body, and wept.

The woman stood silent, like a statue.

At length the King stood up. "He is gone . . . to join his mother. Blest in that, at least. And I am left . . . alone."

"You have your daughters, Sire. And your grandchildren. Even . . . myself."

"He was my son, woman, my only son. Taken! And you – you do not so much as weep!"

"I shall weep later, I think. I wish . . . that I could weep . . . now!"

He peered at her in the gloom, and then stepped over to take her in his arms. "Forgive me, my dear – forgive an old done man in his selfish grief. Your loss is great – the greater, indeed, in that you have to live with it for long. And I, pray God, not very long. Forgive me. Henry could not have had a better wife. He will be waiting for you, one day, to tell you so."

She turned from his grip and hurried out of the bedchamber, leaving her husband to his father.

In the morning they would have to tell the children.

In the morning, in fact it was David who was strong and Ada who was weak, stricken; David who lined up the three boys and three little girls and told them that their father had been called to God – who was a much greater king than he was – to undertake a very long journey in His service. They called the departure on such journey death; but this was a foolish, unsuitable word for what was in truth a splendid new start, a great adventure, sad only for those left behind, in that they would not see him until one day they too would start their journeying.

Great-eyed they listened, until the youngest girl began to cry. That was little Ada.

David gathered her to him. "Not for tears, little one," he said. "Your father has not stopped loving you because he is sent on this journey. He will love you the more, indeed. People can go on loving each other from far, far away. You do not stop loving them just because you do not see them – do you? But he is going to need you much more than before – to help your mother. And to help me, too. For we both need much help, now. Your mother to manage all here, as it should be. Without him. And me to manage my kingdom." He pointed. "And this young man, Malcolm mac Henry, especially is going to have to help me much. For he has to take his father's place, you see. Scotland must always have a king; and when I start *my* journeyings, like your father, Malcolm will be King of Scots. Until then there will be much to do. Will you all help?"

The chorus of affirmation ranged from the strong to the tremulous.

"Now, here is what we shall do – some of us, at least. Malcolm and William and I shall go journeying too, together. Not such long journey as your father's, but all round Scotland. And we shall talk to people and let them see who is to be king after me, and who is to be Earl of Northumbria too. To make them glad that your father left fine sons to continue his work, and fine daughters too, to help them – for there is no queen, you see. Will you do that? Come riding round Scotland with me?"

There was no doubt about the answer to that, from the boys at least, Malcolm nearly eleven, William nine and David six. The girls, younger, were still doubtful, Margaret, Matilda and Ada.

*   *   *

So, without any great delay after they had interred Henry's body in Kelsaugh Abbey across the river, they set out from Rook's Burgh. Scotland was stunned at the death of the popular heir to the throne, with no other adult heir in sight, save for Malcolm MacEth, a convicted rebel and William of Allerdale, who had never shown any interest in the succession. Moreover David, at sixty-eight, was increasingly conscious of the pressures of time and the uncertainty of human life. Delay was inadvisable, however little he felt like jaunting round his kingdom.

The thing was carefully planned nevertheless, a royal progress such as Scotland had never before seen. The two young princes were the heart of it, of course; but the supporting cast was important too, to be seen by all as the power and dignity and experience of the realm upholding and surrounding these young children, continuity assured. All the great of the land were summoned, only sickness and extreme age accepted as excuse, the mormaors and earls, the great officers of state – including Hugo, now Great Constable, his cousin having died – the justiciars and sheriffs, the lords and chiefs great and lesser, the bishops and abbots of both Churches, the chief magistrates of the new burghs. It made a vast company, with all its attendants, posing major problems of commissariat, supply and shelter. But it was July and tents and pavilions could be used. Whole herds of cattle were driven along behind, to be slaughtered as required, and a corps of foragers was always out to purchase food and drink. There was no great hurry, and a holiday atmosphere prevailed in the genial summer weather. The boys especially enjoyed themselves; and the King endeavoured not to let his sorrowing heart put any damper on the proceedings.

David had, as ever, a practical and immediate, as well as a visionary purpose, and used this tour to check on the progress of his parish developments, their judicial corollaries of shires and sheriffdoms, the burgh structures and the work on the new

364

abbeys and priories throughout the land. Apart from those completed, or at least already functioning in some degree, he had other abbeys founded and abuilding at Newbotle in Lothian, Kilwinning in Cunninghame, Dundrennan in Galloway, St. Andrews in Fife, Restenneth in Angus, Kinloss and Urquhart in Moray and Fearn in Ross. All these were, to be sure, to the glory of God; but they were also necessary training colleges for the supply of priests for the parish system. It was not all religiosity and abstract piety but sound and careful planning. If no king had ever founded so many abbeys, neither had any ever tried, in one reign, to convert a backwards-looking, tribal and patriarchal kingdom into an up-to-date, systematically-administered state where law ruled rather than might. If twenty-eight years was scarcely sufficient time for this, at least the foundations should be laid for those who came after. David would have liked to take his colourful cavalcade right up into Moray and Ross. But such distances were scarcely practicable; moreover it would have demanded a vastly larger escort, almost an army, for the Moraymen in particular still favoured the alternative line of the royal house, even though they no longer had an earl to lead them. It would have been a pity to spoil all with possible fighting and bloodshed.

So, starting from Edinburgh, they progressed through Lothian and Calatria to Fife and Fothrif and Gowrie, to Angus and the Mearns, across Stormounth to Atholl, down through Lennox and across Strathkelvin to the Clyde – where at Glasgow the new cathedral was almost finished, although Bishop John had not lived to see it – and on down through Renfrew of the Steward, Cunninghame and Kyle and Carrick to Galloway – where Fergus, only a little mellowed in his old age, took the opportunity to found another new abbey at Soulseat, to demonstrate that the King was not the only one who could make gestures. And so to end at Caer-luel where, at a moving ceremony, David created Malcolm Prince of Strathclyde and Cumbria, William, Earl of Northumbria and announced that six-year-old David would be titular Earl of Huntingdon – only titular meantime, since Stephen had confiscated that earldom and its useful revenues, and David refused to go to war to redeem it.

Thereafter, tired and feeling his age, but reasonably satisfied, the King returned to Rook's Burgh.

The news which awaited him there was important, although he was little moved by it – and realising the fact, recognised that he was indeed growing old. Recognised also that it could be dangerous for a realm to have a monarch, weary of life and failing to react adequately to news and events which, however distant, might affect his kingdom. The sorrow was that there was only an eleven-year-old boy to succeed him – or he would be glad to leave it all and cross the river to his abbey of Kelshaugh, there to become a simple monk until his due time came. But clearly that was not for him, too easy a road.

Was he, then, of all evil fates, growing sorry for himself? That, at least, he could still fight.

The tidings which sparked off this train of thought were that the Empress's husband, Geoffrey of Anjou, had died, and their son Henry Plantagenet – or Fitz Empress as he was being called – had declared himself to be Duke of Normandy as well as Count of Anjou, marching into that dukedom to consolidate his claim. He had, moreover, threatened to invade England on his mother's behalf if Stephen failed to accept the situation. Clearly there was a new force manifesting itself in that weary struggle – a force which might one day bring itself to bear on Scotland. David did not fail to see the writing on the wall.

Nor apparently did Stephen who, after Maud had retired back to France in 1146, had sat precariously on the English throne. For shortly afterwards there was further news from the south that that unhappy man had not only acceded to the Plantagenet grab of Normandy but had entered into a solemn treaty, ostensibly with Maud, that he should retain the English crown only for his own lifetime, but that on his death it should go, not to his own son but to Henry Fitz Empress.

David pondered this development for long. Perhaps he should have been well enough pleased that his niece's cause was vindicated, at last, with England spared the almost certain consequences of Maud's own misrule and arrogance. This Henry Plantagenet he knew. He had indeed come visiting Scotland a few years before, only in his sixteenth year but a spirited, indeed somewhat noisy youth, but no weakling – on whom David, in fact, had been persuaded to confer knighthood. But – King of England? Which would be best for Scotland? A weak, unreliable, inimical but dispirited Stephen? Or a young, strong and ambitious if brash Henry? David had little doubts as to the answer to that.

With a mere child to succeed him, could he possibly force himself to live for another ten years, to give Malcolm time, time? Ten more weary years, God help him . . . !

*   *   *

Whether God was helping or hindering or entirely neutral in the matter, David mac Malcolm mac Duncan did not reign another ten years, nor even one. On the ninth day before the Kalends of June 1153, in the early morning he was found by Alwin his chaplain, kneeling at his bedside in the castle of Caer-luel, in the posture of prayer, but dead. It was his seventieth year and the thirtieth of his reign. His expression was happy, Alwin told Abbot Ailred. He had gone to find Matilda and Henry.

In those thirty years he had changed Scotland more than any other man before or since. Although later canonised, like his mother, and known to succeeding generations as David the Saint, it was as a sore saint that his descendant James the First categorised him. He would have been the last to claim the first title but might well have accepted the second.